MW01127375

You will feel the shock reverberate through your body as author Jackie Glover grabs the breath from your chest and smashes it into the ground!

In *Walnut Hearts*, Glover takes the reader directly into the cauldron of child sexual abuse. But this is not a book about bad guys and good kids. She takes us there from a different direction.

Walnut Hearts is an extremely powerful account of the lives of four generations of Abelard women—all affected by one man. Readers will fall in love with Gussie, an unschooled but very knowing woman. As they watch her grow up, they will understand the traps she falls into—and may even fall into them along with her. The lines between seduction and control, between wanting to please and being afraid not to, and between love and guilt, are blurred and confused. The reader does not see tragedy coming any more than the characters do, and so can genuinely feel the emotions of the characters.

Through her story, Jackie Glover cries out in confusion, in pain, in fear, and finally, in victory, as she finds a voice for the thousands of children who are subjected to that voiceless crime of sexual abuse.

You will not want to put this book down. But even after you do, you will keep the Abelards with you.

Mary E. Shea, Ph.D.
Clinical Psychologist
Columbia Veterans Center
Columbia, SC

Walnut Hearts

By Jackie Glover

ISBN 0-9754922-6-8
First Printing 2004
Cover art and design by Anne M. Clarkson

Published by:
Dare 2 Dream Publishing
A Division of Limitless Corporation
Lexington, South Carolina 29073
Find us on the World Wide Web
.http://www.limitlessd2d.net.

Printed in the United States of America and the UK by

Lightning Source, Inc.

Acknowledgments

With greatest respect I wish to thank the following very special people who patiently and lovingly pushed and prodded me along the path to publication.

My brother Al and his wife Lynn, my brother Gary, my husband Bill, my son Steven and his wife Becky and my daughter Jana each encouraged me to write this particularly difficult story.

Kay Stovall moved an old computer into my apartment after Bill's death and insisted that I finish the manuscript, then helped edit the first draft.

Sue Turner read the resulting one hundred and forty thousand words and told me the last 40,000 were garbage, and she was absolutely correct.

Daisy Reno recognized some errors in time and geography that would have made me look incredibly stupid had they gotten into print.

Irene Grant called me at dawn on a rainy Sunday morning, crying, saying she had spent the entire night reading the revised manuscript and that it had to be published. She edited it then and suggested one very critical change.

Mr. Cowan, my Freshman English teacher at Grants New Mexico High School, told me forty-five years ago I was a talented writer and made me believe it for decades.

Douglas R. Thompson, a fellow student in Mr. Cowan's long-ago class, patiently assisted me with the bewildering technical tasks involved in cyberspace communication with my publishers and hardly ever laughed at my ignorance.

Richard Jones converted my Mac text to Word and put the disks in return mail the same day.

Anne Clarkson and Samantha Ruskin, the wonderful women at Dare2Dream, promised to treat my manuscript with honor and respect and possessed the courage to sign an unpublished author.

"This here is our real honeymoon. We can bury all them bad memories and get on with living."

"Leo was tiny, skin and bones, really, and too weak to hold his head up."

"We can be a real family, this time. We've all had enough bad things happen. Now we're due some good times."

A Storyteller's eyes are always filled
with ghosts of the Walnut Hearts.
It is a sad thing, to have lived amidst such evil.
It can not be helped, for it is
the Great Spirit's plan for the Storyteller.

- Cherokee Legend

Jackie Glover

PROLOGUE

Theresa Abelard was conceived in California during the first weekend her parents, Varina and Leo, lived in Los Angeles. The young couple visited Chinatown on Saturday, where they purchased a small brass Buddha. On Sunday, they went to the beach and got sunburned, even though the sky was overcast. On Monday, as Leo left for his job at the defense plant, Varina huddled in their tiny bathroom, throwing up. Within forty-eight hours of her conception, Theresa was causing Varina considerable discomfort. Fun loving Leo immediately had no place in his wife's evolving, adult world.

"I think we're going to have a baby," Varina groaned.

Theresa, a precocious child by nature and the self-appointed family historian, could never recall a time when she did not know the story of her own beginning. She measured her existence from the moment her mother said, "I think we're going to have a baby," believing that Varina's words had summoned her from some fascinating corner of Chinatown or, even better, from the Pacific Ocean. The mystery of actually coming to life was a subject she often pondered, on her own, until she fell to the floor in what her mother described as "a dead faint". At those awful moments, her Grandmother Rice splashed cold water on Theresa's face to restore her senses.

"She just faints to get attention," Varina declared, after the doctor failed to find a medical cause for the incidents.

Theresa was born in Tisquah, Texas, rather than in

California, because Leo received his draft notice, "Greetings, etc.," wherein he was directed to report for induction in his home state of Texas.

"Well, this is it," he cheerfully announced, handing the notice to his pretty blond wife. "I gotta go fight the Germans or the Japs."

World War II was, for Leo, the ultimate Boy Scout camp out. If he was apprehensive about some details, he steadied himself in the belief that someone was in charge of his destiny and that he would just have to make the most of it.

Varina, three months along and still throwing up all day, every day, immediately made plans to move to her parents' farm near Tisquah. She was frantically eager to return to the childhood home she had haughtily referred to, ten months earlier, as "a hillbilly dump". Though she hated the thought of living in the drafty old farm house, Varina wanted to escape from California, a state she had begun to suspect was populated entirely by lunatics.

"Californians wear their pajamas to the grocery store," she wrote to her friends in Tisquah, "and they dress their dogs in bathing suits and sun glasses!"

Leo shipped out for basic training on his twenty-first birthday, his usually happy nature subdued by the presence of Varina, his mother Gussie and sister Summer, all crying. The three women almost tore him apart on the depot platform in their efforts to be the last one to hug him good-bye, indicating by their actions, if not their words, that they did not expect to see him alive again. Leo escaped the tearful trio's clutches and quickly found a seat on the crowded troop train among hundreds of other Texas draftees. He loved trains and was whistling "Chattanooga Choo-Choo" before Tisquah slipped over the flat, endless horizon.

Theresa always knew she was supposed to have been a boy, patriotically named for her soldier father, after the fashion of the times. Varina had been so certain she would produce a son that she neglected to select a girl's name. After the birth, she was too depressed to think about it, faced with such lack of control. She languished in her hospital bed, received visitors bearing baby gifts, and cried for hours.

"That young lady is a deep well of tears," the head nurse told Varina's friends and family, "a deep, deep well".

When the nameless baby was three weeks old, Dr. Khroner insisted on dismissing mother and child from his new clinic, at which time he filled out the birth certificate.

"Name her Leona, after Leo," he instructed the weeping Varina, "and Theresa, after my mother."

Theresa loved the manner in which she was named. Of course, she wished she had been a boy, since it would have made Varina happy. Each time Varina entered Theresa's latest growth statistic or cute saying in the blue Tree of Life Baby Book, she was obviously disappointed.

"If I'd known you were going to be a girl," she repeatedly explained, "I would have asked my shower hostesses for a pink book. Oh well," she always sighed, "we'll just have to make do with what we have, won't we?"

Theresa adored her maternal grandparents, Robert and Cathy Rice, who spoiled her and did not care who knew it. Though a blue star hung in their front window, indicating the household had a soldier engaged in the war effort, Robert and Cathy seldom mentioned Leo. From her earliest days, Theresa was aware of silent looks exchanged between Robert and Cathy whenever Varina's conversation focused on her absent husband. Theresa thought her grandparents simply grew weary of Varina's tireless recitation of Leo's Pacific Theater activities. Though unaware of their true feelings for their son-in-law, Theresa knew exactly how they felt about Leo's mother, Gussie Abelard.

"That snuff-dipping bitch should be stropped with a buggy whip," Robert once growled, despite Cathy's admonishing glance.

Until Theresa learned to read, she thought her grandfather's remark was recorded in her baby book, along with other milestones of her young life. The book, its blue cover embossed with a family of nearly nude Greek statues, assumed great importance in her mind. It was the only place where she, her hysterical young mother and her absent G.I. father ever came together as an entity. By the time she outgrew her childhood misconceptions, Theresa realized she was in serious trouble. She sensed that she was stretched much too thin, holding onto Varina's version of her life on the one hand and the cold facts, as Theresa knew them, on the other. At five years of age, Theresa resolved to learn the truth about life, hers in particular, and she set about it in the only way she knew. She asked countless questions, mostly about Leo.

Leo's mother, Gussie, always expressed surprise that he lived past infancy.

"I wouldn't of bet a wooden nickel on him pulling through," she said.

Gussie kept a framed snapshot of the infant Leo, bald and frail, which she always dusted with the corner of her apron before showing it to Theresa. Leo had been a sickly baby, possibly dying, which was the only reason Gussie had allowed her uppity sister-in-law, Phoebe, to take his picture in December of 1921.

"Phoebe was showing off, acting smart with that new Kodak camera," Gussie explained, each time she showed Theresa the resulting snapshot, all those years after the fact. "Of course, you know Phoebe and her sisters was all named after birds, so they thought they was special, from the get-go."

Leo, three months old and known to have an affinity for all things mechanical from his earliest days, stared into the camera as if he understood how it worked. He squinted a bit, because his Aunt Phoebe had carefully aligned herself so the sun shone over her shoulder directly onto Leo's pale, pinched face. Years later, peering at the photo, Theresa was fascinated by Phoebe's long, leggy shadow stretched across the yard and up the front of the unpainted farm house.

"Phoebe, Miss Know-It-All is what I called her, told me to squat down behind the chair, under the blanket, and hold him up. She promised me I wouldn't show in the picture. Well, she flat-out lied, as usual, and you can see my hands, plain as day. Look at that, will you?"

Gussie's tiny hands were so delicate and perfectly formed that Theresa, peering intently at the snapshot, imagined a child not much larger than baby Leo was crouched beneath his blanket, struggling valiantly to support his skinny body.

"He was starved to death, almost," Gussie explained, shaking her head, her narrow lips compressed into a straight line, "and don't you dare say I didn't try to feed him! No, sir! He just couldn't keep nary a thing down, 'cepting light bread. Three months old and starved to death on light bread, that's the truth!"

Tucked into one corner of the tarnished frame holding Leo's only baby picture was a small, murky studio picture of a young G.I. who resembled the singer, Frank Sinatra.

"That's your daddy on his twenty-second birthday, in Honolulu. He looks like your granddaddy, with that black hair and them blue eyes. I never thought Leo would come home alive from overseas." Gussie's eyes seemed to focus on some mental map of 'overseas', forever trying to sort out the geographical complexities of a war she never fully visualized. "Well, it don't do to dwell on what might have been, I guess. The good Lord brought Leo home, safe and sound, and that's His will."

At that point in Gussie's oft-told biographical sketch of Leo, the first child of her union with the beloved, handsome, deceased Michaul Abelard, Theresa instinctively understood that Gussie felt something other than gratitude for Leo's survival. It seemed to her that Gussie wished God had killed Leo on some exotic tropical island. Theresa wished the same thing, with all her heart. The mystery was whether she and Gussie shared that unspoken desire for similar reasons. Gussie was not very helpful, no matter how astutely Theresa tried to pry additional information from her. After telling of Leo's almost starving to death on light bread, Gussie usually fixed her shiny black eyes on Theresa and asked her own questions. Conversations between them always ended in a deadlock, their gaze frozen across a chasm of facts about Leo that neither felt able to divulge to the other.

Theresa was two and a half years old when Leo returned from the war. She remembered every moment of the day she first saw him, so it wasn't as if she didn't know what happened between them, from the first. She just didn't know what it meant. Or how to make him stop.

Varina, who viewed World War II as a grand, fitting backdrop for her married life, told everyone how she wished a motion picture camera crew had been there to capture on film Leo's dramatic return to civilian life. Always maneuvering around her husband's possessive mother and sister, Varina had secretly arranged to meet Leo in Big Springs.

"I just felt our little family needed a few days alone, to get acquainted," Varina later explained to the irate Gussie and Summer.

Leo, thin as a reed and yellow from years of taking quinine to prevent malaria, was delighted to be home, alive and well, at long last. Varina told witnesses to their bus station reunion that Leo had been the first in his home town of Tisquah to be drafted and the last to come home, as if the war's outcome somehow hinged on those facts. In a room on the third floor of Big Springs' best hotel, Leo unpacked his bulging barracks bag and proudly displayed souvenirs collected during three years of Pacific warfare. He draped Theresa's neck with shell necklaces and presented her with a chunk of snow-white coral from Christmas Island, his duty station on the day of her birth. He opened a wooden cigar box filled with foreign coins and currency, then identified each item for the curious Theresa. A black man, resplendent in a gold-trimmed red uniform, brought them dinner on a squeaky cart, compliments of the management. After they ate, Varina whispered into Theresa's ear, cueing her in a part they had rehearsed on the bus trip from Tisquah.

"Daddy," Theresa obediently lisped, "I love you."

Leo scooped Theresa up and carried her to the room's only window, opened to catch the listless September breeze. He sat her on the window sill and pointed out cars, as small as toys on the street below, three floors down. Varina, in the authoritative tone she always affected when relating her personal history, often recounted what happened next.

"Theresa was wearing that plaid outfit I made for her, the one with the red vest. She was a little scared of Leo, at first, because his skin was so yellow from taking quinine. Leo should have waited a while to pick her up, but he just had to hug her. They were looking out the window when I stepped into the bathroom and Theresa started screaming! Oh, Lord, it made my skin crawl! The screen was unfastened and Theresa almost fell out the window! It would have killed her, and I told the manager so. I came right out and said that we would have preferred safety over the fancy two dollar meal they gave us. Thank God, Leo caught her leg! He was cool as a cucumber. The Army Air Corps trained Leo not to panic, otherwise Theresa would have died, right then and there!"

Varina eventually recorded the event in Theresa's baby book. After Theresa learned to read, she prayed for the courage to erase her mother's story and replace it with her own. She wished she could write about how, after Varina went into the bathroom that fateful day in Big Springs' best hotel, the yellow-skinned Leo hooked his thumbs into Theresa's cotton panties and pulled them down to her ankles. He winked at her, then lowered his head and stuck his tongue right smack into her tee-tee place. Theresa sat on the window sill, stunned into absolute silence, as her heart beat so hard it seemed to crawl up her throat. She stared at the back of Leo's head buried between her legs, noting the tops of his yellow ears. Pain, sharp and unexpected, pierced her body. She screamed, terrified. With a mighty effort, she twisted her body and lunged against the window screen, then slipped right out of the window, since the latches were unhooked. The only point where her memory of that terrifying moment matched Varina's story was when Leo grabbed her ankle just as she fell toward the pavement.

Leo's homecoming marked the beginning of a silent, fierce struggle between Theresa and Varina, regarding which of them knew the real Leo and what his presence in their lives meant. As the years passed, Theresa watched with growing resentment as Varina periodically recorded her experiences and achievements in the Tree of Life Baby Book. She yearned to rip out all the pages and deface the smug statue family on the embossed blue cover.

"Leona Theresa Abelard had two and one-half good years in her life," she wanted to write, in large, black letters. "Then her daddy came home from the war!"

Jackie Glover

Walnut Hearts

GUSSIE
1920 - 1942

CHAPTER ONE

"I might be a fool for love," Gussie whispered. "If a body loves too much, God will take that loved one away from you! It says so in the Bible, and my Daddy told it to me often enough!"

Phoebe, standing close behind, made a sympathetic noise. Gussie continued speaking, not really caring what her hired hand's young wife thought but still glad to have her company in the shadow-filled parlor. The moment was, for Gussie, too meaningful to witness in solitude. She was about to meet the man of her dreams. The one man on earth she wanted.

"In the month of November, in the year of 1920," she continued, "I believe I am finally in the right place, at the right time. I know now why God has kept me planted for so long in Maverick County, Texas against my will. Michaul Abelard is just passing through! Yes, just passing through Maverick County, and I am right here, waiting for him. It must surely be God's plan, that's what I think! My lack of faith has been forgiven and the Lord has provided me with something grand!"

Gussie knew she sounded like her father, speaking in his most awe-inspiring hellfire and brimstone cadence. On any other day, she would have despised herself for mimicking his preaching voice, but she was in a state of great agitation. Less than twelve hours had elapsed since she had abruptly understood God's plan for her life. In a blinding moment, she had felt the fragments of her pitiful past fall together like wooden blocks. Her senses were infused with pure joy, each nerve so touched that she felt truly alive for the very first time. She'd heard years of loneliness compress into something worthy inside her heart, and it grew into a wonderful sound, like a chorus of angels. Her life, rearranged and pressed into a new shape, burned suddenly bright and wonderful, illuminating the abandoned corners of her existence. Her dark eyes were sparkling and she did not have to examine her reflection in the parlor mirror for proof. She could feel the sparkle, right down to her toes.

"Well, Phoebe, you get the prize for bringing Michaul Abelard here, and I ain't about to forget it."

"Uh, well, mmmm...." Phoebe whispered.

Gussie walked to the pier glass tilted in its oak frame to reflect her from head to toe. She had to admire the figure she cut, even if it was vain to do so. Dressed in a two-piece gray outfit, the skirt cut daringly above her ankles, she might have stepped from the pages of McCall's magazine. Her hip-long black hair was wound in a fashionable chignon, weighty and sensuous against her slender neck. Her snow-white skin made her thankful that her deceased husband had always admonished her to wear broad-brimmed hats against the south Texas sun. Gussie's eyes, jet black and intelligent, were filled with anticipation. She had made the right decision, she thought, to choose clothing other than widow's weeds for this day. The best day of her life.

"I may be a fool for love," Gussie said again.

"Here they come!" Phoebe hissed, from her post at the front window. "Lord, they've been out driving around for hours! I am about to have a fit!"

The young women hurried to the south side of the parlor, then stationed themselves on either side of a window set in the two-foot-thick adobe wall. They watched through immaculate lace curtains as a Model-T Ford automobile bumped across the cattle guard, turned into the ranch yard and drove past the enormous old adobe house. The Ford clattered to a stop beside the main horse corral. A trailing dust cloud caught up to it and showered its emerging occupants with honest, red, Texas dirt.

"Why didn't they stop at the house?" Gussie wondered. "My heart is about to bust!"

"I guess he doesn't want to look like he's in a hurry to

meet you," Phoebe replied. "I mean, there isn't anything settled between you two. It's not like you've even met each other! I mean. Well, you know what I mean."

"No, I don't know what you mean. Why, didn't you come running over here last night and drag me through the dark to look at him? Didn't you say he was perfect for me? That God must have sent your husband's brother here for a visit just so we could fall for each other? Didn't you say he wants to meet me? That he's a Mason who wouldn't ever wrong a widow-woman with a young child? Wasn't that you, the one and the same?"

"Yes, yes, that was me," Phoebe whispered. "And I meant all I said. I just didn't know you would fall so fast, what with not actually meeting him."

"We are meant for each other. Speaking won't make no difference! It's a done deal!"

"Good grief, Gussie!"

"Well, ain't I right? Did you say them very things last night?"

"I guess," Phoebe admitted.

"Then get out of here and go home. We got to pretend like this is the first time I ever met him."

"It is the first time you've met him," Phoebe warned. "Think about that! Don't blame me if you are getting your hopes up too high!"

Gussie did not take her eyes off the two men who stepped from the Model-T and ambled to the corral fence. Tall, lanky, broad in the shoulders and slightly awkward on their feet like the cowboys they really were, they were difficult to tell apart. Then the dust cleared and Gussie recognized Claude, her hired hand, a bit shorter and heavier-set than his visiting older brother. Gussie's heart pounded as she watched Michaul lean into the fence, one booted foot resting on the lower rail. Just twelve hours earlier, she had never laid eyes on her true love, she thought, and now there he was, big as life, right in her yard.

As she stared through the lace curtains, Gussie thought about the wedding ceremony she would soon share with Michaul Abelard. She wanted a satin dress, something extravagant that could be packed away in the cedar trunk, the sleeves puffed with tissue paper. Shoes to match. Flowers, too, even if they had to be shipped from San Antonio on blocks of ice. A lengthy write-up on the society page of every newspaper in the Rio Grande valley. Of course, she thought, her ten-year-old daughter would be a flower girl, dressed in some delicate fabric to enhance her gray eyes and auburn hair. The newlyweds would leave town in a car draped with white crepe paper ribbons, driving through showers of rice as they passed envious onlookers. It would be perfect in every detail.

Not at all like her first wedding.

Gussie had been raised in virtual seclusion and given in marriage at age fourteen to a man old enough to be her great-grandfather. She was unschooled, except for basic tutoring by her father from old copies of McGuffey's Readers, and of course, the Bible. There were no other books in her parents' house, for they frightened her mother, a beautiful Cherokee named Josephine.

Josephine's greatest fear was that she might be forced back onto the Indian Reservation in Oklahoma. As a young woman, she had fled her parent's farm, riding Avery's big black horse, holding onto her beloved's coat tails as her family gave chase. Josephine and Avery lived on the run for years after their marriage, apparently believing their whereabouts was of enormous importance to the Bureau of Indian Affairs. For Josephine, books represented the Indian Rolls, in which her name was indelibly inscribed. For Avery, book knowledge represented sin, which he seemed to have recognized sometime after kidnapping Josephine and taking her to Texas. In fact, Avery worried so much about sin that he answered the call to preach when Gussie was a mere toddler.

Gussie's young mind was often confused by the contradiction of her parents' deep beliefs. Her mother's quiet presence spoke eloquently of the Cherokee Way in which all things fall naturally into order. Her father's paranoia belied his professed faith in God, no matter how loudly he shouted the Gospel. Gussie simply did not know what to think about most things.

Eventually, Avery and Josephine produced so many

children that their incessant roving became impractical, and they managed to buy a ranch in Maverick County, Texas, near the Mexican border. After moving to the ranch, Gussie never had a playmate other than her siblings. She grew fond of recalling the days when her family had lived in East Texas, surrounded by Jefferson cousins. She taught the games she remembered to her younger sisters. Picking up Paw-Paws, London Bridge, Annie-Over, Simon Says and Nah, Nah, Nah, Said the Little Fox were their favorites. Gussie loved the sound of their clear, little girl voices in the twilight as they frolicked beneath the giant cottonwood trees surrounding their ranch house. Their father seldom allowed his sons, after the age of five or six years, to join the girls. Avery believed play would soften the boys, causing them to grow into useless young men.

"I defy anyone to show me where the scriptures advise us to let little boys play sing-song games with their sisters," he said, whenever anyone dared defy his edict. "Here is the Bible! Look for yourself!"

Since his challenge was usually made to his illiterate wife and children, all terrified of his legendary anger, no one ever proved him wrong.

Gussie's only friend on the ranch was a large stray dog she called Champ, who guarded the ranch with devotion far out of proportion to the occasional scraps of food he found in an old tin plate beneath the back porch. Gussie, who mothered him and worried about him, sometimes crawled under the porch and left a bit of meat for him. After Mexican rustlers shot Champ dead, Gussie cried her eyes out. Avery then whipped Gussie with his razor strap as her brothers and sisters bore silent, wide-eyed witness, because she had shed tears for an animal.

"Animals do not have souls," he said, "and you will remember that fact in the future, my lovely Gustine. They were put on this good earth by a loving God for the use of godly men. Do you understand?"

Gussie did not understand, but she promised she would never again cry over the loss of an animal.

Shortly after her fourteenth birthday, Avery arranged the marriage between Gussie and Mr. Peters, a wealthy, elderly rancher whose vast property holdings practically surrounded the much smaller Jefferson spread.

"Mr. Peters is a Civil War veteran, a Captain in the Army of Northern Virginia. Why, the man knew Robert E. Lee personally! Called him 'Marse Bob', right to his very face," Avery explained. "Mr. Peters is a walking history book, a treasure, a high-born gentleman! I give you my word!"

Gussie had no knowledge of history, and though the name 'Robert E. Lee' did sound vaguely familiar, she did not feel it sufficiently qualified Mr. Peters as her prospective mate. She looked to her mother for help. Josephine lowered her gaze and stared at her feet in a peculiarly Indian manner, signifying total submission. Gussie had never defied her father, other than sneaking a few chunks of meat into Champ's plate. She, too, looked down at her bare feet, submitting to Avery's will.

"Well, then, it's settled," Avery announced, as if there had been a discussion or any doubt about the outcome. "Next Saturday, at Mr. Peters' house will be just fine. Josephine, get our eldest daughter rigged up in some wedding finery."

Gussie was married wearing one of Josephine's old dresses hastily cut down to fit her slender body. She wore an outgrown pair of her own shoes that pinched her feet, causing so much discomfort that she could hardly follow the brief wedding rites performed by Avery. After partaking of hearty servings of wedding cake and apple cider provided by the chuck wagon cook, Avery and Josephine took their leave, along with their many children. Gussie watched the departing wagon as it disappeared in a cloud of dust. She had never spent a night away from her family. She had never felt so forlorn.

"Well," said Mr. Peters, "I think we should get better acquainted."

"We ain't acquainted at all, by my reckoning," Gussie whispered. She turned from the window and inspected her new husband, wondering exactly how she should feel about him. He was the oldest man she could recall ever seeing. He could not possibly be her husband. "See here, Mr. Peters," she blurted out, "this here just don't seem right! Ain't you awfully old to be marrying?"

"Madam," Mr. Peters gallantly replied, "age need not be a detriment to the fulfillment of the marital duties, neither on my part nor your own."

Gussie had no idea what the old man meant. Within days, though, she knew she hated him, pure and simple. She hated his incessant retelling of the many battles he had fought on the soil of his precious Virginia, as if Gussie cared or knew if such a place really existed. She hated his habit of smoking a clay pipe after their evening meal. She hated the sound of his coughing in the early morning hours, every day, rivaling the rooster's call as a reliable alarm. She especially hated watching him eat, using the tines of his fork to mash the vegetables she had so carefully cooked. Most of all, she hated what he called "beddie-bye time", a Southern euphemism for intercourse, an act Gussie found totally disgusting.

In the second year of their marriage she became pregnant. At first she had no idea what was wrong with her, not even after Mr. Peters gleefully informed her that she had been "caught". Finally, when she could no longer fasten her skirts over her swelling belly, she realized she was taking on the shape of a pregnant thing, like cows, ewes, mares and most of all, like Josephine. She had not imagined that she would ever have a baby. It was unthinkable. Babies, she well knew, were the source of endless work and total boredom. Gussie possessed such wisdom by virtue of regularly assuming responsibility for her mother's toddlers as each new baby was born.

"I've had enough of taking care of snot-nosed brats," she screamed at Mr. Peters, after she faced the truth about her condition. "I'll not have it! Take it yourself, after it's born, if you think a baby is such a grand thing!"

"Gussie, you are the most adorable thing when you carry on," Mr. Peters laughed. "I swear, had I realized how much I missed feminine companionship, I would have remarried much sooner. It was a long, dry spell for me, alone in the marriage bed. You will have this child, and you will love it. And all the others that follow, mark my word!"

Mr. Peters was right, in a sense. Gussie delivered a ruddy little girl whom Mr. Peters promptly named Lorena. Within moments of the birth, Gussie felt a shock of almost unbearable love for the child. She had not imagined her heart could contain such a mighty emotion, and she admitted that she might never have known love's majesty had she not borne a baby. There were no other babies, though, for after Lorena's birth Gussie declared war on Mr. Peters.

Gussie knew beyond a doubt that all she needed in her life, then and forever more, was her perfect infant, Lorena. She wanted no other child in her arms, for it would surely weaken and perish in Lorena's shadow. Suspecting that beddie-bye time was responsible for conception, she set out to confuse her husband to the extent that he would not think of such activity. She embarked on a program designed to wear the old man down, believing she would succeed without a hitch.

Gussie loved to cook on the massive, oil-burning kitchen range Mr. Peters had bought for her shortly after their wedding. Though a good cook, confident and reliable in the kitchen, she began deliberately burning Mr. Peters' food. What was not burnable, she flavored with odd combinations of spices and extracts. Mr. Peters soon began to think that something was terribly wrong with his taster and sniffer.

"Taste this," he fervently demanded, offering a spoonful of food to his wife, "and dare tell me there's not something odd about it!"

Gussie dutifully tasted, savored, then shook her head apologetically. It seemed just fine, her expression indicated.

"Poor old thing," she said, patting his blue-veined hand. "Here, let me get you another plate. I'm sure this one will taste better."

Eventually, Mr. Peters lost interest in eating food prepared by Gussie, preferring instead apples from the scrawny tree beside the back porch. He then developed a case of the runs and ceased eating much of anything. Gussie mentally chalked up one victory for herself and her campaign but knew she should not ease up just when the enemy was feeling the sting of defeat. She had learned that much from listening to her husband's nightly recollections of military campaigns.

She cut off Mr. Peters' pants legs and hemmed them with

old thread, so they seemed to have shrunk while hanging in the cedar wardrobe cabinet. Next, she replaced his shirt buttons with slightly larger ones from her button box, so he was unable to fasten them no matter how hard he tried.

"Damn it, Gussie," Mr. Peters begged, "tell me what's going on with my clothes!"

"They look just fine to me," she observed.

Gussie's most effective tactics evolved when she decided to hide things Mr. Peters depended on, beginning with the wickedly long razor he used each morning and the horn-handled pocket knife he always carried in his left pants pocket. She reset the heavy gold pocket watch he wore tucked into his vest, each day if she had the opportunity, until Mr. Peters stopped looking at because it was always wrong. On one sultry washday, she bleached the ink from all Mr. Peters' legal documents. Three days later the unshaven old man, dehydrated from diarrhea, dressed in pants cut off at the high-water mark, shirt unbuttoned, and gold watch set at least four hours off the correct time, sat at his enormous roll-top desk and opened a drawer from which he extracted the deed to some property he wished to sell. To his great dismay, all he found were blank pages, wrinkled and damp, smelling ever so faintly of chlorine.

Gussie's plan, though causing general chaos in Mr. Peters' daily life, did not result in his losing interest in beddie-bye time. In fact, he grew more determined to avail himself of conjugal rights.

"Open up, damn you," he panted, night after night. "I've been there before!"

Gussie kept her legs clamped tight, her arms crossed over her hard little breasts, and her lips sealed. Only her eyes were open to her husband, because she wanted to watch him suffer. She thought, hoped, even prayed, that he would just die. That was all she really wanted. To be his widow.

Mr. Peters next did what Gussie had never imagined. He told her father what had been going on during the months following Lorena's birth. Avery came to visit and sat across the kitchen table from her one morning, calmly discussing the matter.

"My lovely Gustine, the Bible says you must honor your

husband,"

"I hate the nasty old thing," Gussie replied, indignantly. "You should have let me find my own husband! Someone my own age!"

Avery considered the situation for a moment, then took a slightly different approach. He rose from his chair, leaned across the table and hit Gussie square on the jaw, like a barroom boxer.

"You will honor your husband, Gustine," he repeated, hitting her again as she struggled to stand. "You will also honor your father, who was guided by the hand of God to choose Mr. Peters for you. If you defy your husband and your father, you defy God in Heaven. Do you understand?"

Gussie nodded. She understood, though she did not agree with her father.

When Mr. Peters came home and found her with a black eye and split lip, he was shocked.

"I never thought he would hurt you, Gussie," he moaned. "I just wanted him to talk to you and find out why you turned against me!"

Gussie knew she had a much better chance of surviving a discussion with Mr. Peters than another encounter with her father, so she decided to come clean and own up to her feelings.

"I wanted to choose my own husband," she admitted. "Why would a girl my age want to marry some old man with one foot in the grave? You shouldn't of asked for me. It ain't right!"

She waited for his response, watching as he walked to the sink and pumped fresh water into the tin drinking cup he favored. He sipped it, then offered it to Gussie, who refused, though her throat was parched. Mr. Peters squared his shoulders. Gussie experienced a moment of insight into how he must have appeared in his younger days, when he still possessed a full head of auburn hair and wore the gold-trimmed uniform packed in cedar chips, secure in the trunk at the foot of their bed. His gray eyes, she noticed, still held the power to command one's attention, to make one squirm.

"Gussie, my first wife and child died during the war. Maybe I never told you, I can't recall if I did. They died of simple starvation, from having to finally eat boiled shoe leather."

Mr. Peters' voice thickened with emotion, and he passed one blue-veined hand over his eyes. "My second family was taken by the cholera. Just dreadful, the way cholera victims die. I hope you never witness that kind of agony. The third wife and babies were attacked by a swarm of hornets right down there on the creek bank. The little girl lived for two days after the others, but nothing would get her over the venom. In all, I lost three wives and six children, Gussie. I came to believe that I just wasn't meant to be happy. I don't know how to justify our marriage, Gussie, other than to say that Virginians are gentlemen. Virginians do what they can to help a lady. That's what I did, try to help a beautiful lady."

"What lady?"

"Why, you, Gussie," Mr. Peters said, softly. "I never asked for you. Never! Your daddy was offering you to anyone who owned property. Said you were old enough to marry and he couldn't afford to go on feeding you. I thought if I took you it might save you from somebody worse. I supposed you knew what he did."

Gussie considered Mr. Peters' story for a moment, though she immediately recognized the truth in his words. She blinked away hot, shameful tears and held out her hand.

"I apologize for thinking poorly of you, sir," she whispered, "though I do believe my feelings was plumb natural."

Mr. Peters solemnly accepted her hand, shook it and nodded.

"Well, Gustine," he said, kindly, "I'll give you a divorce, if you desire to sever our bonds. You think it over and let me know your decision."

"I'm not right certain what a divorce is," Gussie whispered, "so I don't reckon I should take one from you."

"A divorce is a legal action to end a marriage," he explained, "after which, you would go your way and I would go mine."

"I don't hardly know which way is mine, sir," Gussie replied, "other than here, with you and Lorena."

"Then let us start over, Gustine," Mr. Peters suggested. "If I will make a proper proposal of marriage and if you accept, then we will go to San Antonio and have us another wedding."

"You'll need some new clothes," Gussie noted, casting a critical eye upon her smiling husband. "Them don't seem to fit."

"Madam, I could not agree more!" Mr. Peters sighed.

Mr. Peters was apparently happy during the last ten years of his life, though he never actually said so. Gussie knew he adored their daughter, Lorena. She suspected he loved her, too, though he died with his first wife's name on his parched lips. Gussie knew she did not love Mr. Peters, though she did respect him. Her feelings for her husband were a thing apart from her heart's desire. He was just too old to love, too lost in his memories of events and places long gone.

When it was all said and done, Gussie was simply happy to be his widow. It was, after all, the first goal she had ever set for herself. Her second goal was to fall in love with a handsome man of her own choosing. She hadn't counted on the Good Lord enough, she thought, who had simply led someone as perfect as Michaul Abelard to her.

"God done the picking," she whispered, shivering with delight, "and I didn't have to do 'nary a thing except peek in through Claude and Phoebe's kitchen window. I knowed right then that Michaul was the one!"

She opened the door as Claude knocked, pretending surprise, aware that the two tall men on the porch were also pretending. It was fun, she thought, almost like a stage play.

"This is my brother, Michaul," Claude said. "He's right interested in the sorrel."

"You a horse man, sir?" Gussie asked.

"I've rode a few in my time," Michaul answered, looking straight into her face.

An unruly shock of black hair fell across his forehead as he removed his hat. His face was gaunt, and his suit seemed about to slide off his thin frame. His eyes were the bluest eyes Gussie had ever seen. Blue as bottle glass. Bold, too, they were, boring into her insides. Her scalp prickled and she felt for an instant that she might swoon, though she had never before fainted.

"Well, Claude," she heard herself say, "why don't you

leave your brother here to discuss the sorrel while you go to Eagle Pass and pick up the supplies?"

"Uh, it is a little late in the day, ma'am," Claude stammered. "I mean, I wouldn't get back before dark if I leave now, in the wagon."

"Take the Ford," Michaul said, "and take your time."

His eyes never left Gussie's face. Neither noticed as Claude stumbled from the porch and cranked the Model-T to life, then clattered down the road, headed for Eagle Pass.

"Are you a coffee drinking man, Mr. Abelard?" she asked.

"I am that," he admitted, shaking his head as if it was a mortal weakness to crave coffee. "A man can't ever get too much good coffee."

Gussie invited Michaul into the kitchen. She saw right away that he felt immediately at home. She was thankful, for she did not admire shy men. He sat across the table, silently observing as she arranged cups and saucers, the sugar bowl and creamer.

"That is mighty fine china, ma'am."

"What?" Gussie was momentarily confused, then realized he was talking about the dishes. "Oh, this old stuff? It belonged to one of Mr. Peters' dead wives. I forget which one. I been thinking I should throw it all out and buy something new. Something not so old-timey, you know."

"Something modern?"

"Yes. Modern. That's what I been thinking."

"Well, ma'am, I was thinking myself, as we walked through that imposing parlor, that a young woman like yourself doesn't belong in a stuffy old museum like this."

"You thought that? About me?"

"Sure as I'm sitting here," Michaul grinned. He looked younger then, almost playful. Gussie wanted to touch him, to press her hands to his face. "Why don't you sell this junk and start all over?"

"Well, I declare, I might do just that!"

"I know people in these parts who would pay a pretty penny for this," Michaul said. "So, if you decide to sell, I would be glad to put you in touch with them."

24

"Just what line of business are you in, Mr. Abelard?"

"Call me Michaul, why don't you? Oh, I just went bust in the oil boom down south. Trying to find my place since I came home from the war. Looking around."

"Well, I wouldn't want to sell anything before my daughter comes home from boarding school. San Antonio, that's where her school is. She thinks all this old stuff is right out of a storybook. You see, her father filled her head with so much nonsense about Virginia, and the war. I don't know what all he told her, it made my head spin!"

"You need your daughter's permission to sell your things?"

"No, it ain't like that," Gussie stammered. "She just loves the old dishes and furniture, from the old days her daddy told her about. More so, since he died. She was just the apple of his eye."

"What's her name?"

"Lorena," Gussie said, smiling. "After an old Civil War song Mr. Peters recalled his men singing around their campfires at night. He bought Lorena a piano for her third birthday, just so she could learn to play that piece of music. Mr. Peters hauled her around to every place you can think of, so she could play for a bunch of old veterans. She'd have them all in tears. Did it ever make Mr. Peters proud! I was right proud of her, too, of course."

"But?"

"But, well, Mr. Peters put too much on her little shoulders, taking her to them old historical meetings. Them old soldiers, crying, showing each other their scars, their bits of battle flags, I couldn't stand it. I don't know how to say what it made me feel, but I didn't want Lorena to feel the same way."

"It gave you the heebie-jeebies?"

Gussie laughed, nodding her head, though she had never heard the phrase.

"Something like that, I guess," she agreed.

"Still get the heebie-jeebies myself, sometimes," Michaul said, as if confessing a very solemn secret. "I saw some things in the war I can't explain to this day. Some things that still make me feel strange, just remembering."

"Was you was wounded?"

"Just gassed," Michaul said, bitterly. "Though some might say it's the deepest wound of all!"

"I didn't mean to pry," Gussie assured him. "Ain't been many veterans of this latest war around here."

The subject of wars confused Gussie. She never knew when or where, let alone why, they took place. Mr. Peters said she had no head for politics. She had always been too ashamed to admit to her ancient husband that she hadn't a clue as to what part politics played in wars. She haltingly explained to Michaul her lack of understanding, praying he would not think she was stupid.

"Well," he said gently, "it's no wonder a fine lady like yourself is confused. Most everything politicians say about war is an outright lie. I make you out to be a lady who likes to deal only in the truth."

"That's true," Gussie admitted. "I ain't so good at figuring out what's true from the lies. Can't seem to lie, myself. No good at it!"

"Then tell me the truth, right now," Michaul said, teasingly. "You knew I'd be over here this morning, didn't you?"

"Yes, I knowed. Phoebe told me before breakfast that you wanted to meet me. That you might be interested in getting married, to the right woman. That you had a feeling that God sent you to my ranch on a mightier purpose than just visiting your brother and his wife." Gussie paused, then breathed deeply. She squared her shoulders and looked into Michaul's eyes. "Well, I reckon you already know I sneaked a peek at you through the window last night."

"Were you happy with what you saw through the window? Before you answer, you should know that Phoebe showed me your picture and I said right then that you were a handsome sight."

"Yes. I was right happy with what I seen. I seen them blue eyes of yours and knowed you for my own true love. It don't bear explaining. God put us here, believe that. It warn't none of our doing. Please, don't think I'm stupid, but He did, even if I can't explain how I know. It feels true in my heart! I'll just come out and say it, that's how it is! If it don't suit you, all you need do is go on your way."

A deep silence grew between them, fragile as a mirage on a scorching, summer horizon. Gussie could not force herself to say another word, occupying long, shimmering moments by stirring her coffee with a heavy silver teaspoon. The antique clock in the foyer boldly ticked off each minute. Outside, the great windmill in the back yard caught a sudden breeze and clanked into action, spinning its metal blades, driving the pump shaft deep into the alkaline earth. A horse nickered. The sorrel, Gussie thought. The kittens under the back porch mewed, then hushed, muffled by their mother's milky warmth. Beads of sweat ran down Gussie's spine, caught finally, pooled in the gathers at her waist. She raised her eyes and met Michaul's blue gaze.

"Come here," he said, holding forth his arms.

Gussie stumbled to her feet and slowly walked around the table as Michaul pushed his chair back. She assumed he was preparing to stand and embrace her but as she cleared the corner of the table, she realized he had unfastened his trousers. His penis was exposed to her view. Gussie stopped. Stared.

"You want it, don't you?"

Gussie could not answer, nor take her eyes away from Michaul's penis. Huge, pale and waxy, like a thick candle. It seemed in all ways to be a nocturnal thing, unaccustomed to daylight. Dangerous. She moved forward until she was near enough for Michaul to reach out and clasp her hands.

"Take off your bloomers," he whispered.

Gussie dropped her drawers right then and there. Michaul lifted her skirts with one large hand as he pulled her closer. Gussie was aware of his smell, strong and masculine.

"Straddle me," he whispered. "Ride me like a horse."

Gussie obediently lifted one leg across his lap and sat upon his organ, aware that she was wet between her legs. Michaul entered her and she screamed in pain, then fell against his chest, expecting he would understand that he was much too large for her opening.

"Stop!"

"Not yet," Michaul gasped, clasping her narrow waist.

"Ride me!"

Gussie took a deep breath and began moving against him, opposing his rhythm, feeling that she was about to split in half, incredulous then at the pleasure she felt. She moved faster, catching her boot heels in the chair rungs, grasping Michaul's broad shoulders. Gussie closed her eyes and imagined she was riding the sorrel across the prairie. An unfamiliar sensation, a pleasurable cramp, crept down the inside of her legs as she moved faster, straining for something she did not comprehend. Michaul groaned, then pulled her hard against his thighs, squirming in the chair until he found release.

They held each other, gasping, until Gussie realized he was lifting her off his lap. She did not know how to act, could not believe she had done such a thing. He is my true love, she told herself. God sent him to me.

"Let me get rid of this," Michaul whispered.

Gussie stared at his penis as he appeared to peel it away from his body. She could not believe her eyes.

"Never seen one before?" Michaul laughed.

"What in tarnation is it?"

"A French letter, honey," he replied. "You know, a prophylactic."

"A what?" she whispered. Her only thought was that perhaps he had a detachable penis.

"Something men wear so they don't get women pregnant," he explained, as if he did so every day. "It's like a little glove."

Gussie clamped both hands over her mouth and bent closer to inspect the French letter. Sure enough, Michaul was removing a thin membrane from his organ. He held it up for her inspection. The bottom was filled with creamy liquid she recognized as his man stuff. His penis, she noted with great relief, was still attached in the proper place, though shrunken and harmless enough, by then.

"You got a trash sack I can throw this in?" Michaul asked, as he fastened his trousers with one hand.

Gussie felt no embarrassment, just an overwhelming curiosity. She supposed Michaul had learned some things in France that ordinary people did not know. She hoped again that he did not think she was stupid. She quickly scooped up her bloomers and stuffed them into her skirt pocket. She then freshened their coffee and set out the cookie jar full of tea cakes. She felt weak with hunger. Michaul returned from the back porch and sat down, grinning at her.

"Tea cakes," he commented, helping himself to one of the large, thin cookies, "my favorite."

"My husband always said a true Southerner called them 'tea cakes' instead of sugar cookies," Gussie said.

"Well now, he was absolutely right," Michaul agreed. "You can tell. Everybody's mama and grandma made tea cakes."

"Not mine," Gussie replied.

"Your ma's Indian or something," Michaul commented. "Claude told me."

"No, that ain't right," Gussie lied, though she did not know why.

"No matter," Michaul said. "Come back over here."

He held her in his lap like a treasured child, then kissed her upturned face and lips. She felt herself relaxing against his chest, not the least bit self conscious. He placed one hand beneath her skirt, then caressed her leg.

"You are like a little girl," he whispered. "Not big as a minute."

He placed one finger between her legs and began massaging her, slowly at first, then more rapidly. Without knowing why, Gussie gently rocked against his gentle thrusts.

"Your husband ever do this?"

"No," Gussie whispered, "what is it?"

"Just rubbing your place, sweetheart. Didn't you ever do it to yourself?"

"No, but I plumb wish I had."

"Did your husband ever make you come?"

"Come where?"

"You'll see," Michaul promised.

She did.

By dusk, they had made love on the horsehair sofa in the parlor, the Persian rug in Mr. Peters' office, and in the big tin bathtub they dragged from the porch into the kitchen.

"I never knowed people could have beddie-bye so many times, especially in the daylight," Gussie confided. "Let's do it one more time."

"We can't do it again until Claude gets back with the Ford," Michaul told her. "I'm out of French letters."

They gorged themselves on cold roast beef from the ice box, followed by smooth, golden peach halves they ate from the can, juice running down their arms as they giggled like children. Wrapped in a towel, Gussie sliced fresh lemons and squeezed them to make lemonade. Michaul chipped ice from the burlap-wrapped block beneath the ice box.

"We'd best get dressed," Michaul said, draining his glass. "Claude may get back from town any time."

They set about finding their clothes, which became a source of merriment, since they had to search in several rooms before reassembling their outfits. Together they carried pails of bath water outside, pouring it onto the flower beds even though it was autumn and nothing was blooming. Gussie refused to waste water, having been taught since childhood that it was more precious than liquid gold. Michaul, also raised in West Texas, obeyed her instructions without question. They saw, then heard, the Model-T heading towards the ranch yard. They waved at Claude, who blushed like a schoolboy.

"Will you be leaving me?" Gussie whispered to Michaul.

"Do you want me to leave?"

"No."

So, he didn't. It was that simple.

Gussie did not sleep that night, though Michaul dropped off the moment his head touched the feather pillow. She wanted the darkness to herself, in order to ponder the day's events. No matter how hard she tried to organize her thoughts, though, she could not get past how she had felt when Michaul first looked at her. Those blue eyes had, somehow, burned away her former self. A newer, better Gussie lay beside Michaul in the bed she had formerly shared with Mr. Peters. In the dark hour before dawn, as the roosters first crowed, she nudged Michaul awake.

"Do you reckon we're sinning?" she asked.

"Sin means what you want it to mean," he sighed. "Does

it feel like sin to you?"

"No," she whispered. "It feels plumb right to me. I just can't figure out if God wanted us to act like married people on the very day we met. Maybe He put us together and then tested us. Maybe we failed the test, that's all I'm wondering about. I know we was supposed to love each other, but maybe not in every way. My brain ain't worked right since I looked in the window and seen your blue eyes. It scrambled my senses."

"Then what we did was right."

"I'm worried most about what my daddy will do to me," she confided. "He hit me when I went against Mr. Peters. I don't figure he'll be much kinder if he finds out about us jumping the gun."

"He won't lay a hand on you," Michaul promised. "You don't care what that old fogy thinks, do you?"

They were married in Eagle Pass on Thanksgiving Day, at the home of a Baptist minister. The pastor's pimply, teen-aged son played a desultory, greatly abridged wedding march on the parlor organ. The delicious smell of baked turkey and mince pie wafted from the kitchen, along with a staccato of Spanish spoken by the Mexican servants. The atmosphere was a bit too homey for Gussie's taste, not at all like the wedding of her dreams. As far as Michaul was concerned, the ceremony was unimportant. It was the state of matrimony, of being one entity, that he was in a great hurry to attain.

Phoebe and Claude stood up for them, acting like proud peacocks. Gussie knew they took full credit for the marriage, but she didn't care. All she cared about that day was Michaul.

"I feel guilty about not inviting my parents," Gussie admitted to Michaul.

"Don't worry about them," Michaul replied.

Michaul's elegant, white-haired mother, Bitsy, and Gussie's daughter, Lorena, were the only guests. Lorena, adorable in a blue cape and dainty red patent leather boots, wept as the little group left the parsonage and prepared for the trip back to the ranch.

"You are behaving like a spoiled brat!" Gussie hissed. She attempted to grasp Lorena's arm as they climbed into the

Model-T, but the girl angrily pulled away.

"Why did you do it?" Lorena sobbed. "Why did you plan all this without letting me know?"

"Because I don't need to ask for your say-so to live my life," Gussie said, deliberately.

"I hate him," Lorena cried. "I want my father!"

"Lorena, your father is dead and buried, and you know it!"

"I know you wanted him dead and buried, that's what I know!"

"Now, you listen to me, Lorena," Gussie warned. "I want you to stop this temper tantrum. Right now! This is a happy day for me. I don't want you to ruin it!"

"You will be truly sorry you married him. He is no gentleman!"

"He ain't old and he ain't sick, Lorena," Gussie snapped. "That's what you think it takes to make a gentleman, because you don't know better!"

They fell silent as they realized Michaul and Bitsy were listening intently to their hushed argument. Michaul deliberately leaned over and kissed Gussie full on the lips, a lingering kiss that left her breathless and confused. As usual. His touch, even his glance, had supreme power over her mind and body.

"How about we get acquainted," he suggested quietly. He leveled his bold, blue eyes on Lorena.

"You should go directly to Hell, sir," Lorena spat back. It was a remarkable imitation of Mr. Peters. Gussie shivered.

"Lorena!" Gussie cried. "You tell Michaul you don't mean that!"

Michaul, too, was obviously startled by the girl's rudeness. Gussie, recalling her own father's immediate, violent reaction to any impolite behavior from children, was afraid Michaul would slap Lorena's face. She tensed, uncertain which side she should take, and was grateful when Michaul simply shook his head and grinned. He walked to the driver's side and entered the Model-T.

"Well, Lorena," he said, as Claude cranked the automobile to life, "I've decided you should go to Tisquah with

Walnut Hearts

us on our wedding trip. It will do you good to see your new home."

"I'd sooner walk unarmed into a Yankee encampment," Lorena replied.

"Does she ever talk like a kid?" Michaul asked, still grinning.

"She's been raised to act like a little lady," Gussie sighed. "I reckon she's plumb forgot it, from the way she is carrying on!"

Claude and Phoebe squeezed into the Model-T and the six of them rode to the ranch in silence. Gussie ignored the sting of tears in her eyes. All along, she had known it would be hard for Lorena to accept another man in their life. That much was normal and was to be expected, but she was truly amazed at the force of Lorena's instant, apparent hatred for Michaul.

Gussie had wanted to write to Lorena about the marriage plans, but Michaul convinced her to wait and talk to the girl when she arrived home for the Thanksgiving holidays. Lorena would get used to the idea, Michaul had said. She was just a kid, and kids learn to accept their parents' decisions, he said. Well, Gussie thought, it's all in the kettle now. We'll just have to see what cooks up.

At the ranch, Claude and Phoebe helped Bitsy descend from the Model-T. The three of them planned to stay at the main house until Gussie and Michaul returned from Tisquah, a period of about a week, according to Michaul's plan. Gussie was no longer certain any of their plans would work out as they expected.

"Gussie, you and Lorena wait here," Michaul said, as he followed his relatives into the ranch house. "I'll make sure Bitsy gets settled in."

Gussie was not sure just what he meant, for Bitsy had arrived unannounced and made herself perfectly at home the day before. Just for the wedding, Michaul had assured Gussie. Gussie suspected that Bitsy might be planning to visit for quite some time, judging by the pile of luggage she had brought with her.

Michaul returned in a few minutes, carrying Lorena's little valise, which he casually tossed onto the back seat. Lorena resumed sobbing and Gussie sighed.

"My romantic plans is about to get a kick in the pants," Gussie whispered. "Just as plain as the nose on my face."

The honeymoon trip was, at best, a nightmare in Gussie's opinion. Lorena refused to speak, eat or change her clothes and so far as Gussie knew, the child did not sleep at all. Thankfully, Michaul seemed unaware of Lorena's behavior. His mind was on more important things.

"Farm land," he announced on the second day of the trip. He pointed at the flat expanse of tilled earth stretching over the horizons in every direction, broken by occasional clumps of wind-whipped little trees. "Why, before the war, Claude and I worked cows all over this area. We never imagined it would ever get broken up into sections and sold as farms."

He affectionately patted Gussie's knee, grinning, and shook his head, obviously recalling something amusing. "We were some kind of wild men," he laughed. "I started riding for the Slaughter outfit when I was eleven years old. Claude, he was an old man before he started work. Bitsy made him wait until he was twelve, 'cause he was her baby."

"I already own a ranch, free and clear," Gussie pointed out. The idea of selling it and buying new land made her uneasy. "I don't see what the advantage will be in owning a farm way up here on the plains."

"Well, Gussie," Michaul replied, seriously, "I see your point. I do. But, did you ever wonder who will buy your horses now that the war is over? More and more people are getting rid of their horses and buying automobiles. Think about it."

"I never had no idea of that," Gussie admitted, "but what would we grow on one of these farms? What crop can grow in this windy place?"

"Cotton," Michaul replied, nodding his handsome head. "Old king cotton! That's what. Maybe some maize, even some wheat. We can make a fortune, I promise. We'll have to go ahead and put down some money," he explained, "in order to get the perfect place. Lucky for us, we have just enough time to move and get settled before planting time."

"When is that?" Gussie asked.

34

"When the weather gets warmer," Michaul answered, happily, "but we can move as soon as the ranch is sold."

She did not reply, for she was listening to Lorena, who was sobbing in the back seat. In Gussie's shirtwaist pocket was a crumpled note she had watched Lorena furtively place beneath a peanut jar at the cafe where they stopped for lunch. The message, written in Lorena's round, school girl copperplate, was the most alarming thing Gussie had ever read.

"HELP! I am held against my will by my mother, who has taken leave of her senses. Her new husband is a most cruel man. He is no gentleman, I assure you. We will spend the night in Tisquah, Texas. Please tell the sheriff to come get me. A five dollar compensation is offered.

Lorena Delphina Peters, daughter of Cpt. Esau Peters, CSA"

The note lay like a sliver of ice against Gussie's heart.

CHAPTER TWO

"I will never live in this terrible place," Lorena whispered. "Oh, Mama, you will be so very lonely without me! What will you do?"

"It's gonna be better than you imagine," Gussie insisted. She tried to sound confident, though her own spirits were sagging. "Look. Some paint and curtains will spruce it right up. Michaul can build some shelves in your room for all your baby dolls. We can plant flowers in the yard, and there's two elm trees purt near big enough to hang swings in. I know what we ought to do! Let's bring some cuttings from the lilac bushes at the ranch. Come spring time, they'll most likely be blooming!"

"It won't matter. Nothing will make it better. You will be so lonely. You will cry and cry!"

"Lorena, you just hush, right now! I swear, you are going to get brain fever if you don't stop all this gloomy talk!"

Gussie turned in the seat and studied her daughter. The listless child lay across the back seat of the Model-T, scarcely resembling the confident little girl who, only days earlier, had arrived from boarding school for the Thanksgiving holiday. Her normally ruddy complexion had paled, accentuated by dark circles beneath her large, gray eyes. Her beloved blue cape, the one she said made her feel like a grown-up lady, was wrinkled and soiled. Gussie reached to smooth Lorena's unkempt curls, but the child turned her head.

"Don't touch me," she hissed.

"Lorena," Gussie begged, "please, please don't suffer like

this. Please! I am so sorry I didn't write and tell you I was gonna marry Michaul and sell the ranch. It just happened so fast! I had so much work to do, so much to think about! I ain't got no excuse for myself, other than I thought you would understand and be happy. I wish I could go back and write that letter to you, I do! Please forgive me?"

"It is not your fault, Mama," Lorena sobbed. "It is Michaul's fault, all of it! He is the devil!"

"Why do you say such things about the man I love?"

"Because it is true! It is true!"

Gussie sighed. She turned to look at the shabby house that was to be their new home, imagining the work involved just to make it habitable. It was identical to the square, unattractive houses on all the farms Michaul had inspected during their four days in West County, built in the German manner, with a small porch set into the front. Inside, each room opened onto two neighboring rooms. Apparently, Gussie thought, the houses in the area had been built by a carpenter who had never learned to build rooms opening onto hallways. Gussie realized that, come hot weather, she would miss the ranch house in Maverick County, with its wide verandahs.

Gussie did not blame Lorena for doubting that their new home could be made better. She did wish her daughter would accept their new circumstances and show even a little enthusiasm for the upcoming move. Gussie wished that, and more, wished with all her heart. She wished for it in the Cherokee way.

"Lorena, my mama always said there was a better way of living than most folks realize. She told us to think of the things we want in life," Gussie explained, "as if they were already happening. She said we should just picture ourselves walking into another place, where everything was perfect."

"That is just Indian talk, Mama, about some make-believe world," Lorena protested, spitefully, "but, in case it works, then I wish I was back at Miss Rosemary's Academy in San Antonio. My father wanted me to attend that school!"

"Your father didn't know the market for horses would fall flat," Gussie answered. She had not realized how flat the horse market was, herself, until Michaul used it as an argument for selling the ranch. "It costs a bundle to send you to that fancy school. I don't think we can afford it. You can go to school in Tisquah, after we move, and you can make some new little friends."

"Any new little friends I make in Tisquah will be trash, because it is a trashy town! I want to go back to boarding school. That is my final word!"

"Lorena, I am plumb afeered I'll get brain fever myself if you don't calm down!"

"Afraid, Mama," Lorena corrected, "not afeered. I've told you a thousand times that afeered is not a word."

In the distance, Michaul and the banker from Tisquah strode across the plowed acreage, holding onto their hats against the strong wind. A dust devil danced through the fields, enveloping the two men in a swirling cloud of debris and dirt. Gussie, her heart pounding, leaned forward, peering through the windshield until she made out Michaul's dim figure emerging from the tempest.

"Don't worry," Lorena sighed. "Nothing on this earth can hurt your precious husband!"

The dust devil quickly traversed the farm yard and slammed against the Model-T, rocking it like a boat on stormy water. Gussie suddenly felt seasick, nauseous, fearful of something she could not define.

"I will face tomorrow bravely," she whispered, quoting from the only poem she had ever memorized. "Listen here, Lorena. I love Michaul and I am proud to be his wife. He is the best man I ever met! That's my final word. Do you understand?"

Lorena did not reply, though she did move her head enough to indicate comprehension, if not acceptance.

Michaul shook the banker's hand, then climbed into the Model-T. He hugged Gussie and laughed like a mischievous boy as they followed the banker's Packard into Tisquah. Gussie and Lorena waited outside the bank as Michaul closed the deal for the new farm. He brought papers to the automobile window for Gussie's signature, witnessed by a skinny woman who notarized each document. It was all very mysterious to Gussie, who had been taught that women were not capable of understanding business.

"I reckon," Gussie said to Lorena, as Michaul followed the secretary into the bank, "that there skinny woman don't have to understand what all them papers mean. All she has to do is clamp that fancy seal on the bottom of each page."

Lorena did not reply.

Shortly after noon they were on their way out of town, speeding south towards Maverick County. Lorena, satisfied that they were finally driving in a direction of which she approved, ceased crying and fell asleep. Michaul reached for Gussie, pulled her close and nuzzled her neck, his blue eyes never leaving the road. Gussie rested her head on his shoulder. She said a silent prayer for Lorena, for the three of them and their new life. In all honesty, Gussie doubted her prayers would make any difference. God probably expected her to have enough brains to deal with her own daughter.

They stopped for their evening meal at a brightly lit cafe on the main street of Big Springs. They held hands beneath the table as a weary waitress took their order. Gussie kept her eye on the Model-T parked at the curb, where Lorena continued to sleep. It was nice, she thought, that they had a few minutes alone and the opportunity to act like newlyweds, especially since they had not shared a private moment since the wedding. Gussie, recalling their passionate days and nights prior to the ceremony, wondered if Michaul also missed their intimacy. She did not know how to broach the subject, so she talked about how much she loved him, how desperately she wanted their lives to be perfect.

"I am truly sorry about the way Lorena has been acting," she concluded.

"Don't worry your pretty head about it. She will come around, you'll see."

"I reckon. I just wanted you to see her at her best. She has always been such a little lady. Maybe I just couldn't see how spoiled she was. Her daddy spoiled her. He plumb doted on her. He took her with him every place he went until she started to school. All his old Confederate friends thought she was just the cutest thing on earth!"

"Well," Michaul said, thoughtfully, "Here's an idea that

might help. If Lorena gets on so well with older folks, why don't we ask my mother to spend some time with her? Might calm the little girl down."

"That probably can't hurt. I've been meaning to ask how long your mother plans to visit," Gussie admitted. "I never got a chance to talk to her before the wedding, other than to say howdy."

"She will stay as long as we let her," Michaul said. "She doesn't have a place of her own. She's been with her sister's family in East Texas since I joined the Army."

"I don't rightly know if Lorena will warm up to her, or not. She ain't exactly taken a shine to you."

"It is worth a shot."

They sat, enjoying their companionship, lost in their own thoughts as the meal was served. The waitress managed a wan smile when Michaul asked for an additional butter pat for his rolls.

"Well!" Gussie remarked. "That gal sure has an eye for you!"

"Never noticed," Michaul replied, "but she can't be faulted for having good taste in men."

Gussie loved watching Michaul eat. His movements were so graceful she would not have been surprised to hear music playing as he spread butter on a roll or sprinkled pepper on the flour gravy. Some of Gussie's worst memories of her dead husband concerned his eating habits, particularly after he had grown too frail to chew his food during his last years of life. Gussie shuddered. Just thinking of Mr. Peters made her feel queasy.

"Don't you ever get old on me," she told Michaul. "I can't stand thinking of you any way but strong and handsome."

"I like you, too, just the way you are." Michaul tipped his head back, draining the last drop of coffee from the mug. "Let's get going! We're burning daylight!"

Gussie knew the one thing a cow man hated most was wasting daylight hours. To a large degree, she shared his philosophy. As her husband settled the bill, she quickly spread butter on an extra roll and wrapped it in a paper napkin, in case

Lorena should wake up with an appetite. The couple hurried to the Model-*T* and climbed inside without disturbing Lorena. They drove all evening and into the night, piercing the vast darkness with wavering, yellow headlight beams. They stopped only when Michaul relieved himself beside the road. Gussie refused to leave the car because of her fear of snakes.

"Snakes don't crawl in the dark," Michaul laughed. "Not usually."

"I ain't taking a chance of squatting on one, anyway," Gussie primly replied.

"You're likely to bust before the sun comes up, woman!"

"So be it. I ain't taking no chances!"

Gussie listened to Michaul's footsteps as he crossed the road. He was laughing as he unbuttoned his trousers. She fearfully considered what she would do if Michaul should be bitten by a night-crawling snake.

"You be careful, Michaul!" she called through the open window. "I can't drive this car if you get bit, you know!"

"Woman, I've been pissing in the dark all my life. I've never seen a snake out at night, except for water moccasins."

There's always a first time, Gussie thought, shuddering. She did not want anything bad to happen to Michaul, ever, for he was the man of her dreams. Michaul was handsome beyond her wildest fantasy. He was a gentleman, with manners good enough for any company. He understood business, how to buy and sell property, how to discern the best ways to provide for their future. He was, in Gussie's eyes, absolutely perfect. If only Lorena's attitude would change, she thought, everything would work out. She worried that her daughter's behavior would affect Michaul's pleasant disposition.

"Michaul," she whispered, as he settled beside her and put the car into gear, "you ain't going to lose your temper with Lorena, are you? I know it's a trial, putting up with her, but she really is the sweetest little girl in the world."

"I won't lose my temper."

"You promise?"

"I promise."

They talked through the night. Gussie told Michaul about

her parents and how her mother still worried about being caught and returned to the reservation. Michaul told her stories about his youth as a cowboy on the big Texas ranches. She almost cried, visualizing him at eleven years of age, out on the plains with a bunch of wild cows, in all kinds of weather.

"Didn't your ma worry about you?"

"Never said so, not that I recall," Michaul answered, thoughtfully. "She expected me to send her most of my pay, so I guess you could say she kept up with me. After my pa..."

"Look over yonder!" Gussie interrupted, pointing at the window on Michaul's side.

Across an incredibly wide expanse of horizon, the red light of morning etched a narrow, horizontal line in the darkness. Gussie gazed at Michaul's handsome profile, chiseled against the dawn's glow. Her heart ached with love. She reached up and touched his cheek.

"Well, I worry about you, and I always will."

"You are a good little girl, Gussie," he answered. "It's my luck that I found you."

"I been waiting in Maverick County a long, long time."

Gussie felt a sense of well-being when they arrived at the ranch house and parked beside the back door. Michaul's mother, Bitsy, was sweeping the steps leading to the screened porch. The old woman looked perfectly at home, waving when she recognized Michaul. Gussie decided Bitsy might be helpful with Lorena, after all.

"I've probably been worried over nothing," she said. "Wake up, Lorena," she called. "Look here honey bunch, we're home. You slept all the way from Tisquah!"

Lorena sat up and peered out the dusty window, then began sobbing.

"That old witch is still here!" she moaned. "This is no longer my home! My life is over!"

Gussie realized she would worry for a while longer.

Though she loved Lorena with all her heart, the child's constant whining and complaining wore on Gussie's nerves. The weeks following their return from Tisquah should have been fun, Gussie sighed, as she began packing for the impending move.

Lorena's hysteria overshadowed all the activity. The girl was adamant that not a single item belonging to her father be sold or otherwise disposed of.

"Lorena," Gussie explained, patiently, "we can't take all this old stuff to West County. In the first place, there ain't no good reason to hold onto everything, especially what belonged to your father's other wives. I don't want that junk and you don't need it. You can be a big help to me if you will just calm down. Why don't you go pack your dolls and toys? Let's get this done."

"Mama, your new husband knows my father's belongings are worth a lot of money and he wants to sell them. He can see that you don't have any idea of their real value."

"Don't be so uppity, young lady," Gussie cautioned. "What if Michaul and me do want to sell that stuff? Maybe we want the money instead of a house full of memories of days long gone."

"You have no right to sell those things, and that is my final word!"

"We'll just see about that!"

"I'll be in my room forever, Mama," Lorena cried, "or until you regain your senses!"

Two weeks before Christmas, the big house was emptied of china, crystal, silver, linen, antique furniture and art, all shipped to New Orleans, where Michaul had arranged to have it sold at auction. During Michaul's absence, Claude, assisted by several ranch hands, repaired and shipped to West County anything that might be useful on the new farm. Gussie fervently hoped the move would heal the rift between Lorena and Michaul.

Michaul returned from New Orleans, triumphantly bearing a set of modern dishes for Gussie and a book of paper dolls for Lorena, which the child promptly burned in the kitchen stove. Gussie was outraged at her daughter's ungrateful behavior, though Michaul just laughed. Gussie was thankful for his indulgence. She feared a major showdown between her daughter and husband was only days away, concerning disposal of Lorena's piano. The mahogany instrument, the final piece of furniture that would not be moved to Tisquah, stood in the parlor, like a solitary, cumbersome, petulant animal. Michaul claimed that no room in the new house was large enough to accommodate it. Lorena replied that she would never consider giving up her beloved piano, not even for a smaller, newer model.

Gussie, her luxurious black hair tied up in a linen napkin that had somehow escaped the New Orleans shipment, packed the kitchen items. She was aware that her daughter had finally left her room and was spending time with Bitsy.

"Things will get better," Gussie whispered, trying to bolster her own sense of doom. She had fallen into the habit of talking to herself during her lonely years with Mr. Peters. "I just know they will. My nerves won't take much more of this unhappiness. Why, my stomach is unsettled and my head aches all the time. If I had time to be sick, I'd probably catch brain fever."

Gussie had never seen an actual case of brain fever, but it was a common belief that undue exertion or nervousness could bring on an attack. There was no cure for brain fever, of that she was certain.

That night, too tired to stay awake much past sundown, Gussie took an early wash-off on the back porch and went to bed. She was awakened, how much later she did not know, as Michaul pulled on his trousers and boots.

"What's wrong, honey?" she asked, yawning.

"Don't know. Some commotion out in the horse barn. I'd better see what it is. Might be a snake."

"You said snakes don't crawl in the dark."

"Yeah, or it might be a skunk or maybe horse thieves. Don't know until I look."

"Be careful!"

Gussie fell asleep before Michaul left the room, not because she meant to, but because she was so very tired. She was never clear about how much time passed before she was awakened by the sound of breaking glass.

"Michaul?" she called. There was no answer, so she eased out of bed and walked through the house. "Michaul, is that you?"

"It's Bitsy, and I'm in the kitchen. Don't walk in here without your slippers because I just dropped the lamp chimney.

There is glass all over the floor!"

"What are you doing up, at this hour?"

"It is not all that late," Bitsy replied. "Here. I've found the other lamp."

Gussie waited as Bitsy struck a match and lit the kerosene lamp. Light poured across the kitchen linoleum, reflecting off shards of broken glass. Gussie gingerly walked across the room to fetch the broom from the back porch. She paused for a moment, aware that things were not right.

Not right, at all.

"Did you see Michaul?" she asked Bitsy, without turning to look at the old woman.

"No, I did not see Michaul," Bitsy replied. "I just wanted a glass of buttermilk to settle my stomach. Lord knows, I didn't aim to disturb your sleep."

Gussie was not listening to Bitsy's apology, or to her explanation concerning the soothing effects of a bedtime glass of cold buttermilk. Instead, Gussie listened to the night sounds, hearing with her whole being, the way her mother heard. The Cherokee way. She stood perfectly still until she was certain that Michaul was really in the horse barn and that there was trouble there. Big trouble. She stepped back into the kitchen and climbed onto a stool in order to reach the shotgun hanging above the back door.

"What is it? What do you need that shotgun for?" Bitsy gasped.

"I don't rightly know," Gussie replied, "but I aim to find out."

Tripping on the back steps, stubbing her bare toes, staggering under the weight of the gun, she ran, gulping air like a child who had heard the bogeyman under the bed. The expanse of baked earth separating the house from the barn seemed wider than she remembered, as if it had grown in the darkness and was expanding beneath her bare feet. Gussie wondered if she would ever cover the distance.

"Michaul!" she screamed. "I'm coming with the shotgun!"

Gussie, still running, was aware of Bitsy's presence

behind her. She never forgot the image of the old woman standing in the lamp's halo, though she did not actually turn and look back. Her total attention was focused on the gaping barn doors, where Michaul's tall figure slowly emerged from the darkness. Before Gussie drew near enough to see his face, she realized he was carrying Lorena's limp body in his arms.

"What happened?" Gussie cried. "Let me see her!"

"She tried to saddle a horse," Michaul said, calmly, "and he kicked her. I think her arm is broke."

Michaul carried Lorena into the kitchen and laid her on the table. Bitsy scurried about, lighting additional lamps. Lorena stared at them as if they were complete strangers.

"I don't like her eyes," Gussie said, fearfully. "They are glazed over!" Lorena reminded Gussie of Mr. Peters when he was in the throes of a waking nightmare, towards the end of his life. The old man had frequently believed he was in some old battle, fighting for his life, unaware of his real condition. "She don't seem like herself!"

"She is hurt," Michaul answered. "I saw wounded men look like that in the war. We have to wrap her in a blanket so she doesn't go into shock."

"Shock? Oh, dear Lord, what is shock?"

"When somebody gets hurt, if it's bad, their mind just gives up for a while. Don't worry. I know what to do."

"Here is a wrap I knitted just last year," Bitsy said. "It is a nice wool afghan, blue, you see. Well, I know the color doesn't matter. Just tuck it around her little legs and she will warm right up."

Lorena resembled one of the porcelain figurines from Mr. Peters' recently auctioned collection. There was no color to her face, and Gussie was appalled at how cold, how hard, she appeared. Like a beautiful little corpse. Gussie forced down panic as she examined her daughter, looking for injuries.

"Here," Michaul said. "You can feel the break."

Gussie gently ran her fingers down the length of Lorena's right arm, then nodded. It was a break, sure enough, just below the elbow. It was beginning to swell.

"Should we drive her in to Eagle Pass, to the doctor?"

Gussie wondered.

"I don't see the need," Michaul replied. "We can make a splint and keep her still for a couple of weeks, That's all the doc can do."

"Children do heal quickly," Bitsy added. "Besides, the trip into town, over those rough roads, would only cause the poor little thing a lot more pain."

Gussie nodded her agreement and the trio set about locating the necessary items for treating the injury. Michaul used a hand saw from the wood shed to cut a broom handle into four short pieces. Just as well, Gussie thought, for it was bad luck to move an old broom into a new house. She pulled open her pillaged linen cupboard and sorted through the rag box, finally locating enough wide strips of cloth to fashion a bandage. She folded the linen napkin she had worn around her head all day, satisfied it was large enough to serve as a sling. Bitsy pumped a wash basin full of water and bathed Lorena's face. The three of them then gently stretched Lorena's arm, positioned the broom sticks and wrapped the makeshift splint with cloth strips. Michaul carried the girl to her bed. As he pulled the blanket over Lorena's limp body, Gussie saw blood on his hands.

"Michaul, honey," she said, "you're bleeding."

"I got scratched up trying to pull her out from under the horse. That sorrel was trying its best to stomp her to death!"

"Why would she try to ride that wild horse? Oh, my poor darling girl, my heart of hearts! Has she gone plumb daft?"

Gussie knew Lorena had never before ventured into the horse barn at night. She had to admit that Lorena's behavior had changed since the wedding. Lorena had acted like a little hellion. Gussie blamed herself for letting things get so far out of hand. She felt personally responsible for her daughter's injuries.

"Kids don't know they can get hurt until after it happens," observed Michaul, as if reading her thoughts. "Hell, a kid will jump off a barn roof or into a deep river. You could get the heebie-jeebies, just thinking what all tom-fool things kids might do. Now that Lorena is resting, I'll go out to the barn and put the horse up."

Lorena did not speak until after Michaul and Bitsy left her

47

room.

"Mama," she whispered, as tears rolled down her pale cheeks, "Michaul hurt me."

"He said you were trying to ride your horse in the middle of the night," Gussie replied. "He saved you from a really bad hurt, that's what he said."

"I woke up and he was hurting me," Lorena insisted.

"Well, you fell off the horse and hit your head, I imagine."

"You would imagine that, Mama," Lorena sighed.

"We'll talk in the morning, sweetheart," Gussie promised. "I'll sleep in your room tonight, in case you need me."

"Will you take me to the doctor? I need to tell him something."

"Not tonight. Maybe tomorrow, if the swelling don't go down."

"Don't leave me alone, Mama. Promise me!"

Gussie watched as Lorena fell asleep. She tiptoed from the room, avoiding the squeaky floor boards, and went to the kitchen. Bitsy was still there, scooping up broken glass from the floor. The old woman looked incredibly weary.

"I think I'll have a glass of buttermilk," Gussie said. "I ain't feeling so good."

"Child," Bitsy answered, as Gussie poured the clotted milk into a glass, "if anyone was to ask me, I'd say you are in the family way."

"Oh dear, you may be right!"

Gussie walked onto the back porch, sipping the milk, and waited until Michaul came back from the barn. He held Lorena's little traveling bag in one hand and several dolls in the other. He walked into the kitchen and set the items on the table.

"Here's her stash," he said. "Everything a little girl needs to run away from home."

Gussie unfastened the brass clasp on the bag and opened the lid. Inside, tucked beneath some doll clothes and Lorena's silver hair brush, she found a photograph of Mr. Peters. Dressed in his Confederate uniform, his steady gaze fixed on an invisible horizon, he was impressive. Probably staring at some Yankees,

Gussie thought. She shivered, just thinking about all Mr. Peters' losses, all the death he had witnessed. She unfolded an embroidered handkerchief wrapped around Mr. Peters' military medals, all shiny and new looking. His favorite, an elaborate creation of glass and gold, framed a snippet of a flag from some gory battle. Gussie could not recall just which battle. The frame was surrounded by little diamonds.

"I wanted to bury these with Mr. Peters," she said. "All his old friends said I should keep them for Lorena. I never thought it was healthy for a little girl to be so attached to such."

"Well, she sure is," Michaul agreed. "What do you want to do with them? You could sell them. The gold and diamonds are worth..."

"Give them to the child," Bitsy announced, firmly. "They aren't the problem. That little girl is upset because nobody asked her how she felt about getting a new daddy and moving away from here. She might say yes, if she was asked. If you take every last thing she loves away from her, including her daddy's war souvenirs, she will mourn forever. That's just an old woman's opinion. I don't want to poke my nose where it is not welcome. There's no need for trouble."

The next morning, after she fed Lorena and sponged her off with a damp cloth, Gussie decided to follow Bitsy's advice.

"What do you want me to do now, Lorena?"

"About what?"

"Our lives, the move to Tisquah. What do you want?"

"I want you to love me like you did before Michaul came along," the child replied, whispering. "I never meant to be so unkind to you, Mama. I want you to be happy and I don't really mind moving to West County. I said many unkind things to you, and I am sorry. I just want to be your darling girl, like always!"

"Always," Gussie cried, clasping Lorena's hands, "forever and always! You are my darling girl!"

Gussie sat with Lorena until the child fell into a deep, seemingly peaceful sleep. It seemed to her that life was going to be good, after all, now that she and Michaul had Lorena's blessing. She decided to tell Michaul about her suspected pregnancy that evening, after supper.

"Your French letters didn't work," she said, smiling.

"This is not a good time to have a baby, Gussie," he replied.

"What do you mean, not a good time?"

"We just got married. We've got a lot of work to do in West County. We don't need another complication, not with your daughter causing a ruckus at every opportunity. Get rid of it."

"Get rid of our baby?" Gussie shook her head. She could not believe what she was hearing. "Get rid of it?"

"This is not a good time."

Two days later, a Mexican woman rode a gray mule to the front door, where she patiently waited until Gussie walked outside and asked what she wanted.

"Your husband, he send for me," the woman replied, in heavily accented English. "He say get rid of baby." The woman made the sign of the cross, then kissed her thumb, apparently asking forgiveness for even speaking of abortion. "He say do today."

"I ain't about to get rid of my baby," Gussie replied, "and if you ain't out of my sight by the time I count to ten, I'm likely to blow you to Kingdom Come!"

"Bueno, senora, I go. You pay me two dollar."

"I'll give you a dollar for your ride out here, but I don't ever want to see your face again!"

Gussie angrily strode through the house to her bedroom and rummaged in the depths of her reticule, finally locating a silver dollar. As she walked back to the porch, holding the dollar as far from her body as possible, she realized that the coin weighed more than her baby, who was most likely smaller than a sewing thimble.

"Get off my land," she ordered, as she handed the Mexican woman the dollar.

That noon, after their meal, she told Michaul what she had done. He stared at her with his cold, blue eyes, then nodded.

"If it is a boy, we'll name him Leo Martin," he said, "after my Army buddy. Died in the Argonne."

It was the last civilized conversation they would share for many years, Gussie realized much later, or at least, the last concerning their personal lives. At the time, though, she was only aware of an overwhelming chill settling over her and all her hopes for the future.

The week before Christmas, after the papers were signed concluding the sale of the ranch, Michaul disappeared, without a word to anyone, for three days. Frantic with worry, Gussie told Claude to hitch up the team and report Michaul's disappearance to the sheriff in Eagle Pass.

"Don't get all riled," Claude advised. "Big Brother Michaul knows his way home."

When Michaul returned, he was accompanied by two men and a woman whom he introduced to Gussie as cousins from Louisiana.

"What do you have to say for ycurself?" Gussie demanded.

"Let's have us a Christmas Eve party," Michaul replied, winking at her.

"What?"

"A party, Gussie," he said, calmly, "where your friends have a good time. The Messkins can cook up some bar-b-que and a pot of beans. Mama can whip us up a couple of cakes. Fun, that's what I'm talking about!"

"I don't have no friends," Gussie responded. "Michaul, we are all packed and ready to move. We could have already been in Tisquah, if you hadn't up and disappeared! This ain't the time for a party."

"I'll take care of everything."

He proceeded to do so, with apparent ease. Within minutes, Claude was on his way to Eagle Pass in the Model-T, carrying a shopping list for food, drink, fireworks and guests. Gussie, unaware that her new husband even knew anyone in Eagle Pass, was amazed a few hours later, when several automobiles filled with people followed Claude home. By sundown, the Mexicans were slicing bar-b-qued beef brisket and ladling pinto beans into bowls placed on plank tables in the back yard. Bitsy and Phoebe, flushed from the kitchen heat after frantically baking cakes all afternoon, called for help transporting the fruits of their effort to the tables. Phoebe, her black eyes dancing in the dusk, helped Claude string paper lanterns in the chinaberry tree. Lorena also appeared in the yard. She leaned against the tree, watching the proceedings with great interest. A man Gussie had never seen before tuned a fiddle, obviously preparing to play dance music, inspiring Phoebe to twirl across the yard, finally landing in Claude's arms.

"Come on, Gussie girl," she called. "You and Michaul have to dance first, since it is your party!"

"I ain't exactly in the mood for dancing," Gussie snapped. Michaul caught her in his arms and led her in a wild polka, lifting her off the ground when she faltered. "You are getting on my last nerve, Michaul, I swear!"

"Don't worry about it."

She did worry as the evening progressed. Michaul's behavior grew increasingly strange, until she began to wonder if he was the same sweet man she had married just weeks earlier. She pushed through a crowd of laughing men and women to find Michaul engaged in a card game. She leaned on his shoulder, peering at the hand he held, and was shocked to see naked women on the cards. Naked women posed in lewd positions. She gasped and backed away from the table. Michaul chuckled, as if he had caught her doing some shameful thing.

"I won't have them nasty cards in my house!" she hissed.

"It's not your house," Michaul responded. "We sold it three days ago, remember?"

Shaken and fearful, Gussie found Lorena and told her it was time for bed. She helped her daughter slip into her nightgown.

"Lock this door from the inside after I leave," she ordered. "Them men is drinking too much and I don't know what might happen!"

Lorena, pale and silent, followed her instructions, turning the key as Gussie stepped into the hallway. Gussie searched the house for Michaul, determined to tell him it was time to end the festivities. Finally, she heard his voice in one of the spare bedrooms. Her heart skipped a beat, happy to hear her husband's voice in the midst of so much confusion. She opened the door, prepared to apologize for her earlier behavior.

"Sweet Jesus!" Gussie gasped.

Michaul, reclining on the bed, sat up at the sound of Gussie's voice, like a puppet on a string. Between his legs, crouched on the braided rug beside the bed, was the female cousin from Louisiana. Across the room, her companions, each holding whiskey glasses and smoking fat cigars, stared silently at Gussie. Michaul did not attempt to hide his engorged penis from his wife's shocked eyes.

"Gussie," he mumbled, "I thought you were in here, with me." He leaned nearer the kneeling woman, then held up his hands, as if in surrender. "I swear, Gussie, I thought she was you!"

Gussie stood still, aware of the four pairs of eyes focused on her. She knew Michaul and his cousins thought the whole incident was funny, a joke of such bizarre dimensions that she could not comprehend the beginning or end or purpose.

"I'm going for the shotgun, Michaul," she said, finally, "and your cousins had better clear out before I get back!"

Gussie marched into the kitchen, climbed onto the stool and pulled down the shotgun, then retraced her steps to the bedroom, prepared to do whatever awful thing she might have to do. Inside, she found Michaul, sprawled across the bed on his back, snoring. He was alone. Gussie sniffed the air like a hound dog, identifying cigar smoke, whiskey, cheap hair pomade, perspiration and the unmistakable scent of sex. She decided to shoot Michaul, and would have, had Phoebe not intervened.

"Don't be too hard on Michaul," Phoebe said, gently, as she led Gussie into the hall. "He is real upset because he just found out a few days ago that his children was put out for adoption."

"What children?"

"Oh, he didn't tell you?"

Phoebe clamped her hands across her mouth, obviously wishing she had kept it shut, for once in her life. She stepped away from Gussie, her eyes bulging from their sockets as Gussie pointed the shotgun in her direction.

"I think I will just hear it from you, Miss Know-It-All!"

"I swear to God, I thought Michaul had told you about it!

It is just that he was married before and he has two kids. You didn't know? A boy and a girl? Real sweet little kids? I never met them, of course, that goes without saying..."

"What about their mama?"

"She divorced Michaul while he was in France. Ever since he came home he has been trying to get the money to pay child support."

"Child support? What is that?" Gussie asked, suspiciously.

"I swear, Gussie, you don't know beans about the real world! Child support is money the court says a man has to pay to take care of his kids. His first wife said she would put the kids up for adoption if Michaul didn't pay up. So, Michaul went to Louisiana, to pay it, after the ranch was sold. Uh, honestly, you didn't know?"

"You're saying Michaul took money from the sale of my ranch?"

"I guess he thought it was his, too, since you are married. Anyway, he was too late. His ex-wife had already sent the kids up to Canada."

"Well, missy, it ain't none of your concern what Michaul might be thinking, or where his kids got sent, if he really has kids! If you know any more great secrets about him, even if it's none of your business, you'd better tell me. Now!"

"I don't, Gussie," Phoebe insisted, reaching for Gussie's hands. "I promise! I didn't know about the kids, at first, because I'm new to the family, too. Just like you."

"Do you know who them people from Louisiana are?"

"Claude says they are cousins once removed."

"Why are they here?"

"Uh, well, Claude says they are going to West County with us, to help us with the move."

"Us?" Gussie asked, suspiciously. She hated to ask for an explanation because her brain might not absorb any additional information. "I thought you and Claude and his mama would stay here, to work for the new owner."

Phoebe did not reply, or could not, since her hands were clamped over her mouth. Big tears rolled down her cheeks and across her fingers. Gussie sighed. She should have realized, all along, that Michaul would never leave his brother and wife, let alone his cherished mother, in Maverick County. She took a deep breath, straining to hold the heavy shotgun pointed between Phoebe's plump breasts.

"I thought you knew," Phoebe cried. "Michaul wants us to go with you. We are family, you know!"

"You can't live with us," Gussie replied, firmly. "That house in Tisquah is not big enough for all of us!"

"We have our own place, Gussie. The uh, the farm next to yours. Uh, I thought you knew!"

"Stop saying you thought I knew! I ain't knowed nothing about any of this mess! How did you two come up with money for your own place?" Phoebe did not respond, though her miserable expression confirmed Gussie's worst suspicions. "Michaul bought a farm for you and Claude, didn't he? With money from the sale of my ranch?" Phoebe nodded, obviously miserable, her big eyes about to pop out of her head. "Well, I don't know anything about buying land," Gussie admitted. "I guess if it is already done, it is done. There's nothing else to say! I will tell you one thing, though. You and Claude had better get rid of those so-called cousins before I find them!"

"I will tell Claude right now, Gussie," Phoebe stammered. She attempted a smile, but fear pulled her face into a grimace. "Listen, Gussie, we can have a lot of fun together! I think I am pregnant, too. We can sew layettes for our babies, and help each other and..."

"Who told you I'm pregnant?"

"Bitsy."

"It figures," Gussie sighed. "I don't guess I am apt to have any privacy in my life from now on!"

Gussie returned to the bedroom where her husband lay, still snoring, across the bed. When Michaul awoke at dawn, he was startled to realize that Gussie sat in a straight-back chair, holding the shotgun against his head.

"You lied to me, Michaul!"

"Jesus! About what?"

"You was married before, and you got two kids..."

"I never lied," Michaul answered, "and you never asked."

"...and what is worse, you used my money to buy your smart-aleck brother and his wife a farm in West County, without asking, or telling me..."

"Hold on, Gussie, please!"

"...anything about your plan. You just took my money and did as you pleased..."

"It is our money, now, Gussie! We're a married couple!"

"...without even caring what I might say! I want a divorce, that's what I say! Do you hear me? Get out of my house. Now!"

Gussie pulled the trigger and blew out a section of the floor as Michaul rolled off the bed and threw himself through the open window. In moments, Claude was behind her, pinning her arms as he wrenched the shotgun from her hands.

"I got her!" Claude called.

Michaul, his face pale, climbed through the window and sat on the bed, staring at the damaged floor. He shook his head.

"Crazy bitch could have killed me," he declared.

"Tried to, looks like," Claude agreed.

"Don't you two worthless thieves talk about me like I ain't here!" Gussie screamed, struggling to free her arms. "I want my money back, and I want you two and your wormy relatives off my land! Now!"

"Bitsy," Michaul called. The old woman immediately appeared in the doorway, followed closely by Phoebe, who was weeping. "Stir up a glass of grape juice for my wife. She needs to calm down."

"I already did," Bitsy whispered. She did not meet Gussie's furious gaze. "I got it, right here, ready to go."

Michaul took a glass filled with dark liquid from Bitsy's trembling hand, then without hesitation he pried open Gussie's clenched teeth, tilted her head and poured the drink into her mouth. She gagged, and he repeated the process several times, until satisfied she had swallowed most of the liquid.

"Laudanum," Gussie whispered, her eyes filling with tears. "You gave me laudanum! I know how it smells!"

When she thought about it later, she realized Michaul,

Claude, Phoebe and Bitsy stood watching as she passed out. At the time, though, she was only aware of falling a great distance, into a velvet void.

"Dear God in Heaven," she whispered, "take care of my darling Lorena!"

Jackie Glover

CHAPTER THREE

When Gussie opened her eyes she was lying on her bed. The sun flooded the west windows with buttery light, indicating late afternoon had arrived. She thought about the sun for a long while, also contemplating the pressed tin squares on the bedroom ceiling. Eventually, she realized her tongue was swollen, her lips parched and cracked. Her mouth felt as if it was packed with cotton. She finally forced herself to sit up and swing her legs over the side of the bed. Her head swam and for a moment she feared she would fall onto the floor. She noticed she was still wearing the dress she had reluctantly donned for the Christmas Eve party.

"Things is out of kilter!" she whispered. "This ain't right!"

Gussie managed to stand, steadying herself by holding to the foot of the iron bedstead. She cautiously made her way to the wash stand and wiped her face with a damp cloth. Waves of nausea assaulted her body, unexpected, terrifying in their intensity. She heaved a small amount of vile fluid into the wash basin. Satisfied that the nausea had run its course, Gussie changed her clothing, then brushed her hair and fashioned it into a single braid. She let the braid fall free to her waist, rather than winding it into the customary chignon at her neck. She wanted to look like her mother, like a Cherokee. She sensed she would soon need all the strength and wisdom available, even before she recalled the events that had led to her lying alone in the bedroom in the middle of the afternoon.

Memories of the party and the subsequent horror came

flooding back, stunning Gussie. She recalled Michaul lying across a bed as the woman knelt between his legs. She saw herself fetching the shotgun from the kitchen, her encounter with Phoebe, pulling the triggers as Michaul jumped from the window. Worst of all, she recalled Bitsy appearing like an angel of death, bearing a glass of bitter drink.

"Laudanum!" Gussie whispered. "They are devils! All of them Abelards is devils! Lorena was right! I have been a fool for love!"

Josephine had taught Gussie the Cherokee Way as it pertained to many aspects of life, despite Avery's staunch disapproval. In her confusion and fear, Gussie recalled her mother's basic rule. Calm your mind, then follow the Path. A calm mind makes wise decisions.

"Thank you, Mama," Gussie sighed.

Her first thought was to hold the Abelard family at gun point and force them off her ranch. Common sense told her the shotgun was in their possession and that she would not be able to arm herself.

"Them Abelards have probably been run off other folk's land in the past," she mused. "They won't leave nothing to chance! No siree!"

Gussie slowly opened the bedroom door and listened intently. The massive old house was silent as a cave. She crept into the hallway then made her way to the kitchen. Packing crates littered the house, Gussie noted as she walked past each room. In the parlor, Lorena's piano loomed in the shadows.

"Well, they ain't run off with everything yet," Gussie said to herself. "Of course, they had done shipped all the valuables to New Orleans and sold them! I wish I had listened to Lorena!"

In the kitchen she pumped water into the dented old tin cup that Mr. Peters had preferred over all other cups and glasses. She sipped the cold water, remembering Mr. Peters, wondering what he would make of her situation.

"He would know just what to do," she said. "He could handle this bunch of thieves with one hand tied behind his old back!"

She opened a packet of saltine crackers and ate four of the

crunchy squares, then drank another cup of water. She was surprised that Lorena had not stashed the old tin cup away with the other items she was hoarding.

"Poor little girl," Gussie said, her voice wavering with emotion, "how she has suffered, watching her mama let everything slip through her fingers. Lorena has Mr. Peters' good head on her shoulders, thank God! I got to find a way to get Lorena away from here so I can deal with them devil Abelards! This ain't no place for a little girl. Not these days!"

She went in search of Lorena, but the child was not to be found in the house. Gussie cautiously went outside, then inspected the barn, all the outbuildings and even beneath the porches. Lorena was not in any of her usual play places. When there were no options remaining, Gussie turned her attention to the little clapboard house occupied by Claude and Phoebe. Resolutely, Gussie marched across the yard, her fury growing with each step. She did not knock before entering the one-room dwelling.

"I ain't aiming for politeness," she reminded herself.

She pushed open the door and saw Claude, Phoebe and Bitsy casually sitting at the little table. The trio was eating what appeared to be leftovers from the Christmas Eve party.

"Where is Lorena?" Gussie demanded, before any of the three surprised Abelards greeted her. She was trembling, but she forced herself to speak forcefully. "Where is Michaul?"

"Oh, hello there, Gussie," Phoebe said. "Welcome back to the world! We thought you were going to sleep your life away! You missed Christmas Day. Can you believe it?"

"Cut out the cute talk, bird brain," Gussie snarled. "I want some answers!"

"Oh, have a bite to eat," Bitsy suggested, "and you'll most likely feel better. You've been asleep for too long. My lands, you slept around the clock twice!"

"I was drugged, thanks to you devils! You people know what happened! So don't play innocent with me!"

"Well, that was on your husband's say-so," Claude explained. He looked very uncomfortable. Phoebe looked guilty as sin, though Bitsy seemed thoroughly at ease. "Michaul thought you were getting too upset for your own good, being pregnant and all."

"Where is Michaul?" Gussie demanded. "Where is Lorena?"

None of the three answered her questions, though they did exchange glances among themselves. "I am just about to lose patience with you skunks!"

"Ah, Gussie," Claude finally said, just as Gussie had given up expecting an answer, "it's no big thing. Lorena was begging to go visit her daddy's grave before we move to West County. So, Michaul, well...he, uh, he drove her over there in the Model-T."

"When?"

"This morning. Don't know what time, exactly. I reckon they drove on to Eagle Pass. Maybe Lorena wanted to say good-bye to her grandparents. They will probably be home any minute now."

Gussie considered Claude's explanation and found it full of holes. True, she thought, Lorena might have wanted to visit her father's grave. She simply would never have consented going there with Michaul, whom she thought was a devil. Gussie also doubted that Lorena would have asked to visit Gussie's parents because she was uncomfortable around Avery.

"That there story just don't wash," Gussie told Claude.

Claude did not meet her gaze, and Gussie knew she would learn nothing useful from him or the two women. She left the little house, backing away from its inhabitants as she would from a ball of rattlesnakes. She crossed the yard, heading toward the barn with the intention of saddling a horse. She then remembered that all the horses, even the high-spirited sorrel, had been sold. She had no way of leaving the ranch other than on foot.

Gussie stood still, breathing deeply, as her mother had taught her, deliberately clearing her mind. She had to make a plan. There were no familiar sounds, other than a tentative clanking of the windmill. Gussie thought she heard a voice from a great distance, rushing toward the ranch, then inside her head. She shivered, then closed her eyes, listening in the Cherokee way.

"Mama, you will be so lonely without me!" Lorena cried, plain as day, inside Gussie's head.

In that instant, Gussie's heart shattered into a thousand pieces, for she knew Lorena was dead. Her daughter's voice was borne across the prairie by love. Love alone. That was how the dead spoke to the living. So Josephine had taught.

"You are my darling girl!" Gussie shouted. "My heart's true love! Forever and always, always! My darling girl, I love you most of all!"

"Mama! Mama!"

Lorena's voice faded, vanished, and Gussie held it in her memory, for she knew she would never hear it again. She fell to the sun-baked earth, weeping, aware that Claude, Phoebe and Bitsy were hurrying in her direction. She could not bear looking at her in-laws, so she forced herself to stand and run to the house. Inside, she locked the doors, then fell to the floor, weeping, as Claude tried to force his way in.

"Leave me be!" Gussie shouted. "I want no part of you or yours!"

The little group of Abelards stood on the porch, whispering among themselves for several minutes before returning to their own dwelling. Gussie pulled herself to a sitting position beside a kitchen window, watching as they walked across the yard. Their shadows were long and thin, like ghosts, stretched across the ground in the late afternoon light. Gussie pressed her forehead against the cool glass window pane, silently weeping.

Hours later, near midnight, the sheriff drove to the ranch to tell her of Lorena's death at the hands of Mexican bandits.

"It surely breaks my heart to have to say the words, ma'am," he said. Gussie saw sincere sorrow in his brown eyes. He was a good man, she thought. She envied his wife and children. "I know how dear that child was to you and to old Mr. Peters."

Gussie nodded, miserably. She had never imagined such pain as she felt at that moment, just hearing the actual words. Your little girl is dead. Killed by Mexicans. Just like Champ.

Dead and gone. Tears won't help. God won't help. Nothing helps.

"What about Michaul?" she asked, finally. She had no interest in his fate, but the kindly sheriff probably expected her to inquire. "Did the Messkins kill Michaul, too?"

"No, they hit him on the head with a big rock, but the doc says he will pull through. He was able to tell us what happened. The Messkins must have been waiting for someone to drive into the cemetery so they could ambush them. Wel'll find them Messkins and hang them!"

"Where is my daughter?"

"Ma'am, I've got her little body out in my car. I just hesitate to bring her in here, with you all alone. Is there someone I can bring out to help you?"

"I ain't alone," Gussie sighed. "If you go through the kitchen and unlock the door you will probably find my husband's family on the back porch. I reckon they're wondering why you are here." Gussie felt herself dying with unspoken grief, anchored to the earth only by her obligation to the small, dead body lying on the back seat of the sheriff's car. "If it will make you feel better, let them in and tell them what happened. Then, be kind enough to bring my darling girl inside. Put her in her bedroom. Please."

Gussie stood at the foot of Lorena's bed as Bitsy and Phoebe bathed the child and dressed her in a blue challis dress. Pink embroidered rose buds trimmed the outfit, one of Lorena's favorites. Gussie was afraid to think of Lorena in happier days, fearing her grief would overwhelm her senses. Hold on, hold on, she told herself.

Claude accompanied the sheriff back to town, promising to check on Michaul's condition and drive the Model-T to the ranch. He would also bring back a coffin, provided the undertaker had a child's coffin in stock.

"If he don't have one, he can get one built by late afternoon," the sheriff reassured Gussie. "I'll tell him to make it real nice."

Gussie dismissed Bitsy and Phoebe, then locked the bedroom door. She sat with Lorena's body throughout the night, talking out loud, just in case her daughter's spirit still hovered near enough to hear human sounds. Josephine had said it happened that way, sometimes, when love bound a dead person to a particular place. Gussie carefully arranged Lorena's favorite dolls on either side of her cold body, calling each doll by name.

"Here's Queen Victoria, dressed in her velvet cloak," she crooned, smoothing the doll's ermine-trimmed garments. "Oh, look here, Lorena! Here is Belle. And this here is your favorite baby doll, Silly Sally! Did you know, Lorena, that I never had a real doll when I was a little girl? Just scrap babies my mama sewed when she had any cloth scraps to spare. I learned to make corn husk dolls in the summer. That's why I loved your dolls so much, honey. I wanted you to have everything I never had. You were better than I ever hoped to be!"

Gussie then opened a cloth covered box containing Lorena's paper doll collection. She dressed each cardboard doll in her daughter's favorite paper dresses, carefully bending the tabs around the figures. She tearfully recalled the fun she and Lorena had shared in times past, sitting on the parlor rug, arranging paper doll families around Mr. Peters' feet. She and Mr. Peters always exchanged happy glances across their beloved child's curly head, for they enjoyed the play time as much, if not more, than Lorena.

"Those were the good times," Gussie sobbed, "and I was too stupid to know it! Oh, Lorena, I am so sorry, sorry, sorry!"

Gussie pulled the remaining items from the box, then noticed several lines of Lorena's handwriting on the back of the last doll.

"Michaul hurt me and Mama doesn't believe me. I am afraid. I pray to God and to my Daddy in Heaven but no one helps me.

Lorena Delphina Peters
daughter of Capt. Esau Peters, CSA."

Gussie wept again, for she knew that Lorena truly believed that Michaul had hurt her.

"I don't know what it was all about," Gussie whispered, "but I should have paid more attention to Lorena. I should have kept her beside me, watched after her, instead of letting them devil Abelards take over our lives!" Guilt poured out of Gussie's heart, filling every part of her being, as she realized she had been lying in a drugged stupor when her daughter went to her death. "I should have been a better mother!" she cried, sweeping the paper dolls into their box. "What good are dolls and pretty clothes when the most precious child that ever drew breath is lying here on a crocheted spread, her life snuffed out by Messkins?"

At dawn, Bitsy and Phoebe returned and helped Gussie comb Lorena's auburn hair. Gussie shaped the curls by memory, for her tearful eyes were swollen nearly shut. She caught the curls in a pink satin ribbon, tied in a double bow.

"Claude's here with the coffin," Phoebe said, miserably. "It's white with a pink satin lining. Gussie, oh Gussie, I called Lorena a brat once, but I want you to know I didn't mean it! I was just jealous of all the nice things she had. I asked God to forgive me."

Gussie silently watched as the women and Claude arranged Lorena's body in the elegant little coffin. The four of them then carried it into the parlor, placing it on a make-shift platform of boards lying across saw horses. The only furniture in the room was Lorena's piano and the few kitchen chairs that had not been sold. Gussie changed into her black dress, combed her hair, then sat alone beside the coffin as neighbors arrived to pay their respects.

"They already caught three Messkins hiding out in an old barn," one woman told Gussie. "The sheriff says he thinks they are the ones who outraged your little girl and hurt your poor husband. The sheriff says he may not be able to keep the Messkins alive until their trial. Folks are upset about this! This is a terrible thing! Just terrible!"

Gussie closed her eyes, trying not to think about what had actually happened to Lorena. There was no denying the truth, though, for the images of her long vigil beside her daughter's body were etched forever in her mind. She knew there was no way to ignore the awful reality of Lorena's neck, broken like a doll's. Nor could she deny the presence of blood dried inside the child's tender, most private parts. Nor the bruises, evidence of the brutality visited upon an innocent child by those filthy Messkins. Gussie could not speak, though she wanted to scream out the facts. It was rape and murder, she wanted to shout. That darling little girl had her broken arm in a sling, and that linen sling was wrapped around her broken neck! It was much more than a terrible thing! It was the end of the world! Terrible thing, terrible, terrible!

Gussie's parents, Josephine and Avery, arrived and promptly knelt beside the coffin. Avery read aloud from his Bible for a very long time, though Gussie refused to listen to his words. Something much worse than her father's wrath had entered her life. An evil only she could identify and deal with had sprouted and grown with her love for Michaul. She had no hope that words printed on any page, even in the Bible, could help her.

Michaul, his head wrapped in thick white bandages, was driven to the ranch by the sheriff. He walked into the parlor, paused at Lorena's coffin, then swept Gussie into his arms.

"I am so sorry, Gussie," he wept. "I never saw the Messkins! They just sneaked up and hit me on the head. I would have fought to the death to protect her!"

"I reckon I'm the one who is sorry," Gussie replied, "since I just lost the dearest thing in my life and I'll never get her back!"

"You loved that child too much, Gustine," Avery interrupted, waving his Bible in her direction. Heads turned, then swiveled back. No one in the room wanted to be the object of Avery's attention. "I told you, many, many times that our Lord is a jealous Lord, but you refused to listen! Your pride brought this tragedy on all of us! My granddaughter's innocent blood is on your hands! You were warned!"

"What do you mean?" Gussie asked, wearily. "Are you saying it is my fault that Lorena is dead? That the Lord picked out my only child and killed her because I loved her?"

"Loved...her...too...much!" Avery replied, knowingly. "The Bible says it is so! You would know that if you had listened to me, or if you had read your own Bible. It was your choice to ignore God's teachings." He dramatically gestured at Lorena's white coffin. "You see the results!"

"I don't believe you!" Gussie cried. "If the Bible really says such a thing, then I don't believe God, either. A mother is bound to love her child. Who can measure if she loves too much? It don't make sense!"

"May God have mercy on your soul, Gustine," Avery replied, sadly. Gussie knew he was playing to the audience. Avery never passed on an opportunity to preach, especially to a captive congregation. "You will bring down God's wrath on your house, forever, if you don't humble yourself!"

Josephine gently clasped Gussie's hands and led her into the bedroom. She forced Gussie to lie on the bed, then pulled a blanket up to her chin. Josephine massaged her daughter's forehead, talking softly as Gussie relaxed.

"Do you remember the story about the walnut hearts?" she asked.

"I think so, Mama, but I don't believe I ever understood what it meant."

"The Cherokees believe some people forget how to love. Maybe they are hurt, or alone, or maybe they just turn away. After a while, their hearts shrivel to the size of a walnut. When they die, the Great Spirit looks inside and finds those shriveled hearts. He changes them into rotten walnuts and drops them under walnut trees. They are a warning to humans who find them, reminding us that love is necessary for all people. Fill your heart with love, Gussie, always. That is a woman's only strength."

"Papa says God doesn't want us to love anyone too much."

"There is no such thing as too much love, if it is pure, my daughter," Josephine whispered, fiercely. "I don't ever want you to believe anything else, no matter what anyone says!"

Gussie cried then, great, gulping sobs which released a fountain of tears. She tasted the salt and wondered if she could die from crying. Her mother held her and sang in the Cherokee language, sad, nasal little tunes from a bygone era.

Gussie did not weep again, not even at Lorena's funeral when a group of Mr. Peters' old friends gathered around the diminutive coffin and sang

"Lorena", the song they all loved so dearly. By then, Gussie had cried herself dry, though she longed for the comfort of tears. She could no longer recall the mechanism by which she might release any portion of her unbearable pain and guilt.

After the funeral, Gussie lingered beside the Peters family tombstones. She had insisted upon burying Lorena beside Mr. Peters, rather than among the graves of his long-dead children because the old man had loved Lorena more than his other offspring. She hoped, with all her broken heart, that he had met their darling girl at the heavenly gates. Finally, the last guests left the windswept cemetery.

"I ain't about to go off to West County with you," she informed Michaul. "There's no way I'm moving away from here, not ever."

"Why not?" Michaul asked. Gussie detected panic in his voice. "It is all set. You don't have a choice!"

"You know why! It's because you hurt Lorena!" Gussie did not waver before Michaul's arrogant, domineering gaze. "You tricked me, something awful, but that don't matter as much as how you hurt that precious little girl!"

"Why do you think I hurt Lorena? I got my head busted open trying to protect her! You've gone off your rocker, woman!" His eyes were like ice, cold and hard, bluer than Gussie had ever imagined.

"Because she left a note in her paper doll box," Gussie retorted. "Lorena never lied to me, not once in her life. I believe what she wrote. I can see, plain as day, that she was afeered of you, all along. Now Messkins have kilt her because you didn't take care of her!" Gussie fought for breath, determined to rationalize her decision to remain near Lorena's dear body. "I can't leave her here, knowing how alone she felt after we got married. She needed me and I ignored her! Oh, God, she must have felt even more alone when them Messkins put their filthy hands on her. My daughter needed me, and still needs me!"

Michaul picked Gussie up and walked to the Ford, where he carefully placed her trembling body on the front seat. He silently drove back to the ranch house then led Gussie into Lorena's room. Gussie hoped he was considering her decision, that he wanted to talk out their differences and make plans to go their separate ways.

"Show me," he whispered.

Gussie's heart, already broken into a thousand hurtful pieces, fell into a hopelessly deep abyss when she grasped the meaning of Michaul's words. She knew it had been a dreadful mistake on her part to tell Michaul of Lorena's note. There was no way out of the situation. She hesitated, reluctant to produce the paper doll and its dismal message. Michaul grunted, then pushed her aside and quickly gathered up Lorena's toys. Gussie protested, snatching Silly Sally from Michaul's arms as he left the room. She had to run, just keeping up with his long stride, as he walked into the back yard, piled the toys high and poured kerosene over the lot.

"You can't burn my Lorena's toys," Gussie screamed. "They're all I have left of her! Don't do it!"

She watched, horrified, as Michaul struck a match and ignited the pyre. The flames instantly claimed Lorena's toys. Silently, furtively, Gussie stuffed Silly Sally into her shirtwaist pocket. As the dolls and toys twisted in the flames, Bitsy joined Gussie. The two women watched the sparks and ashes fly across the barren yard on a gentle breeze.

"I don't know how to talk to Michaul," Gussie said. "He won't listen to me. I don't want to go off and leave my daughter buried here. I know her soul is in heaven and I do reckon her daddy is looking after her, but all I have is her body, buried in this earth. I can't go off and leave her grave! Now, look at what Michaul has gone and done! He has burned up all her dear toys, all the sweet things she played with, all them memories! It feels like she's dying again, right before my eyes!"

"You have another child to consider," Bitsy reminded her. "Why don't you just go along with Michaul's plans for now? See if things don't get better. You can always move back here if you decide to."

"That's your advice?"

"For what an old woman's notion is worth, yes. When you get to be my age you'll realize that life is about moving on. You can't afford to lie down and mourn when you lose someone you love. It's best to keep going, to see what is coming up next."

The following morning, when Michaul told Gussie they would begin the move that day, she did not argue. She would go to West County and wait for things to get better, as Bitsy advised. Gussie did not honestly believe that her life might improve but she had not the faintest idea what else she should do.

"This will help you, for now," Bitsy whispered, as they prepared to close up the house and drive away. "Use all you need. We can buy the ingredients at any drug store." The old woman pressed the bottle of laudanum into Gussie's hands, and Gussie clasped it tightly. "Southern women always knew how to make laudanum," Bitsy explained, as she guided Gussie to the Model-T. "Why, without a little help, they would have gone mad. Just imagine setting out in the country, waiting for the next party or entertainment, just waiting for weeks and months. My family owned plantations down in East Texas, and let me tell you, my mother got mighty bored just looking at pine trees day in and day out! You know what I mean?"

"I don't know what you're talking about, not really," Gussie sighed. "My mother had too much work to do. She never seemed bored, not that I recall."

"Well, I guess Indian women don't look at life like white women."

"Are you saying my mother ain't a white woman?" Gussie gasped. "Why, her skin is no darker than mine!"

"Child, I declare, you know she is a Cherokee Indian!"

"But, she is white!" Gussie cried. "Oh, you Abelards are the most wicked folks on earth. Devils, that's what you are!"

"Maybe you should have a sip now," Bitsy suggested. She gently uncorked the bottle and offered it to Gussie. "It is helpful when a body is upset."

"I guess a little sip can't hurt me," Gussie sighed. "Lord knows, I am all done in."

Gussie grew pale and thin in the months following their move to West County. In spite of her advancing pregnancy, her clothing hung loosely on her small body. She ceased minding her appearance and doubted that she would ever care how she looked. She depended on Bitsy's laudanum to get her through the hard times and all her times were hard. She existed by clinging to the hope that there might come a day when the mere thought of Lorena did not reduce her to helpless tears. She slept for long periods of time, often for days, without dreaming. Eventually, Gussie no longer heard Lorena's sweet voice in the treacherous void between waking and oblivion.

"I'd better get hold of myself," she said frequently, though she did nothing to improve her condition.

In June, Bitsy persuaded Gussie to accompany Phoebe into Tisquah for a prenatal visit. A young doctor had recently opened a practice in the bustling little farm town. According to Bitsy, it was Gussie's civic duty to become his patient.

"You also need to think about your baby," Bitsy chided. "You are old enough to expect some complications, if you know what I mean."

"I don't ever know what you mean."

"I'm talking about your age! About the way you are neglecting your health and your baby's health! If you don't care about yourself or that little baby, then you ought to give some thought to your husband. Or to your house! Why, without the work Phoebe and I do around here, you and Michaul would starve to death. You are living like pigs in a sty! What would your mother say if she knew what is going on? I've got a good mind to write her and tell her!"

"Don't!" Gussie cried. "It would scare my mother to death if you sent her a letter! Lord, have mercy, if it will shut you up I will see that new doctor!" Gussie ignored Bitsy's pleased smile. "I don't know what a doctor can do that I can't do for myself. It's plain that the baby is a boy because I'm carrying it so high and it kicks so hard. It's going to be plumb bald because I ain't having indigestion. What else does a body need to know?"

The doctor, a tall, slim young German named Zolta Khroner, advised Gussie to take long walks, eat light meals and be prepared to pay him a ten dollar delivery fee. He then asked if Gussie had any questions. She snorted in derision, then stomped behind the privacy screen.

"I reckon I remember how to do it," she snapped. "Ain't

nobody ever claimed what women already know about childbirth is worth ten dollars!"

Phoebe, driving them home in her recently purchased Buick, was a fountain of information about the doctor.

"Dr. Khroner said you need to stop using laudanum," she announced. "He said your baby may have birthmarks, or incurable colic or worse, if you keep using drugs."

"What drugs?"

"Laudanum*!*"

"What was the point of dragging me in to see him if you were going to butt into my business?"

"I'm worried about you, Gussie," Phoebe patiently explained. "We all are."

"Ha!"

"Oh, don't be such a sorehead, Gussie. Anyway, don't you think Dr. Khroner is handsome?"

"I reckon," Gussie said, "if your fancy runs to skinny men who can't speak good English."

"Well," Phoebe said, raising an eyebrow, "I'll tell you something, if you promise to keep it strictly between us. If Claude should die before Dr. Khroner gets married, I'm going to marry him. We're going to live in a big brick house and have servants. We'll travel to Europe. And have manicures. Maybe we will have twins after we see Europe."

"Does the good doctor know about your plans?"

"Don't be silly, Gussie! Don't you ever play-act in your head, like when you were a little girl?"

"I don't reckon I ever play-acted in my head, except to pretend my dog Champ hadn't of got killed by Messkins. I used to think about how he could have stayed alive until I married and took him with me when I left home. What makes you think Claude might die any time soon?"

"Oh, I don't think he will," Phoebe replied, thoughtfully. "But, heck, you never know! Farmers die in terrible accidents, people catch the influenza, things like that happen every day. I just meant that if he dies young, I know what I'll do. It's smart to have a plan, to think ahead."

"Well," Gussie sighed, "I had me a plan when Mr. Peters

was sick and dying. Just be careful about what you wish for, that's all I can tell you."

"Don't be so gloomy, Gussie. Let's make some plans, just you and me. Our babies are due about the same time, so we won't be able to help each other during our lying-in. I thought I might get my little sisters to come stay for a few months. They can cook and clean for both of us. What do you say? Wouldn't you like to have some help?"

"It might make a little sense," Gussie mused, "when you put it like that. Just don't set your sisters to butting into my personal business, You better make that clear to them!"

"Oh, good!" Phoebe squealed. "I'll write to my mother tomorrow and tell her to send Robin and Dove and maybe Wren on out here! They can come early and help us sew our layettes, too. It will be good practice for them! Let's go back to Tisquah, right now, and buy some batiste and some blanket flannel. The dry goods store has a new shipment. Pastel colors!"

"Never heard of a layette in colors," Gussie replied, suspiciously. "Layettes is always white so they can be washed with bleach. Won't colors fade?"

"Don't be such an old hen, Gussie," Phoebe coaxed.

"Why not? All your people is named after birds. Reckon I can be an old hen."

"Gussie, I do believe you are smiling! You're wrong, though. My brothers aren't named after birds."

In the following weeks, Gussie fought hard to overcome her laudanum dependency. There were times when she thought the need was gone, and she rejoiced. At other moments, the pain of her loss was so devastating that she changed out of her clothing and crawled into bed with the dark blue bottle, drank its foul contents and wept as the velvet sleep overtook her senses.

Early in her ninth month, Gussie brought on her labor while straining to have a bowel movement. She sat in the outhouse, bathed in sweat, as her water broke and waves of pain radiated from her lower back. She wanted to scream but recalled her mother's admonition that screaming during labor scared the baby, making it afraid to come into the world. She didn't know if it really mattered, for she was uncertain if she even cared what happened to Michaul's baby.

"I got to do the right thing," she told herself through gritted teeth. "I decided to keep this baby way back when Michaul wanted to get rid of it. The least I can do is get it borned alive."

She managed to walk to the back porch and ring the brass dinner bell, summoning Michaul in from the fields. He was cool and distant, as always, but he did gently help Gussie change into her nightgown before he left the house. Minutes later, he brought Bitsy to sit with her, then drove to town to get Dr. Khroner.

"Land's sakes," Bitsy sighed, "it's not even the full moon! You are going to suffer, that's for certain!"

"Can't say I'm surprised," Gussie admitted. "Nothing about this baby seems right. Now it's coming early and all I wanted to do was use the toilet."

"It was all that laudanum," Bitsy said, knowingly. "It can cause constipation."

"Now you tell me."

Two days later, on the kitchen table padded with old newspapers, Leo Martin Abelard was born. He was an ugly baby and seemed unhappy about life from the moment he drew breath. When Gussie's milk came down, Leo greedily tasted the first drops, shuddered, screwed up his pinched little face and shrieked. Gussie stared at him as if he were an exotic animal in a roadside exhibit.

"I seen a two-headed calf once," she mused. "The mama loved it just the was it was. Loved both little heads. Seems like I could love this baby, but I don't! It don't feel natural!"

"It takes longer, sometimes," Bitsy commented. "Love doesn't always start out easy."

"I loved Lorena the moment I saw her," Gussie recalled. "It weren't no chore. Couldn't stand for anyone else to touch her, I loved her so much!"

"There's all kinds of love."

"I guess," Gussie sighed. "Look. This baby looks like a little rat. No hair, and that pointy little face. Don't look human, I swear."

"You'd best find something your little rat will eat," Bitsy

advised, "even if it is just light bread soaked in warm water. That baby needs nourishment. He'll fill out and look prettier, you'll see."

Gussie did not love Leo until he was almost four months old, and then only because Phoebe ridiculed him. Phoebe's brothers, who were all named for Old Testament prophets, sent Phoebe a Kodak box camera as a baby gift. Phoebe immediately began to chronicle her family's life, with an intensity approaching religious zeal. Gussie, naturally suspicious of cameras, especially one operated by a silly female in-law, did not easily consent to having Leo photographed.

"Come on, Gussie," Phoebe insisted. "Suppose Leo dies and you don't have a picture to remember him by. How will you feel, knowing you could have had a picture taken right on your front porch and you turned it down?"

Gussie had to admit it was a valid point. Leo was tiny, skin and bones, really, and too weak to hold his head up. She nodded her agreement and watched as Phoebe dragged a kitchen chair onto the front porch, then draped it with a baby blanket. Gussie placed Leo on the chair and watched him slowly topple onto his side, for all the world like a rag doll. He lay there, passive and silent, gazing at Gussie with his bright blue eyes.

"Good grief," Phoebe commented, "he can't even hold his head up. Why, my Bobby is already trying to sit alone, and he's two weeks younger than Leo. My, my, my..."

"Leo was borned too hard and too soon. He's near about starved to death on water and light bread," Gussie explained, "so he ain't exactly got the energy to play catch-up with your precious Bobby!"

"Well, if you say so," Phoebe muttered. She sidestepped across the yard until the sun was directly behind her, casting her shadow across the yard. "Just prop him in the chair and get down behind him, under the blanket. Try to hold him up straight. You won't show in the picture and it will look like he's sitting alone. This picture will look professional if you just do what I tell you!"

Gussie obediently crouched beneath Leo's blue blanket, supporting his thin little body through the thick cloth. Phoebe finally pressed the shutter button.

"All done," she sang out. "Nobody will guess that Leo was limp as an old sock."

Gussie shrugged off the blanket's folds then carefully picked up Leo and held his head against the curve of her neck. A fierce emotion seared through her body, settling around her heart, a feeling so unexpected, so enormous, that she thought she might faint. In that moment of raw emotion, she understood what Bitsy meant when she said there were all kinds of love. Gussie realized that she could love Leo because of his ugliness, not in spite of it. She should love him because he couldn't help the predicament into which he was born. He did not seem to expect love and that made him precious in Gussie's estimation. Leo, with a baby's wisdom, was simply clinging to life in case things got better. Within a moment, Gussie felt herself grow wiser and stronger. She faced Phoebe with courage to fight for Leo's dignity.

"You listen to me, Phoebe," she shouted. "Don't you ever make fun of Leo again, do you hear me? I'll likely scratch those big eyes right out of your little bird face if you ever let on like Leo ain't the most perfect baby you ever seen! Ain't nothing wrong he can't outgrow!"

"Good grief, Gussie," Phoebe gasped. "You don't have to bite my head off! You aren't taking laudanum again, are you?"

"No, I ain't taking laudanum," Gussie hissed. "I ain't needing to hear about how dangerous laudanum is, either! You Abelards didn't worry about it when you forced it down my gullet!"

"Whatever you say, Gussie." Phoebe held the Kodak at waist level, squinting one eye as she scanned the yard through the top-mounted view-finder. "Let's take a picture of Bobby and Leo together so if Leo dies, Bobby will have a keepsake for his scrapbook."

"Leo ain't gonna die! You can write that in Bobby's scrapbook and write down that I said it! Leo's mama says he ain't gonna die!"

It seemed to Gussie, from that moment of her declaration of love, that little Leo knew she believed in his ability to live. He slowly gained weight and took notice of his world. He cooed a bit now and then and finally smiled when he saw his mother's face. By six months of age Leo was a truly handsome infant. His eyes changed from baby blue to Abelard blue, though he looked more like Gussie's side of his family, slim and dark. Leo had an endearing way of tilting his head ever so slightly, like a kitten watching a yarn ball, reminding Gussie of her younger brothers and sisters. Small for his age, and very intelligent, Leo attracted attention when Gussie took him out. There was something about Leo that people loved. Women seemed unable to keep their hands off him.

"What a little angel," they usually gushed, holding out their arms for him. "Why, I could just eat him up, he is so sweet!"

Gussie agreed and as time passed she realized her initial lack of feeling for Leo was attributable to her guilt about Lorena's death. She discovered that she could love Leo without diminishing her devotion to Lorena's memory. She rapidly began her journey back to good health, to the inner strength that had always seen her through the bad times. Gussie gained weight, repaired her wardrobe, brushed her hair one hundred strokes every night and rubbed chicken fat into her chaffed skin. Michaul did not seem to notice and Gussie did not care. They had seldom spoken and had not touched since the day of Lorena's funeral.

Leo adored Gussie and especially delighted in watching as she brushed her long, black hair.

"Mama pretty," was his first sentence.

Gussie never allowed Leo out of her sight during the first year of his life. She knew from bitter experience how quickly a child's life could go down the drain if its mother was not vigilant. At fourteen months Leo took his first steps, walking straight into Michaul's arms. It seemed to Gussie that the child instantly forgot her. He toddled after Michaul like a faithful puppy. Leo cried hysterically whenever Michaul left him with Gussie.

"He'll most likely calm down, in time," Bitsy observed.

"I hope so," Gussie replied. "Why, he runs right into the fields if I don't watch him every minute! I can't spend my whole life holding onto this child's shirt tail! I ain't got the time, what with all the work I have to do! I ain't complaining, but he is a handful!"

Gussie knew there were other women in the community who lived in less comfort than she, though her own routine began before dawn and provided little chance for rest until well after sundown. She had never been one to avoid work but she missed the lifestyle she had shared with Mr. Peters. She missed having time to embroider and tat lace, skills learned at Josephine's knee. She often thought of how sad it would be to lose herself in the hypnotic repetition of endless chores, then to finally die without having left a mark upon the earth. Nothing of her life would remain, except Leo, who would soon forget his mama.

In the spring of Leo's first year, Gussie purchased a bottle of Black Draught Elixir at the Rexall Drug Store and was delighted when the pharmacist gave her a complimentary calendar. She hung the calendar in the kitchen and carefully studied the boxes for each day of the month. The calendar noted the phases of the moon and various information such as the best days to catch fish, cut hair, plant seed and butcher animals. Inside the square of the Sunday following the full moon, Gussie penciled in, *"Doss of Black Draught"*. It occurred to her that the notation would serve not only as a reminder to dose the family with spring tonic but also as a record for future reference.

"I can keep myself a daily diary, just like Lorena's," she mused. "Lorena's was in a satin covered book with a little gold lock, but that don't matter. I ain't writing down no secrets. At the end of the year I can roll up this here calendar and store it in the quilt box. It don't have to look pretty." Gussie wondered what had happened to Lorena's diary, but she dismissed the depressing thought. "The past is dead and no good will come from trying to figure it out now. I can't get a clear picture in my mind of them awful days, nohow!"

Each day, Gussie recorded the facts of her life in terse, misspelled messages, mostly concerning the effects of nature. *"Corn ruint by worms,"* she noted, *"dont see how we kin feed the stock all wintur." "Tornado blue down windmil. Fell on pig sty, pigs all cut up." "Cotton fetched good price. Michaul took off with money. Not heer from him in 3 weeks. Dont no where he kin be. Mebe Lusana." "Michaul home, ain't talking." "Garden ruint by hail size of my fist. Leo dip hail in sugar and say it ice kreme."*

"That there is my life," she told Leo, as the years passed and she accumulated calendars in the quilt box. "What's wrote on them pages is all I am. It ain't much. Someday you can read it and know all about your mama."

Leo, ever cheerful, always pointed to the illustrations of Black Draught and wrinkled his cute little nose. "Taste bad!" he always said, seriously, as if his mother was unaware of the fact. Gussie laughed and hugged the child.

"Well, sir, if medicine don't taste bad it ain't doing you no good! I believe in Black Draught twice a year, every year, spring and fall. It keeps you and me from getting sick, don't it? If your stubborn daddy took his Black Draught, he wouldn't be plagued with that nasty old cough."

Gussie realized, after years of silent cohabitation with Michaul, that they probably appeared to be a happily married couple. They attended church on Sundays and seldom missed an ice cream social, political rally, band concert or baseball game. Like their neighbors, they had been relatively affluent when they moved to West County and they shared a deep sense of responsibility for building a thriving community. Gussie had no close friends and would not have confided details of her married life even had she known anyone she trusted. She doubted that Michaul divulged details of their peculiar lifestyle, either, for he was diligently attempting to become a community leader. He hoped to someday run for political office.

Michaul was a member of a group of West County men selected to travel to Austin in search of funding for a hard-surface highway. Gussie could not have been prouder had he been elected governor; she even swallowed her pride and asked Phoebe to take Michaul's picture as he posed in front of the courthouse. She tacked the photo to the kitchen wall beside a clipping from the West County News. *"Local Group Petitions State Legislature,"* she read, sounding out the long, official sounding words.

She wrote on her calendar, *"Michaul name spelt rong in West Cty News. Dont matter, cause he is important man now."*

Though the state denied the petition for a new road, the committee was greeted by a cheering throng just because they had gone to Austin and tried. Everyone knew it was just a matter of time before the main roads would be paved. *"Michaul says he felt rite to home in Austin and would like to live there,"* Gussie wrote. *"That is where a man can make his mark."*

"Dont no where a woman can make her mark," she added, wistfully, *"'cept on a Rexall kalender."*

CHAPTER FOUR

Gussie lived from day to day, governed by the ages-old seasonal rhythm of farm life. She dwelt neither upon her past nor future. Her calendar notations concerning Leo mostly described predicaments in which he wound up whenever they went out in public.

"4th of July piknik at fare grownds. Leo head stuk in fence."

Entries about herself showed a marked competitiveness of spirit she had not experienced in her younger days.

"Git blue ribbin for dill pikils at fare. Growed dill at home. MY NAME in West Cty News."

Occasionally, she wrote about Lorena, for she never met a little girl who measured up to her lost child.

"Christmas show at church. Sure miss Lorena. West Cty. ain't got a pianer player kin hold a candil to MY DARLING GURL."

Bitsy, whom Gussie had first thought of as a nuisance, was usually pleasant, helpful company. The old woman divided her time between her sons' houses, remaining several weeks then moving her trunks and chifforobes back and forth. Gussie wondered if Michaul or Claude ever thought it might be easier on them all if Bitsy left the larger items in one place and moved only her necessities. She never asked. The Abelards had their own way of doing things and she was content to let them be. Even if it made no sense.

Gussie never knew if she looked forward to spring each

year or if she dreaded it. She fervently joined the congregation at church in praying for rain in the early spring, but she feared each cloud, knowing it might conceal a deadly tornado. In terms of dangerous weather, the summers were also treacherous, but Gussie loved the heat and the harvesting of her vegetable garden. Michaul bought her a new pressure cooker and she learned to can vegetables, fruit and meat, though the gauges and valves on the cooker terrified her. On many summer days, she donned her sunbonnet and took Leo to the fields, carrying a hoe over her shoulder. Michaul never asked for her help with the crops, but her own eyes told her the weeds would overtake the young cotton and maize plants regardless of how many Negroes were hired to perform the backbreaking work. Bitsy, elegant in her long black skirts, a Mexican sombrero atop her white hair, sometimes joined them, to Leo's delight. Chopping cotton, they called it, though it was really chopping weeds.

"Claude doesn't want me wearing myself out," Phoebe explained. "He doesn't want his wife doing a hired-hand's work. I'm just supposed to run the house, and he is in charge of the fields."

"Reckon Claude knows you lay up in bed all day, eating chocolates and reading astrology magazines? Your little bird sisters run your house, for a fact! Seems like you forgot to send them girls back home."

"Don't be spiteful, Gussie," Phoebe replied. "Wren was the only one who wanted to go back home. Robin and Dovie like it here. Anyway, if I was half Indian, I suppose I could work in the fields without breaking a sweat, like you. I've had three babies in a row, you know, and they weakened my constitution. I come from delicate stock!"

"The kind of stock that goes 'moooo'," Gussie laughed.

Bitsy used their time in the cotton fields to tell Leo of her family's history. Gussie sensed the stories of a grand, historic past were grounded in fact, unlike Phoebe's vague allusions to her blue-blooded ancestors. Bitsy's family had moved to Texas when the whole place still belonged to Mexico, becoming Mexican citizens and Catholics with the stroke of a pen. The very thought made Gussie shiver; Messkins had killed Champ and Lorena, and

Gussie believed they were all evil.

"My grandfather brought one hundred and thirteen slaves from Mississippi to Texas in the 1830's," Bitsy said, one August morning as they walked up and down the cotton rows, chopping each weed from the soil. "Land 'o Goshen, but we sure could use some of those slaves today!"

"What is a slave?" Leo asked.

"Somebody who does all the work when you tell them to."

"Like Mama?"

"Well, I declare," Bitsy laughed, "I just don't know how to answer that! You are a scamp, young man, a scamp and a blue-eyed little rascal!"

Each autumn, if the weather had been ideal and the insects not too bad, the cotton they gathered and took to market brought enough money to pay off the previous year's debts and buy a few extras. Regardless of their profit, though, Michaul unfailingly came home each autumn with new kid gloves for Gussie, wrapped in tissue paper and tied with string. The ritual baffled her, for she and Michaul seldom spoke and never touched. They lived like strangers, though they shared a bed.

"A lady should have fine gloves," he said, each year. "That's what my daddy told me."

"I thank you," Gussie always replied. The annual gift moved her almost to tears, the poignancy of the moment so like their first wonderful weeks of marriage. She carefully untied the package and wound the string onto her string ball. "Waste not, want not," she sighed. "That's what my mama told me."

Winter was Gussie's favorite season, because Michaul had more free time to spend inside with her and Leo. Though they existed with very little communication, Gussie felt that Michaul's presence in the house somehow affirmed a basic bond between them. Watching Michaul play with Leo made Gussie indescribably happy, for the child seemed unaware of the rift between his parents.

Gussie suspected that Michaul was not a particularly good farmer, though she possessed scant knowledge about agriculture herself. Most years they made very little money, which meant they started off each new year already in debt and doubly dependent on a good crop the next year. It made her head ache, just thinking about the financial complexities, wondering about their fate if future crops failed.

She could get through the lonely days without worrying too much if she pretended that Lorena was alive and well.

"Oh, Mama," her fantasized Lorena said, "I just love my school in Tisquah! I have so many new friends! I am so glad we moved here!"

Gussie knew she was play-acting inside her head, the way Phoebe imagined a life with Dr. Khroner, and she finally understood the value of using her imagination. She eventually kept the imaginary Lorena beside her most of the time, helping with chores and caring for Leo.

"Your big sister would have loved you to pieces," she often told Leo.

"Big sister here?"

"Kind of," Gussie answered, vaguely. She felt in her heart that Lorena's presence was as strong as Leo's, but she did not want to confuse the boy. "She ain't far off."

Gussie never made a trip into town without looking at piece goods and mentally choosing a length from which to sew an imaginary frock for Lorena. The clerks in the dry goods store grew accustomed to her silent assessment of the fabric bolts. They ignored her as she wistfully touched the ribbons and lace laid out in the long glass display cases. Gussie supposed they thought she was crazy, but she didn't care. Her mental images of Lorena dressed in the outfits she pretended to sew were too fulfilling to give up, no matter what some ignorant store clerks might think.

In time, to Gussie's great surprise, she included Mr. Peters in her daydreams, thought not exactly the Mr. Peters she had lived with all those years in Maverick County. She imagined sharing her life with a greatly improved Mr. Peters; younger, more vital, with a full head of auburn hair and all his teeth. Sometimes, lying beside Michaul at night, knowing he would not reach across the bed to gather her into his arms, she invited imaginary Mr. Peters into their bed. Mr. Peters always told her how beautiful she was. He stroked the insides of her thighs, sending warmth all the way to her lonely heart. He whispered endearments and showed her new ways to enjoy beddie-bye time. Gussie supposed it was a sin, but she didn't care much about that, either. Michaul did not appear to notice.

"Michaul probably wouldn't pay no mind if I put Mr. Peters' dead body in bed with us," she said aloud, one wash day as she changed the sheets.

On the really bad days, the lonely days, when the wind swept across the plains, whistling around the corners of the house, chilling her soul, Gussie thought she heard Lorena playing the piano. Practicing scales in a distant parlor, up and down, up and down.

"What Mama hear?" Leo asked, one windy spring day.

"A pianer," she whispered. "Listen, maybe you can hear it, too."

"Can Leo see pianer?" He stood still, listening, mimicking Gussie.

"Oh, it's way off yonder in Maverick County. Your daddy give it to a preacher, after your big sister's funeral."

"Long way off?"

"Longer than little boys can imagine."

In early spring, when Leo was three and a half years old, Michaul came home from town with the back seat of the Model-T stacked full of ventilated boxes of baby chicks. Placing them beside the newly constructed brooder house, he instructed Gussie in the care of the delicate, fluffy creatures.

"They must be kept warm," Michaul explained, "or they will die in no time flat. I'm depending on you to make sure they live. Out of these two hundred, I expect maybe a couple of dozen will die. If we lose more than that, it won't be profitable to go to the trouble of raising them ourselves."

Michaul showed Gussie how to light the kerosene heaters around which the fragile chicks could huddle for warmth. Under Michaul's watchful eye, she then filled one shallow pan with fresh water and another with finely ground feed. They carefully transferred the noisy chicks to their new home. The tiny brood pecked at the feed immediately, their spidery feet etching frostlike paths of grain dust across the plank floor.

"In about six weeks," Michaul promised, "we'll invite the neighbors and have a pullet party."

"What's that?"

"We will spend the day killing pullets and dressing them, then we will fry some of them and have a big party. What we don't eat, we will can in your pressure cooker. You better go ahead and order some extra quart jars, so we'll have enough. We will be eating canned chicken meat all winter long!"

"These here babies will be big enough to eat in just six weeks?"

"You just watch them grow," Michaul answered. He winked at Gussie, for the first time in years.

"Six weeks, then," Gussie mused. Her cheeks grew warm under Michaul's steady gaze. She wondered if things would change between them, if a simple project like raising a couple of hundred chickens was all they needed to mend their broken relationship. "Thank God for pullets," she whispered. "Maybe."

Michaul sat Leo on the ground and gave him a chick to hold. Leo, his eyes glowing with pleasure, carefully cupped his hands around the bright-eyed baby, placing his cheek against its pale yellow fluff.

"Leo love chick," the little boy sighed.

"Let him hold it for a few minutes," Michaul instructed Gussie. "When he gets tired of it, put it in with the others. Just don't let him rough it up."

Gussie busied herself with the kerosene heaters as she waited for Leo to tire of holding the chick. He showed no signs of doing so.

"We got to put it back inside its little house," she explained, reaching for the chick, "so it don't get cold and die."

"Leo hold chick," her son said, solemnly.

"You can hold one again, later, but right now we got to put this one back. Your daddy said so."

"Not now." Leo scooted on his bottom, turning his back to Gussie. He hunched forward, sheltering the chick beneath his chin.

"Yes." Gussie caught Leo's elbows and turned him to

face her. His body felt as hard as steel, unyielding, cold.

"No."

With great determination, Leo tightened his grip on the chick and crushed its fragile body. Gussie winced as she heard the little bones break.

"No, Leo!" Gussie exclaimed. "You've done gone and killed the baby!"

"Leo hold."

"Let me have it," Gussie demanded, between clenched teeth. She tried to pry the dead chick from Leo's fingers, but the child held on too tightly. "Let go, right now! Mama's going to spank you if you don't let go!"

Michaul appeared, laughing, and quickly took the chick from Leo's grasp. He hoisted Leo onto his shoulders and walked toward the barn, still chuckling. Gussie, her heart pounding, stooped and retrieved the dead chick from the floor. Its almost weightless body was still warm. Droplets of ruby blood dripped from the tiny beak. One thread-thin leg was broken in several places, bent under a curved, downy wing. Gussie was almost overcome with remorse for the helpless creature.

"Animals ain't got souls," she reminded herself, recalling her father's admonition not to shed tears for animals. "Anyway, we was planning to kill it later, in six weeks. Leo didn't know what he was doing. He's just a little boy."

Gussie walked across the yard and pitched the dead chick into the hog trough, washed her hands at the pump and walked to the house. She felt like a party to murder, as if the chick's innocent blood must surely hang over her head.

"Chickens ain't got souls," she said. "The Bible says so."

In the years since her dog Champ's death, Gussie had often struggled with the question of exactly what a soul was, and how people ascertained which creatures possessed one. Were souls visible, or palatable? How big was a soul, and where in a body did souls latch on and live? She grew dizzy just thinking of all she did not comprehend about such a fundamental issue. Apparently, she thought, someone knew the answer, for her own father was not the least bit confused about the subject.

"I wonder," she whispered, suddenly suspicious, "if my

daddy knowed it for a fact, or if he just said so?"

Though the death of one chick caused Gussie to question her knowledge of souls, the next few days swamped her ability to figure it all out. Leo was, from the moment he first saw the chicks, obsessed with holding them, then killing them, one after another. He became a tiny, human, chicken murderer.

"You have to watch him," Michaul chided, as he disposed of the latest of a dozen dead chicks, all crushed in the manner of Leo's first kill. "We need every single one of these chicks to live. Don't let it happen again!"

"I try," Gussie protested, "but he sneaks out here every time I turn my back."

"I'll put a second latch on the door, out of his reach," Michaul proposed. "Maybe he'll lose interest if he can't get inside."

The little boy cried constantly for three days, pitifully begging to be allowed inside the brooder house.

"Son," Gussie explained, "you know you can't go in there. You kilt too many babies!"

"Leo hold babies! Now!"

Fortunately, the chicks grew rapidly. Within weeks they were leggy and white, their fluff forever gone. They regarded Leo with glittering black eyes and to Gussie's great relief, Leo seemed afraid of them. When they were five weeks old, she let down her guard and told Leo he could play in the dirt beside their pen as she hung out the washing. That evening as she herded the pullets into the brooder house, she realized several were missing. She found them soon enough, dead, their gangly necks broken, all stuffed beneath the brooder house.

"Leo," she asked, "did you kill these here pullets?"

"Leo hold."

"Your daddy's likely to wring your neck," she threatened. "Or mine."

Gussie considered what course of action she should take, finally deciding she would bury the pullets and hope Michaul would not notice their absence. She furtively dug a hole behind the cow shed, then waited until Michaul, who was plowing the field near the house, turned the mule team in the opposite direction. She collected the dead pullets and quickly carried them to their mass grave. It was a waste, she knew, since they were nearly large enough to cook, but she didn't want to explain her carelessness to Michaul. Afterward, she felt heartsick and dirty, as if she had done something terrible.

"I'll wind up with a walnut heart," she told Leo, "if I have to hide any more dead pullets."

Two weeks later, the day before their scheduled party, she found another pullet, dead, tied to Leo's toy cast iron locomotive engine.

"Leo!" she screamed. "Did you kill this here pullet!"

"Leo tie string," the child explained, patiently. "Leo big boy." He placed his hands on his hips and beamed with pride.

"I'm gonna show this one to your daddy, little man," Gussie promised. "You done got on my last nerve!"

She suffered through the afternoon, dreading the awful moment when she would have to show the dead chicken to Michaul. Michaul had never lost his temper with Leo and it broke her heart to think of what punishment he might deem appropriate for the boy.

"Listen, Mama loves you, no matter what, but you got to stop killing chickens. Why, if you was a dog, you'd already be shot! You can't be acting like no hen-house dog, because you are a little boy. Your daddy is going to whup you, but you have it coming! Do you hear me?"

He nodded happily, apparently delighted to be included in the company of chicken-killing canines.

"Leo big boy!"

"I told you to keep him out of the brooder pen," Michaul said, when she showed him the carcass.

"Well, mister, I tried," Gussie argued. "I swear, I don't know when or how he done it! He's just a little boy and the pen is locked tight. Are you going to whup him?"

There was no further discussion about punishing Leo, for Michaul casually lifted his hand and slapped Gussie's face. Hard.

"I can't believe you done that," Gussie gasped, backing away from her husband. "You hit me! Why?"

"It was just a backhanded swat," Michaul responded,

wearily. "If I had hit you, you would be on the floor looking at stars." He sounded exhausted, as if slapping Gussie had sapped all his energy.

The next morning, Gussie arranged her hair to cover her bruised cheek. She was up and laboring at her chores earlier than usual because it was the day of the much-anticipated pullet party. At breakfast, she found the courage to confront Michaul.

"I'm telling you right now, Michaul," she said, "don't you ever hit me again!" I'll tell the sheriff, I promise, if you ever hit me!"

"You had best boil up a big pot of spuds," Michaul commented. "We'll need lots of mashed potatoes and gravy. Get those lemons squeezed, too, so I can set the lemonade in the well house to cool before noon."

Gussie sighed. As usual, she had no idea if she had communicated with Michaul.

"You're getting on my last nerve, too, Michaul," she whispered, as her husband left the kitchen.

Their neighbors arrived early, while there was still dew on the grass, and began the wholesale slaughter of the pullets. Dressed in work clothes because it was such a bloody business, they found spots in the shade and set to work. Michaul and Claude, assisted by four men, took the hysterical pullets from their pen, quickly wrung their necks, then allowed the headless bodies to run in the dirt, spurting blood until they toppled and died. A laughing group of older boys followed the headless birds, mimicking their blind dance of death, then dragged the lifeless bodies to a group of men gathered around planks laid across saw-horses. The pullets were quickly gutted on the makeshift table. The steaming entrails were emptied into tubs for sorting; the livers, gizzards and hearts would be deep-fried for lunch. Additional boys transferred the gutted carcasses to an area where Gussie's two enormous wash pots filled with boiling water sat over wood fires. Bitsy was in charge of the women who dipped the birds into the hot water.

"Don't take them out too soon," Bitsy instructed Phoebe, who looked as if she had never seen a dead chicken, let alone touched one. "It is the hot water that loosens the quills. If you leave them in the water too long, though, it cooks the skin and makes them hard to handle. You'll get the proper time figured out by the time you dip a few more." Several older women were responsible for plucking the feathers from the limp bodies. Soon, the ground around their feet was heaped with mounds of smelly feathers. "Too bad it's not ducks," Bitsy complained. "I surely would like to stuff some down pillows for my bed. Ah, well, let's give thanks for what we have!"

Within minutes of their death, the pullets were cooked until their flesh could be easily removed from their immature bones. The pans of tender meat were passed to Gussie, who packed it into clean quart jars. She spent the next few hours nervously watching the pressure cooker gauges, praying with all her might, for she was always fearful that the contraption would explode.

Long before Gussie set the final jars into the cooker, Michaul and Claude cut up twenty pullets, rolled the pieces and giblets in seasoned flour and deep-fried the lot. The crowd quickly cleared away all evidence of the morning's gore, then split into two groups and changed into clean clothing. Gussie suspected the men, gathered on the far side of the cow shed, passed around a bottle of whiskey. They looked awfully sheepish when they carried their soiled clothing back to their cars and wagons.

"I guess a little snort ain't much to worry about," she whispered, "but I better not see any Abelard cousins driving up, 'cause I still have the shotgun."

Michaul then urged the guests to fill plates with fried chicken and potato salad. Claude and Phoebe poured glasses of cool lemonade as they chatted with the guests. Bitsy proudly sliced four cakes she had baked a day earlier. They were having a wonderful time, Gussie marveled, while she was exhausted and worried that the pressure cooker would explode and kill or at least maim them all.

"We ain't much alike," she muttered. "Me and them Abelards is like oil and water."

After the last morsel was eaten, the men regrouped behind the cow shed to play poker; Messkin Draw, they called it. The women gathered around Gussie, watching as she canned the last jars of pullet meat. They discussed local events, at first, then relaxed and talked of their own experiences, mostly about men and babies.

Gussie removed the last jars from the cooker and set them in the shade beneath the largest elm tree to cool. She then excused herself and began walking the quarter of a mile to Claude and Phoebe's house to fetch Leo. Halfway there, she was met by a tearful Robin. Or Dovie; she could never tell them apart.

"Come quick, Gussie," the girl cried. "Leo's done killed all of Phoebe's calico kittens!"

"Have mercy!" Gussie gasped.

She hesitated as she considered turning back to get Michaul, thought better of it, then gathered her skirts in one hand. She ran.

"Hurry!" Dovie gasped. "Those kids are after Leo!"

Dovie pointed to a knot of children gathered in the shade. They were solemnly looking at a rope swing dangling from a large elm tree. As she drew nearer, Phoebe saw four kittens, Phoebe's prized calicos, hung by their little necks with bits of string tied to the plank swing seat. The children turned and stared at Gussie. She saw tears in the eyes of three little girls.

"Where is Leo?" she demanded.

"Under the porch," Bobby announced, pointing his chubby finger in that direction. "My ma's gonna skin Leo alive for hanging her kittens! I'll bet she is!"

Gussie walked to the porch and stooped to look for her son, squinting into the gloomy recesses until she finally saw him crouched in the far corner.

"Leo," she ordered, "come to Mama." Leo dutifully crawled to her, hesitating when he saw the children gathered around the porch. Gussie snapped her fingers, catching his attention again. She pointed to the ground at her feet. "Come on, Leo. Mama will take care of you."

Gussie could feel the children's morbid curiosity directed at Leo, saw it reflected in her son's blue eyes. She picked him up, then turned to face Robin and Dovie, who looked slightly sick.

"You big girls go get them kittens down and bury them," she instructed. "I know Phoebe will be mighty upset, and I don't blame her. Let's wait until the neighbors go home to tell anybody what happened. Do you girls understand?"

The girls nodded, then obediently headed for the swing and its grisly cargo. Gussie walked home, carrying Leo all the way in spite of his weight. The party was breaking up when she arrived, so she sat Leo in the corner of the parlor and joined Michaul as he waved farewell to their guests. She sighed. It seemed to her the day had lasted forever and might never end.

"I got to tell you something, Michaul," she said. "But first, you got to promise you won't hit me, 'cause we need to figure out what to do."

"Tell me," Michaul sighed.

"Leo kilt all of Phoebe's calico kittens. Hung them by their necks with string."

"So?" Michaul asked, one eyebrow raised.

"So. Leo is killing things all the time. It is all he thinks about. I thought you would be riled up about it."

"I was riled up about him killing chickens," Michaul agreed. "I don't see why I should be riled up about cats."

"Well, mister man," Gussie replied, with great certainty, "I promise you Phoebe will have a conniption fit when she hears about them kittens!"

"So?"

"So...what...are...we...going...to...do...about   LEO KILLING THINGS? Are you drunk? Are you deef? This killing ain't right! Leo is just a little boy!"

"Boys kill things," Michaul explained, patiently. "It's natural. Now, listen to me. So long as he doesn't kill things we grow to eat, or anything we spend money to raise, then it's not a problem. O.K.? Kittens, puppies, birds, rats, mice, lizards, snakes, wild rabbits, coyotes. They're all varmints. Understand?"

"No, I don't," Gussie sighed, "but to tell the truth, I don't think it's natural for Leo. I think there is something mighty wrong with him!"

"Well," Michaul laughed, bitterly, the tone of his voice

cutting Gussie's heart, "you're the one who stayed doped up on laudanum the whole time you were pregnant with Leo. If there is something wrong with him, you have yourself to blame. Where is he, anyway?"

"In the parlor," Gussie replied. "I made him sit in the corner."

"Bring him here," Michaul ordered. "I'll try to explain things to him, since you are so worked up about those kittens."

Gussie walked through the darkened house to the parlor, where she had left Leo sitting in his little red rocking chair. The chair was empty.

"No, Leo!" she cried.

Her heart began pounding but she forced herself to listen in the Cherokee way. She paused, then ran out the front door, around the house and into the back yard. In the lengthening shadows she saw Leo, his back turned to her. He was sitting among the jars of canned pullet meat she had earlier placed in the shade to cool. As she approached, she saw blood on his hands and clothing, dripping into the sandy earth. The blood looked black in the twilight. Broken glass from several Mason jars was scattered in the grass around her son. Leo was clasping portions of pullet meat in his bleeding fingers.

"Leo," Gussie called, softly, "what are you doing?"

"Leo hold chick," the child explained, as tears glistened on his cheeks. "Leo hold! Leo hold now!"

Gussie knelt beside her son and gently pried open his bloody hands. She untied her apron and ripped it in half, then quickly fashioned make-shift bandages. She heard Michaul walk across the yard and she actually felt his heart skip a beat when he saw the blood.

"What's all this?" he asked.

"Leo broke open some jars to get at the pullet meat."

"Christ Almighty!"

"We got to drive him to Tisquah so Dr. Khroner can stitch up his hands. This is too big a job for you and me. There's glass in some of them cuts, too."

"I'll get the Ford," Michaul said.

"Michaul?" Gussie whispered, as he turned away. "How

do you reckon he knowed it was the pullets in them jars? He wasn't here all day. How did he know?"

"I don't know," Michaul replied. He hesitated, his gaze fixed on the darkening horizon, then looked down at Gussie. His expression softened and she saw her confusion and wonder mirrored in his eyes. "Why don't you ask your Cherokee spirits? Maybe they told him!"

That night, after their return from the doctor's office and after Leo finally fell into an exhausted sleep, Michaul reached across the bed and wrapped his arms around Gussie. She stiffened at first, from the sheer unexpectedness of his movements in her direction. She slowly embraced him, then held on for dear life, amazed at how quickly her body responded to his hard, driving need.

"I thought you'd never want me again," she gasped.

"I thought you hated me."

"Well, I declare," Gussie said, softly. She wondered briefly what moment in the strange day had wrought such a dramatic change in their relationship. "I reckon we was both wrong."

"This here is our real honeymoon," Gussie told Michaul, a week after the pullet party and their sweet reconciliation. "We can bury all them bad memories and get on with living."

"You betcha," Michaul agreed, pulling her close to his body, just like old times. "We're on the right path this time."

I believed we was on the right path years ago, Gussie thought. She told herself she had obviously missed some important road signs from the start of her relationship with Michaul, though after all the intervening years she had not reached a personal understanding of just what went wrong. She did not try to discuss her confusion with Michaul, lest the bad memories drive them away from the comfort of each other's arms. Resentment about the treatment she had suffered at the Abelards' hands had, long before, paled beside the crushing, heart rending loss of her daughter.

It was enough, at the moment, to lie beside her handsome husband, to be cradled in his strong arms.

In spite of Gussie's reservations, the days and nights

passed in absolute bliss as she and Michaul fell in love again, sweeter and more profoundly than the first time. They could not touch often enough, could scarcely endure any separation, no matter how brief.

"That was a mighty fine meal," Michaul whispered, hugging Gussie as he left the kitchen after lunch. Five weeks into their new happiness, they continued to linger with each parting. "Bring me a cool drink this afternoon."

Gussie loved watching Michaul as he rode the plow behind the mule team, turning up precise, straight rows of black sod. At the far end of the row he was plowing, he turned the team and Gussie felt the very moment he noticed her and Leo. Her heart skipped a beat, her throat tightened and she gasped, so strong was the connection between them. She thought she might fall to the ground, her legs grew so weak.

"Your daddy sees us," she told Leo. "He's tugging at our heart strings. Do you feel it?"

Leo, his hands still bandaged, stood quietly, occasionally waving at his father in a distracted manner. His blue eyes, so like Michaul's, brimmed with confusion. When Michaul reached them and guided the mules onto the turn row, Leo suddenly skipped away, his bare feet splattering little dust clouds in his wake. Poor thing, Gussie thought, he ain't never seen his mama and daddy act like married people. He probably can't figure out what is going on.

"Leo," she shouted, "you wait for Mama in the back yard. We'll play for a while before nap time." Leo did not indicate that he heard her, so she shouted, louder than before, "Mama still loves her little boy!"

She hoped that Leo would marry some day and understand how joyfully love could bind a husband and wife, how that love did not diminish their feeling for their children.

Michaul made a great show of unscrewing the metal ring on the Mason jar she'd brought him, smacking his lips in anticipation of the cool lemonade. Gussie watched her husband drink as he held the jar in one hand, gulping its contents, his Adam's apple bobbing up and down. She vaguely recalled a verse from the Bible about a woman watching a man drink water in a wheat field.

"Did people in the Holy Land call each other 'mister' and 'missus', or 'honey?'" she asked Michaul.

"Danged if I know," he laughed. He unwound the damp tea towel from the Mason jar and wiped his face and neck, smiling as he looked into his wife's eyes. "What's that you're thinking about, now, woman?"

"Oh, I just wonder, sometimes, about people who lived way back then, in the Bible. I wonder what they thought about."

Michaul winked at her, then strode to the mules and gently guided them into position for the next row. He beckoned to her and she ran to his side, anticipating a kiss. Michaul laughed and winked again, then bent to whisper in her ear.

"What this man is thinking about is buying a tractor."

"Mercy!" Gussie gasped. "A tractor! What for?"

"So's I can tend to these fields in half the time and loll around in bed with you, Missus Honey Abelard! Step up there, Mose, Tom!"

Michaul slapped the reins across the mules' backs, then leaned into the plow as the metal bit the earth.

"You scamp!" Gussie laughed. She dropped the Mason jar and ran to snap the tea towel at her husband's backside. He made a show of leaping into the air, almost spooking the complacent mules. "Can we afford a tractor?"

"We'll talk," Michaul replied. His happy laughter rolled across the fields.

Gussie took her time walking back to the house, enjoying the warm afternoon as she picked a bouquet of wild flowers. Leo sat at the edge of the yard, surrounded by his collection of hand-carved wooden toys. He was hammering nails into a board. Gussie paused in the elm tree's scant shade, arranging her flowers, watching Leo from the corner of her eye. She considered taking the hammer away from him, afraid he might cause further injury to his slashed hands. She decided to distract him, rather than confront him about the hammer.

"Son," she called, "come inside and have some lemonade with Mama. I'll stir in some extra sugar!"

He obeyed without comment and joined her as she walked

from the shade into the house. Leo washed his hands in the basin on the back porch as Gussie poured a jelly glass full of lemonade. She added three spoons of sugar and busied herself in the kitchen as he drank.

"Mama is afeered that hammer will hurt your hands. Why don't you play with something else?"

"Leo will, Mama," the boy agreed. "Can Leo have a ribbon?"

"Ribbon? What do you want with a ribbon?"

"Make something pretty."

Smiling, Gussie watched as Leo sorted through her scrap bag. After careful consideration, he chose a length of tattered pink satin ribbon. She watched as he returned to his play area and knelt in the sand beside the wooden toys. When he showed no inclination to pick up the hammer and resume pounding nails, Gussie returned to her chores.

The following week, when Dr. Krohner removed Leo's bandages and pronounced him healed, Gussie was skeptical. Her son's hands looked incredibly fragile, crisscrossed with pink scars and puncture wounds from the sutures.

"Do you have any questions about the boy?" Dr. Krohner asked.

Gussie wondered if she should ask the physician about Leo's obsession with the pullets and his kitten-killing spree, but she decided it was pointless.

"No," she said, "I reckon he is just a little boy, doing what boys do. Leastways, that's what his daddy thinks. I don't rightly know what boys do."

"Didn't you have brothers?"

"Yes, plenty of them," Gussie replied. "My daddy didn't let the boys play with us girls, so I never knowed much about them."

"Do you want to ask me a question about your son?" His accent had grown less pronounced with the passing years, Gussie noticed, though he still sounded distinctly German. "Anything else?"

"No, I guess not," Gussie sighed. "But I do believe I will be paying you ten dollars more." She opened her reticule, then counted out ten silver dollars. "I believe I am pregnant."

"Ah," Dr. Krohner replied, peering down at her. "How long?"

"Almost a month, I figure," Gussie said.

"Come back in another month and we should know, for certain. You can pay me then. My fee is now twelve dollars."

"Good grief!" Gussie exclaimed. "Did you learn two dollars more about delivering babies?"

"Ha, that is funny thing you say," Dr. Krohner laughed. "No, I learned nothing new, but I now own an automobile. It costs to operate it."

Gussie dropped the silver dollars into her reticule and closed it. She recalled how, long before and far away from Tisquah, she had paid a Mexican midwife a silver dollar to go away and leave her unborn baby alone. She had imagined that baby weighed less than the silver coin. The baby was Leo, whom Michaul had not wanted. Thank God, she thought, things is different, this time around!

"He said to come back in a month," Gussie told Michaul, who was waiting in front of the clinic. He had purchased a licorice whip for Leo, who was happily sucking on one end of the soft, black candy. Michaul put his arm around Gussie and slipped a jaw-breaker into her mouth. She laughed around the huge, hard candy ball.

"We'll have us a girl this time," Michaul promised.

He popped a jaw-breaker into his own mouth, smiling and winking at Gussie. Gussie felt faint, and she clutched Michaul's arm to steady herself.

A girl!

For a moment, Lorena's memory overwhelmed Gussie, but she swallowed the sweet, runny jaw-breaker juices and pushed the horror of Lorena's death into a far corner of her mind. We can be a real family, this time, she told herself. We've all had enough bad things happen. Now we're due some good times.

Long before another month passed, Gussie was certain of her pregnancy. She was even more certain she should have consulted Dr. Krohner about Leo's behavior.

Gussie was fanatic about keeping their outdoor privy

clean. She felt great contempt for women who kept dirty privies, no matter what excuses might be offered for such neglect. Early on the Saturday following the removal of Leo's stitches, Gussie mopped the kitchen linoleum. As part of the weekly cleaning ritual, she then carried the soap bucket across the back yard to the privy and scrubbed it down with an old broom, ceiling to floor. She sprayed coal-oil around the rims of the two adult and one child-size holes in the wooden bench, to discourage spiders and scorpions from lurking there.

"I don't want a scorpion to bite my backside," she whispered. "It would surely make me nervous every time I had to go."

When the interior was dry and the oil fumes aired out to her satisfaction, she filled a lard bucket with snow white lye crystals from a barrel in the barn and liberally sprinkled the lye through each hole, onto the waste pit beneath the privy. Gussie then used a sharp kitchen knife to cut a roll of toilet paper in half, placed the halves on three-penny nails hammered into the privy walls, swept the path clear of twigs and pebbles, then closed the privy door.

Her weekly efforts typically produced a fresh-smelling privy, but on that Saturday morning, Gussie detected a distinctly unpleasant odor. She returned to the barn, scooped additional lye powder into the lard can and walked behind the privy in order to gain access to the waste pit at the ground level opening. She stooped to pour the lye, then screamed and dropped the lard can, spilling its white contents across her shoes. At the corner of the edifice, a swarm of large flies buzzed around the most horrifying object Gussie had ever laid eyes upon.

Retching, she ran down the path until she reached the elm tree. She wrapped her trembling arms around the tree, unmindful of the rough bark scraping her flesh. When she gained control of her breathing, she wiped her mouth with the corner of her apron and resolutely returned to inspect the fly-blown object propped against the rear of the privy.

The buzzing, darting flies were drawn to the rotting carcass of a cotton-tailed rabbit scarcely old enough to have ventured out of its den. The creature was nailed, belly up, to a piece of wood. Gussie saw immediately that it must have been alive at the time the nails were pounded through its tiny limbs. There were five nails, one through each frail leg, the fifth and largest piercing its genital area. The rabbit's eyes bulged almost completely from its head and the tiny pink tongue extended an impossible length between perfect little white teeth. What she had first thought was a block of wood was, in fact, one of Leo's wooden toys. The locomotive engine. Around the toy and the rotting rabbit, tied in a lopsided bow, was a length of tattered, bloody, pink satin ribbon.

"Dear Jesus," Gussie wept, "Leo, oh Leo, what have you done now?"

The discovery was so awful, so unexpected, that Gussie had trouble taking it all in. She knew, though, that the macabre display was Leo's handiwork, that he had been working on it the day she lured him inside to drink a glass of sweet lemonade. He had asked her for a ribbon to make something pretty. Gussie searched her memory, forcing herself to recall his every move. Every word. Try as she might, she was unable to remember any indication that he had been the least bit upset. He had been calm, happy. Busy. No trouble, at all. A good boy.

"Leo," Gussie whispered, "what kind of good boy are you, exactly? This ain't the work of a good boy. No, siree!"

The thought of telling Michaul about her grisly discovery filled Gussie with trepidation, for she imagined he would lecture her, again, about how all boys killed little animals. If he did, Gussie realized, they would undoubtedly argue, for she knew that Leo's behavior was anything but normal.

"If I tell Michaul about this here poor little rabbit," she said aloud, "it will drive a wedge between us, it will for certain! I can't bear to lose his love again, not after all the time we've been so distant. I won't tell him! I will watch Leo every minute, until he outgrows this nasty habit! It is all on my shoulders now, but I can do it. It can be done with my sweet Savior's help!"

She fell to her knees behind the privy, before the rotting rabbit. She closed her eyes and prayed harder than she had ever prayed. She prayed for strength to keep Leo's awful secret. For strength to watch over Leo every moment. For strength to carry and bear the child in her womb, who did not yet weigh as much as a silver dollar.

Gussie then went to the tool shed, found the garden spade and buried the evidence of Leo's madness deep in the earth behind the barn.

At noon, when Michaul and Leo returned from the feed store, she watched from the kitchen window as her husband unloaded the heavy sacks of chicken feed and as her son disappeared behind the privy.

Later, Leo silently entered the kitchen, where he and Gussie regarded each other for long, heavy minutes. Their silence rang in Gussie's ears until she feared her head would explode. Their shared secret lay on her heart, cold and sharp as ice, just as had Lorena's note, snatched by Gussie from beneath a peanut jar in a roadside cafe.

"Mothering," Gussie wrote on the Rexall calendar for that day, "ain't all its kraked up to be!"

CHAPTER FIVE

Gussie's pregnancy proceeded uneventfully, though she was often exhausted. She watched Leo every waking moment of his life and learned to sense when he seemed compelled to revert to his killing behavior. At times, she imagined she saw gratitude in her son's eyes when she pulled his rigid body onto her lap and whispered to him.

"Mama loves you, Leo," she told him. "Mama loves her little boy! You're Mama's little honey bunch!"

Phoebe was also pregnant, and the two women passed many autumn afternoons in their parlors, seated around the kerosene stoves their husbands had purchased with the first of the year's cotton money. After they mended their layettes and sewed some tiny new gowns, Bitsy announced plans to teach them the art of crochet. Gussie surprised herself and quickly mastered the hook and thread. Phoebe struggled with her first attempt, which she finally hid in the bottom of her sewing basket.

"Phoebe, stay with it a bit longer," Bitsy urged, "and you'll get the hang of it."

"I doubt it," Phoebe pouted. She watched Gussie's flying fingers. "I don't have generations of basket weaving and beadwork in my family."

"Let's talk about names for the baby," Bitsy suggested, obviously attempting to head off an argument between her daughters-in-law.

"Phoebe and Claude are about to use up all the names in the book," Gussie observed. "Now, Phoebe says they're having twins, so they will need four names, just to cover all the bases."

"Don't be mean, Gussie," Phoebe sighed. "Anyway, I told you I might have twins someday."

"You told me a lot," Gussie recalled, watching Phoebe's eyes widen in panic. Gussie smiled, savoring Phoebe's obvious apprehension that her imaginary life with Dr. Krohner might be revealed. "I was just funning you, Phoebe. My baby is due around Valentine's Day, so if it is a boy we will call him Valentino Jefferson. If it is a girl, and I think it is, we will call her Lacy Heart."

"It is a girl," Bitsy agreed. "You're carrying it much too low for a boy. She won't have much hair, because you haven't been bothered with indigestion."

"We could hold your wedding ring on a thread over your umm, uh, your stomach and see if it turns in circles," Phoebe suggested. Phoebe often correctly predicted an unborn baby's sex by suspending a pendulum above the mother's abdomen and interpreting the movements. Circles meant it was girl and a straight line indicated a boy. "I personally think it is a boy. Oh, I hope it is! I just swoon over the name 'Valentino'."

"It's a girl, I know it is," Gussie said. I'll call her Lacy and sew a bit of lace on everything she wears."

"We ought to send that idea in to Ladies' Home Journal," Phoebe commented. "You might start a fad!"

On the afternoon of December fourth, a fierce dust storm struck from the north with very little warning. From the kitchen window, Gussie watched Michaul struggle with the barn door as he attempted to pen the livestock. She ran to help him, gasping in the cold wind as she crossed the yard, actually breathing dust. With her help the cows, mules and pigs were safely penned inside the small barn. Michaul raked down feed, filling the hay rack and feed troughs. Gussie climbed onto a nail keg to reach the pipe extended from the windmill through an opening four feet above the water trough. She turned on the faucet, watched as the trough filled to the brim, then cried out in dismay as the faucet handle broke in half. Water quickly overflowed the shallow trough and spilled into a broadening puddle on the barn floor.

"Look what you've done now, you bitch!" Michaul yelled.

"It just happened, Michaul," Gussie explained. "It warn't my fault!"

Without a word, Michaul kicked loose two boards from the wall between the barn and the adjoining tool shed. He entered the smaller room and soon returned with wrenches and a hammer. He dropped the tools beside the nail keg upon which Gussie stood.

"Fix it," he demanded.

"Michaul," Gussie cried, "I'm way into my seventh month. I can't climb up there in this storm and fix that faucet!"

She watched in absolute terror as her husband's eyes turned steel blue. She was certain he was about to hit her, but he pulled his lanky frame onto the water trough and quickly closed the tap. In a matter of seconds he tightened a length of baling wire around the faucet stem as a make-shift handle. He dropped to the floor, shoved the tools through the opening in the wall and replaced the loose boards.

Before Gussie realized what was happening, Michaul picked her up and carried her outside, leaving the barn door flapping in the wind. He stomped into the kitchen and dumped her on the floor. As she got her bearings, Michaul returned to close the barn door, then reentered the kitchen.

Michaul then kicked Gussie until she lost consciousness.

She opened her eyes several hours later, still lying on the kitchen floor. The linoleum pattern looked different from eye level, she realized, as she followed the pattern across the floor. It was oddly beautiful, shaded in the flickering glow of lamp light.

"Mama hungry?"

Leo's voice came from beneath the round oak table that had once belonged to one of Mr. Peters' wives. The one who starved to death during the war, Gussie thought, the one who boiled shoe leather for soup. Leo loved to sit upon the wide legs which extended from the center pedestal. Gussie couldn't see him, but she knew he was on the opposite side of the pedestal, concealed by the table cloth.

"Where's Daddy?" Her voice was a mere thread, weak and bubbly. She ran her tongue around her mouth, tasting blood. "Dear, sweet Jesus!" She remembered why she was on the kitchen floor. She tried to sit, then crumpled to the floor again as pain jolted every nerve in her body. "Leo! Where is Daddy?"

"Daddy cry," Leo answered, still concealed beneath the table. "Daddy make Leo bread and butter."

"Leo, come help Mama sit up."

"I'll help you, Gussie," Michaul whispered, from behind Gussie. "Don't be afraid. I'll help you."

Gussie was speechless with fear, but she knew she had no choice but to let her husband to whatever he wished. Think, she told herself. Think. This is bad, but if you make a mistake, things can get a lot worse. She recalled her mother's gentle voice.

When you are in danger, keep quiet. Your body will know what to do, Josephine whispered, somewhere inside Gussie's battered head.

"Thank you, Mama," Gussie sighed.

Michaul's strong hands reached through the air and gently lifted her to a sitting position. My baby, Gussie thought. Please be alive. I'll get us through this, I promise, if you just stay alive.

"I'm sorry, Gussie," Michaul sobbed, kneeling beside her, holding her upright. He rested his head on her shoulder, sending waves of pain through her with each sob. "I don't know what came over me! It was like the whole world turned red. It started when I couldn't get the stock in the barn. The wind, that wind...wind kept ripping the door out of my hands...I was glad you came to help but I knew you shouldn't be out in that wind. I got so mad! Mad at the wind, at something I can't...mad! I wanted to hit something, to kill something, someone! I don't know why! Now, I'm afraid I've killed you and the baby! Why? Why?"

"Michaul," Gussie whispered, "I know you couldn't help it. I know! Listen to me, you listen!" She pointed to the sink, wincing in pain. "Pump me some cool water, for my face!"

Gussie struggled to breathe, thinking Michaul had probably broken her ribs, how many she couldn't guess. Her head was bleeding, as were her mouth and nose. She gingerly moved her feet, then her legs, relieved that her spine wasn't crushed. Her left arm didn't respond well, but she found no obvious break as she examined it with her right hand. Probably been laying on it all this time, she told herself, it's probably just asleep. Michaul knelt again and offered her a damp cloth, then a basin of fresh water. Between them, they cleaned her wounds. Leo sat beneath the table, happily eating his bread and butter.

"Did Leo see you hurt me?"

"No, I don't think so. I hope to God he didn't," Michaul replied. His voice was choked with shame, with tears. "When I came to myself, after the madness left me, I found Leo asleep on his bed."

"Can you get me to our bed?" She was shivering, perhaps had been all along. She was suddenly aware of intense pains in her lower back. "I think I'm in labor! You've got to go to Tisquah and bring the doctor. I'm going to need him, soon!"

"I'll get Bitsy and Phoebe, then drive to town," Michaul suggested.

"There ain't time to get nobody but the doctor!" Gussie stifled a scream. "This here is going to be quick!"

"Gussie," Michaul gasped. "The doc will see what I've done to you! I might go to jail!"

"Michaul Abelard, on any other night I'd say you should go to jail. But, this here is an emergency. I need that doctor! Listen, when you get back, I'll say I went out while you were gone and the cows trampled me when I tried to pen them. Nobody will ever know different."

"Gussie, oh Gussie, I don't deserve your understanding! I promise never to raise my hand to you again! I promise! I'll make this up to you, sweetheart, just don't die! Don't die!"

He carried Gussie to their bed, piled quilts and afghans around her shivering body. She hurriedly gave him instructions on preparing for the delivery.

"Quick, Michaul, before you go, put the leaves in the table and cover it with the oilcloth. Then unroll them newspapers I been saving for padding. Fill all the lamps with oil before you go, and pump all the buckets and pans full of water. Set two buckets on the stove...make sure the oil tank on the stove is full, so the fire don't go out. Come here and help me get into my old gown! Then go! Go! I can't wait!"

Michaul immediately followed her instructions, then donned his heavy coat, gloves and wool cap.

"What about Leo?" he asked.

"Stir ten drops of paregoric and four spoons of sugar into a glass of warm milk," Gussie whispered. "He'll fall asleep in a few minutes. He don't need to be awake tonight. What's about to happen ain't for little boys' eyes!"

In moments, Leo appeared beside her bed, greedily drinking milk from a glass. He climbed onto a ladder-back chair beside one of the bedroom windows and peered outside. Gussie raised her head and watched, too, as the Model-T's yellow lights bounced into the dusty night. She and Leo were suddenly more alone than she had ever imagined. Michaul had not said farewell before he left.

"Leo sees snow!" her son gleefully announced.

"Ain't snow, son, it's dust."

"No. Snow. Snow and dust."

"You be a big boy and put on your perjamers," Gussie suggested. "Then go to bed. If it does snow, you can play in it tomorrow."

"Leo play?"

"Yes! Now, go to bed!"

Leo obediently went into his room and climbed into bed. Gussie knew the child was sleeping in his clothes rather than pajamas, in order to waste no time dressing the next morning. About some things, her son was smart as a whip.

Her labor progressed rapidly, as she had predicted. She was not overly concerned at first, believing that Michaul would return with Dr. Krohner within the hour. Or, at the most, two hours. Three hours after his departure, she knew it would have been wise to have allowed Michaul to fetch Bitsy and Phoebe. Her water broke, soaking the old blanket she had directed Michaul to place beneath her buttocks. After that, the pains came so fast she hardly had time to breathe.

"Oh Michaul," she wept, "hurry, hurry! I can't do this all by my lonesome!" She fought the panic rising in her throat. "I don't dare make enough noise to wake Leo! God, let my little boy sleep through this!" She was hardly able to breathe; it seemed that the blankets, the bed itself were sucking her into a soft, airless pit. "God! Please hear me now! Get me up out of this here bed and onto the kitchen table. I need something firm to hold on to, something to brace against, even if the doctor ain't here! Please help me!"

A warm, peaceful feeling swept over her pain-wracked body. With absolute clarity, she knew she was able to rise and walk into the kitchen. As she slipped from the bed covers, the icy floor felt wonderful beneath her bare feet. She took small, shuffling steps as she made her way out of the bedroom and into the kitchen. She glanced through Leo's bedroom door and saw he was safely snuggled beneath the quilts.

"Keep Leo asleep this night, Lord, I'm begging you!"

She placed two porcelain basins on the buffet beside the oak table, then filled them with hot water from the buckets Michaul had placed on the stove. Her strength held as she made several trips from the buffet to the stove, carrying water by means of a smaller bucket. She returned to her bedroom for blankets and pillows, then for scissors and crochet thread. Debating whether she should close the bedroom door to keep the heat in the kitchen required all her concentration. Finally, she went to the bed and pulled all the quilts, pillows and afghans into the kitchen, then closed the bedroom doors to Leo's room and to the kitchen.

In spite of believing that Michaul would return at any moment, she had to admit that the baby would probably arrive before its father and that she would have to keep it, and herself, warm. The house seemed to spin on its foundation as she rolled onto the oak table.

"I've done all I can do, God," she whispered.

She squirmed onto the newspaper padding then raised herself into a sitting position, pushing down with all her remaining strength.

"God! Help me, now!" she prayed. "And keep Leo asleep! I ain't even asking why Michaul ain't come back yet! Just help me!"

She clenched her teeth against the pain, looking at the ceiling and gulping great droughts of air. Cobwebs had accumulated in the corner over the stove, she noticed, making a mental note to sweep them down as soon as she felt up to it. Once again she pushed, keening with pain as the baby slipped easily onto the newspaper padding. Before Gussie reached for it, it flailed its miniature limbs and mewed like a kitten.

Gussie was afraid she would faint, from pain and relief, but she quickly tied off the cord with two twists of crochet thread. In moments, the umbilical between the two ties paled. She snipped the tough, rubbery tissue with her embroidery scissors. Gritting her teeth against the pain, Gussie then sponged the tiny infant clean.

"So tiny," she cooed, as she worked. "You got to be strong, and I pray to God there's a big heart in that tiny body. I had a baby sister named Tiny because she was borned too soon, just like you. She's a big girl now, and I know you can make it, just like she done!"

The newborn was a girl, Gussie noted, though its sex didn't seem important at the moment. She wrapped it in a soft receiving blanket, then an afghan, before placing it onto the buffet beside the table.

She endured the pain preceding the expulsion of her afterbirth, then rolled off the newspaper padding and cleaned herself the best she could. She was desperately weary, but terrified of falling asleep upon the table. With greater determination that she knew she possessed, she slid off the table, onto her knees, then crawled to the pile of blankets and formed a nest within their soft depths. She returned to the buffet, carefully grasped the baby's wrappings and pulled the newborn into her arms. She crept backwards until she was in the nest she had fashioned. Her vision was fading, and she knew she should have something to drink. But she was too tired to do more.

"Thank you, God," she sighed, snuggling her baby against her neck. "Thank you for this little baby. Thank you for keeping Leo asleep. Bring Michaul home with the doctor as soon as you can. And let me remember to explain about how the cows trampled me, and...please don't let Michaul get mad at me again. Jesus' sweet name, Amen!"

She slipped into the deepest of all sleep, thinking as she

drifted away that she had seldom been tasked to such a hard day's work.

Gussie opened her eyes to absolute stillness, to such quiet and cold that, for an instant, she feared she had died during the night. The baby, still curled against her neck, moved gently. Brilliant sunlight shone through the kitchen windows and fell across the floor. The kitchen door stood open, accounting for the extraordinary cold. She considered her situation for several minutes, hoping against hope that she would hear the familiar sounds of the Model-T as Michaul drove into the yard.

As her thoughts grew more coherent she knew she had to cross the floor and close the door. Carefully, biting her lips against the pain, she placed the baby in the depths of the quilts and covered it. She took her time stretching her arms and legs, for she was unbearably sore and stiff. She crawled to the cabinet and pulled herself to a standing position.

The pan in which Michaul had warmed milk for Leo still held some liquid, which she drank in three gulps, aware that she should sip it.

"I can't afford to get sick on this here milk," she cautioned herself. "So, I just won't."

Her stomach knotted and she gagged, but the milk stayed down. In seconds, or so it seemed, she felt stronger. Holding onto furniture and leaning against the wall, Gussie gradually worked her way to the open door. She scarcely believed her eyes when she looked outside.

A deep, pristine layer of snow undulated across the landscape, its brilliance bringing tears to her eyes before she had the presence of mind to blink.

"Leo did see snow," she whispered. "Lordy, it must have snowed all night, and in a hard wind, too, judging from the size of them drifts." Gussie pushed the door shut, then leaned against it, trying to organize her thoughts. "I know the wind was blowing, hard, when me and Michaul left the barn. It was blowing when Michaul left us to fetch the doctor, too, and it must have blowed hard all night. I never heard it. Lawsy, I didn't think about it because I was so busy birthing the baby. Them roads to town must be all drifted over. That's why Michaul ain't got back yet! We could be here for days before he gets through!"

She walked back to her pallet of quilts, holding to the cabinet so she wouldn't fall. Her feet were numb from the cold. She wanted nothing more on earth than to crawl into the quilts, snuggle her baby and drift off to sleep. Her mother's voice came to her, softly.

Death beckons women with a smile, Gustine. The more it smiles, the harder we must fight!

"I'll get some socks on and try to make breakfast," Gussie whispered. "That's about all the fight I got left."

She opened her bedroom door and shuffled across the braided rug to the bureau. She found two pairs of her own woolen stockings and two pairs of Michaul's, then sat on the ladder-back chair and pulled them on, Michaul's over hers. She could barely move her toes but did not feel the cold as she walked back to the kitchen, closing the bedroom door behind her.

Gussie dipped milk from a large crock, filled the little pan, then warmed it on the stove. She filled the coffee pot with water from a bucket, aware without wasting her energy that the pump was frozen. As the milk warmed and the coffee brewed, she scrambled a dozen eggs, fried a slab of bacon and sliced a loaf of bread she had baked two days earlier.

"I don't know when I'll feel up to cooking again," she said. "I'm tired enough to sleep all winter." She placed the food in the warming oven, then opened a jar of canned peaches. "I got to turn off the stove in the parlor and bring that oil in here for the cook stove. I'll never make it out to the tool shed for more coal oil. I don't know when Michaul will be back, and I doubt that his shiftless brother will even think to come see about us. Them Abelards who live up the road ain't good for nothing!"

Gussie made her way into the parlor and turned off the heater. She carefully removed the oil tank and poured the contents into the larger tank mounted on the rear of the cook stove. She then went to wake Leo.

"Sweet boy," she called. "Wake up now. Mama has breakfast all cooked. After you eat, I got a real surprise to show you!"

Leo did not move, so Gussie made her way to his bed,

then turned back the quilts. Leo was not there. In disbelief, Gussie fell to her knees and looked beneath the bed, then in each corner of the room. No Leo.

"Oh, sweet Jesus! Leo, you went outside! That's why the door was open!"

Her brain seemed split in half. She thought, on the one hand, that she did not have the strength to go outside and search for Leo. On the other hand, she was already gathering up the quilts and pillows from Leo's bed, dragging them into the kitchen so she could warm him after she had him back inside. Gussie closed Leo's bedroom door, then the door between the kitchen and parlor. She quickly ate a spoonful of scrambled eggs and a slice of bacon, then drank a scalding cup of black coffee. Bright lights swirled before her eyes. She knew she was risking all their lives if she went outside in her weakened condition, but she had to do it. She pulled on her coat, then Michaul's work boots.

Gussie left the baby as it was, opened the door and called for her son. The only sound was the lowing of the milk cows.

"Yeah, you need to be milked," she said. "Well, you'd best get in line, because I got a lot to do before that happens."

"Leo!" she called, again, hating the weak, feminine sound of her voice across the glistening landscape. It was as if the snow swallowed up her words. "Leo, answer Mama!"

She looked down then and realized she could follow Leo's small footprints, which lead straight to the barn, through snow perhaps a foot deep. On the north side of the house and barn, snow had drifted to the rooftops. Thankfully, she noted that her son had not walked towards the deeper drifts. She struggled to the barn and pulled open the door, grateful for the warm, beastly smell that greeted her. The pigs huddled together in their pen near the door, snuffling expectantly. Chickens roosted on the rafters, heads comically turned, peering down with bright, black eyes.

"Chicken coop must have blowed over," Gussie said. "Some of the hens somehow managed to get inside the barn." She located a bucket containing about an inch of chicken feed and scattered it on the barn floor. "Use your heads, you stupid birds," she called up to the chickens, "and hop down here if you

114

want to eat."

Mose and Tom, the mules, regarded her suspiciously, as if they feared she would harness them and lead them outside, into the snow. She scratched their faces, then moved around the stalls. She saw Leo then, valiantly attempting to milk one of the four milk cows.

"Let Mama help you, Leo!"

His face red from his efforts, the boy ran to her and wrapped his arms around her knees.

"Leo played in snow!" he shouted. "Cows cry and Leo milk! Leo big boy!"

"You are a good boy," Gussie whispered, fighting back tears. "Let Mama help you with the milking. I cooked breakfast, so we need to hurry! You are a good, big boy. Mama's right proud of you!"

She simply did not have the heart to make her little son leave the milking undone, so she gingerly sat on the three-legged milk stool and finished the job. The cows' udders were swollen with milk, jagged blue veins protruding through the fine hair, crisscrossing delicate, baby-pink flesh. At first, Gussie doubted she had the strength to grasp the warm, swollen teats, but after a few tentative pulls, she fell into the rhythm. The cow was visibly relieved and Gussie also benefited from the repetitious movement. Soon, she had much more flexibility to her movements and the exertion warmed her through and through. Again, Gussie heard her mother's voice.

Simple efforts solve all problems, daughter. All things are simple, unless we stop trying.

Gussie dragged the two large buckets of milk to the pig pen and poured one into the feeding trough. It was a shame to waste it, for she would normally have separated the cream and churned butter. She knew she was unable to carry both buckets through the snow.

"Wake up, pigs," she said, softly, "this is your lucky day."

"Lucky day!" Leo laughed, clapping his hands.

The pigs tested the milk with their soft snouts, then greedily drank every drop. Leo imitated their happy snorts.

She let Leo help her carry the heavy bucket to the house,

though it meant spilling great drops onto the snow. She had seldom seen the boy so proud of his efforts and she did not want to diminish his sense of accomplishment. Inside the warm kitchen, she hung their frozen clothing over the chair backs, then braved the cold in each bedroom to fetch them dry garments. She bundled the oilcloth and soiled newspaper padding and stowed it in her bedroom. Outside, it would surely attract coyotes and other predators, and she already had more problems than she could deal with.

Gussie had never felt so weak or exhausted, not even when she was doped on laudanum. She served herself and Leo plates of hot eggs, bacon and bread, and they each drank two glasses of milk, still warm from the cows. Her breasts felt like hard knots beneath her gown and she hoped the food and drink would start her own milk coming in. Her stomach accepted the food, so she joined Leo in dessert - bowls of canned peach halves topped with warm milk and sugar. She had never loved the taste of anything so much.

"Leo," she told her beaming son, "you done a good thing by going to the barn. But, listen, you don't go out again without telling Mama. I'll go with you next time. Understand?" Leo nodded, solemnly. "Promise Mama? Cross your heart?" Leo crossed his heart, mimicking her movements, and nodded once again. "Good boy! Now, Mama has a surprise for you."

Gussie led Leo to the quilts piled beside the cook stove. She gently uncovered his baby sister, marveling herself at how very small the infant appeared. The little boy was enchanted. He looked at Gussie with such wonder in his blue eyes that Gussie felt her heart lurch with the pure joy of her son's discovering an unexpected, beautiful thing. She guided his hand to the baby's wrinkled, fuzzy cheek. He stroked it gently, his mouth a perfect "O".

"This here is your new baby sister," she explained.

"What her name?"

"Well, I don't rightly know," Gussie mused, smiling. "It was supposed to be Lacy Heart, but she come before Valentine's Day. What do you think we should call her?"

"Lacy Summer."

"Summer? Why?"

"Summer warm. No snow. Snow hurts Leo's hands and toes!"

"Then her name is Lacy Summer. Let's call her Lacy, and Mama will sew a bit of lace on all her little clothes."

"No," Leo argued, patiently. "Let's call her Summer!"

Leo sat calmly beside Summer as Gussie gathered some of his toys and a pencil and tablet. She pulled the quilts from Leo's bed near her own and made a nest for him. He snuggled in, holding the toys in his arms. His eyelids drooped and Gussie saw that he would soon sleep.

"Don't open the door without Mama," she whispered. "We got to keep the kitchen warm."

Leo mumbled something about the cold snow.

Gussie cleaned herself with warm water and pinned folded pads of cloth inside her undergarments. To her great relief, she had not bled heavily after the birth, though her trip to and from the barn might have increased the flow.

"I think I done good, without a doctor or any help," she said. "Now I just have to keep us all alive until Michaul gets home." She crawled into her quilt nest and put the baby to each breast, with little result. The infant showed no interest in suckling. Gussie's breasts, if possible, were harder than ever. "Something has to give," she mused. "I either got to make milk or this baby has to suck. Summer, honey, we got to help each other out of this mess."

They slept throughout the afternoon. At dusk, Gussie lit the kitchen lamps and prepared chicken soup, using a jar of canned pullet meat and the last of a box of egg noodles. She gave Leo the box, instructing him to copy the lettering onto his tablet.

"You better learn your letters," she admonished, "if you want to go to school next year!"

They ate on the floor, wrapped in quilts, for Gussie did not want to waste the energy required to properly clean the table. Leo proudly showed her his tablet. Gussie smiled.

"Them's real good letters, Leo," she acknowledged. "But, you got most of them upside down and backwards. Try again."

She tidied up the kitchen, willing her sore limbs to reach and lift, demanding more of her battered body than necessary. In a far corner of her mind, she acknowledged that her husband might be stranded in the snow. That he might never return. She asked herself, in the Cherokee way, if Michaul was alive, if he was trying to come home. She sensed no answer. Perhaps, she admitted, it was because she did not know if his return would be a good thing. Or a very bad thing. Leo tugged at her skirts, eager to show her the tablet again.

"That's better!" she said. Leo beamed, then gave her the box to compare to his work.

"Read to Leo," he demanded.

"Real good noodles for little boys," Gussie pretended to read. She was always embarrassed to read aloud, even to Leo, because her literacy was so limited. Except for crochet instructions, which for some reason she could follow. She was startled by Leo's work, for he had correctly copied the Hebrew emblems on the noodle box, though his version of the English lettering was mostly upside down, as usual.

"Sweet boy," she asked casually, "how come you drawed them Bible letters right when you have trouble with the regular letters?"

Her son carefully considered the box, shrugged, then looked at her as if she was daft.

"Pictures," he said, pointing to the Hebrew words. "A, B, C," he explained, pointed to the English words. "Not same, Mama, look and see."

Gussie then attempted to nurse the baby, delighted that the infant sought her nipples and actually sucked. The pain was intense, like a hot wire inside her body, running from her nipples to her privates. She gritted her teeth and switched breasts after a few minutes, though she was afraid she would faint. The alternative would be much worse, she thought, determined that she would not raise another child on light bread softened in warm water.

Leo, who was only briefly curious about the nursing procedure, played an imaginary game of baseball on the kitchen linoleum, running from invisible base to base, sliding into home, then scurrying to the pitcher's mound to deliver another fast ball.

Gussie tore a diaper in half and folded it to fit her tiny baby. She then prepared a pan of cocoa, mixing paregoric and extra sugar into Leo's cup. She needed a good night's rest and it was obvious that Leo had no interest in going to sleep. The potion worked; in half an hour, Leo was sleeping in his quilt bed. Gussie blew out the lamps and snuggled beside the baby.

At dawn, Gussie nursed Summer, then put the coffee pot on and slipped out the back door. She milked the cows, again pouring half the milk into the pig trough. She found a grain scoop and cleared a narrow path to the chicken house. Inside the small structure lay most of her hens, frozen, gnawed at by something wild. Pole cats, she thought. She filled a bucket with feed from the covered barrel in one corner and dragged it back to the barn. The surviving chickens scurried around her feet, pecking the seeds from the barn floor, clucking happily. Gussie wondered how those few chickens had escaped the hen house and gotten into the barn. Her search for an opening proved futile. She pulled down more hay for the cows and mules, broke the ice covering the water trough and rummaged in a tool box for a tin of udder cream. She tucked the tin in her pocket and left the barn, securely closing the door. There was no sign of life at Claude and Phoebe's house, so far as Gussie saw.

The kitchen's warmth enveloped her as she painfully lifted the bucket of milk to the drain board. Leo, she noted, was already awake, sitting beneath the table, singing.

"Nah, nah, nah, said the little fox," he warbled, "singing merrily!"

Gussie removed the udder cream from her coat pocket, turned her back to the table, opened her dress and rubbed the soothing ointment on her nipples. The relief was instant and wonderful.

"I won't ever again tolerate nobody letting a cow suffer with sore teats," she said.

Gussie quickly scrambled eggs, fried bacon and mixed up a batch of biscuits. She called Leo from his perch beneath the table and they ate breakfast, sitting on Leo's quilt pallet. Gussie then straightened the kitchen, confident enough in her recovery to use some of the water from the bucket to wash dishes. She would melt snow later and refill the water supply. Leo returned to his play place beneath the table and Gussie, armed with a small bowl of warm water, knelt on her pallet to clean and change the baby.

Summer was gone!

"Leo!" Gussie screamed. "Where's the baby?"

"Leo and baby play Little Fox."

On her knees, speechless with dread, Gussie crawled across the linoleum and looked under the table.

"OH, GOD!" she screamed.

Her voice startled Leo and he toppled backward from the table leg. His head hit the floor, he gasped, then was silent.

The baby was perched in a very odd position on a table leg, one of four extending at right angles from the pedestal base. In an instant, Gussie crawled across Leo's unconscious body and tried to lift the infant. Moaning, she realized the tiny body was tied to the table leg with crochet thread, loops of which crisscrossed Summer's body, holding her more or less upright against the pedestal. Gussie fumbled with the thread, then blindly groped for the embroidery scissors lying on the floor. She freed the baby, then scuttled backwards across the linoleum until she reached the quilts. Only then did she dare look for signs of life in her daughter's face.

"Oh, Summer honey," Gussie wept, "if Leo hurt you, I promise I'll kill him! The devil himself is in that boy!"

Amazingly, the baby seemed unharmed, except for slight indentations marking the path of Leo's haphazard looping of crochet thread around her body. She was cool to Gussie's touch, but alert and moving on her own. Gussie wept as she inspected the little arms and legs for damage, afraid to believe she was not harmed. She looked at each miniature finger, each perfect toe and ear lobe, then removed the little diaper, unable to erase the memory of the mutilated rabbit she had found, months earlier. The baby was fine, she eventually admitted. Gussie pinned a dry diaper on Summer, nursed her at each breast, then placed her in the quilts.

Only after her daughter fell asleep did Gussie direct her attention and energy to Leo. She located her twine ball in the catchall drawer and deliberately tied Leo to the pedestal legs, allowing enough extra length for limited movement. She dragged Leo's quilt bed, his toys and tablet beneath the table. She lifted him onto the pallet, then felt his head, locating a large bump on the back side. There was no bleeding, so she covered him with a quilt and returned to her own bed.

Gussie spent the day deep in thought, leaving the quilts only to check on Leo. He continued sleeping and Gussie eventually realized he probably had a concussion.

"Ain't nothing more I can do for him," she said, aloud. "Maybe he's gonna die. Maybe he should die!" Thoughts of Leo's death did not shock Gussie, for she had carried them deep in her heart for months. "Leo ain't normal. He's cute and I love him, but he ain't normal. He's dangerous, that is a fact! I can't watch him close enough to keep everybody and everything on this farm safe from him!"

The baby was awake, sucking her tiny fingers. Gussie looked into her eyes, as she stroked her downy face.

"Your big brother ain't right," she whispered. "I swear I'll protect you from him, Summer, no matter what it takes!"

Afternoon shadows stretched across the kitchen floor as Leo roused. Gussie watched from her quilt bed, her eyes narrowed. She kept perfectly still as Leo attempted to free himself from the twine bindings she had fashioned. She waited for him to panic, but soon realized he was not going to fight the bonds after he found himself unable to escape.

"Leo?" she called. "Mama had to tie you up, so you don't hurt the baby."

"Leo not hurt baby!"

"You tied her to the table leg, Leo! You could have broke all her little bones!"

"Mama tie Leo," the boy answered, reasonably, "but Leo not hurt."

"It's different," Gussie sighed, aware that Leo was about to defeat her with his five-year-old's logic.

"Mama kiss Leo?"

"No, Leo, I ain't gonna kiss you, not right now. Mama is tired. You play with your toys."

"Daddy kiss Leo!"

"Daddy ain't here."

"Other time, in barn, Daddy kiss Leo."

"Well, Daddy loves you," Gussie replied.

"Daddy tie Leo. Daddy kiss Leo," the boy said. "Leo tie baby. Leo kiss baby. Same thing!"

Their conversation was interrupted by the howling of a band of coyotes, very near the house. Gussie's skin crawled. She had never heard them so close. Automatically, she looked at the gun rack above the back door, where the shotgun normally rested. The rack was empty!

"Michaul must have knowed the blizzard was coming, before he left," she whispered. "He wouldn't have taken the gun unless he feared he'd be caught out where the coyotes could get him!"

"Bad dogs get Leo?" her son asked. His voice vibrated with fear.

"No!" Gussie shouted, rising from her quilts. She lit the lamps and put her face close to the window glass. Her heart almost stopped. At least ten coyotes were in the yard between the house and the barn, noses skimming the packed snow as they circled each other. They looked like pure hunger, Gussie thought. She checked the door, though she knew it was shut tight. "Nothing is going to get us, Leo. Mama is going to make us a peach cobbler, right now! Would you like that?"

Leo whimpered as Gussie prepared the cobbler batter. Before the dish was fully cooked, the animals in the barn began the worst commotion she had ever heard. The braying of the mules and the desperate lowing of the cows was almost drowned out by the frantic, high-pitched squealing of the pigs. They would go for the pigs, Gussie thought. The mules and cows could kill a coyote with one swift kick. Pigs were, essentially, helpless.

Gussie dipped a bowl of hot cobbler for Leo, poured milk over the thick, sugary contents and crawled beneath the table. Leo was curled in his quilts, his twine-bound hands on either side of his little face, shielding his ears. Purest terror shone in his blue eyes. Gussie set the bowl aside and curled around her son's shivering body. She covered him with kisses, rocking him back and forth until he fell asleep. She stayed beside him until the terrified pigs ceased their squealing. They were all dead, she was certain.

It was the longest night of her life, longer than the night she had spent alone with Lorena's corpse. Longer and more frightening than the night, just forty-eight hours earlier, when she had birthed Summer.

"Nights like this," she observed, "make a body wonder if God really cares. Of course, God is a man. If God was a woman, things would be a heap better!"

When the morning sun was high, she went to the barn. Ignoring the signs of carnage, the frozen, partially eaten pig carcasses and the prevailing sense of doom in the small building, she searched for the opening through which the coyotes had gained entrance. At the dark side of the barn, beyond the hay rack, lay one of the boards Michaul had kicked loose when he was in his rage. She crossed the blood-soaked floor and looked into the tool shed. The outside door stood ajar, probably blown open during the blizzard.

"Them fool chickens didn't find their own way in," Gussie said. "The same wind that took the roof off the hen house must have blowed open the tool shed and plopped them birds inside. Lucky old things, them few chickens."

She found the hammer and some nails, then repaired the loose boards, adding extra nails for good measure. She didn't think the coyotes could get back inside. She wished she had some way of passing that information on the terrified cows and mules, who regarded her with glazed expressions. She quickly spread feed and milked the cows.

"Less than one bucket full," she said. "I reckon them coyotes put us all off making milk. I never spent such a purely awful night!"

As she walked back to the house, she felt a warm, south wind whirling across the snow. She stood still for a moment, luxuriating in the unexpected warmth. If it continued, the snow would melt in a couple of days. Gussie sensed that Michaul would return home that day. She hurried inside, her mind setting out a schedule of things she had to do before his return.

"Empty the chamber pots," she whispered, mentally counting off the looming chores, "burn them bloody newspapers, put bread dough on to rise, get the beds made, wash down the kitchen table with lye soap. When all that is done, I'll untie Leo."

Mid-afternoon brought real warmth, causing huge sheets of snow, six inches thick, to slide off the roof. Gussie completed her chores, changed into a clean dress and sat at the table as she nursed Summer.

"My real milk ain't come in yet, honey," she whispered to the baby. "It will soon, though, and you can get fat and grow big. Lots of babies your size, even smaller, have made it!"

Her reverie was interrupted by furious knocking at the front door. She ran through the house, flung open the door and found Claude standing on the porch. He stepped inside, slack-jawed when he saw Summer in Gussie's arms.

"Before you ask," Gussie laughed, bitterly, "Michaul ain't here, he went to get the doctor the night of the blizzard. I birthed this here baby all by my lonesome. Coyotes got in the barn last night and kilt the pigs, so if you and Michaul was going halves on them, you're out of luck. Leo is tied to the kitchen table, drugged on paregoric because he just about kilt the baby with crochet thread. He may have a concussion, too, but I ain't sure. That's about it!"

Claude continued standing in the parlor, gaping at Gussie, so she returned to the kitchen. Her milk suddenly came down, soaking her clean dress, dripping onto the linoleum. She didn't know whether to laugh or cry. Claude finally stumbled into the kitchen, wiping his fog-shrouded glasses.

"I came over to see if Michaul wanted to hunt coyotes," Claude explained. He shrugged. "I'm sorry I didn't come down the first day of the blizzard, but we just figured you were all right. Dang!"

"Yep," Gussie agreed. "Dang!"

They regarded each other for long moments, neither knowing what to say. Gussie broke the impasse by handing Summer to Claude. She went to her bedroom and changed into a dry dress. As she fumbled with the buttons, she heard the unmistakable sound of automobiles on the road.

"It's Michaul!" Claude called, from the kitchen. "Dr. Krohner is driving him. Two other guys are driving Michaul's car."

"I can see that with my own eyes," Gussie snarled. "You Abelards are such know-it-alls!"

Claude returned Summer to Gussie's arms then plunged out the back door, into the drifts. He returned with Dr. Krohner and Michaul, whom they half-carried up the steps and into the kitchen.

"What now?" Gussie asked.

"Your husband has pneumonia," Dr. Krohner explained, breathlessly. "His car was stuck in the snow until yesterday morning. I tried to keep him at the clinic, but he said you were alone and in labor."

"I was," Gussie admitted. She ran ahead of the men and turned down her freshly made bed. Claude removed Michaul's boots and coat, then pulled the quilts up to his chin. "I birthed the baby myself," Gussie explained, "the night he left to fetch you. How sick is Michaul?"

"He's dying," Dr. Krohner replied. "He knows it. His lungs were ruined in the war, when he was gassed. He knew it was only a matter of time. The dust and cold just speeded up the process." The doctor led Gussie to a chair and gently pushed her into it. "He is worried about you and the children. About how you will survive without him."

"I'll bring Bitsy down," Claude whispered. "I can drag her on the sled. Gussie, you're going to need some help!"

Gussie sighed. "I reckon I will need all kinds of help!"

"I must go soon," Dr. Krohner said. "I need to examine you and your baby. The baby is small, but I believe she will thrive. You handled the birth very well, I'd say."

"Real well," Gussie replied. "But then, I didn't have no choice."

"I will leave some medicines to keep your husband comfortable. I speak plainly when I say that I am aware of some of the problems you have experienced with him. He has been talking to all the ministers in Tisquah."

"Ministers? You mean to tell me that Michaul has been talking to all the preachers in town? Why?"

"As I said, he knows he is dying," Dr. Krohner said, firmly. Gussie heard the finality in his voice. "He wants his conscience clear while he can still talk, I would imagine. It is not unusual. He has asked the ministers to come here, to your home, as soon as the roads allow."

"Why?"

"He wants to hold a family prayer meeting," the doctor explained. "Some people want to get things in order when they know they don't have much time to live."

Three days later the ministers arrived; Methodist, Baptist, Presbyterian and Foursquare Gospel. They were covered in mud from head to toe, the result of pushing and pulling the Baptist minister's auto through the swampy mire left by the melting snow. Bitsy sat on the bed, holding Michaul's hand as the group took turns offering prayers on behalf of her oldest son's soul. They blessed him, anointed him, baptized him and dedicated him to God, in Jesus' name. Amen.

Gussie sat stiffly on the ladder-back chair beside the window, uncomfortable with the proceedings, certain that everyone in the room shared knowledge she did not possess.

Michaul was perspiring and his eyes were glazed from high fever and medication. His face, though pale and waxy, glowed as if bathed in light. Twin spots of red accented his cheeks, like rouge.

"Lungers always get that sheen on their faces just before they die," Claude informed Gussie, tearfully. "He's on his way out, for sure. My big brother is leaving us! It's the worst thing in the world! Dang!"

"I reckon," Gussie replied. Claude's only contribution, other than moving the stock to his barn, had been to repeatedly relate his scant knowledge about lung patients. "He's is mighty sick, even I can see that!"

No one had asked Gussie what she thought or how she felt, or if she needed anything. No one praised her for having delivered a baby without assistance in a terrible blizzard. No one offered her a word of condolence, not even the ministers. It seemed to Gussie that Michaul's illness had taken over their world, which was only right, she supposed.

The four ministers drank copious amounts of coffee and devoured one of Bitsy's famous pound cakes.

"That pound cake recipe is from England," Bitsy called, from Michaul's bedside. "My family had it in Mississippi, before they came to Texas in the 1830's."

"Cake is cake," Gussie muttered. "Big deal."

She showed the ministers to the door and watched as the Baptist minister's Buick slipped and skidded down the road, a mechanical prisoner to the muddy ruts. She could not imagine what they did to earn their pay, other than hang around for cake and coffee during the week and preach a sermon or two on Sunday.

"Vultures," she whispered, "just waiting for people to die."

Claude appeared beside her at the door, dressed in Michaul's heavy wool jacket.

"I'll bring down whatever milk you need every day," he informed Gussie. "Eggs, too, if the hens ever lay any. They are still nervous."

"I'm still nervous, too," Gussie said, sadly. "Look, you just remember them cows and mules is ours. Don't get too attached to them, and don't think I will forget."

Claude left the house, slamming the door so hard the windows rattled.

Leo, his health restored, dragged a chair to a living room window and watched his uncle walk down the muddy road.

"Gussie," Bitsy called, from the bedroom, "Michaul has something he wants to tell you."

Gussie walked to the bedroom, feeling like a lamb to the slaughter. Something awful was in the air, something all her Cherokee blood told her she did not want to know.

"Gussie," Michaul whispered, "I've got blood on my hands. I killed Lorena."

"Dear God!" Gussie said, holding her hands over her ears.

Michaul's voice was weak, but there was no doubt about what he said. The room began spinning beneath Gussie's feet.

"I did things to her. I lied to her and said you wanted her to submit to me. The night her arm got broken, I was doing things to her. I had been carrying her to the barn at night from the time she came home from school. That day at the cemetery, she bashed me in the head with a rock. I raped her then and broke her neck because I got so mad. You've seen me mad, you know how it is."

"It was Messkins that killed Lorena!" Gussie shouted. "Everyone said it was Messkins! They hung them murdering Messkins!"

"They were wrong, Gussie. I killed Lorena. The Mexicans' death is on my hands, too. And other death and hurt you don't know about. It comes up from my insides, Gussie, and it can't be stopped. I do...things."

No one spoke for several minutes. The silence in the room grew so intense that Gussie thought it would crystallize inside her ears.

"It can't be true!" Gussie said. She backed away from the bed, bracing her back against the rose patterned wallpaper. "Why? Why?"

"All my life, I've done things to little girls, Gussie. I don't know why, except my daddy used to make me watch him do things to my sister when we were little kids."

"Things? What things? I can't stand this!" Gussie cried. "Bitsy, make him stop saying these things! He don't even have a sister!"

"Oh, he had a sister," Bitsy replied, sadly, "but she died. Her daddy killed her before he ran away and left us to fend for ourselves. I didn't know it could be passed down, from father to son. How could I have known? I was a righteous young woman, raised by good, God-fearing people! When I realized that Michaul had the same problem, it was too late to do anything!"

"Michaul," Gussie said, turning to her husband, "if there is anything more you want to get off your conscience, you'd best say it now. I won't be speaking to you or hearing your voice from now on, no matter how sick you are!"

"I did things to Leo, too," Michaul whispered, miserably. "I showed him how to kill animals. I think I drove him crazy."

"Dear God!"

"I had to tell you, Gussie! I can't die with it!"

"Did them preachers know?"

"Yes. I told them right after the doctor said I had pneumonia. I had him send for the ministers. I told them all about my life, what I've done. I begged them to pray for me, to keep me out of hell. I'm guilty and scared, Gussie! You have no idea!"

"I reckon you will go to heaven, Michaul," Gussie said. Michaul could not hold her gaze; his blue eyes shifted to the wall, the ceiling, then fluttered shut. Gussie leaned near her husband's perspiring face, breathed in his decay and fear, and whispered. "Go to heaven, Michaul Abelard. Go on! I'll be the one living in a perfect hell. I bought me a ticket straight to hell the day I first looked into them blue eyes of yours. You will never know how much I loved you, what high hopes I had for us! I was fool for love! Now...now, I will go to the end of my days hating you! I vow I ain't ever gonna forget the misery you brung to my life! How dare you? And your greedy family, all of you ruining my life, taking my land, poking fun at me? Looking down at me, calling me a red Injun! Laughing at my ignorance! You go on now, go fast! Go, before I kill you with my bare hands!"

Gussie left the room without looking at Bitsy. She stumbled into the kitchen, trying to breathe, trying to organize her thoughts. Something she had to do was nagging at her mind. She suddenly remembered the cobwebs in the corner above the kitchen stove, the ones she had seen while she was in labor. She grasped the broom in both hands, climbed onto a stool and swept the corner clean. Her mother's voice seemed to permeate the warm kitchen.

The smallest tasks keep our feet on the path of right living, daughter. Never let a chore go undone.

Tears filled Gussie's eyes and she angrily brushed them away.

"I'll get on the path of right living as soon as Michaul Abelard is dead and in the ground! That there is my promise!"

Michaul's burial was a grand affair. Tisquah businesses closed their doors from 1:30 to 3:00, as customary for local funerals. The Tisquah American Legion Post performed a drill at the cemetery, delighting Leo so that he clapped his hands and cheered. Gussie stood perfectly straight and quiet, oblivious to the wind whipping her skirts above her ankles. The ministers who had baptized Michaul pushed and shoved each other for the superior position at the head of Michaul's coffin. Like pigs at a trough, Gussie thought.

It was a wonderfully clear day, the kind of day Texans expected after the passage of great storms, summer or winter. The azure sky was only slightly marred by threads of whitest cloud speeding from west to east. The wind, perfumed by wet soil, was unbelievably cold and sharp, cutting through Gussie's Sunday coat.

Someone had laid planks across the muddy ground from the road to the grave site. Gussie was almost mesmerized by the yellow, gleaming angles of new lumber against the velvet black mud. Her only words at the conclusion of the service were about the pine planks, though anyone hearing her thought otherwise.

"It looks like the black earth plumb cracked open," she whispered, several times. "I never seen the like of it!"

Gussie stood beside the open grave, shaking hands with neighbors and strangers. If any of the guests knew what her husband had done, or what he was, they did not reveal it by their sympathetic murmuring. Gussie did not know what her future held, but she had decided she would leave Tisquah if she sensed that people there knew about Michaul's evil ways.

Her father had sent two of Gussie's youngest brothers by train to stay until she could sell the farm and decide where she would live. Jim and Lee stood on either side of her, slim and dark, shining with their mother's calm assurance. How was it, Gussie wondered, that a violent man like her father could raise such good children? She hoped it was because of their mother's guidance, for that was all she had to offer her own children. She thought of Summer, left in the care of Phoebe's little sisters, and the memory of her tiny daughter caused her breasts to fill with milk. Summer was tugging at her heart strings, calling her home, inspiring her to keep a clear head.

"I have to do the best I can for Summer," Gussie

whispered, as the services ended. "I have to do proper by Leo, too, but I don't know what that might be! His daddy ruint him for a normal life!"

Selling the farm turned out to be no problem, for she soon discovered that she owned only one-fourth interest in it. Michaul and Claude shared the other three-fourths, with their share going to the other in event of death. It was much too complicated for Gussie's comprehension. She bitterly recalled the day she had signed the papers as she and Lorena sat in the Model-T outside the Tisquah bank.

"I should have read them papers," she lamented. "Even Lorena knowed enough to warn me about Michaul. Them Abelards used my money to set themselves up real fancy. That's for certain. Not one of them came to my ranch with much more than the clothes on their backs! Now I'm the one who's left out! It ain't right! Oh, I was a fool for love!"

Claude was too cowardly to face her, preferring to negotiate with notes delivered by the bird sisters to Jim and Lee, halfway between the two farm houses. Two days after the funeral, Claude offered to trade, free and clear, a four room house in Tisquah he had won in a poker game. All Gussie had to do was sign over her fourth interest in her farm.

"Tell him I'll take it, but only if he signs the deed to the house and we file it at the courthouse," Gussie instructed Jim and Lee. "I'll take back my best Jersey milk cow, too, and all my laying hens. I'm taking them to town, and he can like it or not!" Her brothers donned their jackets in preparation for the trip down the road to their rendezvous with Robin and Dovie. Gussie thought they looked much too eager. "You sweet boys listen here," she warned. "Don't go making eyes at them sisters of Phoebe's! You boys can do better for yourselves!"

By week's end she and her children, as well as the best cow and the surviving hens, had moved from the farm to the house in Tisquah. The house, though much smaller than the farm house, was better constructed and had water piped to the kitchen sink. It was wired for electricity, too, and featured a single light bulb dangling in the center of each room. Leo was fascinated with the light switches and occupied himself by constantly turning the lights on and off.

"Leo!" Gussie repeatedly said, her eyes bright with concern. "You'll wear them things out before it gets dark. Now, stop it!"

Jim and Lee were immensely helpful in the following days, locating enough scrap wood around town to build a small cow shed and chicken coop and to fence the back yard. They reconditioned the privy at the back of the lot, then smilingly showed Gussie where they hid Michaul's tool box in the garage. Shovels, rakes and hoes hung in neat rows along one wall. On a shelf above were arranged all her brooder pans and jars, along with many implements she had not thought to retrieve from the barn and tool shed.

"Is that coal oil I smell?" Gussie asked. The boys pulled back the corner of a tarp, revealing several cans, their wooden handles lined up straight as soldiers.

"Yep. We brought everything from the farm we thought you might be able to use in town," Jim explained. "You have to get what belongs to you now, or kiss it good-bye. That Claude has his eyes on everything."

"You don't know the half of it," Gussie agreed. "He ordered that fancy coffin for Michaul and I know he don't intend to help me pay for it. All I have to my name is fifty dollars and that canned food we moved from the farm. I'll have a bill for the water and the electric, so I'm told, every month. Dr. Krohner has to be paid, and the drug store, for Michaul's medicine. I don't know how I will support these younguns and myself, but I know for sure that no Abelard will offer me a red cent! I want you boys to know how grateful I am for your help. There ain't nothing like family, in times of need!"

"We can stay until the end of the month," Lee explained. "Daddy said you would pay for our train tickets back home."

At the end of the month, Gussie gave her brothers the Model-T, with enough cash to get them back to Maverick County. The boys left Tisquah before dawn, then made a quick raid on Claude's place, Cherokee style. They stole Phoebe's little bird sisters, Robin and Dovie, and all their clothes, conveniently packed in Bitsy's favorite cowhide trunk and hidden under the porch.

"Your sneaky Indian brothers kidnapped my innocent little sisters," Phoebe wailed. She and Claude had wasted no time driving into Tisquah after the young girls' farewell note was discovered. "That worthless sheriff says there's nothing he can do since they are probably halfway to Maverick County by now! Oh, I don't know what I will do without my sweet little sisters!"

"You might have to learn how to do housework," Gussie replied.

"That Model-T should have gone to me," Claude said, fixing his watery blue eyes on Gussie. "Me and Michaul had us an understanding!"

"Then go on down to Maverick County and take it back," Gussie said. "Maybe we will have two Abelard widows around here before the week is up! Best pay for your own coffin before you go!"

"Claude!" Phoebe screamed. "You aren't about to go bothering those savage Jeffersons! No car on earth is worth getting scalped for!"

"Keep that in mind, Miss Know-It-All," Gussie warned, scowling. She managed not to laugh at the pure terror on Phoebe's face. "My daddy has a train load of boys he can send up here, any old time I ask!"

"I thought you hated your daddy," Phoebe said.

"Maybe so," Gussie said, "but I hate you Abelards even more!"

CHAPTER SIX

"Summer can't be pregnant!" Gussie stared at Dr. Krohner's face, desperately hoping for a sign that he might have any doubt about her daughter's condition. "She ain't even twelve years old!"

"I wish I could tell you otherwise," the doctor said, "but I can't. The girl is at least four months pregnant."

"It can't be!" Gussie walked to the window of Dr. Krohner's tiny office. Sheets of rain poured onto the wooden sidewalks and the unpaved streets. She and Summer would have to wade mud on their way home. Their shoes would be ruined. Everything got ruined, sooner or later, Gussie thought, miserably. "I don't believe it!"

"It is a difficult situation, Mrs. Abelard. We must address several issues at this time. Her delicate health, her tender age and, of course, paternity. Won't you please sit down?"

"Tell me what to do," Gussie sobbed. "I'm sorry for crying like a fool! I ain't shed nary a tear since before Michaul died." She sank onto a sturdy wooden chair and grasped the arm rests. "Summer is my darling girl. I promised her nothing would ever hurt her! I promised!"

Dr. Krohner spoke gently, explaining the problems and possible solutions in layman's terms. Because Summer had suffered extensive heart damage after a bout of scarlet fever, and because she was so young, the doctor felt she was a candidate for legal abortion. To spare Summer's reputation, he recommended taking her to San Antonio for the procedure. He explained he

134

would need to obtain three additional physician's opinions in order to stay within the law. Gussie agreed and returned to the window as Dr. Krohner placed a long distance call to San Antonio. Her world had already fallen apart and washed down Third Street towards the little house she and her children had shared since Michaul's death. The doctor left her alone in his office as the local telephone operator routed the call from town to town, into the heart of Texas. Fifteen minutes later, the phone rang several times as Gussie stared at it with dread. In a flurry of white jackets, a nurse and the doctor entered the office simultaneously. Dr. Krohner spoke into the telephone for several minutes, then joined Gussie at the window.

"If I know who the father is, I will have to report him. For statutory rape."

"Rape," Gussie nodded. "It was rape, no matter what it's called. I'll get back to you on that, after I have time to think on it. Right now, I have to find somebody to drive me and Summer to San Antonio."

The trip and the doctors' fees cost her all her savings. Claude furnished the car and gas, but pointedly allowed Gussie to pay for his meals and lodging. Phoebe, pregnant again, chose not to make the arduous journey, and for that small blessing Gussie was grateful. She sat erect in the passenger seat, head held high, and spoke not a single word to Claude during the two-day ride to San Antonio. The afternoon before the abortion, Claude escorted Gussie and Summer on a tour of the Alamo. Inside the crumbling old church, Gussie felt so breathless that she turned and fled out a side door. Moments later, Claude and Summer joined her, their faces white with concern.

"Don't worry," Gussie gasped. "I ain't gonna get sick. Nobody needs to take care of me. It was just that old church! I think it is full of dead people, and they ain't too happy!"

On the return trip to Tisquah, Gussie sat in the back with Summer, holding the child's head on her lap. The roads were wet and dangerous. Gussie thought the best thing that could possibly happen would be for Claude's fancy car to plunge off a bridge and sink beneath the muddy, roiling surface of the Llano River. She would die holding her darling Summer in her arms. Claude, too, would drown, and good riddance. Phoebe wouldn't waste much time mourning before she married Dr. Krohner, honeymooned in Europe and gave birth to twins. Good luck to them, Gussie thought, miserably.

"I didn't know how to tell you what Leo was doing to me," Summer whispered, clinging to Gussie's hands. "It started last year, after I had scarlet fever and you had to work in the cotton fields to earn money for my medicine. Leo came home from school every day and got in my bed with me. I always cried and begged him not to touch me, but he just smiled. He said you wanted him to do it, that it was good for me! I knew he was lying! He scared me, Mama, but I know I should have told you. I just didn't want you to find out because I thought it would break your heart."

"I should have killed Leo when you was borned," Gussie replied, sadly. "I knowed he was all wrong and nothing but pain would come from letting him live. I loved him, though. I was a fool for love! It ain't the first time I was fool!"

Gussie's anger stemmed from much more than Summer's immediate condition. The years following her daughter's birth had been a constant ordeal, due to Leo's behavior. Leo had been sent home from grade school hundreds of times, for reasons ranging from his inability to learn the alphabet to his killing of the school mascot, a purebred English Bulldog puppy. Tisquah citizens were divided in their opinions of Leo; some thought he would benefit from mentoring by older boys and Christian men, while others were in favor of shooting him on sight if he set foot on their property. In reality, Gussie was the only person in town who actually believed that Leo might grow into a normal young man.

She always tried to impress her son with the seriousness of his transgressions. When he was small, she whipped him, hard, with switches cut from the sweet locust tree in the back yard. She took him to church every Sunday and rejoiced when he was baptized. She read to him from the Bible until they were both so confused they could barely discuss the Christian message concealed in the difficult language. Nothing worked. Leo remained as inscrutable as ever, a handsome boy with startling blue eyes and absolutely unpredictable behavior. The only thing Gussie could count on was that Leo would frequently run away from home and be found hours or days later at his father's grave.

"Why do you go to the cemetery?" Gussie asked, when Leo was younger.

"Talk to Daddy," the boy answered, as if she was daft. "Daddy talk to Leo."

If Leo was a thorn in Gussie's side, Summer was a jewel in her crown. Summer grew into a shy, blond little girl, always at Gussie's side. She was a good student and musically talented, to Gussie's delight. When Gussie won a hard-fought battle with the Veterans' Administration for a thirty-two dollar a month pension, she purchased a piano. Summer mastered it on her own, with the help of a mail order course.

"That there pianer is our salvation," Gussie told Summer, on the long drive home from San Antonio. "You and me can live together forever, and you can teach pianer lessons. We will be just fine!"

"I want to get married someday, Mama," Summer answered. "I can't live with you forever. I want my own home."

"We'll see, honey." Gussie wiped her eyes, recalling the surgeon's words. Summer was damaged by the pregnancy and the abortion. She would almost certainly never lead a normal life. She should not marry and would never have children. "Things will work out fine, Summer. Getting married ain't the only way to have a life."

Gussie did not allow herself to fall into despair during Summer's ordeal. She had learned well the art of holding her emotions at bay until a crisis was resolved. Two weeks after Summer's abortion, Gussie knew she had to deal with the horror Leo had caused in Summer's young life. She had sorted out all the issues in her own mind and formulated a plan to hold Leo accountable and to protect Summer.

"I'm telling you to move out of my house," she told Leo. He regarded her with his usual steady gaze, tilting his head to one side, just like when he was a little boy. "There ain't no way around it. You broke God's law and Texas law by having intercourse with your sister. It is called some kind of rape. Her life is ruint and can't ever be fixed! You are might nigh a growed man now, and you better get out!"

Leo calmly packed his few belongings and left the house, whistling some new-fangled band tune as he jauntily walked down the street. Gussie heard gossip that he was living east of town, working on an outdoor skating rink everyone was talking about. He had been hired, according to the gossip, to run the rink after it was completed.

Two weeks later, he walked into the house and winked at Gussie.

"What are you doing here?" she demanded. "You ain't supposed to be here! Why ain't you at your high-powered new job?"

"Got fired," Leo explained. "I'm moving back."

"You ain't!"

"I am. I asked a lawyer. He said this is as much my home as yours and I have a right to live here. You can leave if you want to but you can't kick me out."

"What lawyer?"

"A lawyer from Lubbock."

Gussie considered Leo's news. Finally, grudgingly, she nodded. Men knew about consulting lawyers and how to work the law. She did not even know where they found the law, let alone how they comprehended its meaning. Leo was smart about what mattered to him, always had been. She followed Leo into his room as he unpacked his belongings.

"If a lawyer said so, then I guess I can't argue. But you listen here, Leo! I'm nailing that door between our bedrooms shut, and you can believe it! If you plan to live here, you'd best plan to stay in school so I can go on collecting that VA pension. Otherwise, you will have to go to work!"

"What's for supper, Mama?" Leo asked. He picked Gussie up and swung her in circles as he walked through the parlor and into the kitchen. He stopped in front of the stove, where a pot of pinto beans had been simmering all day. "Ummm-ummm, red beans with ham hock and corn bread, my favorite! It sure is good to be home!"

Gussie ran to the privy and vomited. She then fetched the

hammer and some three-penny nails from the garage and nailed the connecting door between the bedrooms shut. Leo was the devil, she knew, and he had always sneaked into her room through that door.

To her eternal shame, she had to admit that she had sensed Leo's silent presence, many times, in the bedroom she shared with Summer. At times, Gussie feared he had touched her private parts, for she often woke with a moist, keen craving between her legs, her nipples hard as peach pits. Regardless of how long she lay in the darkness, listening, willing Leo to reveal himself, she never saw nor heard him. Not once. Yet, she knew he was there, or had been there, knew it in the Cherokee way. Her thoughts ran to murder as she lay in the darkness, but by morning, she had always locked the shameful secret in her heart. She had never imagined he was also touching Summer. It was unthinkable, until the day Dr. Krohner confirmed that the girl was pregnant. Then, in a miserable instant, Gussie knew the whole story.

"I promised Summer that no Abelard would ever hurt her," Gussie wept, time after time in the months following Summer's abortion. "I should have killed Leo when Summer was borned! It's all on my head now! Well, at least no one in Tisquah knows what happened!"

Summer's recovery was slow, but obvious. The week before Christmas, Gussie baked one of her special fruit cakes and carried it to the Rexall drugstore fountain. The owner exchanged two dollars worth of store goods for the cake, and Gussie carefully chose gifts for Summer and Leo. Bath power for her daughter, a wild extravagance, as well as a scrapbook for her collection of art work and magazine clippings. After considerable thought, she picked out hair pomade and a hairbrush set for Leo. Though she was exceedingly unhappy about Leo's presence in the house, she did not have the heart to exclude him from what had always been their special family celebration.

As she left the store, someone clasped her elbow and whispered urgently into her ear.

"Sheriff Stone wants to see you in his office. Now!"

"What?"

"Now! Go to the courthouse and see Sheriff Stone!"

Gussie hesitated, standing motionless on the sidewalk, wondering who had whispered the ominous message. There were many men gathered in front of the drug store, out of the cold north wind's reach, but not one of them seemed to be looking at her. She wanted with all her heart to turn west and hurry home, but instinct told her the message had something to do with Leo. Clutching the little paper bag of Christmas gifts to her chest, she took a deep breath and crossed the street, then hurried into the massive courthouse. The location of the sheriff's office was familiar, for she been there on numerous occasions to fetch Leo and take him home. She didn't feel inclined to rescue him any more, she thought, as she trod the waxed marble floors. In fact, if he was in trouble again, she'd exchange his Christmas gifts at the Rexall on her way home. Her heels clicked a steady tattoo that seemed to echo forever.

Gussie paused in the anteroom to the sheriff's office, noting the absence of the deputy who also acted as secretary. Shrugging, she pushed open the door to the main office, expecting to find Leo standing in front of the sheriff's massive mahogany desk.

"Sweet Jesus!" she gasped. Sheriff Stone sat on one corner of the desk, alone in his office, his khaki trousers unbuttoned to reveal his engorged private parts. "What in tarnation is going on here?"

"Close the door, honey," the sheriff growled. "We have some legal business to work out."

"There ain't nothing to work out with you," Gussie whispered. "I'm going home!"

"You are going to jail, along with those brats of yours, if you don't work with me," Sheriff Stone said. His voice made Gussie's flesh crawl. She wanted to gag, just looking into his little bloodshot eyes. "Now, come here, woman!"

Gussie stepped closer, averting her eyes. "Tell me what you want, and be quick about it," she whispered.

"I want you to lift your skirts and bend over this desk," he said, pleasantly. He casually unholstered a massive revolver and laid it on his desk, then picked it up and twirled it on one stubby finger. He chuckled as it came to a stop with the muzzle pointed at Gussie.

"And what if I don't? Are you going to shoot me?"

"Naw, but you're going to jail, and so are your kids, if you don't work with me."

"We ain't broke no laws!"

"The hell you ain't! The three of you has broke the heaviest goddam laws known to the state of Texas! All of you stacked up in bed in your cozy little house! Incest is against the law. So is poking it to a minor. So is letting it happen. You are all three in contempt! You even got an abortion for your daughter! What have you got to say about that?"

"I can't figure what you mean, all them words is too hard to understand!"

"Don't you dare play simpleton with me! I got your number, yes ma'am, I do! We're talking about Leo doing it to his little sister when she was eleven years old! That is against the law in so many ways you ought to go straight to the electric chair!"

"He raped her, but she warn't to blame! She was helpless!"

"Helpless or not, she was a minor and she was his sister. It's all illegal, and you, ma'am, are at the heart of it!"

"It ain't happening now. I didn't know about it when it was! That's the truth, I swear! It won't ever happen again!"

"Listen to me, woman," his voice dropped, and Gussie was forced to lean nearer to hear him. "If I take this mess before the Grand Jury, you will go to jail and them hot-blooded kids will go to reform school. That is a fact! I am trying to do us all a favor by working out a deal we can all live with!"

"Summer can't go to no reform school! She is just a little girl who can't help what happened! She has rheumatic fever! She has to be cared for, has to take her medicine! What do you want me to do?"

"Ma'am, I want you to lift your skirts and bend over this desk. You come here every Thursday at this time and do the same. I will try to keep you and your kids out of prison. Is it a deal? 'Cause, if you don't agree, then I can't force you to do anything. Let's be clear about that. Let's hear you say that."

"It is a deal," Gussie sighed, "and you ain't forcing me."

Gussie carefully placed her bag of gifts on a chair, stepped out of her drawers, lifted her skirts and bent across the desk, face down on its polished surface.

"You tell no one, understand?" Sheriff Stone growled.

His pudgy red hands closed around Gussie's waist as he moved behind her. She felt the starched khaki waistband of his trousers against her buttocks. He thrust into her vagina, a rough, dry entry that would have made her cry aloud had she not already fled to a safe place in her mind. There was no indignity she could not hide from in her mind, the Cherokee way. It was one of her skills.

Back home, Gussie wrapped the Christmas gifts in red tissue paper and tied them with ribbon saved from previous years.

"Honey girl," she called. "Come in here and look under the tree! It looks right pretty. I got us a bag of hard ribbon candy for the candy dish!"

Summer woke from her afternoon nap, solemnly inspected the tree and selected a small piece of ribbon candy. She joined Gussie in the kitchen, watching as her mother marked the calendar with a red pencil.

"What is that about?" she asked.

"Just something I have to do every Thursday," Gussie answered. "It ain't nothing for you to worry about."

They opened their gifts on Christmas Eve. Summer immediately set to work filling the scrapbook with clippings and art work she kept in a cigar box. Her little jar of school paste had dried out and Gussie softened it with a few drops of hot water. She wondered if Summer would ever be healthy enough to attend classes again or if she was doomed forever to the isolation of their home.

"Summer, do you miss going to school?' Gussie asked, as if the question had just then crossed her mind.

"I used to miss it, Mama," Summer replied. "Now, I know I'll probably just stay here with you until I get married."

Leo went to his room, applied pomade to his black curls, then left the house without saying a word.

"Just like his daddy," Gussie told Summer. "Them Abelard men just come and go as they please, without a good-bye or a howdy-do."

"Why didn't we sing Christmas carols?" Summer asked. "It doesn't seem like Christmas without singing."

"I'll sing with you," Gussie said. "Let's put on happy faces! It's Christmas Eve!"

Later, Gussie inspected Summer's scrapbook. Her daughter definitely had artistic talent, Gussie thought with pride. The pages were cleverly decorated with various articles and colorful letters cut and pasted to spell out headings. It was pretty, but the total effect made Gussie's blood run cold. Her daughter's interest undoubtedly ran to the macabre, for the articles were reports of various deformities and strange illnesses. Several bizarre clippings of "Ripley's Believe It Or Not" articles, illustrated with outrageous images, were also pasted on the black pages. One item in particular seemed important to Summer, for she had pasted it on a separate page and embellished it with snips of red Christmas wrapping ribbon.

TEN YEAR OLD GIRL GIVES BIRTH

Bogota, Columbia. *Local officials confirm that a ten year old Indian girl gave birth this week to a normal, healthy baby boy in Zipiquia, a mountain village fifty miles north of Bogota. Identity of the baby's father is not known, according to the Catholic priest who performed the baby's baptism.*

"The ten year old is the youngest mother known to have given birth to a viable baby. She is reported to believe that an evil mountain spirit put the baby into her mouth as she slept. Villagers constructed a shrine to the young mother and baby in the apparent belief that they are blessed. A brief riot ensued when the priest destroyed the improvised tribute.

"'These are ignorant people,' says the priest, 'who do not understand the social or moral implications of this situation. For them, it is a special event, beyond their comprehension.'

"Plans are pending for the girl and her baby to be moved to a convent in Bogota."

Gussie labored over the article for an hour, moving her index finger along each line as she sounded out the unfamiliar words. When she was certain she understood their meaning, she wept.

"Oh, Summer! What can you be thinking about yourself? About all of us? Damn them Abelard men to hell!"

Each Thursday afternoon right after lunch Gussie douched with vinegar and resolutely walked downtown to keep her bargain with Sheriff Stone. Occasionally, he was out of the office, on sheriff's business. The first time Gussie almost fainted with relief, but as the months passed she found that it was easier on her nerves if he was waiting for her in his cigar-tainted office. She did not allow herself to think of the words "rape" or "sin". She considered their meetings only as "deals".

Their couplings were wordless, filled with great tension and severe pain for Gussie. When the sheriff was done with her, Gussie turned away from him, stepped into her drawers,

Walnut Hearts

smoothed her skirt and quickly walked out of his office. She loved the cool, marble hallway that allowed her passage to the fresh, outside air.

A group of old men was always present on the courthouse lawn in warm weather, sitting in the sparse shade of young Chinese Elm trees, spitting tobacco juice onto the ground and whittling on small pieces of wood. Gussie avoided them, though it meant she had to walk around the block. She hated their rheumy old eyes and the aura of ancient knowledge hovering over the benches on which they perched, restless, like predatory birds.

"Old buzzards," she whispered, each week.

Gussie always hurried home and douched again with vinegar, just to be safe. She had not yet gone through the change of life and she could imagine no worse fate than conceiving Sheriff Stone's child.

Summer surprised everyone by regaining her health and returning to classes for the fall term. At first, Gussie walked her to and from school, carrying her books, watching anxiously for signs of exhaustion. Gradually, Summer proved she was strong enough for the task and Gussie grudgingly let her walk with her classmates each morning.

"One of you girls run back here and tell me if Summer gets out of breath," she instructed the group, every day, without fail.

Life in the little house gained a sense of normality, at least compared to the tension of the previous year. Leo went to school each day, too, though he had never been promoted beyond the eighth grade. Gussie did not complain, for she would be eligible for Veterans' Administration benefits for Leo only if he attended school. She had, long before, abandoned all hope that he would be a scholar.

"Leo is a mechanical genius," Summer told Gussie. "He just can't read or write about what he knows. He needs someone to stay with him and read and write for him."

"Summer, what on earth are you talking about?"

"Mama, face the facts! Leo is going to be in this house with us forever if we don't figure out a way to make him more popular with other kids."

"Popular? Have you gone daft?"

"Look, Mama, you don't know what it is like at school. If a kid doesn't have friends, he is treated like he has the plague. I think if Leo had friends he would grow up and stop doing all the bad things he's done since he was a little boy."

"Summer, don't you think I tried to change his ways?" Gussie cried.

"I know you did, Mama, but he walks all over you." Summer stood in the living room, her hands on her slim hips. "He really wants to be popular at school, and I think it's a good idea. I'm going to help him."

"God help you!" Gussie sighed. "You don't know what you're doing! Abelard men can't be helped by human beings. Or maybe not even by God!"

"Mama, Leo goes to agriculture and shop classes every morning, then he leaves school."

"What?"

"He climbs a tree in front of Lebeouf's School Store, across the street from the school building. He sits there until lunch."

"Until lunch? In a tree?"

"He sits in that tree and whistles until lunch. Most days, he is able to borrow ten cents to buy a hamburger and soda pop from Lebeouf's grill. After he eats, he climbs back in the tree until the bell rings and then he hitches a ride out to the skating rink."

"Are you telling me he don't go to class, at all?"

"Yes, Mama," Summer sighed. "He would rather sit in a tree so you can collect his VA pension than get out and find a real job. Do you know why?"

"No. Do you?"

"Well, I think it is because he can't read or write, and he is ashamed to let people know."

"And you think you can fix that?"

"Maybe," Summer mused, "just maybe I do. Do you love Leo, Mama?"

"I love him because he is my flesh and blood," Gussie

admitted. "But I don't think he belongs on this earth. He ain't right! He hurts people! Do you love Leo, Summer?"

"Yes, I love him, because he is my brother and I don't think we're supposed to hate our brothers. I do think he might change, though, if someone gave him the right kind of help."

"Have you forgiven him for what he done to you, Summer?"

"I don't know. I just know that unless things change we aren't going to get rid of him. It seems smart to try to help him act normal, that's all I'm saying, because we love him in spite of everything. We have to try to change things, Mama."

"Well, I was a fool for love, many times," Gussie said, wiping her eyes with the corner of her apron. "You watch out you don't get hurt worse, trying to turn Leo into a normal person."

"I have a plan, Mama," Summer informed her. "I'm not stupid!"

As autumn passed and the cool winter winds swept across the plains, Summer frequently brought her friends home after school. Gussie loved listening to their gossip and their idle girl's talk. She stretched her grocery budget in order to buy popcorn and hot chocolate for Summer's friends, and sometimes joined them around the piano as they sang from Summer's collection of sheet music. Gussie allowed herself to dream that things would continue in just such a manner, that Summer would study hard and get her music teaching certificate and live in the house on Third Street forever. In those dreams, Leo was magically absent and unmourned and Sheriff Stone was rotting in hell, where he belonged.

For two years, little changed in their lives. Gussie met with the sheriff each Thursday. Summer's health, if not robust, remained constant and the girl seemed happy. Leo spent most of each school day in the tree. Then, with no warning, their world turned upside down and Gussie felt like she was drowning.

"I have a boyfriend, Mama," Summer confided. "I love him!"

"You don't need no boyfriend!" Gussie replied. "No need wasting your time with boys, when you know you ain't ever getting married!"

"I love him!" Summer wailed. "You just want to shut me up in this old house with you. You want us to live here together like two old maids, forever! You had your own life but you don't want me to have one! You are selfish!"

Gussie learned the boy's identity from her neighbor across the alley, Cleta Brown. Known as Widder Brown, Cleta was a veritable encyclopedia of Tisquah trivia, past and current.

"It is Brendan O'Meara," Widder Brown confided to Gussie, as they talked across the fence. "Summer loves him."

"One of those O'Meara brutes? Why, that can't be! They're Irish! Summer and one of those huge boys? Never!"

"Brendan weighed sixteen pounds when he was born," Widder Brown recalled. "All those boys were large, because their mother has the sugar diabetes. She's crazy now, too, like a loon! I heard from Mrs. Dilbert that they have to tie her to a chair all day, while the old man works and the boys go to school. Irish, for certain. You're right about that."

"Lord, have mercy," Gussie whispered. "Summer says she loves him!"

"She is young," Widder Brown said. "She'll find someone more suitable."

"Ain't nobody suitable," Gussie cried. "Summer has rheumatic fever and can't be a wife or mother."

"These things work out," Widder Brown said, soothingly. "Why, I was crippled myself, after a horse fell on me when I was eight years old. Nobody thought I'd live. But I married and had six children, all healthy! You got to put your faith in the good Lord."

"That ain't worked out all too well for me and mine," Gussie said, sadly. "I was always a fool for love."

"Amen! We both must have been!"

Summer withdrew completely from Gussie. She spent her spare time writing love notes to Brendan.

"Why do you think Summer writes those long notes to that O'Meara dolt, when she can talk to him every day at school?" Gussie asked Widder Brown.

"I heard that the boy is too shy to speak to Summer,"

Widder Brown confided. "He tells his friends what to say to Summer and she sends back those notes."

"What does he say to his friends?"

"He says he wants to marry her. Says his daddy will give him a quarter section of land and a house the day he graduates from high school. And, a new car."

"When will that be?"

"This spring, if he can pass all his classes. He was held back a year or two, I forget how many times."

"That lout can't have Summer! She's too young! And she is sick!"

"She's as old as you and I were when we first married, I reckon. You'd better face the facts!"

"I ain't never done anything but face the facts, Cleta!" Gussie cried. "It's just that my say-so never counted for squat! Anyway, I ain't facing nothing until that Brendan O'Meara passes all his classes," Gussie retorted. "Them O'Meara boys are pure-dee stupid, from what I hear."

"Oh, he'll pass," Widder Brown assured Gussie. "That Varina Rice is tutoring him, and she is one smart little miss. She says Brendan will graduate this year, even if it kills them both."

"What's her interest in that big dope? I can't imagine her snooty daddy letting her go near those O'Meara boys."

"Oh, Varina is sweet on Leo, don't you know? She is helping Brendan because Summer asked her to. I reckon she thinks she will catch Leo's eye if she helps his little sister's boyfriend."

"Sweet Jesus," Gussie cried. "I can't believe my ears! What does Leo want with a girlfriend? He can't even take care of himself! He borrows lunch money every day at school! He purt near lives up in a tree! All he does is whistle dance tunes! This here is just too much!"

"Well, you aren't the first mother to misjudge her children's needs and wants. They usually want what we would never imagine."

"You don't know my children!" Gussie said.

"I know enough," Widder Brown assured her.

Within weeks, Gussie read in the West County News that

Brendan O'Meara would indeed graduate with the Class of 1941. His senior picture was beside Varina Rice's smiling face. They looked like movie stars in one of Summer's magazines, Gussie thought. She could not imagine what either of them found attractive in her children.

Gussie had no friends in Tisquah other than Widder Brown. She found herself drawn across the alley more and more often, leaning on Widder Brown's rickety fence and pumping the old woman for information about Summer and Leo.

"You'll have pretty grandbabies," Widder Brown speculated. "You'd best prepare yourself."

"No," Gussie argued, "it can't be. Leo and Summer can't have babies!"

"Well, I heard Leo is working three nights a week at the newspaper office, printing the West County News. I also heard he is working at the furniture store on weekends."

"What?" Gussie asked. "Why, I thought he was working at the skating rink for free skates! He don't bring me no money! I don't believe it!"

"He is saving his money to marry Varina Rice," Widder Brown whispered. "It is the biggest secret in Tisquah!"

Gussie fell backwards into Widder Brown's morning glorie vines. She thought her heart would explode.

"Something ain't right with that story!" she gasped. "I just don't believe it! Leo can't be nobody's husband! He can't do it!"

"You'd best get hold of yourself," Widder Brown advised, knowingly.

The following day was Thursday. Gussie kept her appointment with Sheriff Stone, then reversed her usual route and approached the old men who comprised what locals called the "Spit and Whittle Club". She stood patiently in the shade until the old men turned their wrinkled faces to her. It was like peering into eight images of her first husband, Mr. Peters. Her flesh crawled.

"What can we do for you, missus?" one of the images finally asked.

"Tell Mr. Robert Rice to meet me here next Thursday at

this time. Tell him it is a matter of life or death!"

"Whose life or death?" one of the old geezers asked, sending a ripple of gentle laughter through the group.

"None of your concern," Gussie replied, primly. "Get the word to him, understand?"

She marched away without a backward glance though she felt their curious eyes upon her until she found refuge in the drug store. She splurged and ordered herself a frosted Coke. For the first time ever she felt no pangs of guilt for not sharing the treat with Summer. Summer had broken their trust and Gussie was, by damn, going to have a whole nickel's worth of cold, sweet delight! She finished the concoction fast even though it gave her a splitting headache. Then, she hurried home to douche with vinegar, as usual.

One week later, after her visit to Sheriff Stone's office, Gussie again approached the Spit and Whittle Club. Robert Rice, imperious in dark wool trousers and starched white shirt, rose to meet her. He was polite, she had to admit, as he gently guided her to the next patch of shade.

"I don't normally leave my farm during the week," he said.

"This here is an emergency," Gussie countered, "or I wouldn't have asked you to come."

"Spit it out, then, woman," he said, reminding her of Mr. Peters. Old men came from another world, she thought.

"Our kids, Leo and Varina, is planning to get married!"

"To each other?"

"Yes, to each other, man. Why else would I want to talk to you? We got to stop them!"

"Ma'am, it has been my experience with my older children that they will do as they damn well please."

"This ain't right," Gussie said. "Them marrying ain't right. Leo ain't what you want for your daughter."

"I agree," the old man laughed. He was obviously amused. "What do you propose that we do?"

"Can't you think of something? Send your girl off to college? I heard she's real smart."

"I do have it in mind to send her to college, for a fact, if she will go."

"You got to make her go!" Gussie was frantic, sensing her time with Mr. Rice was ending. "She can't marry Leo!"

"Calm yourself, ma'am. I'll look into this matter, be assured." He leaned near Gussie's face and looked into her eyes. "Now, you understand me. Don't ever send for me again. I won't be summoned by one of Sheriff Stone's whores. Do you understand?"

Gussie thought she would surely die there in the shade as Mr. Rice turned and walked to his automobile. A young Negro man behind the wheel quickly drove Mr. Rice around the block and out of sight. The car, Gussie realized, had been running during their conversation. Mr. Rice obviously wanted no one to get the impression that he meant to tarry in her company.

"Old buzzard," Gussie muttered. She took her handkerchief from her pocket and wiped the perspiration from her face and neck. "Old buzzard, calling me a whore! You've done worse, I'll wager that!"

The unrelenting, hot summer months dragged by, bringing a heat wave and drought unprecedented in recorded history. In churches throughout Tisquah, preachers delivered sermons based on end of the world prophesies. Heat and cold, wet and dry, day and night, they warned, would be confused and upside down in the End Times. War would cover the planet and people would suffer unceasingly. Gussie studied her Bible after each sermon, slowly reading aloud the referenced text, knowing in her heart that life was about to get worse.

Summer got a job at the Rexall Drug Store working behind the counter as a soda jerk.

"Is that what they call them kids?" Gussie asked. "Soda jerks? What does that mean?"

"You have to jerk the handles to dispense the drinks and ice cream toppings, Mama," Summer explained. She rolled her eyes, sighing. "I swear, Mama, you are so old-fashioned."

In August, Sheriff Stone was killed by lightning as he fed his favorite bloodhound, Tracker.

"Burned a big, black hole right through his head," Widder Brown gleefully reported, "and down his left side, into the ground! Melted his boots to his fat little feet! Exploded his eyeballs, I'm told! Fried his gizzard! Killed that nasty dog, as well. Who cares? The devil took his own, that's what I think! Straight to hell!"

"I hope it hurt him," Gussie mused. "I hope it scared him before it cooked him. Hope he died scared and hurt!"

"Several other Tisquah women feel the same way, I'll wager," Widder Brown said. "Some would say he was the very worst sort of man."

"They don't lie," Gussie sighed.

The following Thursday, Gussie walked to the courthouse and stood quietly before the acting sheriff, a former deputy. The young man looked into her eyes and shook his head. He was nice looking, Gussie thought, like a normal man.

"You don't need to come here again, ma'am," he said, kindly.

"God bless you and yours!" Gussie answered. "God bless!

It was the happiest moment of her life.

She learned, through Widder Brown, that Varina Rice had gone to stay with relatives in the Panhandle and would enter a Baptist college in the fall. Gussie and Widder Brown agreed that such a beautiful, intelligent girl would hardly wish to return to Tisquah and marry an uneducated boy like Leo.

"She'll forget about Leo in a month," Widder Brown predicted.

"She will, if she knows what's good for her!" Gussie agreed.

Gussie knew that Brendan O'Meara occasionally escaped his father's stern supervision and came into town during Summer's work hours. She knew because Summer came home with boxes of Whitman's Assorted Candies on those days. She did not offer to share the fancy chocolates with her mother. Gussie did not mind, for she would sooner have eaten rattlesnake meat than touch a love offering from the O'Meara boy. She held onto the hope that Summer and Brendan would grow tired of each other.

That fall, Leo refused to return to school.

"You'll have to pay rent, if you want to live here," Gussie informed him. "I can't afford to feed you without the VA pension."

"No problem," Leo said, affably. He casually handed his mother five dollars.

"I'll need money from you every week," she cautioned him, "not just today!"

"I said it was no problem," Leo replied. "Ease up, woman!"

Gussie looked deep into Leo's blue eyes and shivered. The Abelard arrogance was all over him, she thought, in spite of having little contact with any other Abelard men since Claude and Phoebe had sold out and moved to New Mexico. Gussie wanted to scream.

On December 7, the Japanese attacked Pearl Harbor. Gussie had no idea who the Japanese were or where Pearl Harbor was, or for that matter, why anyone cared. She was interested only because it meant that Leo would possibly be drafted and taken away from Tisquah. She had never dared hope for such a blessing.

On Christmas Eve, Gussie sat alone in the parlor beside the Christmas tree, waiting for Leo and Summer to help her with the decorations. At ten o'clock, she pulled the delicate glass ornaments from their tissue lined boxes and decorated the tree alone. She straightened the parlor and put away the empty boxes, then put on a pot of coffee.

"Them kids is up to some mischief," she said softly, "and it ain't about surprising me with a fancy new dress."

For the first time in years, Gussie used the Cherokee Way to reach out for knowledge about her children. She closed her eyes, breathed deeply, and felt Leo and Summer immediately. They were in a car. Brendan O'Meara's car. The car was speeding through the darkness, headlights illuminating a narrow highway. She felt their youth, their pure joy and sense of fun. She smiled in spite of her misgivings.

"What are you younguns up to, anyway?" she whispered.

The coffee came to a boil and she removed it from the burner. Gussie sliced a generous serving of her Christmas fruit cake and savored every bite, washing it down with scalding black coffee.

"I think Leo and Summer ran off to marry Varina and Brendan," she said, finally. "I think I'm through with mothering. Fair enough, 'cause it brought me nothing but pain. I'm done."

Two days later, her suspicions were confirmed when Brendan O'Meara's car skidded to a halt in front of the house. The two couples emerged from the car and walked to the front door, where Gussie met them. They were obviously afraid to face her, except for Leo, who winked and gave her a quick hug as she held the door open and they filed in. The tiny parlor seemed too small for all of them, for so much youthful energy. The spindly Christmas tree shivered as they walked across the linoleum. Gussie felt the earth tilt, a Cherokee sign, for sure.

"We got married, Mama," Summer said, nervously. Her eyes begged for mercy and Gussie had a hard time keeping a straight face. "We knew you wouldn't give us permission, Mama," Summer continued, desperately clutching Brendan's massive hand. The boy was a black haired giant, Gussie thought, like something out of a fairy tale. "We ran off to Arkansas to get married, because we can't live without each other! Leo and Brendan may get drafted any day now!"

"Arkansas?" Gussie asked.

"So we could get married without permission," Summer explained. "Or, at least, so I could."

"Am I the last to know?" Gussie asked. The quartet's guilty expressions told her she was. "What do the Rices and the O'Mearas think about this here secret wedding stuff?"

"My parents said I'm old enough to make my own decision," Varina answered, quickly. She was a beautiful blond girl, dressed in a rumpled blue woolen suit. A wilted gardenia was pinned to one lapel. She looked directly into Gussie's eyes as she spoke, every bit as arrogant as her father. "Leo and I are in love. There's nothing anyone can do about it!"

"Brendan's daddy gave us his blessing, too," Summer added.

"What else did Brendan's daddy give you?" Gussie asked.

"You know he gave Brendan some land, a house and a

car, when he graduated. He will let us use a tractor and have all the butane we need. I won't even have to work. I can rest in bed whenever I feel tired. We just need to spend a week or so here with you, until we fix up our little house. It is all settled!"

"I reckon it is," Gussie said. "Can your husband speak for himself, or is he tongue tied?"

Brendan blushed, shuffled his enormous feet and sighed.

"He speaks fine, Mama," Summer replied. "He's just shy. And you're being rude."

"What about you two," Gussie said, turning her attention to Leo and Varina. "What are your plans?"

"We're going to live here with you until we get a place of our own," Leo said, happily. "Or until I get drafted."

"No, I don't think so," Gussie said, thoughtfully. "I think you had all better go someplace else."

"This is my house, too, don't forget," Leo reminded her.

"Stop it, Leo!" Gussie shouted. The four young people stepped back, shocked by the tone of her voice. "It ain't ever been any part your house and you know it! I sweated blood to keep this roof over your ungrateful head, and over Summer's, too! Now, you two have gone and got married without so much as a fare-thee-well to me! Well, let me tell you both, this is my house. You are welcome to visit me any time, but you won't be staying with me tonight or any other night, for a long, long time. You've married into families with plenty of money and room to spare, I'll wager. You better go knocking on their doors tonight. You ain't staying here!"

"What about our things?" Summer wailed.

"Come back for them when you have a place to keep them."

"You are just a selfish old woman, Mama!"

"If I am," Gussie replied, "it's high time!"

The four young people stumbled through the door and onto the front porch. Only Varina turned to look back at Gussie. Her big brown eyes were hard and filled with venom.

Gussie slammed the door and locked it, then marched through the house, across the alley and into Widder Brown's house. The old woman fumbled with her dentures, popping them in as Gussie collapsed onto the horsehair sofa. Half a dozen cats sprang into the air and dashed from the room.

"I got big news to pass on to you," Gussie informed the startled old woman. "I thought I'd tell you first hand, so you will get all the facts straight."

"Your kids eloped with Brendan and Varina," Widder Brown cackled, slapping her least arthritic knee. "Everybody in town knowed about it! You're the last to know!"

"Why on earth didn't you tell me?" Gussie cried.

"Oh, hon," the old woman said, primly, "you know I don't like to meddle."

Within the week, Leo and Summer had moved their possessions from Gussie's house. Gussie insisted on keeping the piano.

"Well," Summer said, "you go on and keep it for us, Mama. Until we get a bigger house."

"I'll keep it until you pay me what it cost," Gussie replied, coldly. "I done without most everything I ever needed so I could pay for this here pianer. I wanted to do the best thing I could for you, no matter what. Pay me and you can have it."

"Come on, honey," Brendan whispered, desperately. "I'll get you a new piano."

"Oh, the big boy can speak!" Gussie laughed.

"Mama," Summer warned, "don't make me hate you!"

"I ain't worried."

In fact, Gussie thought, for the first time since the day she met Michaul, she had absolutely nothing to worry about. It seemed a miracle that without any effort on her part, her children were suddenly independent and capable of supporting themselves. She had never imagined such a turn of events, having always believed she would have to care for them until the end of her life. She had never planned a future for herself other than fending for Leo and Summer.

"The worm done turned," she told Widder Brown, "and I am free as a bird!"

"It is a blessing," the Widder agreed. "I seen it acoming."

Gussie reported Summer's marriage to the Veterans' Administration, ending her already reduced benefits. She had imagined it would be traumatic, but it was liberating. Within days, she had found work as a live-in housekeeper for Old Man Cooper, a wealthy widower whose health was failing. Her room and private bath were on the second floor, overlooking downtown Tisquah. She spent the evenings seated in front of her double windows, crocheting, listening to music on the Philco radio Old Man Cooper had ordered from the furniture store especially for Gussie. Her future seemed as endless and calm as the plains, and for a few months, she had absolutely no worries.

Tisquah boys were signing up for the draft in droves. Leo, according to Widder Brown, was classified 1-A, which meant he was likely to be drafted at any time. Gussie, always confused when it came to geography, had no idea where the boys would go when they joined the service, other than "overseas", a location somewhere between heaven and hell, she supposed. She visualized them all dressed in new uniforms, seated on wooden chairs, listening to a big radio. Who told them when to fight? And where to do the fighting? It gave her a headache.

In May, Leo and Varina moved to California without a word to Gussie. Leo, again according to Widder Brown, immediately found work in a munitions plant, making bombs for the war. Gussie was awed.

"Leo and bombs," she said, again and again. "It ain't right!"

Within three months, Leo and Varina returned to Tisquah, driving an old car filled with baby furniture. Varina was pregnant and Leo had received his draft notice. Gussie thought she would have a conniption fit when she heard the news.

"Leo ain't fit to be nobody's daddy!" she cried. "What is God thinking of?"

She wept for days, spending most nights on her knees, deep in prayer. She begged God for understanding, fearing she would go mad if she did not learn why God had allowed Leo to father a child. On Leo's twenty-first birthday, Gussie accompanied Varina, Summer and Brendan to the depot to bid farewell to Leo. The troop train, filled with other Texas boys headed off to basic training, began moving and Leo tore himself from the fervent embrace of the three women in his life. They all wept, even the stoic Brendan, as the train gained speed and puffed toward the horizon. Gussie alone wept from relief, for she alone had listened to the Lord and knew His plan.

The Lord would kill Leo in the war.

Varina would give birth to a baby whom no Abelard would ever harm.

Gussie would, finally, receive her reward for all the tribulations the Abelard family had brought into her life.

"I'll have a precious grand baby, maybe a girl" Gussie whispered. "Nobody will ever hurt this baby. Nobody!"

Jackie Glover

KENDRA
1979

CHAPTER SEVEN

Kendra had always known she was much more intelligent than her parents, Theresa and Mason Mitchell. Even as an infant, she had easily outsmarted them whenever she wished. She supposed it was her luck to have been born in modern times.

"Bless my parents' pea-brained little hearts," she told her best friend, Samantha. "It's not their fault they were born during World War II. Kids were treated like pets for the first few years of their lives back then. Unbelievable!"

On the infrequent occasions when she experienced a twinge of guilt for feeling so superior, Kendra leafed through one of her parent's many photo albums and looked at Theresa's and Mason's childhood pictures. Mason looked like an nasty-tempered little girl, dressed by his weird mother in girl's clothing, his hair combed into long curls until he was old enough to go to school.

"Pathetic," she told Samantha. "It's no wonder he is so goofy now. His mother called him her 'little girl' until he was old enough to shave!"

Theresa, too, was dressed like a doll in most of her photos, but at least she really was a girl. Kendra hated the way Varina's long shadow fell across Theresa's face in the snapshots. It seemed to Kendra that Varina had dressed Theresa up, posed her, then deliberately ruined the pictures with her shadow.

"Ugh," she and Samantha said in unison, looking at Varina's shadow, "imagine having Varina as your mother! Gross!"

Samantha knew how mean Varina was, having encountered her scowls and whispered insults whenever Varina visited.

It was a very good thing, Kendra thought, that she was the smartest member of her family. Otherwise, she could never have managed to conduct an affair with her parents' best friend for the past two years.

"Of course," she told Samantha, "they will have to be told sooner or later. Calvin and I have discussed telling them. We both think I should finish two more years of school before they find out."

"What do you think they will do?" Samantha asked, fearfully.

"Blame each other," Theresa answered. "That's all they ever do about anything. I'm not worried."

The only cloud on the horizon, Kendra explained to Samantha, was Theresa's constant bitching about the expensive presents Calvin often gave Kendra.

"I'm going to slap her if she keeps ranting about the gifts from Calvin," Kendra told Samantha. "She is trying to make Mason tell Calvin I can't accept any more presents."

"What will Calvin do?"

"He can handle Mason, don't worry. Calvin can run circles around Mason. Mentally, anyway. He'll probably tell Mason that Theresa is jealous of me. That will pull Mason's strings. He loves it when Theresa gets her pantyhose in a wad."

"I wish my life was as exciting as yours, Kendra," Samantha said, wistfully. "My family is so boring!"

Though Kendra did not mention it to Samantha, she suspected she was also smarter than Calvin. It was so simple to control him. All she had to do was plant an idea in his head, then cry or look sad, and he ran all over himself to buy whatever she wanted. Sometimes, Calvin made a big deal out of surprising her with something she had manipulated him into buying. It was a real kick to have such power over a man who was her father's age.

"Theresa is bitching about my closet being too full of clothes," she told Samantha. "Pick out some things you really like. Take enough to clear out some space. Shoes, too."

"Really, Kendra," Samantha gushed, "you are the best friend in the whole world! Are you sure Calvin won't care if you give these things away?"

Clothes and jewelry were too easy to come by, Kendra thought. In fact, she liked the challenge of persuading Calvin to buy the more expensive things, like her pedigreed dachshund, her imported Nubian goats and, especially, the barrel-racing mare, all kept at Calvin's farm north of town. Not to mention the custom-made saddle with her name worked into the leather, a barn full of tack and red suede chaps and hat.

"Calvin won't ever know, or care," Kendra told Samantha. "He's rolling in money."

"Is he rich?"

"Well, I don't know just how much money he has, or how much he makes in a year, but he paid for the last two vacations my family took. He gives us great presents at Christmas and on our birthdays, too, so I guess he knows what he can afford to spend."

"You are so lucky, Kendra!"

"Yeah, I guess," Kendra modestly agreed. "I'll just be glad when I get older, so I won't have to sneak around to see Calvin. We need some time alone. Some time for love."

"When do you think you can spend some time with him?"

"Hopefully," Kendra sighed, "this weekend. Theresa and Mason are going to Tisquah to visit my great-grandmother, Gussie. They want me to go. Actually, Mason doesn't care, but Theresa is pitching a bitch fit for me to go. Look, I want you to call the gang and make arrangements for tonight and tomorrow night. Got it?"

"This is so exciting," Samantha said, shivering. "I feel like I'm in a John Travolta movie!" She scooped up an armful of dresses and shoes, then climbed out the bedroom window Kendra left unlatched for their convenience. "Talk to you later! Good luck!"

"I want you to go with us to visit Gussie," Theresa insisted, for the umpteenth time. "She is getting awfully old and you should get to know her. Learn from her. She's led an exciting life."

"Mom," Kendra replied patiently, though she wanted to set Theresa's hair on fire, "I do know Gussie. She's great, I really mean that, but don't you remember? She already told me those stories about coyotes circling the house during in a blizzard, like Little House on the Prairie. I've heard more about birthing babies on the kitchen table than anyone needs to know. How many times do I have to listen to all that old junk?"

"Oh, Kendra," Theresa sighed. Her face twisted into the miserable expression Kendra especially hated. Disappointment etched ugly lines across her forehead and on each side of her mouth. "I wish you had more respect for family! You could learn so much. Why, when I was your age, I loved being around my relatives."

Kendra almost screamed.

If she wanted to be really cruel, Kendra thought bitterly, she could remind Theresa of the summer when she was seven years old. Kendra had begged to stay with Leo and Varina and several of her cousins at her grandparents' Utah ranch. She had cried, clinging to Mason's neck, until he shut Theresa up and told her it was stupid to tear Kendra away from so much fun. Kendra had squeezed out huge tears, then, sensing victory, actually believing it would be fun. Leo hovered in the background, offering no opinion, pretending it was fine with him, either way, when all along he was the reason Kendra wanted to stay.

Leo had promised to buy her a horse if she stayed on the ranch for two weeks. A horse of her own, because she was so special. A real, live horse, because Kendra lived in town and couldn't have a horse at home. Leo had kept his promise. All Kendra had to do in return was sleep out in his pickup camper every night with him and hold his weenie between her legs. And every day, after Varina drove to her job at a curio shop on the Interstate, Kendra had to sit in the bathtub with Leo as he held her in his lap and did things to her body she couldn't begin to comprehend. Her cousins knew the routine because their parents let them practically live with Leo and Varina. They felt sorry for Kendra, having already been down the 'horse of their own' road, but they knew they couldn't stop Leo. Leo was like an evil force of nature, Kendra thought. He ruined me.

So, Kendra thought, she had no reason to want to spend time with relatives. It was all water under the bridge, she knew. Sometimes, she wondered why Theresa had allowed her to stay on the ranch, when her mother had later admitted knowing how twisted Leo was.

"Times change, Mom," Kendra said. "Look, I have all these tests to study for. Just let me stay at Samantha's, so we can study together. I'll go to Tisquah next time, I promise."

"Next time might be Gussie's funeral," Theresa warned, as if it mattered a rat's ass to Kendra. "You'll be sorry, later on, if that's the case!"

"I'll deal with it then, Mom," Kendra said. She managed not to smile when she sensed Theresa's withdrawal from the conflict. "I love the old lady, too, you know. I just need to ace these tests next week, you know that."

"I know, dear," Theresa sighed. "Just be sure you stay at Samantha's house and follow the rules we agreed on. O.K?"

"O.K., Mom, I will."

Kendra helped Mason carry the bags to the car. Theresa had packed enough clothing to travel to Antarctica.

"Think Mom packed enough, Dad?"

"Beats the hell out of me," Mason sighed, as he arranged the bags in the trunk. "You know how she is. I learned a long time ago to just let her have her way. It's easier on all of us."

"You're a good husband to her, Daddy," Kendra said, hugging him. "She is just such a bitch! Honest to God, I don't know how you put up with her."

"Hell," Mason laughed, "I don't hear half of what she carries on about." Kendra's compliment obviously pleased him. "I do the best I can."

Kendra waved as her parents drove away, headed for Tisquah, one hundred miles to the northwest. She went inside and called Samantha.

"Saaaaaammmmy," she sang, "the old faaaaaarts are gone! Did you fix things with your mom?"

"It's cool," Samantha replied, nervously. Kendra felt her friend's excitement and tension actually flow through the telephone wire. "She thinks I am going to Tisquah with you and your parents. Donny's folks think he is spending the weekend at Possum Kingdom Lake with Josh. This is going to work out great!"

"Just don't use the phone," Kendra warned. "I gotta go. Calvin will be here any minute. Remember our deal?"

"Sure, Kendra." Samantha sounded hurt by Kendra's inquiry. "If we get caught we blame it all on Sue Ann, then we go to church for a couple of Sundays and read the Bible until our parents think we are truly sorry."

"Great!"

Life was simple if you just used your brain, Kendra thought. She quickly dropped a couple of maraschino cherries into the aquarium for her iguana, Lizard Boy. Not that he would eat them, she thought. Lizard Boy was, apparently, on a suicide mission. Death by starvation.

"Oh, well," Kendra said, "if you croak, Calvin will buy me another iguana. Or maybe a Ball python. Neat!"

She stuffed her school books into a bag and went out the back door, across the patio and into the alley. Calvin's new king-cab pickup pulled into view and Kendra suddenly felt sick. She knew the sick feelings would pass. It wasn't that she dreaded spending time with Calvin, for God's sake! He was the man she loved! It was just the strain of keeping their relationship a secret. Her hands were so moist with perspiration that she fumbled with the door handle. She just felt so rushed, so pushed around by everyone and everything in her life! But, she really wanted to spend the weekend at Calvin's farm.

"Hi, darling," Calvin crooned. His big blue eyes shone with devotion as Kendra climbed into the pickup cab. He reached across the seat and squeezed her thigh, hard, with his right hand. "We're going to have a great time!"

"I know we will, Cal," Kendra replied. She swallowed the lump in her throat. Damn, she thought, angrily, why do I always feel like I'm going to cry? "I'm starved," she said, because if she had something to eat, maybe the dead feeling in her chest would go away. Sometimes, she felt like her heart had rotted. She could almost smell it. "Let's pull through the Dairy

Queen and get some chili fries and a Pepsi, O.K.?"

"Sure, Punkin, whatever you want."

Calvin never lectured Kendra about nutrition or getting enough sleep or planning her future, like her parents always did. He just let her do whatever she wanted. It was heaven. All Kendra's friends envied her. Envied, hell, she thought. They were in awe of her.

They ate the chili fries on the way out of town as Calvin brought her up to date on her horse, her dog and her goats. He took excellent care of them when she wasn't there, though he was really busy with the farm. Calvin loved animals as much as Kendra did.

They were moved to tears sometimes, discussing plans for the animal shelter they would build and operate when they were finally able to marry. Of course, building the shelter would have to wait until after Kendra graduated from Texas A&M School of Veterinary Medicine, but it was a dream they would realize. Whenever Kendra saw a stray kitten or dog, she silently promised God she would make it all better in the future, when she and Calvin would rescue every lost and sick animal in Texas. Later, after they raised their children, they might even buy a boat and patrol the tuna fishing industry, saving dolphins and endangered turtles from drowning in the evil nets. Their love would make it all possible. They would probably be on the cover of People Magazine someday. Theresa would just shit a brick then, wouldn't she?

"Better get out of sight, honey," Calvin said, breaking her reverie. "We can't take a chance that anyone will see us."

Calvin's former in-laws lived across the road from his house. The former mother-in-law spent a great deal of time watching Calvin's activities with a pair of expensive binoculars Calvin had given her husband years earlier. Calvin said he had never imagined he would be in the embarrassing position of having to sneak into his own house with the woman he loved. He had truly believed he and Maria would be married forever. Maria was such a bitch, Kendra thought, always with her hand out for more money. Of course, Theresa and Maria had been good friends, just to make matters worse for Kendra and Calvin.

Kendra slipped onto the floor of the cab and Calvin covered her with his jacket. She buried her face in its folds, breathing in the earthy odor of the man she loved. He was so clean and blond, so perfectly formed, with such beautiful pale blue eyes, that Kendra could barely look at him without feeling faint. That such a perfect man had fallen in love with her seemed the greatest miracle on earth.

Calvin drove the huge pickup into the double garage attached to his brick house. Kendra remained on the floor until he closed and locked the garage doors. She listened for his footsteps, and just as he approached the passenger door, Kendra cried a few big tears. Calvin gently removed the denim jacket and gasped in dismay when he saw her tears, which he naturally assumed were because Kendra had to hide on the floor like a criminal. He was so easy to fool. Calvin carefully picked her up, as if she was no more than an infant, and carried her into the house.

"Don't cry, honey," he begged, "don't cry. I can't stand it!"

"I'm sorry," Kendra sobbed. "I just hate hiding our love. I wish we could tell everybody!"

"We just have to be patient, darling," Calvin crooned, smoothing her hair, kissing her tears away. He held her in his arms as she wrapped her legs around his waist. "It will be worth the wait, I promise!"

Kendra nodded, then rested her head on his shoulder as he carried her into the master bedroom. He sat her on the edge of the king size bed and disappeared into the bathroom. He would fill the garden tub and pour in lots of her favorite bubble bath, Kendra knew. He liked to undress her in the bedroom, then carry her to the foaming tub in his arms. As if she was a toddler.

The master bedroom, decorated by Calvin's ex-wife Maria, looked like a Juarez whorehouse, in Kendra's opinion. Red shag carpet, red crushed velvet bedspread, flocked red wallpaper and massive wrought iron light fixtures. Oh, well, she thought. What had Calvin expected when he married a fifteen year old Hispanic girl who had never been out of the county?

Maria had smartened up, Kendra thought, by the time Calvin asked for a divorce. She demanded, and received, a new car, all the heavy, Mexican-made furniture (except the bed) and twenty thousand dollars cash, in return for an uncontested divorce. Kendra was wise enough to keep her mouth shut about the dreadful decor, aware that Calvin liked it, that he was even proud of it. She would redecorate in due time to her own taste. She planned to use unicorns as her decorating focal point. Something American, anyway, and definitely no crappy pinatas. And no red anything.

"What are you smiling about, darling?" Calvin had removed his clothes, except for his glasses, and stood in the doorway. "I hope it is because you love me."

"I do love you, Calvin," Kendra replied, sincerely.

Calvin was in fantastic physical condition, Kendra noted, proudly. The sight of his nude body always made her weak with desire. He had been a Marine in the Viet Nam war and liked to keep himself in shape. Kendra was glad. She did not think she could love a flabby older man. Calvin was perfect, except for being terribly nearsighted. Kendra thought it would be nice, too, if his dick was longer and maybe not so thick. She had once made the mistake of teasing him about his square dick and he had cried. Men were real babies about some things.

The weekend was perfect, except for having to stay indoors the entire time. Kendra desperately wanted to ride Topsy, her horse, but Calvin cautioned her that someone might mention her presence to her parents. Then it would all hit the fan, Calvin said.

"Maria's folks would just love to get the goods on me," Calvin added.

Kendra was safely home in time to clean the house before Theresa and Mason returned from Tisquah.

"Samantha, you bitch!" Kendra said, later, when she called her friend. "You guys trashed my mom's house! What were you thinking of?"

"Oh, God, Kendra," Samantha moaned. "I'm sorry! Sue Ann and Andy showed up with booze and we all got smashed. I puked until I thought I would die! I think we all did it with each other, but none of us can remember exactly what we did. Anyway, they all left the house for me to clean up and I didn't feel like it! I practically crawled home! Don't be mad!"

"You owe me, Sammy," Kendra snarled. A little menace always kept Samantha in line, especially if she felt guilty. She was an idiot, basically, but trustworthy. "Don't forget it!"

"Well, how was your weekend?" Samantha asked.

"Great," Kendra replied. "I can't tell you what happened, over the phone. Maybe someday."

Actually, Kendra thought, if she was totally honest with Samantha, she would admit that the weekend was boring. Calvin apparently lived for the long hours they spent in the garden tub or lying in the king size bed as they ate microwave popcorn and watched television. Kendra was always annoyed because he laughed at the same stupid things that her parents found funny. After the news and weather report, which he refused to miss because weather determined his work routine, Calvin checked all the locks, turned out the lights and cuddled Kendra in the dark. He liked to lick Kendra's body from head to toe, particularly her genitals. It was mind-numbing, really, when she only wanted him to push his square little dick inside her hot body. Just do it and get it over with! He had a lot of will power, she had to admit.

"It will mean more to us after we are married," he explained. "You'll see."

Well, she thought, it was a good thing she loved him so much. Otherwise, she would be looking elsewhere. Samantha and her drunken boyfriend, Donny, had more actual sex than she and Calvin.

Kendra sensed a change in the status quo before Theresa and Mason entered the house. Something was different, her sensitive antenna told her, really different. She turned her jam-box off and lay on her bed, listening. Her parents walked down the hall, straight to her room and entered without knocking. God, Kendra thought, panicked, they know about me and Calvin! I'm dead!

"What's up, guys?" she asked, as perky as any television sit-com idiot. "How were things in Tisquah?"

"Everyone was fine, but they were disappointed that you didn't go," Theresa replied, gently. "Your father and I have something to discuss with you."

"Cool," Kendra said, swinging her legs off the bed. She needed to be able to run if things got bad, because Mason was prone to hitting her. "What do you want to discuss?"

"Your father and I have decided to get a divorce," Theresa said. Her words sounded like little rocks hitting the wall. Kendra was shocked into silence, which had hardly ever happened to her. "We have some personal issues we can't resolve."

"Huh?" Kendra whispered. Theresa had tears in her eyes. Mason was seriously studying the light fixture. "Divorce?"

"We just aren't meeting each others needs," Theresa replied.

"Needs?"

"We don't feel comfortable discussing the details with you, dear," Theresa said, primly, and in that instant, Kendra knew she was referring to sex. "We just want you to know we both love you. We love you dearly, isn't that right, Mason?"

"Yeah," Mason replied, still looking at the ceiling. "Dearest, or whatever your mother said, Kendra, that's how it is."

"Mason," Theresa practically yelled, "we agreed on how to break this news to Kendra! We love you dearly, Kendra. You may talk to us any time you have questions or if you feel sad about the changes we will experience. For now, we want you to be thinking about which of us you want to live with. It is your decision. There won't be any fights concerning your custody because we both love you. Dearly."

Kendra burst into tears, mostly from relief, having feared the jig was up for her and Calvin. Also, her friends had said it was important to act distressed if your parents said they were divorcing. It could be a real scam if you played your cards right.

"Is it something I did?" Kendra sobbed. "If it is, just tell me and I'll never do it again! I promise!"

Her parents hugged her and swore on all they held holy that their decision had nothing to do with her behavior. Theresa began sobbing, too, and even old stone-face Mason looked rattled. Mason never showed much emotion unless he was watching a sports event, especially a Dallas Cowboys football game, so Kendra knew he was truly upset.

"Well, I think I should stay with Mom," Kendra said, thoughtfully. She really preferred living with Mason, but she knew Theresa would block that, no matter how fair she professed to be. "That is, if I can see Daddy real often." Mason was visibly relieved, so much so that he turned his head to hide his expression. He was such a simpleton, Kendra thought. "I just want to do what you two think is best, for us all."

Within the week Mason had rented a snazzy apartment on the west side of town. Kendra played it cool for a few days, moping around whenever Theresa was at home, trying to look depressed about the whole farce. She was not surprised that her parents were finally divorcing. It was a mystery to her that two such radically different old geezers had ever married in the first place. She began testing Theresa's boundaries, bit by bit, and was amazed at her mother's ditsy behavior.

"Mom, what is going on with you?" she asked. "You can talk to me."

"Oh, Kendra, honey," Theresa replied, "I didn't want to tell you this yet, but there is a new man in my life. We are in love. We are talking about getting married! I hope you won't be upset."

"A man?"

"Yes. A very wonderful man," Theresa said. Her eyes glistened and her face was very flushed. Kendra wondered if the old gal might be coming down with a virus. "Please don't get upset, Kendra. Please be happy for me."

"Sure. O.K., Mom, I am happy for you. When did this happen?"

"I can't discuss the details yet, honey. I'll tell you all about it after the divorce is final. Just trust me for a few more weeks."

"Yeah, whatever," Kendra said. Her mind was in high gear, compiling a mental list of men whom her mother might love. She came up with a big, fat zero. "Where did you meet this guy?"

"I said I'll tell you later, Kendra. That's a promise. You'll be surprised!"

Kendra's friends cautioned her that Theresa would go through a period of 'bonding' with her after Mason moved out of the house. Sure enough, Theresa bugged the shit out of Kendra, insisting on taking her shopping, out to eat, to the movies and to church. They even had their hair done together, the most humiliating experience of Kendra's life, made bearable only because the fag hairdresser was so interesting. Kendra was suffocating and out of patience with Theresa. She experienced two basic emotions for her mother. Boredom and hatred. She didn't know which felt worse. Kendra endured all the togetherness because her friends said it would cease after the divorce was final and Theresa was free to see her new man.

"Get what you can from her before she lets some old dickhead start bossing you around," they advised. "Once another guy is in the picture, she will forget all this mother-daughter bullshit. Things won't ever be the same between you and your mom."

A week before the divorce was to become final, Kendra got sick at school. She threw up twice in the rest room, then managed to stagger to the nurse's office.

"Shall I call you mother or your father to pick you up?"

The nurse waited patiently as Kendra considered the options. What the hell, she decided. If she calls Mom, I'll wind up in the doctor's office all afternoon. Dad will just pick me up and drop me off at the house. I can have the rest of the day to watch TV.

"Call my daddy," Kendra whispered. "Please."

Mason pulled up in front of the school in a company truck twenty minutes later. He hardly looked at Kendra as she climbed inside. He drove with one hand and held a clipboard in the other, moving his lips as he read the delivery schedule to himself. God, Kendra thought, he looks absolutely simple when he moves his lips like that.

Mason dropped her off at the house and did not offer to help her inside. Sympathy was never her father's strong point. Kendra let herself in through the garage, surprised to see her mother's car parked inside.

"Maybe she got sick with the grunge, too," Kendra said. "God, I hope she is asleep. I absolutely do not feel up to talking to her!"

Kendra took a can of soda from the fridge and walked down the hall, past Theresa's room. Theresa was moaning. She sounded sick enough to die.

"Great," Kendra whispered. "I guess I have to see if she needs anything."

She opened the door to her mother's room. She froze perfectly still. Her mother was in bed with a man and they were humping like elephants. Theresa's flabby boobs bounced around like tennis balls. The man's butt looked like a baboon's, with wrinkled, red testes scooched between his muscular thighs. Sickening! Kendra immediately stepped back into the hall and pulled the door shut. She felt faint.

"Something is definitely weird here," she whispered, "really, really weird!"

Kendra tiptoed to her room and crawled into the closet, a habit from her childhood when she was afraid of thunderstorms. She shivered all over.

"Calm down," she told herself. "Figure this out!"

She breathed deeply and forced herself to replay the scene in her mind's eye. She already knew the truth, but it was too hard to believe right away.

The man in bed with Theresa was Calvin Wolfe!

It was perfectly clear in her mind as she thought about it. Her mother's puke-green pant suit and polyester blouse were strewn across the orange shag carpet. One of her yo-yo sandals lay beside the night stand. Kendra had always coveted those sandals but the bitch wouldn't share shoes. Not sanitary, she claimed.

A pair of Wellington boots sat at the foot of the bed, white tube socks neatly draped across each boot. Worn jeans and a denim shirt, carefully folded, rested on the bedside chair, topped by a pair of thick lensed, gold-framed glasses.

"Calvin!" Kendra whispered. "Oh, my love, what are you doing in bed with my mother?"

She lay on the closet floor all afternoon in unbearable agony. Every emotion she had ever experienced flooded through her body like acid. Eventually, her mother and Calvin went into the kitchen and nuked something in the microwave. Kendra wept then, her face buried in the carpet, hoping Calvin and Theresa would choke to death on frozen pizza. Half an hour later, she heard Calvin's footsteps as he crossed the patio. His pickup must be parked on the far side of their block, Kendra thought.

She had no idea what she should do. It hurt so much! The pain was like a massive internal bruise that must, surely, be seeping through her skin. She heard the sound of her mother's bath tub filling and decided to pretend that she was just getting home from school.

"Hi, Mom," she called. "I'm home."

"Oh, Kendra, honey? I didn't hear the school bus."

"Dad gave me a ride home. I'm sick."

"Well, sweetie, I'm sorry! Go to bed and I'll take your temperature when I get out of the tub."

"Swell," Kendra replied.

Hours later, after Theresa had ministered to her and just about driven her mad, Kendra called Samantha.

"Sammy, get over here! I've got the biggest problem you can imagine!"

They pretended to do their homework, for Theresa's sake, as Kendra told Samantha about finding Calvin in her mother's bed. Neither of them had the slightest idea of what Kendra should do, other than talk to Calvin.

"O.K., Sammy," Kendra sighed. "Go out and keep my mother busy while I call Calvin."

"Sure thing," Samantha agreed. "I'll ask her to help me write my English theme. That should keep her busy. The last time she helped me, she wrote the whole thing!"

"Calvin," Kendra whispered into the telephone, "I can't talk for very long."

"What's wrong, Punkin?"

"I came home early today, Cal. I saw you and my mother in bed."

A velvet silence whooshed across the distance between

Calvin's farm house and Kendra's room. Kendra felt faint. Calvin did not say a word. For the first time since she had fallen in love with Calvin, Kendra felt fear. At that moment, she wanted nothing more on earth than to run into Theresa's arms and tell her everything about the past two years. It was much too late for that, Kendra knew. Theresa would probably send her to juvenile hall.

"Don't jump to conclusions, Punkin," Calvin whispered. "Remember, I'm on a party line."

"Fuck that," Kendra remarked, angrily. "What conclusions are possible, Calvin?" She was afraid she would start weeping, so she summoned up all the anger she could manage. Calvin was not going to get off the hook just because their conversation was taking place on a party line! "Like, maybe you thought she was me?"

"No, look, honey, you've got it all wrong! Your mom has been chasing me for months. She keeps making things for me, bringing me gifts and baking cakes, you know that. Hell, she even brought me some grape vines to plant! She won't leave me alone, I swear!"

"So you fucked her to be polite, is that it?"

"No." Calvin sighed, sounding like a man about to fall apart. "Listen to me. I got to thinking about our situation. I thought if I married your mom, the two of you could move out here. I could see you every day, every night. Then, in a couple of years, I could divorce Theresa and marry you. Don't be mad, Punkin, please! It could work out, don't you think?"

"I think it would drive me crazy!"

"Just think it over, won't you?"

"Suppose we can't wait two more years, Calvin? What if she figures out how much we love each other? She can be a real bitch! What if she tells Dad?"

"Don't worry about Mason," Calvin laughed. "He doesn't care what Theresa says. He thinks she is crazy, you know that."

"Calvin," Kendra said, patiently, "he thinks she is crazy because she is crazy! That's my point! No one knows what she will do at any given time. She's a walking nut case!"

"If it starts to turn nasty," Calvin said, softly, "your

mother might die."

"Die?"

"In an accident. If you get my meaning."

"That scares me," Kendra replied. She really felt like crying. She had never, ever, been so confused. Not even when Leo molested her and Varina ignored her pleas for help. "What do we do now?"

"Leave that to me, darling," Calvin crooned. "You don't have to be concerned. I know how to handle this, you'll see."

Kendra experienced a moment of absolute certainty that Calvin's plan would ruin her life. She had never opposed him, other than slyly manipulating him to buy something for her, but she instinctively knew it was time to take a stand.

"Calvin, you break it off with my mom or I will tell her everything! I mean it!" Kendra was weeping, but for real, not to influence the tender-hearted Calvin. "BREAK...IT...OFF!"

She slammed down the receiver as Theresa, followed by Samantha, rushed into her room.

"Kendra, honey," Theresa cried, "what was that all about? Who was that? Why are you so upset?"

"It was an obscene phone call, Mommy," Kendra wept. Theresa sat on the edge of the bed and wrapped Kendra in her arms. "I told the freak to break it off or I'd tell you to call the cops!"

"Oh, dear, I am so sorry! The best thing is to not talk to them. I read an article just the other day. It turns them on if they know you are upset. Imagine! Anyway, honey, if he calls back, just blow this whistle into the mouthpiece. It will explode his eardrums."

Her mother removed a gold necklace from her neck and handed it to Kendra. A small gold whistle dangled from the chain. Kendra had never seen anything so ridiculous. Geez, she thought, why do I ever worry that she might see through my lies?

"Thanks, Mommy," Kendra whispered, tearfully. She clasped the whistle to her breast, as if it was the most precious item on the planet. "You always know what to do."

"Well, that's my job," Theresa replied, modestly.

Samantha, standing uncertainly behind Theresa, pursed

her lips and rolled her eyes up until only the whites showed. Kendra almost burst out laughing. She managed to sob, instead.

Theresa had a really bad week following the final divorce hearing. Kendra almost felt sorry for the old hag, but really, it was what her mother deserved. True to form, Theresa went to work right away spreading her misery around, ruining life for them all.

"She's such a bitch!" Kendra told Samantha. "I wish she would get hit by a train!"

Two days after the divorce hearing, Kendra was awakened by Mason, who was apparently sitting on the doorbell. Kendra watched from the hallway as Theresa opened the door. Mason burst inside, swinging a baseball bat, which seemed to upset Theresa. Kendra watched as Mason smashed the bat into several pictures hanging in the foyer. Theresa backed away from him, silent, for once in her hysterical life.

"You bitch!" Mason yelled. He smashed the bat across the coffee table, sending Theresa's cherished collection of antique butter presses flying across the room like a fleet of wooden UFOs. "You cunt!"

"Good Lord, what...what on earth?" Theresa stammered. She did not approach Mason, a tactic she had, no doubt, learned from his pervious, legendary explosions. "Mason, calm down. You'll wake Kendra!"

Mason wilted onto the sofa, panting. The bat rolled beneath the splintered coffee table. He ran his fingers through his wavy brown hair. Kendra was glad she had inherited her father's hair, as well as his double eyelashes and strong fingernails. Theresa hardly had enough hair on her head to cover the scalp. Kendra could not imagine going through life with thin, old-lady hair, almost no eyelashes and tiny, fragile nails. Gross!

Mason grew calmer and the scarlet flush of pure rage drained from his face. Kendra knew he would probably insult Theresa a few times more, then slink off and go to bed. Her parents were such morons!

"I drove over here last night with my shotgun," he snarled. "I was going to ring the doorbell and blow your frigging brains out! What do you think about that, you bitch?"

"I think you would have regretted killing me in front of Kendra," Theresa replied, evenly. "Maybe we should go to family counseling and resolve some of these issues."

"We aren't a family anymore!"

"We are, Mason. We could get separation counseling. It's the modern way. Talk things out. There's no reason for violence."

"Fuck it," Mason sighed. He stood and stumbled out the door, coming down off an adrenaline high, shaky as a drunk after a binge. It was so lame, Kendra thought. "Go to hell! I don't know why I ever trusted a goddam woman! It won't happen again, I promise you that!"

"Go home and get some sleep," Theresa said, as she closed and locked the door.

The next morning, Calvin met Theresa at the Saddle and Sirloin for coffee and broke off their secret engagement. Theresa took another day off work and collapsed on her bed, sobbing. Kendra found her there after school.

"It's all over," Theresa wept, holding on to Kendra like a drowning woman. "I was engaged to Calvin Wolfe, Kendra, but it's all over! I could just die!"

"Wow," Kendra replied, softly. "I don't know what to say, Mom."

"It's nothing for you to be concerned about, honey. I don't want to worry you with my adult problems. It's just that we had such wonderful plans and now they won't ever come true."

Bet your fat booty they won't, Kendra thought. Not if Calvin wants to be with me!

"We have to stop seeing Calvin, Kendra," Theresa sobbed. She wiped her face and composed herself. Kendra would have fled the room had she known how to escape. "I think Calvin has a mental problem of some kind. I really think he's nuts, Kendra! He just blows hot and cold, without any warning. Maybe it's because of something that happened to him in the war, post-traumatic something or other, they call it. It's something we can't deal with! Just forget about him!"

"Mom!" Kendra shouted. "What about Topsy? Where will I keep her if we don't see Calvin again? We can't afford to

179

stable her anywhere else! What about Ducky? Our lease says 'no dogs', you know that! I can't live without seeing my horse and dog! And my goats! Don't you care about any of my animals? No! No! We can't stop seeing Calvin just because you broke up with him!"

"Calvin broke up with me," Theresa snarled. "I'll see what arrangements I can make for the horse and dog, but you can forget about those stinking goats. You pay attention to me, now, Kendra. We will not see Calvin Wolfe again. That is a fact of life you can take to the bank!"

"You can't do that to me, Mom," Kendra wept. "I'll live with Dad. He won't keep me from my animals!"

"Don't make any rash decisions, Kendra! I read an article just the other day that said people usually live to regret hasty decisions. Think about this for a few days. Be sure of what you think and feel."

"Mom, there isn't a magazine article in the world to cover what I think or feel! I am going to live with Dad! You can take that to the bank!"

Kendra moved to Mason's apartment the following weekend, in spite of Theresa's rabid opposition. Mason did not seem inclined to follow Theresa's instructions regarding Calvin. In fact, he seemed to enjoy allowing Kendra to spend as much time as she wished on Calvin's farm. At first, Kendra felt a sense of triumph at having outsmarted her mother. As the weeks passed, though, Kendra sensed a great difference in Calvin's attitude. They didn't seem to really have fun, not like before.

"What's wrong, Cal,?" she asked. They were in the garden tub, as usual, soaking in a mountain of bubbles. "Is there something I should know?"

"I don't know how to tell you this, Punkin," he replied, sadly. "Your mother is threatening to get a court order to prevent you from coming out here."

"Can she do that?"

"She may be able to. She says you can't spend any more time out here unless I start dating women my own age. She thinks I have too great an attachment for you. She says it doesn't seem healthy for me not to have friends of my own. Junk like that, you know."

"Can't you stop her?"

"Not without killing her."

"Do you want to kill her?"

"Not now, since she has stirred up such a fuss. It might look suspicious. She even has Mason upset. You know how he can be."

"So, what do we do?"

"We stop seeing each other. We hide our love until you get older. It's the only way, Punkin. I've done a lot of thinking about this situation. I'm sorry."

A week later, Kendra overheard a furious, whispered conversation between Theresa and Mason.

"Mason, I don't want to publicly accuse you of homosexual behavior," Theresa hissed. "But, so help me God, if you don't follow my lead in this matter with Kendra and Calvin, I'll do it! I swear I will!"

"You bitch!" Mason replied. Kendra could not see either of her parents, but she felt their intensity, even though she was on the balcony outside her bedroom. Her new friend, Sissy, had taught her how to climb onto the balcony from outside by balancing on the patio fence below. Sissy frequently fled her own parents' wrath and spent the night in Kendra's room. "Theresa, I'm warning you," Mason snarled, "I'll kill you if you accuse me of being queer!"

"Do as I say, Mason," Theresa said. "Keep Kendra away from Calvin and vice versa. Otherwise, I will let it be known that you prefer men to women. In fact, I've sometimes wondered about you and Calvin, if you want the truth. What do you think of that?"

"I wish I had killed you a long time ago! You don't know anything about how men feel about each other! You think women know about friendship? You're a stupid cunt if you think women know! Men have an understanding that would stun your brain, if you had a brain! Sure, I love Calvin! Is that what you want me to say? I love, love, love him to goddam death! I would die for that guy, but that doesn't mean I'm queer for him! You're too stupid to know the difference! Go to goddam hell! I hate you! You're so fat it makes me puke!"

Kendra almost toppled off the balcony as Theresa stormed out of the apartment and Mason slammed the door. She thought she would never be able to breathe again. Kendra could not believe she had just heard such a dramatic conversation between her parents. They actually hated each other, in fact, they loathed each other. It was stunning. She could not imagine they had ever been close enough to conceive her, or that either of them cared a rat's ass what happened to her life. She sat on the balcony floor, where she remained until she was certain Mason had gone to bed. She then tiptoed to her room and called Samantha.

"Sammy, things have gotten so much worse! You can't imagine what I just found out!"

"Tell me, Kendra," Samantha whispered. "Maybe I can help."

"I just heard my parents arguing about Calvin. My mom is threatening to tell people that my dad is a fag!"

"Shit! Get out of here!"

"No shit! Look, I have to go. I've got to figure out what I'm going to do with this mess. My frigging parents have just ruined my life, forever! I hate them both more than you can imagine!"

"O.K." Samantha replied. Her voice was so sympathetic it almost moved Kendra to tears. "Oh, hey, Kendra? What are you going to wear to school tomorrow?"

"I don't know. Maybe my black handkerchief skirt and black feather earrings."

"The black widow outfit?"

"Yeah, I feel like a frigging widow. Or maybe my Wranglers and my pink satin 'Grease' jacket. Depends on the weather."

"You are so damned brave, Kendra," Samantha sighed. "I'm really worried about you."

"Thanks, sweetie," Kendra replied, bravely. "Somebody should be worried about me! I think I may have to kill myself!"

"O.K.," Samantha said. "See you in the morning."

Kendra filled her bathtub with scalding hot water and eased her body into its fiery depths. She gritted her teeth against the heat. In one hand, she held her father's disposable razor. In the other she held a snapshot of Topsy taken the day they had ridden in the Grand Entry at the Stamford Cowboy Reunion Rodeo.

"Good old Topsy," she whispered, as tears filled her eyes. She kissed the picture, remembering how thrilled she had been to ride in a world-famous rodeo, thanks to Calvin. "I won't be riding you this year, old gal. Everything is all screwed up!"

Kendra dropped the picture on the floor. She positioned Mason's Bic razor on her left wrist, applying just enough pressure to hurt. Tiny droplets of blood popped up along the blade's length.

Kendra knew, without a doubt, that she was the most miserable eleven year old girl in Abilene, Texas.

CHAPTER EIGHT

Kendra thought it was the oddest thing in the world, really, but the only reason she did not slash her wrists was because of a magazine article her mother had read and endlessly discussed. The previous year, a neighborhood girl Kendra barely knew, a girl who took tennis lessons and owned two Great Danes, left school one afternoon, walked home and blew her brains out with her daddy's pistol. Naturally, Theresa felt it was her duty to talk to Kendra about suicide.

"I read an article just the other day about the national epidemic of teen suicides," Theresa began. "I can't explain why, but I had a strong feeling that I should clip it and file it for future reference."

"You had a feeling?" Kendra asked. It was best to pretend she was interested and let the old hag spin out her dreary tale. "Cool."

"Well, I'm glad you think so, dear. The article said teens don't realize that death is permanent. You know how little children think because cartoon characters survive explosions, an actual explosion wouldn't kill real people? Well, a group of psychologists did a study and found that most teens who admitted they had suicidal thoughts really just wanted to punish their parents or teachers. They all said they daydreamed about coming back and resuming their lives once they made their point. They wanted to kill themselves as a means of communication. They did not think they would be permanently dead!"

"Wow, Mom," Kendra said, "that is really, like, you

know, interesting! You think Laura maybe thought she would just blow her brains all over the den and wake up later? No headache? Maybe she would just get grounded for a couple of weeks?"

"Don't be sarcastic, Kendra," Theresa sighed. "Honey, I just mentioned it because I know your friends confide in you. If anyone tells you they are thinking of suicide, you should tell them what the article said."

"Cool, Mom," Kendra said. "You think of everything."

The spooky thing was, months later, as Kendra sat in the bath tub contemplating Mason's orange and white Bic trace a line of blood on her wrist, she recalled the article on teen suicide. Her mother had been thoughtful enough to share the information with her, which was more than any of her friends could say about their moms. In fact, her friends thought Theresa was a great mom, except for ruining Kendra's life with Calvin, of course. Kendra wished she could tell Theresa how miserable she was at that very moment. It was impossible, and Kendra did not honestly blame Theresa. She blamed herself. She had finally outsmarted all the important adults in her life. The joke was on her, though, for she had created a world in which she had no adult to whom she could turn for help.

"Oh, Mommy!" Kendra wept. "I won't kill myself just to hurt you! I don't want to be really dead, not even for a minute! I just want someone to take care of me again. I'm sorry I've been so bad! Sometimes I think Calvin is just a pervert like Leo! He knew I wanted a horse of my own, and he just wanted a little girl he could feel up in the bath tub! I think I've been stupid! Nothing is working out right! I want to be your little girl again!"

Since she was already in the tub, Kendra shaved her legs and under her arms with Mason's razor. She didn't have much body hair, but she practiced shaving so she would be good at it once she got her periods and started sprouting bushes in her pits. She shampooed her hair, got out of the tub and took her blow dryer onto the patio. Her hair was almost dry when Sissy clambered over the railing and fell to the floor beside her.

"Hi," Kendra whispered.

"Hi," Sissy whispered back. "I'm gonna sleep here

tonight, O.K.? My old man just broke my mom's nose again. I don't want him to find me."

"Cool."

"What's up?"

"Not much," Kendra sighed. "I just decided not to cut my wrists, but that's not big news."

"Yeah, I know where you're coming from. Hurts, don't it? Is there anything in your apartment we can eat? I'm starving!"

"We can find something. If you're going to eat here, you have to take out that pile of trash in the kitchen. Mason thinks it's my job because I'm a girl."

"O.K."

Kendra missed Calvin so much it hurt. Her appetite dwindled and she hardly slept. She fell behind in her school work and was forced to sit through a goofy session with her school counselor, Mrs. Muncie.

"You seem to have a problem, Kendra," the counselor announced, peering over her glasses. "Let's talk about it."

"My parents got divorced."

"How does that make you feel?"

"Like I don't want to do my homework."

"Do you think it will help your situation to fail this grade period? You've always made very good grades."

"I don't see what difference it makes."

"What difference what makes?"

"What?"

"What?"

"Kendra," Mrs. Muncie said, patiently. She gave Kendra a look that plainly said she had seen it all. "Are you just trying to get your parents' attention by failing in school?"

"No, but that's a good idea, Mrs. Muncie. Thank you."

"You aren't as smart as you think you are, missy," Mrs. Muncie sputtered. "Some students avoid dealing with their problems by pushing my buttons. You can do it, but it won't help you with whatever is bothering you."

"Well," Kendra said, "it hasn't made me feel any worse."

A month later, Mason told Kendra that Calvin was engaged to be married. Kendra's heart dropped to her shoes.

"He asked me to be his best man," Mason said, proudly. He was as empty-headed as a cartoon character, Kendra thought. "You'll need to stay with your mother that weekend, O.K.?"

"Sure, Daddy," Kendra shrugged. She felt like an ice cube. "Who is Calvin marrying?"

"A nurse he met when he had hemorrhoid surgery last month. He went to school with her husband. The poor old boy got killed in a car wreck. She has two little kids, a boy and a girl. Calvin sure is excited! He's building a swimming pool for the kids and buying another horse, so they will each have one."

"What do you mean?"

"Hell, I told Calvin he could keep Topsy since you don't go out there anymore. He sure appreciated it and I felt damned good to be able to do something for him. Now, he only has to buy one horse."

"You told Calvin he can keep my horse?"

"Kendra," Mason snapped. His blue eyes narrowed. Kendra shivered. "Calvin paid for Topsy and the saddle and the tack, so they belong to him, anyway. Don't act like your mother. I'm not in the mood for any temper tantrums!"

"God!" Kendra screamed. "I'm surrounded by total, fucking idiots!"

Mason hit her with the back of his hand. Stars exploded in her head and she fell to the floor, whimpering. She tried to stand.

"Daddy," she pleaded, "don't hurt me!"

"I said no temper tantrums, you little bitch!" Mason kicked her in the backside, sending her sprawling. "I am goddam sick and tired of your behavior! I ought to send you back to your fucking mother! That's where you learned to act like this!"

Mason stormed out of the apartment and Kendra crawled to the sofa. She dialed Calvin's number.

"Is it true?" she wept, when she heard his voice. "Please say it isn't true. Say you aren't marrying a nurse with two kids. Tell me you aren't giving my horse to a little kid I never met!"

"Face the facts, Punkin," Calvin sighed. "It wasn't working out for us. We just have to move on. I'll always love you, but we have to go our separate ways, at least for now.

Maybe we can get together, later on."

"I hate your guts, Calvin!" Kendra screamed.

The weekend of Calvin's wedding, Mason drove Kendra to her mother's house. They had not spoken a word since the night he told her of Calvin's impending marriage. Kendra unloaded her books and clothes as her father sat in the car, glaring at her. She had decided to ask her mom if she could move back home, but she hadn't mentioned it to Mason. No sense burning her bridges before she knew if her mom would take her back. Her life was a real drag, she thought, fighting back tears. Theresa met her at the door.

"Honey!" she cried. "You've lost so much weight! You're not anorexic, are you? I read about anorexia in The Reader's Digest. What is going on?"

"Dad doesn't feed me, Mom," Kendra wept. "I'd eat more if he ever had any food in the apartment."

"Well, I'll mention it to him. He should be able to afford groceries since he doesn't pay child support while you are living with him. Good grief! Let's order a pizza right now. You are nothing but skin and bones!"

"Great," Kendra replied.

Kendra was angry with herself. She was hardly in the door and had already managed to put herself in a position where she would have to eat a greasy pizza. Mason would beat her again after Theresa inquired about why there was never any food in his apartment. She was a total screw up, Kendra thought, miserably. She hadn't done anything right for months, for years! Her whole life was one long, nasty joke.

"Kendra, I am so glad you are here this weekend!" Theresa said, as they ate pizza. "There is someone I'd like you to meet."

"Who?"

"A man I really like, honey. He lives in Lodestone. We are talking about marriage. I know this is sudden, but I hope you like him!"

"Geez, Mom, you sound like you want my approval, or something."

"Of course I do, Kendra," Theresa replied. She reached

across the table and covered Kendra's hand with hers. "You're the most important person in my life."

Kendra felt the love flow between them, just like when she was a little girl. Before they had turned away from each other and grown so far apart. Before Leo had molested her, leaving her feeling so dirty that she hated herself. Before she was involved with Calvin. Kendra stifled a sob. There was no point in getting emotional about an issue for which there was no possible remedy. She wanted to cling to her mother's hand.

"Cool," Kendra said.

Theresa was obviously relieved. Kendra felt as if she had given her mother a valuable gift. She hated herself for not being able to carry on a conversation with Theresa. God, Kendra thought, my mother is happy and I can't tell her I'm miserable. I can't eat or sleep. I can't think! I can't win!

Her mother's new man, Devon Fulton, arrived in time to share the last of the pizza. Kendra was grateful because she was able to push her last slice onto his plate, unobserved by Theresa. Devon seemed nice enough, good looking, dressed in Levi's, a starched white Western shirt and gray Stetson, the well-dressed West Texas man's courting uniform. Naturally, he wore black boots, polished to a mirror sheen. He called Theresa 'darlin'. He helped Kendra clear the table as Theresa went to respray her beehive hairdo.

"I'll be up front with you, Kendra," Devon said. "I hope you will be up front with me."

"About what?"

"Well, I want to marry your mother. I'll take good care of her. I'll take good care of you, too, if you need me. I'd like to know how you feel about me."

"I don't know you."

"I'm a simple man," Devon answered. "I've been married twice and I have three boys I don't see very often. I used to drink too much, but that's under control now. I own a big old house in Lodestone I've been fixing up most of my adult life. I also own some ranch land. I make custom saddles for a living, mostly, and sometimes when money is real tight, I refinish antique furniture and remodel old houses. I watch cartoons on Saturday mornings,

I like horses, dogs, windmills, sunsets and Willie Nelson. That's about it."

"Wow," Kendra commented. She really hated her parents most of the time, but Devon sounded O.K., for an old geezer. "It's cool, I guess. I just don't know how I feel about my parents getting married to other people."

"Reckon you've been hoping they would get back together, huh?"

"Something like that," Kendra lied.

"I know how it feels. My folks divorced when I was six years old. Seems like I spent my whole young life hoping they would remarry."

Kendra wondered if maybe, somewhere deep inside, she also wished her parents would remarry. Thinking about it made her want to cry.

"Did they remarry?" she asked.

"Naw," Devon replied. He winked at Kendra. "They didn't. They each married people I still don't like."

They were laughing as Theresa returned to the kitchen. Kendra saw her mother's expression relax.

"I didn't run him off, Mom," she said.

"Good," Theresa laughed. "We're going to see the remake of a movie we both saw when we were kids, Kendra. 'Invasion of the Body Snatchers', if we can get tickets. It's such a smash hit. You may ask Samantha over to spend the night, if you wish. We won't be late."

"Good night, Kendra," Devon said, politely.

"Good night, Mr. Fulton," Kendra responded. "Oh, I should warn you not to light a match near my mom's head. She's wearing enough hair spray to go up in flames."

"Thanks for the tip."

"Kendra!" Theresa gasped. "What a thing to say!"

Kendra called Samantha and invited her to spend the night. In minutes, Samantha crawled through the bedroom window, like old times. Kendra thought it was hilarious that her safety conscious mother had never, not once, discovered the unlocked screen and window.

"Don't be fooled, Kendra," Samantha said. "Devon will

turn out to be just like the others."

"What others?"

"Calvin, Mason, all men."

"You know that for sure, Sam?"

"I've had two stepfathers and I have an older brother. They all think with their dicks, I promise you."

They were lying on the floor in Kendra's room, eating microwave popcorn and drinking Pepsi. The girls had discovered a box of vaginal suppositories in Theresa's bathroom. Their plan was to experiment with insertion of the little wax triangles after the popcorn was devoured. It was not much in the way of entertainment, they agreed, but it was free. Best of all, it would drive Theresa nuts if she found out. Anyway, they might learn something in the process.

"I guess you are right about some men," Kendra admitted. "You did warn me that Calvin might mess up my life."

"They're all the same," Samantha said, wearily. "They lay out a good story about wanting to be your friend, then turn their backs on you. All men."

"Screw them," Kendra sighed. She read the instructions on the suppository box out loud, whooping along with Samantha at the really funny parts. "It tells us everything we need to know except what these little fuckers are actually used for."

"Freshness," Samantha said, solemnly. "Feminine freshness."

They finished the popcorn and eventually used half a dozen of the suppositories. The first two were total failures, mostly because the little plastic tongs were impossible to manipulate. They used their fingers for the second try, with little success because the wax melted. The third set they inserted into each others vaginal openings. They played around for a while, kissing and rubbing each other, finally bringing themselves to climax with perfume bottles from Kendra's dresser.

"How did you learn to do this?" Samantha asked, as they masturbated with the bottles.

"Calvin showed me. He said it was the way women can have sex and not worry about getting pregnant."

"So, I guess Calvin was good for something, after all."

"Yeah, I guess," Kendra agreed.

Kendra felt awful, as if some invisible beast was eating her insides. She had an image of Baby Jesus watching as she and Samantha writhed on the shag carpet, holding perfume bottles between their legs. She knew she shouldn't do anything that would shame the Baby Jesus. But, she thought, as she neared her climax, if Baby Jesus cared, he would have already puked from watching Leo and Calvin mess around with her. She really did not know the source of her unease, because she did not believe she was doing anything wrong. She and Samantha were just curious. Just being girls. But, she still felt just awful.

The girls gathered the pieces of foil suppository wrapping and flushed them down the toilet. They returned the box to Theresa's hiding place.

"I feel like shit," Kendra said. "I don't know why."

"Oh, I know," Samantha answered. "You need to have sex with someone your own age. Get over Calvin! I think he is warped, if you want to know the truth. He is way too old for you! Why don't you do it with a young guy?"

"Who?"

"My brother?"

"Shawn?"

"Yeah. Why not? He's home tonight, baby-sitting our little cousins. He's grounded for driving my mom's car without permission. I'll call and tell him we're on our way over."

Shawn was a hunk, Kendra thought, fifteen years old, with shoulder length blond hair he wore in a ponytail. He probably already had to shave because Kendra had seen underarm hair sticking out of his tee shirt. He smoked, too, right in his mom's living room. Kendra felt a charge of energy course through her veins, just thinking about Shawn. Maybe he wanted to date her or go steady and had asked Sammy to set them up. Maybe he would ask her to go skating next Saturday night. Maybe things were going to get better.

Half an hour later, Samantha and Kendra were at Samantha's house. Three small blond girls, the cousins, lay on their stomachs in front of a huge color television console. They did not seem to notice as Samantha led Kendra down the shadowy hallway to Shawn's room. She shoved Kendra inside and closed the door. Before her eyes adjusted to the darkness, Kendra sensed Shawn's presence. She gasped as he pushed her onto the bed. Immediately, she realized they were not about to share a romantic interlude.

Fear and panic washed over her in the instant it took Shawn to rip her jeans open. He pushed the denim down her left leg and the garment's awkward weight pulled her right foot to the edge of the bed. Shawn crushed his lips to hers and his tongue filled her mouth, gagging her. He was panting, growling like a dog. She caught his scent then, a pungent mix of stale cigarettes, perspiration and cheese crackers. With one hand, Shawn ripped her panties in half and pulled them off. He immediately drove his penis into her opening. It hurt, but it was bearable. She did not cry out.

Kendra did not fight Shawn. This is how a woman feels, she thought. This is how it feels when two people want the same thing. She sensed Samantha hovering in the hallway, listening, excited, fearful. The three cousins were still sprawled on the green carpet, like bugs in the grass, Kendra thought. She recalled their dirty little feet, toes dug into the rug. Their oblivion seemed unbearably poignant to Kendra. She hoped no one would ever molest them. She was lost in Shawn's dirty sheets, buried beneath his sweaty body as he thrust into her. His rhythm was familiar, but he was deep within her flesh, working towards something Leo and Calvin had never sought. Abruptly, Shawn grunted like a pig, panted for a few seconds, then rolled onto his back.

"Cig?" he gasped.

"Sure," Kendra answered.

They shared a Marlboro and Kendra was relieved when she did not cough like a goofus as the smoke hit her lungs. Thank goodness, she thought, she had practiced smoking in private.

"Beat it," Shawn said. He sat on the edge of the bed and zipped his jeans. "Uh, I just wanted, uh, well, you ain't half bad."

Kendra fumbled with her jeans, finally getting both legs right, then rushed from the room. Samantha met her in the hallway, then led her into the bathroom. They were silent as Kendra cleaned the blood and ooze from between her legs. Samantha found a panty shield in the cabinet and handed it to Kendra.

"Hurry!" Samantha hissed. "I just heard my mom's car in the driveway!"

The girls ran through the living room, leaping like greyhounds over the little cousins, reaching the front porch as Samantha's mother entered the kitchen. They ran to Kendra's house and were soaking in a bubble bath when Theresa returned from her date.

"Well, Kendra," Theresa asked, eagerly, "what do you think?"

"About what, Mom?" Kendra asked. Her heart was still racing. Theresa's voice might have been broadcasting from outer space.

"About Devon!"

"Oh." Kendra replied. "He's cool, Mom, really nice. I liked him."

"I'm so glad you did! I read an article about remarriage and I want you to know I would never marry anyone you didn't like. Oh, look at the time! You girls had better get to bed."

"Sure, Mom," Kendra agreed.

Long after Samantha fell asleep, Kendra cried into her pillows. Shawn had practically raped her. It was her own fault. He said she wasn't half bad. God! What had he expected? Hadn't he understood that she needed his help? That it was her first time? She felt stupid. She realized, with a sinking heart, that Shawn would probably tell everyone how ignorant she was. She felt worse than she had ever felt in her life. Lying in the darkness, she mentally listed all her failures. It seemed she had never done anything right. Everyone and everything had always been against her.

Her parents were divorced. Her mother wanted to marry Roy Rogers and move to Apple Valley. Calvin was married to a fat nurse with two brats, one of whom was riding Topsy. She would probably never see her dog again. Calvin had actually barbecued her expensive, beautiful Nubian goats for his wedding reception. Mason hated her and beat her and called her a bitch. She was making really bad grades at school. Her feet were too big, like a clown's, and everybody noticed them. Her teeth were crooked and she had never been to an orthodontist because Mason refused to spend the money to have them straightened. Lizard Boy was sick. Shawn had practically raped her.

"What's wrong, Kendra," Samantha asked, sleepily. "Are you hurt?"

"Fuck, I don't know what's wrong. Everything!"

Kendra recited her list of misery to Samantha. Her friend was silent for a moment.

"Look," Samantha said, solemnly, "there is something I should have said a long time ago. I think your problems are your mom's fault. I've thought so for ages, but I didn't want to hurt your feelings. If your mom was doing her job, she would have kept your life on track. My God, Kendra, she left you in Utah with your grandparents when she knew what they had always done to little girls! What kind of mother does *that*? She asked Calvin to spend time with you because Mason didn't know how to be a father. I can't believe she didn't have some clue about what kind of person Calvin is! She threw you to the dogs and expected you to handle it. Don't you see?"

Kendra pondered Samantha's ideas. They made sense. Theresa spent too much time reading magazine articles and too little time acting like a mom. She had, essentially, abandoned Kendra years ago.

"You're right," Kendra sighed. "My life is shit and it is mostly my mom's fault! I hate her!"

GUSSIE
1997

CHAPTER NINE

"This is middle C, Mama," Lorena said. "Just strike the key. It won't bite you!"

Gussie stood at the kitchen sink, staring out the window. Lorena's sweet voice still spoke to her across the years since her violent, untimely death. Lorena was her closest companion, her solace.

"My dearest heart," Gussie whispered. "My darling girl."

Gussie dried her breakfast dishes and placed them on the table. She liked to keep her favorite everyday dishes, the old ones from long ago, on the table so she would not have to reach into the cabinets. She covered them with a clean cloth. They would be gritty with dust, otherwise.

"I do hate the dust," Gussie muttered, "but it's part of life."

People might connect to the internet on their fancy computers and fly up into outer space, but in Tisquah, the dust would always blow. "Man ain't learned knowledge enough to keep the dust from blowing," Gussie said, knowingly. "No help for it."

Gussie smiled. No help for dust, no help for anything, when a body got right down to it. Things either happened or they didn't.

Like her birthday plans. She had carefully written down a list of things she wanted to do on her birthday, when her precious Theresa would drive to Tisquah and help her celebrate. Now, her plans were ruined because Theresa was coming a week early. A week! Wouldn't be spending the night, either, because she had to drive to visit Kendra. Gussie knew it was Theresa's duty to place her daughter's needs above her ancient grandmother's birthday wishes. Knowing it didn't keep it from hurting, a knife in the heart kind of hurt. Jealousy, Gussie felt in the knife's wound, green-eyed jealousy. She was jealous of her great-granddaughter, her flesh and blood.

"No help for it," Gussie sighed. "Just got to make the best of it and do the best we can. Kendra moves around too often, always trying to do too much."

She had worn her new dress all night, lying perfectly still on top of the quilted satin bedspread so the dress wouldn't wrinkle. Esperanza, her plump Mexican health aide, hadn't blinked an eyelid when Gussie told her to get the dress, a pretty blue challis, from the closet and help her put it on. Esperanza came five days a week, at 4:00 p.m., to prepare Gussie's supper, help her bathe, then get into bed.

"Messkin girl don't think I know she cooks enough food for four people, every day. Oh well, I guess I can afford it if she sneaks some food home every now and then. I keep forgetting that I'm rich! Old and rich, what a mix! I better go powder my tail before Theresa gets here."

Gussie walked slowly to the bathroom, pulled down her bloomers and carefully sat on the padded toilet seat.

"Fancy, smancy," she muttered as she squeezed out a few drops of urine. She wouldn't have to waste time going to the toilet after Theresa arrived. "Lawsy, when I think of all the Saturdays in my life when I had to scrub down privies after I cleaned the house, it gets me plumb mad. This indoor stuff is lots better!"

Gussie dusted herself with a cloud of fragrant bath powder. She adjusted her clothes and rearranged the powder box on the back of the toilet.

"Powder cost a king's ransom, down to the Rexall," she said. "Pretty gold box, pretty yellow puff, gold ribbon and butterflies on all of it. Cost too much! But, I guess it don't matter."

She didn't know when she had begun to realize that there was no help for life's little occurrences. Or when she had begun to understand that most things didn't matter. All her life, she had firmly believed that God was watching her every move, that God cared about what she did and what happened to her as a result of her actions. She had believed her life was important to God. The Bible said the hairs of her head were numbered, so she had believed it meant she was valuable. Lately, though, she had decided it just meant God had counted each hair and didn't give a hoot about what happened to the head upon which it grew. She had also decided all that talk about resting in the Lords' hands was bullshit.

"Bullshit," Gussie said, laughing, "and I ain't afraid to say it out loud! God don't even know who his people are, that's what I say! I care more for my soap operas than God cares for this world!"

She dearly loved the characters in her soap operas. She watched every afternoon on the big color television Summer had given her, no matter what. The home healthcare agency had once sent her an aide who came at 1:00 p.m. each day. Said one o'clock was the only time she could work Gussie into her schedule. Bossy young woman who often tried leading Gussie from room to room, grasping her arm as if she was a toddler instead of one of the oldest women in Texas. For sure, the oldest woman in West County. Hovered around, sneaking peeks at the TV, then had the nerve to try to discuss the stories with Gussie.

"Reckon I put a stop to that nonsense," Gussie recalled. "Got me an aide to come at four in the afternoon. Don't want to be bothered. I reckon I care more about Nick and Sharon Newman, bless their hearts, than God ever cared about me! Care about their little baby, Noah, and long-lost little Cassie, too, more than God ever cared for one of my babies! They better watch out for that sneaky Grace, I'm telling you, or they are gonna be in a heap of trouble!" Gussie pursed her thin lips in disapproval. The introduction of a blond villianess into the script of her favorite daytime drama, "The Young and the Restless", filled her heart with foreboding. "I never trusted a long-necked woman, and that Grace has a neck like a swan!"

Gussie went to the buffet and carefully removed two settings of Moss Rose china, then set them on either side of the table. Nice dishes, the china, she thought. Nice gift from Summer and Brendan the Christmas before they died in that airplane crash.

"They fell from the sky in a ball of flames! God didn't care, or He thought it couldn't be helped! Bullshit!"

Gussie returned to the buffet and opened a hardwood chest, from which she removed two place settings of beautiful silver. Oneida, the best, she thought, as she polished the heavy pieces with the corner of her apron. Summer never bought anything but the best. Always had good taste, even before Brenden got rich in the oil business. Lawsy, Gussie thought, then Summer had really spent the money. Had a pure-dee talent for spending! Houses, cars, furs, jewels, you name it, Summer bought it. But none of their money or possessions had kept that airplane in the air. Couldn't be helped.

"Ha," Gussie sighed, thinking of her second-favorite soap. "I worried more about Marlena being shut up in that secret room than God ever worried about Summer! If I was God, I'd fix Stephano Dimera's wagon, don't think I wouldn't! I wouldn't let him go on hurting people!"

Gussie considered whether she should climb on the kitchen stool and take down two glasses from the Danish crystal collection, also a gift from Summer. She decided not to risk it. Broken hips, that's what killed old women!

"Broken hearts kills 'em, too, if they don't watch out," she whispered.

Well, she thought, she was old. Old. One hundred and two, next Thursday! More years than Gussie could imagine, let alone realize she had actually lived. Must be some good years in there, somewhere, she thought. But none came to mind.

"Don't matter. I'm just drawing breath now. That's all the fun I need. Just outlasted all them bastards, and all their walnut hearts, too! Old buzzards!"

"Gussie?" Theresa's voice interrupted Gussie's reverie. "Are you awake?"

"Awake and kicking!" Gussie called. She rushed to the

front door and fumbled with the latch on the storm door. Finally, the new-fangled metal pieces slid together, and Gussie pushed the door open. "Come in here! You are a sight for sore eyes!"

"Happy birthday, Gussie," Theresa said.

Theresa was putting on too much weight, Gussie noted. Her legs were too short to carry those excess pounds. Gussie didn't mention it. Didn't matter. What mattered was having her precious girl, her Theresa, in the house for the day. Or for part of the day.

Theresa carried in a bakery cake decorated with pink roses. Beautiful! A big carton of French vanilla ice cream! A fancy gift bag full of wrapped packages, too! Goodies the likes of which Gussie had only imagined when she was a girl. Gussie wondered if she had ever told Theresa about her childhood, about learning the alphabet from McGuffey's Reader and about crying over Champ? About not loving anyone too much? Surely, she had. She just couldn't remember.

"Them pesky television people ain't coming again, I hope," Gussie said. "I didn't mind so much for my hundredth birthday, but it looks silly to have them here every year. Asking me the secret of living so long, like I done it 'a purpose.'"

"No, they won't be here today." Theresa said. "They may come next Thursday, on your actual birthday. They like interviewing you, Gussie. You've got a following."

"Better not come during my soaps," Gussie said. "I ain't missing my shows. Stephano Dimera is loose in Salem again!"

"What would you like to do today, Gussie? Theresa asked.

"Well, I made out this here list for Thursday, my real birthday," Gussie replied. "I doubt we'll have time to do it today, since you can't spend the night."

Theresa studied the list. Her dark brown hair, so luxurious in her youth, was getting thin on top, Gussie noted. At least, she did not appear to be using hair dye. Good thing, Gussie thought, because you could see the dye on her scalp, if she used it. Tacky. Theresa finished reading the list and looked into Gussie's eyes. She tilted her head and smiled.

"You look like your daddy," Gussie said.

"I know I do, Gussie," Theresa sighed. "What is this list about? I'll be glad to take you to these places, if you want to go, but this list doesn't make sense to me."

"Makes sense to me," Gussie said. "Drive me around, then maybe I'll explain when we come back here for cake and ice cream."

Theresa drove two blocks to the Rexall Drug store and parked in front.

"This place has run plumb to seed," Gussie observed. "Used to be a going concern."

"The drug store or the town?"

"Both, I reckon. The drug store was the center of life back in them days. Everybody shopped here. Greyhound bus stopped several times a day, right at the front door. Surely you remember it?"

"I remember, Gussie," Theresa replied, softly. "I remember Aunt Summer bringing me here when I was practically a baby and feeding me Coke floats at the soda fountain."

"Summer loved you, honey," Gussie said. "Loved you like her own. I kept a daily diary on Rexall calendars from this very store. I wrote something down every day, for years and years."

"Do you still have them?"

"I reckon I do, somewhere," Gussie replied. "They're likely turned to dust, just like me. My life will someday just blow away in the wind."

Theresa then crossed the intersection and slowly circled the block. The courthouse, once the pride of the county, sat like a wounded war veteran in the center of the shabby little farm town. The huge elm trees had died off years earlier, victims of age and exotic elm diseases, according to the West County News.

"If you was to ask me," Gussie told Theresa, "them trees died from all the tobacco spit that landed around their roots. Them old spit and whittle men pisined the best shade trees in Tisquah, sure as I'm sitting here! Nasty old vultures, watching and laughing at decent folks!"

Without the elms, the red brick courthouse looked like a fat lady caught without her clothes on, Gussie thought. She motioned as they drove near the east entrance, indicating Theresa should stop the car.

"What's so special about the courthouse?"

"I went through hell on earth in that building, for years," Gussie mused. She took off her wire-rimmed glasses and wiped her eyes with a pop-up tissue from the console. "I was finally redeemed, right down that hallway, right there!"

"In the courthouse? Don't you mean in the church?"

"No, ma'am," Gussie insisted. She stabbed the air with one delicate finger. "I mean right there, in that very building, down that marble hallway! Church, ha! Nothing big ever happened to me in church!"

"Gussie!" Theresa said. "I thought you loved church."

"Reckon I thought so, too," Gussie said. "I don't now."

Theresa was silent as she drove to the cemetery, the third location on Gussie's prepared list of places to visit. Gussie held onto the seatbelt and looked out the window, thinking. She wondered what her own life would have been like if she had ever owned such a magnificent automobile. Theresa's car was shaped like an egg, all pale blue, formed and fitted on the inside like a sea shell. Like it could give birth to another of its kind, it was that complete, Gussie thought, in awe. Gussie noticed a cell phone lying on the blue carpeted floor. She knew a cell phone when she saw one, from watching her soap operas. That evil Kristen used one every minute of the day, calling her stepfather, Stephano Dimera. What use did Theresa have for a cell phone? Whose voice did Theresa hear when she placed the strange little instrument to her ear?

"There's Michaul's grave," Theresa said, solemnly. "Do you want to get out of the car and walk over there?"

"Yep," Gussie replied, "I do. I'll reckon I'll have to lean on your arm."

At the grave, Gussie tried to pray for Michaul's soul. She wanted to give God another chance to make her feel something, even if it was not actual forgiveness. She and Theresa stood beside the crumbling concrete curb surrounding the burial plot as the wind whipped Gussie's dress above her knees. She realized she was not wearing stockings. Not that it mattered. She leaned forward after a few silent minutes and spat onto the slightly sunken earth. Beside her, Theresa gasped.

"I'll tell you later. Or, maybe I won't," Gussie said. She pointed to the narrow road on which Theresa's car sat like a wondrous new species of blue beetle. "That there path shone in the sun like it was paved with gold the day your granddaddy was buried," she said. "I was so tuckered out, it looked like the path to another world."

"What made it shine?"

"Yellow pine planks from the lumber yard," Gussie said. She was silent for several moments, remembering that day. "The ground was so muddy from melting snow they had to pave a path to the grave with new lumber. My little brothers come back after the burial and took them very planks. Built me a cow shed in the back yard."

"I wish I had paid more attention to your stories when I was a little girl," Theresa commented. "I want to know everything about you, now."

"It don't matter now," Gussie sighed. "You know what you know and you can live with it, I reckon. Stories are just stories. They don't matter a lick. Living! That's all that matters!"

"I'm not a little girl, Gussie," Theresa whispered. "Don't you think it's time you told me the truth?"

"Truth about what?" Gussie parried. She sensed a demand in Theresa's question. What was the proper response? Tell Theresa some truths no one had ever spoken? Or bury the secrets deeper than Michaul's emanciated body? "Truth ain't always easy to hear."

"Gussie, it's sometimes easier to hear than it is to speak."

The wind whistled through the headstones, moving the countless evergreen trees planted by generations of Tisquah's bereaved. Gussie sighed. This day in Tisquah's cemetary, she decided, the truth would be told.

"Your grandfather, Michaul," Gussie began, hesitantly, "he was the only man I ever loved. Truth is, I loved him too much. Too much. That's how it began. He used my love for him as a way to take all I loved away from me."

"What was that, Gussie? What did Michaul take?"

"He took my darling girl," Gussie said, softly, remembering the pink satin bow she'd tied into the little corpse's abundant auburn curls. "He kilt Lorena. Raped and kilt her. Had been doing things to her since we got married. She told me and I didn't believe her. She finally wrote it on her paper dolls. I was a plumb fool!"

"Gussie!" Theresa placed her hands on Gussie's frail shoulders and looked into her misty eyes. "Do you know that's what happened, for certain?"

"I know it. Michaul confessed it to me on his deathbed for fear he'd go to Hell."

"Oh, my God, Gussie! You never told anyone?"

"No. By the time I knew for certain, I had Leo and Summer to take care of and Michaul was dead. Who would I have told? You don't know what this town was like back then, Theresa. All them old vulture men sitting around the courthouse, laughing and passing judgement. You don't know!"

"Gussie," Theresa whispered, "did you know Leo molested me my whole life? Starting with the day he came home from the war?"

"I don't reckon I knowed it, for a fact," Gussie sighed. "But I prayed awful hard that God would kill that boy in the war. I guess there was so much killing going on Leo was able to slip through the cracks, 'cause he come back here all full of himself, same as always."

"Did Aunt Summer know any of this?"

"I took Summer to San Antone for an abortion when she was not quite twelve years old," Gussie said, shaking her head as if she was still amazed that she had done so. "Them doctors done away with the baby, because it was Leo's baby, forced on Summer. Me and that no-good Claude Abelard, we took care of it."

Gussie swayed and Theresa embraced her. "Let's get back in the car, Gussie," Theresa instructed. "This is too much for us both!"

"Reckon the weight of all them dirty old secrets is all that's held me to this earth for a mighty long time," Gussie observed. "I feel light as a feather now."

Theresa efficiently snapped the seat belt around Gussie's thin body, then walked around the car and stood staring at Michaul's grave. Her face was impassive, unreadable. She took a deep breath and slid into the driver's seat.

"What now, Gussie?" she whispered.

"Cake and ice cream."

They drove back to Gussie's house and ate cake and vanilla ice cream. They drank coffee, though Theresa didn't really care for it, because Gussie loved the taste of coffee from china cups.

"Coffee tastes better from china cups," she told Theresa.

"I love your china," Theresa replied.

"It's yours when I'm gone."

"Then I hope I don't get it for many more years," Theresa said. She was about to cry, Gussie realized.

"Come in the spare bedroom," Gussie said, briskly. "I'll give you some things to take home with you. You can give some to Kendra, too, when you want to. Where is she now? I forget!"

"She is in North Carolina, managing a beauty salon."

"I thought she was in California," Gussie said, "or was it Florida?"

"Both, at one time or another," Theresa said. "She took singing and acting lessons in California and operated a swimming club and spa in Florida. You know, I told you about the men she was involved with after her first marriage broke up."

"Seems like she lives in a soap opera. Does she have a cell phone?"

"Probably."

"Wonder who she calls?"

"I can't imagine. Her life is so different from mine. I don't think I know her now."

"Honey," Gussie replied, "don't none of us ever know our children."

"What did you want to give me?"

"This here picture of your daddy," Gussie said. She held two small, tarnished frames in one hand and wiped the dust from each with a corner of her gingham apron. "That there is your daddy, when he was starved to death on light bread. Phoebe, Miss Know-It-All is what I called her, took this here picture. Her and her sisters was all named after birds, you know. This here little picture stuck in the corner is your daddy in Honolulu on his twenty-second birthday. He looked just like your granddaddy, with that black hair and them blue eyes. This other one is your granddaddy Michaul, when he was in the Army, before I met him. I'm going to give you these pictures now."

"Won't you miss these pictures, Gussie?"

"I reckon I've just been keeping them until I told somebody what they done to my girls." Gussie looked into Theresa's eyes. "I never protected any of you girls, honey, and I don't know what to do about it now. You fix it with yourself any way you can, you hear me? Don't carry around all them filthy old secrets. Them Abelard men was pure evil!"

"Gussie," Theresa said, her voice breathless with concern, "are you all right?"

"I suppose so," Gussie replied. "Who can say how an old woman should feel at my age? Here, Theresa, here is a box of things I want you to take and share with Kendra."

"Well, I hate to leave you if you are not feeling well. Maybe we did too much walking today."

"Maybe it warn't the walking, but the talking," Gussie said. "Do you hear that singing?"

She heard Lorena's sweet, pure voice again, singing that old song her daddy loved so much. What was it called? 'Lorena', of course. In the distance, Gussie heard the sound of a piano, of scales played by phantom little hands, up and down, up and down. Far away, but clear as bells.

"Reckon you don't hear that pianer, either," she whispered. "Maybe we did too much of everything today. You go on, though, if you need to. I'm fine. Esperanza, that Messkin girl, will be here at four, after my soaps. Oh, did I tell you I learned a Messkin word? 'Esperanza' means 'hope'. Wonder how they learn all them words? I'm fine, Theresa, you go on."

"If you're sure," Theresa said. "I do need to hit the road. I'm driving to North Carolina from here, rather than back through Lodestone. Did I tell you Kendra bought a new townhouse and she wants me to help her put things away and do some decorating?"

"You told me."

"Well, I'm driving to Amarillo, then on Interstate 40 through the mountains to Raleigh. Cooler that way."

"Drive careful, now. You hear?" Gussie said, kissing Theresa's cheek. "Will you call me on your cell phone?"

"Sure, Gussie, if you want me to."

"I love you, Theresa," Gussie said. "I always feared for you, feared I didn't do right by you. Like Summer and Lorena. Lorena wrote notes asking strangers for help, did you know that? My own flesh and blood left a note under a peanut jar in a gas station. I didn't do right by Lorena, but what did I know back then? Guess it don't matter now. You call me up on your cell phone and say it's Stephano Dimera calling. Just for fun."

"All right, Gussie," Theresa said. "If you are sure you feel like staying alone until Esperanza gets here."

Gussie watched Theresa's little blue car as it traveled west on Third Street, then north to the Brownfield highway. A cloud of dust hung in its wake, finally sifting to the earth, like brown sugar. Gussie locked the storm door and waved.

"Be sure to call me on your cell phone," she whispered.

She went into the kitchen and tidied up, though Theresa had already washed and dried the china and silver. The birthday cake was in the refrigerator. No telling when she would eat the rest of it. The ice cream was in the freezer, already freezing too hard for Gussie to scoop. Esperanza would dish some up, later. That girl could dip cement from the sidewalk, Gussie thought, if it meant free food.

"I never could abide Messkins," Gussie said, "but maybe I just never knew any. Maybe Messkin rustlers didn't kill Champ. My daddy might have shot him. Lawsy, I ought to learn to like Messkins, because they are taking over Tisquah like it belongs to them. Esperanza's husband is a deputy sheriff. I think Messkins are as good as any white folks, better than some."

Gussie walked to the back door and peered out at her garden. Prettiest it had ever been, she thought, and without a smidgeon of effort on her part. The banker, Woolaver, was executor of Summer's will. He paid a boy to water Gussie's yard every day and mow it once a week. Woolaver had proposed marriage to her, way back in the 'thirties, but she had turned him down. She feared he might be ruined if people started talking about Summer's abortion. Funny how things worked out. Anyway, she thought, it looked like heaven out in the back yard, and she loved it.

"Wouldn't nobody believe now that I growed everything we ate for all them years out in that yard!" Gussie mused. "Hauled water in a bucket, I did, and spread cow manure with my own hands. Growed some fine vegetables and yarbs. But, this is better. This is just fine!"

She pushed open the storm door and stepped onto the little concrete porch. She walked slowly to the shade beside the old garage and inspected the pansy bed. It took a deep shade to grow pansies in late July, practically August. Pansies were a lady's choice, that's what Mr. Peters had told her. Bought her a pansy corsage the day they heard John Philip Sousa play in San Antonio. Took off his hat and bowed from the waist when he gave her the corsage, all tied with blue ribbon. He was a gentleman from Virginia. She had never learned where Virginia was though she had learned that it actually existed. Somewhere.

"This key is middle C, Mama," Lorena said. "Strike it. It won't bite you!"

That child had a way about her, Gussie thought, smiling. And a voice like an angel. Middle C twanged, again and again. She felt middle C in her guts, on and on, like it would never stop. Something else was ringing, too, like Stephano Dimera calling Kristen on a cell phone.

"Hello?" Gussie said, "hello? Here's a silly old woman locked up in the secret room. Hear that pianer? Hear that singing? That there is my darling girl! Whooee, am I ever tired! I got to take a nap. That's it!"

Gussie stooped to pluck a small weed from the flower bed and died, sprawled face down in the purple pansies.

Walnut Hearts

THERESA
1997

CHAPTER TEN

Theresa drove through the virtual ghost town that was once the heart of Tisquah, her childhood home. She could hardly bear looking at the vacant store fronts and cracked, deserted sidewalks. The bank, drug store and newspaper still occupied their original sites, but most other stores and offices had, long before, gone out of business. The white stucco clinic where she and her brothers had been delivered by Dr. Krohner was boarded up. The only new site was a county museum.

Gussie's shocking statements made an hour earlier continued to ring in Theresa's ears. She wondered if what her grandmother had said was true or the dramatic fantasies of a very old woman. Gussie had experienced more than a century of history, as had Tisquah. Maybe living out her life in what had become a ghost town had distorted Gussie's memories. Her history.

"It's all history, now," Theresa said, thinking only of Tisquah. Her grandmother's revelations didn't bear serious thought. Not yet, anyway. "It breaks my heart to see it like this! The state finally got around to building the divided highway and now the town is nearly dead."

She turned north on the freeway, toward Lubbock, twenty-eight miles away. It was impossible to make the journey without reminiscing about her senior year in high school, when she had returned to Tisquah. She had completed the first three years of grade school there and was among the very few children who ever moved away. After enduring many harrowing years with her parents, she had fled back to the Rice farm for her senior year. Her classmates regarded her as one of their own who had been brought back into the fold. Theresa had not revealed much about the intervening years, other than having attended five high schools in three different states. Mason, who had adored her in grade school, was captain of the football and basketball teams. She broke her engagement to a cowboy from New Mexico in order to date Mason.

"I was a fool for love," she said, shaking her head.

How many times had she heard Gussie say the same thing? What if Gussie had spoken truthfully at Michaul's grave? Must have been some heavy truth spoken or intended, or Gussie would not have spit on Michaul's grave. Theresa had never heard of anyone from Tisquah desecrating a grave. After citizens of Tisquah died, they were instantly elevated to sainthood. Those memories always made Theresa shiver. So many old dead people beneath Tisquah's fertile soil, all wrapped up in each other's history, were too depressing to think about.

She thought instead of her first date with Mason. They had felt very sophisticated, driving to Lubbock in his mother's two-toned Ford Fairlane. Mason wore new jeans and a starched, white Western shirt with his boots. According to her Grandmother Rice, Theresa had looked "too cute for words," dressed in a blue wool Bobbie Brooks sheath trimmed with a satin cummerbund and covered buttons.

"God," she whispered, "how I loved that dress!"

She still had her high school scrapbook, filled with trivia, including a page from <u>Seventeen</u> magazine advertising the dress, which she had instantly coveted. Hers was a size 4, she remembered, and almost too large.

"What I wouldn't give to be that size again," she said. She had sensed Gussie's assessment of her weight gain and was thankful the old lady had not mentioned it. "The last thing I wanted to hear today from Gussie was, 'Ain't you putting on weight?'"

On their first date, she and Mason ate at Furr's Cafeteria. She was appalled at Mason's lack of table manners, but willing to ignore that slight flaw because he was the captain of the football team. After the meal, they saw 'Cleopatra', starring Elizabeth Taylor and Richard Burton. Mason slept through most of the movie because he was exhausted from football practice and from working nights at the West County News. Months later, he slept through 'Exodus', claiming his fatigue was due to basketball practice.

As their courtship developed, Theresa learned that Mason managed to stay awake only at drive-in movies, where they had sufficient privacy to make out.

"Yeah, I remember the only thing that kept Mason alert," Theresa laughed. "By Christmas, we were screwing like minks!"

One rainy spring night they attended a drive-in screening of 'Psycho', parked among the curved rows of cars and pickup trucks. In the famous shower scene, when Janet Leigh screamed, at least one occupant of every car on the parking lot screamed along with the actress. In their car, the screaming was done by Mason.

"Why," Theresa wondered, "why, oh why didn't I see then how immature Mason was? God, he cried every Sunday night when Lassie saved Timmy on television. Did I ever wonder when he might grow up? Noooo. I was too excited about going steady with the football captain to worry about his IQ. I didn't even realize he was dangerous when he tried to run over me with his mother's car! He was jealous because I spent the night with Deanna and her brother was home from college. He would have run me down if I hadn't jumped into the shrubbery. I felt sorry for him because he was so upset! God, I was a fool!"

Seven miles north of Tisquah, Theresa passed the road to the old Rice farm. Her mother had been born in the old house and Theresa's happiest memories were of the tree-shaded yard and all her imaginary adventures there. It was her only safe haven. After her grandmother's death, the farm was sold, the house and outbuildings razed, the trees cut and the pond filled in. Long-staple cotton grew in regimented rows over the site, cultivated with massive new air-conditioned farm equipment. For more than thirty years Theresa had refused to turn down that road, refused to so much as look in its direction whenever she drove past.

"In my heart and mind, it is still the same," Theresa said, tearfully, "and I won't ever believe it is gone! It was my only real home! It's not gone!"

She wiped her eyes and groped in the console for a French lesson tape, popped it into the cassette player and shut the door on her Tisquah memories. The authoritative voice of the French instructor began the lesson.

"Comment allez-vous?"

"Comment allez-vous?" Theresa mimicked.

She continued the lesson as she traversed the Lubbock loop and she was approaching Amarillo by the time both sides of the tape had played. She stopped for gas and a burger, then turned east on Interstate 40. She felt fine, full of energy and anticipation for the journey. Except for her eyes. They had felt swollen, watery, as if she was allergic to something, since she wiped away the tears as she passed the Rice farm road.

"Maybe my new hand lotion irritated my eyes," she said. "Oh, well, I'm sure it will clear up. I think I'll try to make Oklahoma City before I call it a day."

The little Ford Escort ate the road as country music blared over the radio. Theresa loved the isolation and the sense of adventure she experienced driving in the dark, listening to a car radio.

All her life, when riding in automobiles, she had imagined she was flying through outer space, learning of earth by gleaning information from its radio broadcasts. She and her brothers had played the radio game throughout their childhood, trapped in automobiles Leo would never pay for, traveling to towns Varina feared and hated.

It was still fun, she thought, pretending to wonder about the mysterious civilization inhabiting the little blue planet orbiting in the darkness. What clues were now revealed in lyrics sung by Garth Brooks and Trisha Yearwood? Or the stand-up dialogs of Jeff Foxworthy? Or the radio D.J. who talked about Reba McIntire as if he showered with her on a daily basis? What did it mean, when talk-show callers continued voicing their outrage over the Murrah Building bombing, long after Timothy McVeigh was convicted of killing one hundred sixty-eight people and sentenced to death?

At El Reno, west of Oklahoma City, Theresa felt weary enough to pull off the Interstate and rent a room. The long summer twilight was nearly gone when she removed her overnight bag. She plugged the cell phone into its charger, then closed here eyes in exasperation.

"Oh, no, Gussie!" Theresa cried. "I forgot to call you!"

She felt guilty, knowing the old lady had waited patiently for the imaginary call from her favorite soap opera villain. It was far too late to call by the time she remembered her promise, for Esperanza tucked Gussie into bed by 7:00 p.m., without fail.

"I'll call in the morning, Gussie, I promise. I'll say it's Stephano Dimera calling. I promise!"

The next morning, when Theresa called Gussie, there was no answer.

"She must be outside, supervising the yard boy," Theresa said. "I'll call later, before her soap operas start. She'll be inside by then."

She ate breakfast in El Reno at a family style restaurant, seated at an indoor picnic table with seven other diners. Her table mates discussed, endlessly, tirelessly, obsessively, one subject only - the Murrah Building bombing. They traded passionate opinions regarding Timothy McVeigh's punishment, methods to prevent future terrorist acts, and the state of the nation in general. Conspiracy theories flew across the table and no one indicated the slightest disbelief.

"Where were you when you first heard about the bombing?" a woman asked Theresa. "What were you doing on April 19, 1995?"

"I was in Cary, North Carolina," Theresa recalled, "just leaving my daughter's house. I heard the first announcement as I closed the door. Later, at the bank, the teller who was waiting on me received a phone call. 'Oh, no,' she cried, 'some Arabs bombed a day care center in Oklahoma City!' It was very strange for a few moments. Everyone in the bank stood still and looked at each other. It was as if we suddenly realized we were all standing on a time bomb. It was sickening!"

"Sick, that's what it was," the woman agreed, nodding her

head. "This is not the world we imagined, is it?"

"No," Theresa whispered, "but it never was, for me. Not after my daddy came home from the war."

Theresa drove to Oklahoma City, deciding at the last moment to leave the Interstate and visit the Murrah Building memorial. She parked and joined a line of people who silently filed through the temporary shelter housing the Murrah Memorial exhibit. As she scanned the displays of newspaper articles detailing Timothy McVeigh's trial and sentence, a woman in line behind her sobbed.

"Death is too good for McVeigh!" she cried. "He ought to be blowed up one hundred and sixty-eight times! The bastard! Oh, my God!"

Theresa felt the unknown woman's anguish pierce her own heart. She was stunned, for she had often said the same thing about Leo. Analyzing Leo's actions always left Theresa feeling helpless and furious because Leo always won. Everyone around him lost.

"Death was too good for Leo," she whispered, wishing Leo was still alive, so she could kill him with her bare hands. How could anyone, Leo Abelard or Timothy McVeigh, casually inflict so much physical and emotional devastation on other human beings? "The bastards!" Theresa hissed. She turned and ran out of the shelter, past chain link fencing adorned with toys, flags and teddy bears placed there by anonymous mourners. "Everyone is still horrified about the bombing," she whispered. "No one knows how to deal with what happened to innocent people, other than keep the story alive for the public!"

Theresa sat in the Ford until she regained her composure. She rummaged in her cosmetic bag, found a plastic bottle of Visine, and squeezed drops into her swollen eyes. The tears finally stopped.

She drove through Oklahoma, Arkansas and most of Tennessee, stopping only for gas and fast food, until fatigue forced her to leave the Interstate at Cookeville, Tennessee. She checked into a motel, carried her bag up a flight of metal stairs and immediately ran the bath tub full of tepid water. A hot bath would feel better, she thought, but Southern girls knew hot baths made them glow. Glow was the Southern euphemism for perspire. Or sweat. A most impolite condition, according to her Grandmother Rice.

Half an hour later, cool, relaxed and dressed in clean shorts and cotton shirt, Theresa walked across the brightly lit parking lot to a restaurant. A real one, not a fast food joint. She had just been seated when the hostess, a slender girl sporting black nail polish, returned to the table. Theresa noticed her name tag, which said,

WELCOME
My Name Is TAMARA

"'Scuse me, uh, ma'am?" the girl drawled. "Uh, ummm, we are just all full-up tonight, and um, I'm supposed to ask if you might be willing to share your table? I, myself, well I wouldn't ask, but my boss says I have to? You'll get free dessert if you say yes!"

Theresa looked into the girl's face and saw herself, forty years earlier:

Working in a roadside hamburger joint near Grants, New Mexico, on Route 66, two years before Bobby Troup wrote about getting your kicks along that fabled highway. She was intimidated by her boss, too, though he was only seventeen pimply years old. Theresa was fifteen, and it was her first real job. Twenty-five cents an hour plus tips and meals. The cafe was little more than a wooden box with a metal awning, set twenty-five feet from Route 66. The view in every direction was of ancient lava flows, dominated by towering Mt. Taylor in the distance. Summer was hot as hell.

Cows ate the air conditioning tubing on a regular basis. Two fat prostitutes got into a fist fight one Saturday night in the minuscule dining room, vying for the attentions of an elderly old man who did not speak a word of English. A caravan of Jehovah's Witnesses bound from California to the east coast drank an entire keg of fermented lemonade. Every Wednesday night, after the conclusion of wrestling matches in Grants, pickup trucks full of Acoma Indians circled the little restaurant, each driver ordering ice cream cones for all his passengers, sometimes as many as fifteen per truck. Theresa's hands ached for hours after scooping the endless dips of rock-hard ice cream. Mountain cones, the Acomas called them.

A courteous young man named Paul, a railroad employee, asked Theresa to marry him, though they never went on a date. He had grown up in the Baptist orphanage in Portales, he said, dreaming of a wife just like her. Theresa declined, saying she could not abandon her little brothers to her parents' violent care.

On pay days, Theresa crossed the road to the general store, cashed her pay check and purchased money orders she immediately enclosed in Montgomery Wards or Sears and Roebuck mail orders. It was the only way to prevent Leo from confiscating her meager earnings. The bastard, Theresa thought.

"Sure," Theresa said, realizing the young hostess was about to burst into tears. Tamara looked so relieved, Theresa thought the girl might faint. "Why not?"

Theresa swallowed a lump in her throat and wiped her eyes with the napkin.

"Girl," she told herself, "you better get a grip. You've been on an emotional roller-coaster since you left Gussie's house! All these old memories are just upsetting you! You know the past is poison, so don't think about it! Stay in the here and now!"

Tamara hurried away and promptly returned, followed by a man wearing rumpled khaki shorts and a denim shirt. Theresa averted her eyes as Tamara handed him a menu and scurried away, chewing the black polish from one thumb nail.

"You are very kind person," the man said. "Thank you for sharing your table. My stomach has been making sounds for many miles!"

His voice was pleasantly accented. Theresa met his gaze, aware that her heart was beating faster. She smiled, but before she could reply, the waitress arrived to take their orders. Theresa stared out the window, watching a steady river of cars turn off the Interstate and flow along the street in front of the restaurant.

"This little town never had it so good, before the Interstate," her table companion said. "It is good location for restaurants and motels."

"Yes, it must be a dream come true for local people,"

Theresa replied. "You have a lovely accent," she said. "Where are you from?"

"Thank you. I am born in Turkey. I leave fifteen years ago. First go to Sweden, then New York, then Salt Lake City. Now, I go to Research Triangle Park, North Carolina. Do you know it?"

"Yes. Actually, I worked for several companies in the Park. My daughter lives in Cary, North Carolina, near Raleigh. Cary has grown by leaps and bounds since the Park opened."

"Ah, Cary!" her companion beamed. "I am to stay there with my friend until I find job! Is nice place?"

"Very nice," Theresa replied. Their orders arrived, along with two complimentary desserts. "Cary is like no other area on earth, or so they say. Many engineers from all over the world, and their families, live there. There is a very high standard of living."

"My friend is engineer for Borg-Tech. Do you know of it?"

"No, I don't. There are many research and development firms in Research Triangle Park. It is very interesting."

"Yes! I plan to enroll in North Carolina State University and complete my degree, like my friend. I grow tired of working as lab tech, making so little money. I am rude tonight, must be so much driving, people are crazy on Interstate! My name is Siyit Yigistoy. Sometimes my English is funny. I am sorry!"

"Theresa Fulton. I am learning to speak French, so I know how hard it is to think in a second language. You speak very well. I mean that!"

Siyit Yigistoy smiled and reached across the table, offering his hand. He was an amazingly handsome man, Theresa thought. His teeth were so white they looked back-lit. His eyes were beautiful, as dark and glistening as obsidian. She found herself wanting to run her hands through his curly black hair, especially where it nestled just behind his ears. Theresa could hardly believe the emotions and sensations coursing through her body as their hands touched. She had not felt so alive since the first few months of her marriage to Devon.

"Good!" Siyit replied. "Tireza, good Turkish name. I

hope not to offend you. You seem like nice person. Nice American lady."

"Thank you."

"I was married to American woman, five years. In Salt Lake City. Nice woman, but her mother ran our lives. I had no peace, always hear, 'Mama need this,' and 'Mama doesn't like.' Bad days, always. Wife says Mama doesn't want us to have baby because I am Turk. I say I can't help that! My goodness! Then my wife says divorce, was mistake to marry foreign man. I feel glad. Sorry thing for man to say about losing wife, but true."

Siyit's full, soft laughter sent chills down Theresa's spine. She could not recall a more pleasant sensation. She had forgotten just how much she enjoyed the company of a truly masculine, nice man.

"I know," she replied. "When my first husband said 'divorce', I was glad, too."

"You have other husband?"

"Yes, I did. He died a year ago."

"A good man, your last husband?"

"Sometimes," Theresa sighed. "Other times, not so good." She shrugged and Siyit nodded, indicating he understood perfectly.

Their checks arrived and they rose to leave the restaurant. Siyit insisted on paying Theresa's check, ignoring her protests.

"Please," he insisted, "it is my pleasure."

"There is no need," Theresa replied, firmly. "We don't even know each other."

"We almost know each other," Siyit said, patiently. "Walk down this street and talk with me for ten minutes only. Then we will know each other. You will see. Ten minutes!"

"You could be a serial murderer," Theresa laughed. "It would be foolish for me to walk with you. Dangerous."

"Ah," Siyit laughed. "You have heard of the famous Turk serial murderer hiding in Tennessee, strong Turkish accent and drives old Volvo? Dangerous Turk in Clarksburg?"

"Cookeville," Theresa replied, smiling.

"Is same, I think. Walk with me, you nice American woman. Tireza."

In spite of her caution, Theresa took Siyit Yigistoy's arm and strolled down the bustling street. They chatted like old friends, and though she was alert to any sign of weirdness about Siyit, she grew more and more comfortable. She studied his reflection in store windows and noticed other women looking at him, as well. He was incredibly handsome. Theresa wondered why he had not found work as a professional model or actor. She was certain he had great screen presence.

"You are look at me in glass," he commented. "Think I am danger?"

"No, not at all. I think you are handsome."

"Ah, all Turk men handsome. Really handsome Turk men have large nose. My mother was very sad because my nose too small. My father think I not his son, not with so small nose."

"Really?"

"Just joke, Tireza. My mother and my father love each other very much. Love all their children."

"How many children?"

"Five. Four girl, one boy, me."

"How long since you saw them?"

"Fifteen years. Big disgrace on my head in Turkey because I run away from Army, leave my first wife. My father was put in prison for months, my mother and sisters in danger."

"What? You ran away? Why?"

"All young Turk men must join Army then. I young, not wise, and marry my officer's daughter, very spoiled girl. When we have no understanding, she tell her father and he break my knees. So, while I am in hospital for knee surgery, another injured soldier and I sneak away. No money, no clothes, scared we would be caught and sent back to Turkey. Finally, beg rides to Sweden."

"Why Sweden?"

"Sweden had organization to help other Turks escape army. Give us money and warm clothes and teach us English. Then help us get political refugee status, send us to safe countries. I say want go to South Africa, but I end up in America. In New York, they think I am Puerto Rican, in Salt Lake City they think I am French. Hope North Carolina is better, hope to meet other Turks.

"I think that will happen in Cary," Theresa said, thoughtfully. "The area is like the United Nations."

They retraced their steps and returned to the restaurant.

"Well, thanks for dinner," she said. "Good luck in Cary."

"You, too, Tireza," Siyit replied. Their eyes met and Theresa felt giddy. "Wait," Siyit exclaimed, "I give you my friend's phone number. If you want, call me and show me around Cary. It would be my pleasure, Tireza."

He wrote on a blank page from a small note book, then handed it to Theresa. Before she touched the paper, she saw Siyit's handwriting. Strong. Beautiful. Exotic.

"I would enjoy that," she said. She hesitated, then explained, "I don't know my daughter's new number. She is moving into a townhouse this week. Her number is always unlisted because her ex-husband stalks her. She works at Beautifica Salon, in the largest mall in Cary. Her name is Kendra. I'll tell her you might come in for a haircut. Oh, dear, I am babbling, aren't I? If I don't call you next week, you can see Kendra and find out if I am still in Cary. If you wish."

"Thank you, Tireza," Siyit said, formally. "I wish."

Theresa walked across the parking lot as Siyit entered his battered brown Volvo and drove away. Before she covered half the distance, she saw the Volvo pull into the motel driveway. As she reached the metal stairway to the second level, Siyit's car parked beside her Escort. Siyit obviously had not seen her, and Theresa contemplated running up the stairs and hiding in her room. She hesitated a moment too long. Siyit looked up, directly into Theresa's eyes. She felt his gaze on her face, his energy actually stinging her flesh like tiny darts.

"This is too silly," she whispered. "Get a grip!"

She waved and walked to the curb.

"I guess we are neighbors for the night," she said. They stared into each other's eyes for what seemed an eternity. "I'm in 210. If you want to visit later, come on over."

"I must bathe, first," Siyit replied. "I will bring Cokes and Bud Light if you have ice. Deal?"

"Diet Cokes," Theresa said, "and I will have ice.

Theresa entered her room thinking what an idiot she was making of herself. Siyit was, easily, fifteen years her junior, a complete stranger. He was from Turkey, for God's sake! She must be losing her mind! As she berated herself for her foolish actions, she hurried to the courtesy room and filled the plastic ice bucket. It was as if her brain and her body were no longer connected.

"Oh, no, no!" she cried, glancing at her watch. "It's too late to call Gussie!"

At that moment, Theresa wanted nothing more than the sound of her grandmother's voice, ancient and mysterious, telling Theresa she was Gussie's honey bunch, Gussie's heart of hearts. Gussie's darling girl.

Theresa returned to her room and locked the door. She sat on the bed and breathed deeply, forcing herself to calm down and think.

"What in the world are you doing?" she asked herself. "This is exactly the kind of dangerous stunt Kendra would pull! Don't be a fool!"

It was settled, she thought. She would not answer the door when Siyit arrived. If he arrived. Siyit might also be reconsidering their "date". It was foolish and risky to get involved with strangers along the highway, male or female. Theresa filled a plastic glass with ice water and drank deeply. The water tasted of a river, murky and earthy. The phone rang, startling her. She quickly answered it.

"Tireza?" Siyit's husky voice asked. "I am now buy Diet Coke, but do not know if you wish caffeine or caffeine free. What is your choice?"

"With caffeine," Theresa answered, automatically.

"Good! I also bring poppy seed rolls, for snack. You like?"

"I like."

Theresa replaced the receiver and shook her head. What was wrong with her? Why had she not told Siyit she had reconsidered, that he should not come to her room? She was unable to answer her own questions.

Siyit arrived minutes later, carrying six-packs of cola and

beer, as well as a bakery sack of fragrant rolls. They faced each other across the room's wobbly round table and discussed the cars driving slowly along Cookeville's main drag. They conversed easily, like old friends. Theresa felt a peaceful, comforting sense of trust growing between herself and Siyit. She smiled.

"You feel relaxed, now?" Siyit inquired, softly. "Are no longer scared of me?"

"I'm just scared of doing something stupid. Of trusting someone who will hurt me or rob me. Or assume anything."

"Me, as well," Siyit replied. "I tell you truth, Tireza. I have no sex since separate from my wife. Eight months, now, little longer. I am afraid of getting AIDS or other terrible disease. I go dancing sometimes in Salt Lake City, dance with many women, never ask them to go home with me."

"Never?"

"Never." Siyit lit a cigarette, illuminating his chiseled features. Ageless, Theresa thought, and beautiful. A beautiful man. "My life is this way, you see, if I fall ill, there is no one to care, no one to help me, impossible for my family to come here. I must keep myself healthy, must not tempt fate. I have maybe used up God's patience, taking chances with my own safety. Even these," Siyit gestured with his cigarette, "must go. I will stop smoking very soon. Is my responsibility to keep well."

"I know that feeling," Theresa replied.

"You have family, yes?"

"Yes. But no one who would take care of me."

"We have different life, different places, but now feel same," Siyit mused. "Interesting, I think. Tireza, will you make sex with me tonight?"

"Yes," Theresa answered. "I will."

Siyit walked to the television set, turned it on and selected the Country Western Music Channel. He listened for a moment, then crossed the room and offered Theresa his hand. She rose and tentatively stepped into Siyit's arms. Wordlessly, he led her in a slow dance, taking small steps because their tennis shoes clung to the carpeted floor. Three songs later, they stood beside the bed, holding hands and kissing.

Theresa had always imagined such kisses. Always, she had hoped to experience a predestined connection between her lips and those of an incredibly gentle, sexy man. A kiss that was meant to be, she thought. Lovely.

They removed their clothing, slowly, savoring each moment. In bed, Siyit was absolutely masterful, fully aware of her needs and able to satisfy them before he took his own pleasure. Theresa had never before been with a man who took such joy in every facet of the act.

"That is good," he whispered, "is excellent!"

They rested, eating the poppy seed rolls with gusto, washing them down with beer and cola. The flickering television screen lit the room like moonlight reflected on crystal water.

"I want to do it again," Siyit said. "Is O.K.?"

"Oh, yes," Theresa whispered. "It's very O.K.!"

"Turn back, baby," Siyit whispered, "turn back." He clasped Theresa's hips and rolled her over. "Trust me, Tireza."

She felt his muscular legs wrap around her calves, silky, curled hair alive against her flesh. Siyit entered her vagina from the rear, quickly, smoothly, hard and hot, so that she gasped with pleasure. His right arm slipped beneath her waist and he cupped her labia. His left hand gently kneaded her heavy breasts. Theresa was unable to move against Siyit's deep thrusts, though she ached to push against his hand as he grasped her mound.

"Feel me inside," Siyit whispered, "feel me, baby." Siyit kissed her neck and shoulders as he moved slowly, deliberately, pausing between thrusts until she was on the verge of crying out. Theresa felt their sweat mingle, soaking their tense bodies. She breathed in the wonderfully masculine, clean scent of Siyit's flesh. "Now, baby, now!" Siyit whispered.

Siyit clasped Theresa's waist with both hands, driving deep into her. So exotic. So unlike any other sexual experience she'd known. Pleasure erupted inside Theresa in ways she had never experienced, traveling down each leg, convulsing her entire body. She cried out as Siyit moaned and tightened his grip on her slippery body. They lay without moving for long moments as their pulse slowed. They slept then, still entwined, bathed in the blue, electronic glow of the television screen. The last sound

Theresa heard was Leann Rimes, singing 'Unchained Melody.'

"Oh, my love, my darling, I've hungered for your kiss a long, lonely time."

Theresa had first heard 'Unchained Melody', the theme song of a black and white, B-grade movie screened in a quonset-hut theater in downtown Chama, New Mexico. She was twelve years old that cool summer night, sitting on rough log benches with her family and most of Chama's citizens. The song became her anthem throughout her anguished teen years, as she unceasingly hoped for true love, against all odds, in the face of absolute depravity.

When Theresa awoke, she was instantly aware of Siyit's measured breath against her neck. He still held her wrapped in his arms and legs, though his penis had slipped out of her vagina. She lay in his sleeping embrace, contemplating how marvelous it would be to feel him harden and enter her yet again. She was awake for what seemed an eternity, memorizing his body, his scent, his essence. Tears blurred her vision as she realized what she must do.

Siyit did not stir as she slipped from the bed and walked to the bathroom. She closed the door and quickly showered, then dressed in the darkness. She blindly located her toilet articles, silently fitted them into the overnight bag, then zipped it shut. She left the motel room, pulling the door closed behind her. Siyit slept on, sated, exhausted. A beautiful Turk man. Alone in the double bed. Alone in Cookeville, Tennessee.

Theresa pulled onto Interstate 40 and drove without thinking for an hour. Impulsively, she exited on Highway 441, headed for Pigeon Forge and the Great Smoky Mountains National Forest. She reached Pigeon Forge before dawn, drove down the main street lined with hundreds of motels separated only by chain link fencing. She parked outside a massive outlet mall, then rested her head on the steering wheel. Her cheeks were wet with tears.

"Stupid!" she said aloud. "Are you trying to get yourself killed? A handsome man says you feel the same about sex and you think it's safe to go to bed with him? You're losing it, girl!"

As the sun rose, huge and red, thousands of vacationing

families emerged from countless motels. Querulous children
pushed each other towards cars and vans as their parents
struggled with tons of luggage. One after the other, the vehicles
streamed onto the street, heading for one of the many area theme
parks. Theresa's reverie was interrupted by a security guard
tapping on her window.

"Ma'am, this parking lot is closed until eight o'clock,
a.m.."

"Thanks," Theresa replied, wiping her eyes. "I'm just
waiting to check into a motel."

It was a lie, but she didn't want to sound suspect. She
could not have explained to the guard why she was sitting on the
empty parking lot because she didn't know. Smiling at her
reflection in the guard's sunglasses, she drove away as his head
swiveled in her direction. Theresa glanced at his image in her
rearview mirror.

"He looks like a giant insect dressed in a cop's uniform,"
she giggled. "Maybe I'm the only one of my species left on
earth."

Theresa drove for three blocks, then turned into a motel
entrance, suddenly aware that the best thing she could do was get
some sleep. She could straighten out her thoughts later.

"Fortunately, we just had a cancellation," the desk clerk
remarked. "We are jam-booked this time of year." Theresa filled
out the registration card and paid the clerk an outrageous amount
of money. "You can't check in yet," the clerk remarked. "The
room won't be ready until at least ten o'clock. But, if you want
to, you may leave your car here until then."

Theresa parked the Ford and walked to a crowded
restaurant. She stood in line, gave her order to a teenager dressed
in a Loch Ness Monster costume, then sipped orange juice and
ate a sausage biscuit while she stared out the window. She wept
as she ate, but it didn't seem important.

"That lady is crying, Mommy!" a small child said,
pointing at Theresa.

"It's just allergies," Theresa told the child's mother. "I left
my prescription at home."

How easily I can lie, she thought. Where does that come

from? Of course she knew if such a trait was genetic then she possessed the DNA to be the best liar on the planet. Leo had never told the truth, not in his whole, miserable life. "Don't lie to me!" Varina had often shouted to Theresa. "Don't you try to take the Abelard way out of things! You'll go to hell for lying!" Well, Theresa thought, leaving the restaurant, I was already there. Biblical hell wasn't as terrifying as life with Leo and Varina. Satan could have taken lessons from them.

Theresa hailed a brightly painted trolley and rode to the outlet mall, where she wandered from shop to shop for hours. She purchased an umbrella for Kendra, who habitually lost hers as well as those she borrowed from Theresa. For herself, she purchased a cassette tape of 'Unchained Melody.' At ten o'clock, she left the mall and walked through the blistering heat to her motel. She carried in her bag, showered, fell into bed and slept until dawn.

Before opening her eyes, she realized every muscle in her body ached. She felt feverish. The pillow was soaked with tears. How could she cry in her sleep, she wondered. But she knew. She knew. In her sleep, she was always closer to the pain she had buried in her heart for so many years. The tears flowed from a river of emotional agony, the result of catastrophes that occurred far from the Great Smoky Mountains. This she knew, instinctively, just as she knew beyond a doubt that Gussie's revelations at the cemetary had fractured her last, vulnerable defense against the reality of her childhood. The thought that the accumulated pain of her lifetime might escape the darkest corners of her psyche was terrifying. No human could withstand the onslaught, she thought. All that pain and fear, concealed and unacknowledged for more than fifty years, would surely destroy her world. But Gussie had carried her secrets for even longer, for dark years, alone on the Texas prarie.

Theresa packed her things and drove to a convenience store where she purchased cookies, Diet Cokes, a Styrofoam cooler and ice. She filled the gas tank, then drove out of Pigeon Forge, past giant signs advertising Dollywood. She joined a river of traffic flowing through the ancient Smoky Mountains, stopping occasionally at scenic overlooks, drinking in the mystical beauty of the mist-shrouded valleys.

Theresa realized she was detouring far from her planned route on Interstate 40, but she wanted to avoid any possibility of encountering Siyit before she reached Cary. She had always been stupid in her choice of men and she would absolutely avoid letting any man get close enough to destroy another minute of her life. She drove to Charlotte then straight through to Cary, munching cookies and sipping cans of cola, stopping only for gas.

She arrived in Cary at nine o'clock and drove directly to the massive mall where Kendra worked. She parked beside her daughter's car, a pale gold Saturn. Theresa ran a brush through her hair, then entered the mall. She heard Kendra's voice as she neared Beautifica, the upscale salon Kendra managed. Theresa's heart leapt with joy.

"Kendra!" she called. "Honey, I'm here!"

Kendra turned to face Theresa, her mouth set in a thin line, her eyes hard, accusatory. She looked like a younger, better groomed Varina. Chills ran down Theresa's spine.

"Kendra?"

"Where in the hell have you been?" Kendra shouted. Theresa was aware of heads turning in their direction. An instant hush swept through Beautifica. "Are you trying to make me crazy? Do you know the highway patrol in six states has been looking for you for the past three days?"

"What?" Theresa gasped. "Why?"

"Gussie is dead, that's why!" Kendra exclaimed. "Like I don't have enough to deal with, running this fucking place and moving into a new house without any help from anyone? Like it's my place to deal with your ancient relatives? Oh sure, look stupid! I'm the one who has been handling your problems, and I told you a long time ago not to dump on me!"

"Gussie's dead?" Theresa whispered.

She staggered to an empty chair and sat down, gasping. Oh, Gussie, she thought. I should have phoned. I should have said it was Stephano Dimera calling. I promised. I am so sorry!

"Don't expect sympathy from me," Kendra said. She pushed a box of tissues into Theresa's hands. "Go wait in the car until I close up. You can follow me home."

Theresa nodded. She wiped her face and walked out of Beautifica. She felt the curious stares of the customers and other hairdressers, watching her departure reflected in the enormous, beveled mirrors.

Kendra did not glance in her direction.

Jackie Glover

CHAPTER ELEVEN

Kendra led the way through a bewildering maze of winding streets to her recently purchased townhouse, located in Cary's newest prestige neighborhood, 'Hampton Court.' Theresa parked her car in a visitor's parking area, collected her bags and followed a curved, beautifully landscaped walkway past rows of elegant, Tudor style homes.

"This place looks like the sound stage for a Jane Austin movie," Theresa whispered. "I wouldn't be surprised to meet Emma Thompson out walking her dog, pining away for Hugh Grant."

No scrap of rubbish nor stray lawn chair marred the uniformly clipped yards. All the cars in the discretely numbered spaces were new, or at least less than three years old.

"Not a pickup truck or a horse trailer anywhere in sight," Theresa whispered. "You're not in Texas anymore, Dorothy!" She always savored the exact moments when she first felt the vast differences between Lodestone, Texas and Cary, North Carolina. "This place is too perfect," she said, as she neared Kendra's open front door. "There is absolutely no sign of life. The home owners' association fees must be out of sight!"

Inside Kendra's house, Theresa walked through stacks of moving boxes and clutter throughout the elegant foyer, living room and dining area. She paused at the foot of the stairs and looked up. Kendra leaned over the railing, her auburn hair reflecting the soft, indirect lighting above the stairwell. She looked like a princess.

"Your room is a fucking mess," Kendra sighed, "but so is the whole house. I have, honest to God, spent the past few days trying to find you, instead of getting settled in."

"I'm sure the room is fine, Kendra," Theresa replied. "I'll unpack and get the house squared away tomorrow."

"Thanks, Mom," Kendra said, softly. She met Theresa at the top of the stairs and wrapped her in her arms. "I'm sorry I was such a bitch at the shop. It's just that I've been so worried about you and not knowing where you were. That old asshole banker in Tisquah somehow managed to get my phone number at work and he has called, I swear to God, every half hour! I was already so pressured, you know, from buying this house and making all the moving arrangements. I'm on the nicotine patches, because I started smoking again during all this moving nightmare! I think I'm expecting a lot from myself. Beautifica, alone, is enough to make me crazy..."

"Kendra," Theresa interrupted, "it's all right. I didn't like you talking to me in public like that, but I do understand your feelings."

"Thanks, Mom," Kendra said, again, as she released Theresa and led her to a small bedroom. "Did you drive out on Interstate 20? If you did, the cops never spotted you!"

"No. I decided to go through Tisquah and take Gussie a birthday cake, just in case I wasn't back in Texas by her birthday next Thursday. Then I just drove up to Amarillo and got on I-40. I didn't call because I knew you were so busy."

"Well, I realize you had no way of knowing we were looking for you. Mom, they found Gussie in the pansy bed, dead as a door nail, the day you were there. They didn't think she suffered. Probably died in an instant."

"Thank goodness," Theresa wept. "I should have stayed with her when I realized how tired she was. Her health aide was due in less than an hour, and Gussie said she would be fine until then, so I just went on my way."

"Esperanza?" Kendra asked. "She's the one who found her. It wouldn't have mattered if you were there, or not, Mom. Don't beat yourself up over it. Look, put your stuff in the bedroom. Let's order a pizza and talk. We have to decide what to do about Gussie."

"What about her?"

"They won't bury her without your permission, according to the banker. It's in her will."

"Oh, no!" Theresa cried.

Theresa showered as Kendra ordered a pizza. She slipped into her robe and unpacked her things. At the bottom of her overnight bag she found the faded old pictures of Leo and Michaul. The tarnished frame holding her father's only baby picture, as well as the dark little portrait made on his twenty-second birthday, had always sat on Gussie's old Singer sewing machine beside the picture of Michaul in his World War I era uniform. Theresa had never imagined looking at them in any other location, especially not in a Tudor townhouse in Cary, North Carolina.

"I always considered Gussie my guardian," Theresa whispered. "I always thought she knew what Leo was really like, and that she would protect me. What a childish notion! I'll bet Leo made her life a living hell, too. No one escaped Leo's destruction."

Her tears fell on the photographs before she realized she was crying. She dropped the frames into the empty suitcase, dried her eyes and went downstairs.

"I really am sorry for treating you so rudely, Mommy," Kendra said, as Theresa entered the kitchen. "I have to be a bitch on wheels at the shop. You have no idea! That attitude seeps into my personal life. That's probably why I can't stay married!"

The pizza arrived and they cleared away a corner of the glass-topped dining table.

"Look," Kendra said, "I have to go straight to bed because I have an eighteen hour day tomorrow. Shop meeting, color classes, then a full day on the floor. Then I have to transmit my weekly report to the main office so they can do payroll. Just sleep in, if you want to. Call that old guy in Tisquah before he has a cow. I swear, I tried to persuade him to go ahead and bury Gussie, but he wouldn't budge. His number is on the desk. If you can find the desk in all this mess."

Theresa was unable to fall asleep until after dawn. She

lay awake all night in the air conditioned darkness, thinking of Gussie and Leo. She was filled with remorse for accepting the status quo concerning her grandmother's knowledge of Leo's behavior. She felt that Gussie and Leo were probably the two major pieces in the puzzle of her life and she had no clue as to how or where they fit.

At dawn, she crept downstairs and sat outside on the miniature patio. The sun, an orange globe emerging from the pine forest, looked sullen and menacing, shrouded through the opaque fog. No sounds drifted across the humid, motionless air. She might as well have been the first, or last, human on the planet. She thought of Gussie and Leo. And of Varina.

Kendra had reminded Theresa of Varina the previous evening. The quick temper, the angry body movements, the cold, judgmental eyes were so like Varina's that Theresa had, briefly, felt the same fear she had always associated with her mother.

"I was actually terrified of my own mother," she said, softly. "I feared her more than I feared Leo. What does that mean? Damn! I thought I had worked all this mess out in counseling! Several times! But just now, it feels as if I never understood a thing about my childhood! How can that be?"

Theresa slipped back into Kendra's frigid little house and curled up on the forest-green leather sofa. She slept deeply for two hours, dreamlessly, unconnected to any events of her life, past or present. Her first thoughts, upon waking, were of food.

She located Kendra's toaster, plugged it in and placed both halves of a gourmet blueberry swirl bagel in the wide slots. As she depressed the toaster knob, she heard Kendra scream. Theresa ran up the stairs and found Kendra in the master bathroom, standing in a pool of blood. A bath towel was clumsily wound around her left arm.

"Shit!" Kendra screamed. "The fucking shower door shattered and cut my arm all to hell! I'm going to sue that bastard contractor! I swear I will! I didn't pay a fortune for a piece of crap! Oh, no, not this girl!"

"Kendra, let me look at it," Theresa demanded. She carefully unwrapped the towel, gasping when she saw the extent of the wound. A long sliver of glass was embedded in Kendra's upper arm, shining like fool's gold through the flowing blood. "Kendra, we have to get you to an emergency room! Now!"

"Fuck!"

"Stand still, Kendra," Theresa ordered, "while I find you something to wear. Here, step into these jogging pants and we will put your robe on your good arm."

"Mommy, I'm scared!"

"No need to be scared, honey," Theresa said, "but we do need to get it sewed up. What hospital does your HMO designate?"

"Cary Med," Kendra whispered. "Take Chatham past the new mall. Mommy, I feel like I'm going to faint!"

"Breathe," Theresa said. She ran to the bedrooms, grabbed their purses, then returned to the bathroom. "Here, Kendra, I'll run this comb through your hair. I know you're worried about going out like this. You might meet an eligible doctor."

"Ha, ha," Kendra laughed, gamely. "Thanks, Mommy, but what I'm really worried about is taking my car. I don't want to bleed on the upholstery. It's brand new!"

"We'll take my car," Theresa laughed, as she guided her daughter down the stairs. "Stay calm!"

The streets were, as usual, teeming with new Japanese and compact American automobiles, carefully following each other at intervals of three car lengths. Cary had an ordinance prohibiting tailgating, which some people felt only created more complications on the streets, especially during rush hours. Theresa pulled into the traffic flow and followed the manicured parkway. The driver of every car on the road honked their horns at what sounded like musical intervals. Everyone was so polite. Why wouldn't they be, when their lives were so obviously perfect? Theresa smiled, in spite of her concern for Kendra. Her concentration faltered and she failed to make the proper lane change in time to exit on Chatam Street.

"Well, great!" Kendra cried. "You missed the turn! What now?"

"I'll get on the beltline and go to Wake Medical, in Raleigh," Theresa replied. "Considering the traffic, it will be quicker than backtracking to Cary Med. They didn't design this town for anyone who needs to drive around the block! It'll be fine."

"Great! Drive me twenty miles to the county hospital! Maybe we will meet some nice street people and hookers! I chose to live in Cary so I don't have to mix with lowlife, Mom. Way to go!"

"It's a good hospital, Kendra. Remember when Devon had chest pains and we took him there? He received excellent treatment."

"Two things, Mom," Kendra whined. "I'm not having chest pains! And my insurance won't pay!"

"I'll pay, in that case, Kendra. That's not the most important issue at the moment!"

Kendra was immediately ushered into a treatment room. Theresa was interviewed by a bored black woman who completed Kendra's admission data at an ancient computer terminal. Theresa then found an empty seat in the public waiting area. She wanted a cup of hot tea, but did not wish to walk to the opposite side of Wake Medical Center dressed in her blood-splattered bathrobe and house slippers. She resigned herself to a long wait and observed the other people in the waiting area. Theresa recalled that Wake Medical still accepted indigent patients. By a wide margin, Wake County had voted to continue treating the indigent, bucking the national trend in hospital management practices. She had always felt safe in the hospital, probably because Devon had received world-class care there after his first heart attack.

A doctor approached Theresa. He was young, Theresa noted, dark, muscular, unshaven and very, very exhausted. She read his name tag.

WAKE MEDICAL TRAUMA CENTER
Antonio V. Cavaleri, M.D.
Resident

"Your daughter is fine," he said. "The x-rays of her wound showed two large pieces of glass, which we removed. We want to keep an eye on her for the next four hours or so, to avoid complications."

"Complications? Like what?"

"There is a slight possibility of additional bleeding," Dr. Cavaleri explained, "because of the position of the wound. She should be able to go home around two o'clock. She, uh, she wants you to call her workplace and tell them what happened."

"She's bossing everyone around in there, isn't she?" Theresa asked, smiling.

"She is doing well," the young doctor replied, his dark eyes twinkling. "She is in no real danger."

"Well, I will go home and get dressed," Theresa said. "Please tell Kendra I will be back by noon."

At Kendra's townhouse, Theresa immediately called Beautifica. The young receptionist put her on hold three times, disconnecting her twice in the process. Theresa finally delivered the news of Kendra's injury, then dialed the banker in Tisquah, Mr. Woolaver.

"Theresa," he said, kindly, "how good to hear your voice. Your grandmother's will expressly states that you, and only you, are to make her funeral arrangements."

"Fine," Theresa replied. She knew, at that moment, that Gussie had intended to explain why she felt compelled to spit on Michaul's grave. She did not wish to be buried beside him, that much was obvious. "Have the services at First Baptist Church. I'm sure they have someone who will sing 'The Old Rugged Cross' and 'Precious Memories.' Buy a gray casket, lined with pink satin. Dress her in a gray silk dress and place a pink rosebud in her hands. No jewelry, just a new lace scarf at the neckline of that dress. Buy an expensive plot in the nicest cemetery in Lubbock. Order a headstone carved with roses. Oh, and will you look into having her daughter's body moved and buried beside her?"

"Summer O'Merea's body?" the old man inquired.

"No. Gussie had another daughter, ten years older than my father. Her name was Lorena Peters. She is buried somewhere near Eagle Pass, Texas.

"Certainly," Mr. Woolaver replied. "I have a contact in

that area who can facilitate this matter." Theresa sensed he was slowly writing Lorena's name on a notepad. Precise as an ancient, unfathomable machine, he seemed. "Will you be flying home for the services? Money is no problem, as I am authorized to advance any amount you might need. From the estate, of course."

"No. I won't be there. My daughter injured her arm this morning. I don't want to leave her. Go ahead without me."

"I see." The old man's voice was cultured. Theresa vaguely recalled his face, bland, secretive, innocent as a nun. She could not imagine why Gussie had placed such trust in him. "All will be done according to your wishes. Please call me, if you think of anything more."

"Thank you. Did you know my grandmother well?"

"I once proposed marriage," Mr. Woolaver replied, thoughtfully, "but I don't think I knew her very well."

"I know what you mean," Theresa whispered. "I don't think I knew her, at all."

Theresa climbed the stairs, cleaned the glass and blood from Kendra's bathroom, then showered in the guest bath. At some point, she began weeping, soundlessly, and was unable to staunch the flow of tears. They fell in streams as she drove to the hospital, like salty little rivers, finally cascading onto her blouse.

The trauma room area was crammed with patients waiting for minor emergency treatment. Theresa found an unoccupied folding chair in the hallway. Across the hall a slender black woman, wearing purple Spandex shorts and an minuscule orange halter top, sat in a hospital wheelchair. One of her impossibly slender wrists was handcuffed to the chair. A uniformed Raleigh police officer, who looked like he would rather be falling from an airplane without a parachute than waiting, idly, for the woman's turn in the trauma room, stood guard.

"You tell this ratfucker to let me out of this goddam hospital WHEELCHAIR!" the woman screamed, as Theresa sat down. "I ain't no nut case ! I ain't no criminal! He be violating my silvel rights! Tell him, why don't you? You a good person, I can see that. He listen to you. Tell him!"

"Simmer down, you," the cop growled. He ignored the

woman's venomous stare. She squirmed in the chair like a circus contortionist, attempting to slip free of the handcuffs. "Be still, or I'll have them put you in a straight jacket."

"Well, make my day, you fuck! Ha! Think I be scared of a straight jacket? Get yourself a clue, you fuck! My whole life be a straight jacket! I can do straight jacket from now on, yeah, I can! You don't know shit!"

"Stop yelling," the cop said, patiently. "You aren't in much trouble. Sit still. Let the doctor examine you and you will probably get off without going back to a cell."

"Thank you very much, you ratfucking self," the woman muttered. She drew her bare feet into the chair, then somersaulted onto the floor, still handcuffed. She sat on the tile floor as the cop glared at her. She looked directly into Theresa's face. "You, nice lady, you, yeah, you. You knows what I mean, I can see it in you eyes. You knows what my life be all about!"

Theresa politely averted her eyes, then leaned her head back until it rested on the wall. The woman's voice washed over her, like hot water, until Theresa was floating in her words. Adrift. In great peril.

"Yeah, you knows. Well, I be want to ast you something. I wants to ast where this fucker be when I a little girl and my granddaddy feel me up ever time I gets close to him? Huh? Where the cops be back then, that's what I be needing to know! I ast you! Listen, I pays my taxes, I pays cops' catfuck salary, that the truff! Where the cops when my mama's doped-up friends be touching me, be kissing me, tongue kisses, too, be holding my little hands on theyselfs? Huh? Huh?"

"Pipe down," the cop ordered. "The only thing you are charged with is walking nude on a convenience store parking lot. Just shut up and nothing is going to happen to you."

"Yeah. I shut up! I can do that, standing on my head! I motherfucking shut up! That be what they ALL say! SHUT UP! Well, this be the day I don't shut up. This be the day, honey. I be laughing at cops, 'cause you don't be no place around, not when I needed you! Nuh, uh! How you think that feel, be a little girl, holding onto her baby doll, while her own granddaddy stick his dirty fingers you-knows-where? Huh?"

Theresa realized she was still crying, that something was wrong with her and that she needed help. It didn't feel like a hormone imbalance, or road fatigue, or chronic depression, conditions with which she had frequently dealt. It felt, well, it felt as if the protective dam she had constructed throughout her life was cracking open. It felt like the preview of a devastating flood. As if the secrets and pain she had so carefully stored behind the dam were, at long last, roiling out of her control. She rested her cheek against the cool tile of the corridor wall, listening to the black woman's ranting.

"The bastard! That what I be saying, all these years. Baaaastaaaard! I too young to write it all down when he be doing it to me, but it be the Lord's truff! That what he done to me!"

Theresa remembered keeping a crude record of each time Leo molested her. Little crayon marks on the inside cover of her first coloring book, one mark for each time he touched her under her panties. She imagined hurting Leo in return for each mark she carefully drew inside the book, 'Little Red Riding Hood and the Big, Bad Wolf,' a fairy tale with significant meaning to her. Bad Wolf Leo.

"What are these marks?" Varina had demanded. Varina wore the green and white striped maternity dress that was practically her uniform throughout Theresa's childhood. Trimmed in wide, eyelet lace. "Don't you turn your eyes away from me when I'm talking to you! What do these marks mean?"

"Every time Daddy puts his tongue in my tee-tee," Theresa whispered, miserably. Leo had told her that Varina would not love her if she knew about their activities. Theresa held onto hope, though, for she adored Varina and imagined her mother felt the same devotion. "Every time Daddy touches me here," she whispered, pointing between her legs.

Four years old, she was, a veteran of a year and a half of Leo's attentions. The coloring book and crayons were birthday gifts, along with sidewalk roller skates. Theresa's most prized possession was the skate key, which she wore on a shoe lace tied around her neck. After her birthday cake, Leo had rolled her in a snow drift, finally landing on top of her, pinning her until Varina picked her way across the little yard and appeared at his shoulder.

Varina's pale face, her hateful voice. Scary. Leo's blue, blue eyes blazing into Theresa's face with an intensity she had understood, clearly, as predatory. Big Bad Wolf!

"Leo! Get up out of that snow, right now! The neighbors are watching! Theresa, go to the kitchen and take off those wet boots. It's your nap time!"

Her father rolled away from Theresa, releasing her, and she ran like the wind, boots crunching the snow. Outside, Theresa heard Varina's angry voice, threatening, fearful, as Leo pelted his pregnant wife with snowballs. Leo drove away in the new chocolate brown Chevrolet he loved as if it were a living thing. He did not come home for supper.

Varina put Theresa to bed on the sofa, then let her listen to The Judy Canova show on the radio. Miss Canova ended her broadcast with Theresa's favorite song:
'Go to sleepy, little baa-by,
Go to sleepy, little baa-by.
When you wake, we'll patty, patty-cake,
Ride the pretty little po-oo-ny!'

Later, in the dark, fearsome hours, someone knocked at the front door, which they never used because opening it allowed the cold, north wind entrance to the tiny apartment. Men called Leo's name, "Sgt. Leo Abelard!" Varina, wrapped in her chenille robe, opened the door, spoke to the men, in urgent whispers.

"Your daddy got drunk and threw a snowball at a pregnant woman, hit her in the stomach. She's in the infirmary..." Varina sobbed, sitting on the end of the sofa bed. Her face crumpled and broke Theresa's heart. It felt like the end of the world whenever Varina cried. Which was often. "The M.P.s are looking for Leo!"

Theresa, speechless, curious about the chaos, lay among all her dolls and stuffed toys. She clutched Suda, the doll her Grandfather Rice had given her on her second birthday. Suda's painted blue eyes stared into the darkness. Suda saw everything, but she was unable to speak through her perfect, rosebud lips. Pink, they were. Perfect.

Suda, whom Theresa clutched in terror whenever Leo crawled, slowly, silently, across the living room floor to the sofa bed, knew everything. She knew all about Leo, about his creeping through the darkness, reaching beneath the covers. Touching Theresa with his hard, relentless hands, kneading, probing. Sliding his head beneath the quilts, between the sheets. Licking Theresa. Sucking.

"Daddy's bad," Theresa told Varina. "Suda sees what he does."

"Don't you ever say that again, young lady!" Varina shouted. "You show respect for your daddy!"

The 'Little Red Riding Hood and the Big Bad Wolf' coloring book vanished. Varina only shrugged when Theresa asked where it might be. Suda knew, of course, but Suda couldn't speak.

"Thaaaaat be right," the black woman moaned, "thaaaaat the truff. I telling the truff. I beg my mama stop my own brother from coming to my bed. My mama, she say I gots to let him do anything he want to do. My own mama say, he the only one gots a job, say she gots to have his paycheck. That what she always say. Do she say I important? Hell, no. She don't say that, 'cause I ain't nothing but a nappy-headed girl chile! Good huntin' dog be worth lots more than a nappy-headed girl chile! Truff!"

"Be quiet?" the cop begged, wearily.

"You be quiet," the woman replied. "I done being quiet. I just wants to take off my own clothes, walk down you pissy street and tell the world I just as important as everbody else! Fack! What you really care I smoke a little dope? You don't care back then, I in my mama's bafroom, three times, motherfucker! Three times, I gets a baby out all by my ownself in the bafroom. I cuts the cord, I wraps the baby, I takes it to my mama. What you care now that I had to get three babies off my own brother, 'cause my mama need his paycheck? All retarded, they all retarded, but what you care? I alone. Always was. Always will be. Will be! You hear that? WILL BE!"

"Mom?" Kendra's voice barely penetrated the din of voices ringing in Theresa's ears.

The black woman handcuffed to the wheelchair yelled at the cop. Varina's countless rules and threats pounded in Theresa's head; so many things she shouldn't do, so many horrible consequences. Leo's sly whisperings, accompanied by his blue-eyed winks, implied that everything he did was a great joke. But his jokes hurt Theresa! She was hurt! Hurt! Still! Nobody had ever cared, or stopped the hurt, or explained it to her. Why hadn't they cared about her? The bastards!

"Mom, what's wrong? Somebody get a doctor! Something has happened to my mother! She's sick!"

"Yeah, she be sick," the black woman agreed, knowingly. "She be know all about sick, that right. She need a little dope, that fix her up!"

"Shut up!" the cop ordered.

"Shut up you ownself," she replied. "I be seeing that look ever time I see my black face in the mirror. That white bitch be needing help she ain't never got before! 'Cause nobody ever cared!"

"Get a doctor!" Kendra screamed. "NOW! Mommy, talk to me, tell me what's wrong!"

Theresa wanted to answer, wanted to explain what was happening to her, but it was just too hard to speak.

All her energy was focused on holding the image of her sofa bed, her dolls, her memories of life on a post-war Army Air Corps base before the Army discharged Leo from its active-reserve ranks. Theresa saw everything in incredible detail, her flannel pajamas, the little white drop-leaf table in the tiny kitchen, the cheap bedspread hanging across a doorless closet.

Like a miracle, her childhood unreeled before her eyes complete with sound and scent. Her baby brother, asleep in his crib, his cloth diaper reeking of ammonia and talc. Leo's winter fatigue jacket and wet boots drying in front of the gas space heater. The bookshelf containing her plastic doll-house furniture, gaudy pink and black, glowing against the white paint. Outside, across the sidewalk in the next row of converted troop barracks housing G.I.s and their little families, two dogs barked. They were like demons, those dogs, waiting beneath flimsy wood steps until Theresa ventured outside, then snaking across the yards, snarling, snapping at her heels as she ran, screaming, to the safety of her back porch. And at night, Leo stalked her. From her father, she had no place of refuge.

"Has she experienced any trauma recently?" Dr. Cavaleri asked Kendra.

"I don't have the slightest idea!" Kendra cried. "She was missing for several days, on her way here from Texas. She didn't say anything about being traumatized. Do something, will you? I can't stand that expression in her eyes! What is she looking at?"

Theresa saw herself, four years old, roller-skating down the sidewalk, holding a fruit jar in each arm. Falling. Bleeding. Mommy!

"We can run some tests to rule out physical causes for her condition," the doctor explained. "My gut instinct is that she is in emotional trouble."

"Meaning what?"

"She may need psychiatric treatment."

"Oh, that's just fucking great!" Kendra replied. "Great! I've just moved into a new house, I've just had twenty-seven stitches in my arm, I'm missing work. Now, my mother has gone bonkers! Why do these things always happen to me?"

"I think you should sign admission papers for your mother, then go home before your pain medication wears off," Dr. Cavaleri suggested. "Call a cab. Look, I realize you won't be able to come back for a while to see about your mother. Just leave all your phone numbers and I promise we will stay in touch. You should also sign those other papers, now, just in case."

"What other papers?"

"Committment papers. We can only keep her here for twenty-four hours without formal committal. She will probably need to be transferred to Dorothea Dix. I may be speaking too soon, but my best bet is that after we run all our tests, the only thing we can do is transfer her to Dix."

"The nut house?" Kendra shrieked. "Oh, this is fucking wonderful! My mother drives out here to help me get settled, she gets lost on the way, my great-grandmother dies and no one but my mom can handle the funeral, I'm cut all to hell, I need a fresh nicotine patch, and my mother decides to go nuts! Great! Why does this always happen to me?"

"You need to stay calm," the doctor said. "I know this is

stressful for you, but it won't help if you get upset. The admissions office will send the papers over here for your signature. Call me tomorrow and I can tell you the results of our tests." He paused, fished a tattered business card from a bulging pocket of his lab jacket and handed it to Kendra. "This is my beeper number. You can use it whenever you want."

Kendra accepted the card and carefully placed it in her purse. She leaned near Theresa's face and stared into her glazed eyes. Theresa saw her daughter with great clarity, as if Kendra was standing behind a giant magnifying glass. She had, in fact, heard the conversation between Kendra and Dr. Cavaleri. She was simply unable to respond, fearing that she would lose the bright images of her four-year-old self.

It was like a trip back in time. Her toys, her clothing, her red tricycle, her plump baby brother, were all displayed on an invisible screen in the center of her vision. The images slowly rolled down, like a television screen needing horizontal adjustment. The pictures were not in chronological order, but they were perfect in detail. She saw Varina's swollen belly where her second baby brother was growing from a seed watered in a special way by Leo, according to her mother's explanation.

Theresa saw the ominous paddle as Leo whittled it from a pine board, then drilled holes spaced evenly down its hideous length. He carved a handle, with finger grips he wrapped in adhesive tape. Like the principal's paddle at Tisquah High School, he explained, before Theresa understood it was constructed expressly for use on her tender young bottom. Applied, without mercy, on those days when Varina told Leo how very naughty Theresa was. Theresa had experienced pain before, but nothing prepared her for the agony of the paddle. Lying across Varina's lap, held motionless by Varina's strong, lovely hands as Leo struck her naked backside with the paddle, time after bone-jolting time. Torture! Each day, Theresa pretended to sleep late, to lessen the hours of another day in which she might incur Varina's wrath, leading to an evening in the closet, lying on her mother's lap as her father beat her.

She understood Dr. Cavaleri's advice. It truly would be for the best if Kendra signed commitment papers. Dorothea Dix, the nut house, as Kendra called it, was a massive psychiatric hospital in an area known as West Raleigh. Just off Western Avenue. Named in honor of a Civil War era pioneer in mental health awareness, Dorothea Dix. Theresa had read that much on the back of a post card.

Theresa stared straight ahead and held her body as rigid as possible, fearing the slightest move would dislodge the images. They were magical, awesome.

"You are ugly!" Varina screamed. She snatched the hair brush from Theresa's small hand and threw it onto the bed. "Don't you ever let me catch you primping in front of a mirror, ever again! Do you understand?" Outside the flimsy barracks walls, a fierce wind blew thick clouds of dust across the flat, Texas panhandle. The wind whistled eerily around the corners, howling like an invisible animal. In the back yard, block-long sections of wire clotheslines zinged like giant piano strings. Theresa had been inside for two days, unable to play outdoors because of the storm. She had tried, unsuccessfully, to stay out of Varina's way. "Vanity will send you straight to hell! It is a sin! You are not pretty! You are the ugliest little girl in the world! Go to bed! Take your nap! Leave me alone! Ugly, stupid, stinking, clumsy little girl! Your daddy is going to paddle you tonight, missy!"

In a hospital room, attended by the unshaven, handsome Dr. Cavaleri, Theresa was aware that she did not feel the needles enter her flesh. No pain. How wonderful. Maybe she could patent the process, when she finished watching her personal memories glide past her eyes.

How small that barracks apartment was! All those young military families, housed in hastily converted troop quarters, all so happy as they began their peacetime existence. Every woman was pregnant, it seemed, and carrying babies in their arms. Every child old enough to walk played incessant war games. Even the girls. Each child favored the area of the planet in which their fathers had seen combat. Theresa was a Pacific Theater child, automatically bonded to others whose fathers had followed General McArthur across the tropical islands. All Theresa's playmates knew their father's duty stations on the day of their births. Leo had been on Christmas Island the day she was born. He was tanned, playing with his pet monkey. Gathering white coral as a keepsake of her birth day. These facts she shared with her peers. Other facts she swallowed, storing them in a secret place in her chest, around which she constructed an enormous wall.

"Look at this picture, Theresa," Varina often demanded, showing Theresa a page torn from a magazine. "Look at the white picket fence and the roses and the grass. That's Bermuda grass, it has to be ordered special. See the white walls and the blue roof? See the little birds? See that little window, that's a dormer window, that's where your room will be."

Varina called Theresa inside late one afternoon to listen to a new song, 'Just Molly and Me and Baby Makes Three.' Theresa counted on her fingers, calculating that the baby in her mother's tummy would make five, but she didn't mention the inconsistency to Varina. Perhaps Varina planned to get rid of Theresa and her baby brother before the new baby arrived. If that was the case, Theresa hoped she would be given to someone back home in Tisquah.

Theresa lived for the monthly visits to Tisquah, when they packed a suitcase and Leo drove them the two hundred miles between the air base and their real home. She sometimes thought she might die from homesickness, that hollow feeling in her chest that vanished only when she saw Tisquah, proudly sitting on the plains, dominated by the square profile of Tisquah High School.

'On dear Tisquah's western border,
Staunch against the sky,
Hail to thee, our alma mater,
and to days gone by!'

Theresa loved singing the school song when she first spotted the skyline, night or day. She had no idea what the strange words meant, but she memorized them in the firm belief that she would, one day, graduate from Tisquah High School. Like Varina and Uncle Brendan. Unlike Leo and Aunt Summer.

Leo never touched Theresa when they were in Tisquah, though he sometimes crept through the old Rice farm house in the darkness. If Varina roused at all, Leo slithered into the bathroom and relieved himself, his strong, yellow urine splashing into the toilet.

Leo took Atabrine tablets, quinine, because he had been exposed to malaria during all those years in the tropics. Theresa once touched her tongue to one of the innocuous little yellow tablets. The vile taste made her fall to the floor and roll, as if her dress was on fire. After that, whenever Leo placed his wriggling tongue inside her tee-tee, Theresa imagined his mouth passed the Atabrine to her private parts. She could smell it. She thought everyone could. The taste and scent of Atabrine lurked between her legs, inside her cotton panties. That's why Varina called her a stinking little girl.

Three days after Kendra's accident, an ambulance carried Theresa to Dorothea Dix. Lying on the stretcher as the vehicle drove around the beltline, Theresa marveled that the city of Raleigh could not be seen, nestled as it was in a forest. In the autumn, the leaves on the hardwood trees turned gold and red, creating such beauty that people frequently ran their cars off the road, stunned by the immense vistas of color and transitory magic.

Theresa believed in magic. Always had, though she had experienced very little in her life. But, she thought happily, a little magic went a long way. Magic had opened the door to a museum of her childhood, perfectly preserved in every detail. In her museum, carefully concealed by her younger self, lay the truth of what really happened after her daddy came home from the war.

CHAPTER TWELVE

"So, why is my mother still crying? Kendra's voice vibrated with a dangerous timbre, not quite like Varina's, but similar enough to frighten Theresa. Her heart beat faster, just listening to her daughter's questions. "What, exactly, are you people doing for her?"

"She is currently receiving medication to ease her anxiety," Dr. Buhudra Patel explained. "For the past week, she has attended two sessions of therapy each day, one is individual and one is group. She also participates in recreational therapy and exercise classes. We are pleased with her progress."

"What progress?" Kendra cried. "She's a vegetable! I don't think she can hear a word I say!"

"We believe she is fully cognizant of her surroundings," the doctor replied.

Dr. Patel was from India, Theresa had learned. He was very chauvinistic with the female staff and patients. His well-honed sense of superiority cut the very air as he walked through the unit. But, Theresa had to admit, he was unfailingly professional. She felt his deep compassion, in spite of his arrogant persona. Kendra should watch herself, if she truly wished to learn anything more from Dr. Patel.

"Why?" Kendra demanded. "What has she done to make you think she hasn't checked out for good?"

"Well, Ms. Santiago, for one thing, human beings seldom 'check out for good', as you so charmingly put it. It is not unusual for someone to exhibit your mother's symptoms when he or she is processing a painful experience."

"Processing?"

"Yes. If your mother suppressed a serious problem or stress-inducing situation from her past, it is possible that she is now ready to rethink the events and put them into the context of her current life."

"Well, she is the poster child for stressful situations, I'll admit that," Kendra said, sighing. "It's always something, with her. She just never seems able to get a grip."

"Perhaps she is now about to get a grip," Dr. Patel replied.

"I hope so," Kendra sighed. "I can't be running out here very often. I lead a very busy life, myself. Is there anything she needs?"

"Why don't you ask her?"

"Sure," Kendra replied. Theresa sensed her daughter's uneasiness, her fear, as she leaned forward, lessening the distance across the table separating them. "Mom, is there anything you need?"

"Yes," Theresa whispered.

She did not look at Kendra, choosing instead to remain focused on the images. The memories filled most of her field of vision, like a film strip unreeling in front of her eyes. The scenes had begun to move in response to her thoughts, with absolutely accurate sound and, at times, physical sensations. Theresa knew she had to keep looking, for if she lost the image, she might be unable to bring it back.

"Yes." Her voice sounded like it came from the grave, Theresa thought. She should speak more often. "Pencils, lots of pencils and colored pens, every color. Uh, notebooks, artists notebooks, if you don't mind. There's money in my purse, in lockup. I don't know how to get the money for you..."

"You want pencils, notebooks and colored pens?" Kendra said. "Is that all?"

"Yes."

"Why?"

"To draw what I see. To write what I hear."

"Is this normal?" Kendra asked. She sounded scared, as if

Theresa's request was too exotic to be considered. "Like, is she in Bizarro Land, or what?"

"Of course, we do not know what she sees because she has not yet told us," Dr. Patel explained. Theresa heard a smile in his voice. He was not without humor, so long as it was not directed at him. "Most of our patients improve and resume their lives after they resolve whatever issue is demanding their energy and focus. Since she is requesting the means to record her visions, I assume she is ready to share them."

"O.K.," Kendra sighed. "I'll drive to K-Mart and buy what she asked for. Will she get them today if I leave them with the receptionist?"

"Of course."

"Look, Mama," Kendra said, firmly. "I'll get what you need. Just get well, O.K.? Fuck, I don't even know if you can hear me!"

Well, Theresa thought, you need to stop using that word. It is not a word I taught you.

Later that morning, during personal time, an aide brought Theresa a shopping bag filled with drawing paper, notebooks, pencils, and an elaborate set of water colors. Though she would be required to check the items out from the nurses' station during her free time, they were hers to use as she pleased. Theresa held each article at eye level, in her peripheral vision, until she had inspected them all. Then, by touch, she opened a sketchbook and began drawing. By group therapy time, she had completed the picture and colored it blue with a map pencil. She held it in both hands so the group could inspect her work. She kept her eyes focused on her images.

"What is it?" Teddy asked. Teddy was in Dix for threatening to kill her mother. "It looks blue."

"Yeah, sugar, what it be? A black woman named Demetrius who, by her own account, had been in Dix at least ten times. "Ain't nothing wrong with blue, Teddy, blue is good."

"Theresa, do you feel like explaining your work?" Dr. Patel asked. Theresa heard the unspoken suggestion in his voice, and knew he meant she should explain it.

"Tree of Life Baby Book," Theresa whispered. "Leona

Theresa Abelard's baby book. Theresa should have been a boy, because the book was blue. I should have been a boy."

"WHO said you shoulda been a boy?" Demetrius shouted. "You is who you is, and that good enuf! Ain't that right, Dr. Paddel? Ain't that what you been saying? Good enuf?"

"What is your name?" another woman asked, as if she was asking for directions to the Holy Grail. Pale as a ghost, fliting from chair to chair, she had maneuvered her way to Theresa's side. "Your name, dear, what is it?"

"Theresa," she answered. "What is your name?"

"Mary, the Mother of Jesus," the woman whispered. "Are you Mother Theresa?"

The group members groaned, and some laughed, until Dr. Patel signaled for silence. In that instant the images in Theresa's vision changed and she was transported to a time and place she had long forgotten.

Her oldest baby brother, dressed in a blue satin sacque, lay on a baby blanket draped across the room's only armchair. A photographer hunched beneath a black cloth, his head apparently attached to the large camera mounted on tripods. Varina hovered nervously in the background, awed by the presence of a professional photographer in her own living room. The flash exploded, once, twice, then a mind-boggling third time. The baby hiccuped and slipped sideways, catching his plump little chin on the chair arm, as the photographer stepped away from the camera. Varina placed money in his hand, in return for a receipt written on yellow paper. Theresa looked at the photographer's boyish face, recognized the self-hatred in his brown eyes and intuitively knew he would never send the baby's photographs to Varina. Theresa watched silently as the man packed up his equipment and walked out the door. He was a bad man, but Theresa kept that fact to herself.

"I kept secrets," Theresa told the group.

"I kept the greatest secret of all time," Mary the Mother of Jesus confided, in a stage whisper. "All of you know what it was, but you don't want to admit it."

"I didn't want my mother to yell at me," Theresa explained, louder. Her throat felt scratchy. "It made me sick when she yelled at me."

"What did you think would be the result of your keeping secrets?" Dr. Patel asked.

"I wanted things to be like they were before my daddy came home from the war," Theresa replied, sadly.

"Viet-fucking-Nam, baby," a former Army nurse named Chris replied. Chris always sat away from the group. Her graying hair was pulled back into a ponytail that hung to her waist. She complained of suffering every agonizing symptom of mental and physical illness known to the medical profession. The cures for her conditions were unattainable, she said, because of the Viet Nam war, because no one truly understood what that war did to people. "Bitch of a war!"

"Not Viet Nam," Theresa argued. "World War Two."

"Very good, Theresa," Dr. Patel said. "Let's move along."

That evening during personal time, Theresa sketched herself dressed in a red dotted Swiss dress, her hair in braids, walking hand in hand with Leo through the streets of Tisquah. It was late June, ten months after Leo returned from the war. It was hot, even though it was early morning, and the cicadas hummed in the trees. She and Leo were going to Dr. Krohner's clinic to see Varina and the new baby, Theresa's first brother.

Inside Varina's room, Theresa stood on tiptoes to peer inside the bassinet. The baby flailed his fat little arms and made sounds like a calf choking. Leo picked him up and placed him on the bed beside Varina.

"SPIDERS!" Varina screamed, frantically slapping at the baby's blankets. "There's spiders all over him, and in my bed! Leo, get them off!"

"Shit," Leo said. He scooped the baby from the blanket's folds, inspecting him as he quickly moved away from Varina's bed. Varina continued slapping the blanket. "Nurse!" Leo yelled. "In room four!"

A white-clad nurse entered the room, calmly surveyed the scene, then snatched the baby from Leo and the blanket from Varina. She unceremoniously pushed Theresa out of her way as she bundled the chirping baby into the bassinet.

"Varina is still full of the anesthetic," she told Leo. Leo

was perspiring and breathing heavily. "Varina is hallucinating. Seeing things that aren't real. I'll take the baby back to the nursery now. Varina needs to sleep. You can go now."

"You betcha." Leo replied. "Let's go, Skipper," he said, as he hurried down the hall. 'Skipper' was one of his pet names for Theresa. 'Partner' was the other. "Come on, let's go over to the Rexall!"

Theresa backed out of her mother's hospital room, memorizing Varina's glassy stare, her matted hair, the little water carafe on the bedside table. Safely in the hallway, she looked for Leo, but he had already gone outside and was standing on the little concrete porch, leaning over the railing. She ran to the glass door but was unable to push it open. Leo, she saw, was retching into the evergreen shrubs. He was crying, too, but when he turned and opened the door for Theresa, he pretended he was just fine.

Leo took Theresa's hand and they walked in silence the half block to the Rexall store. They sat in one of the high-backed leather booths and Leo ordered Coke floats. While the soda jerk prepared the drinks, Leo went to the tobacco counter and purchased a box of cigars, Dutch Masters. Theresa asked if she could have the box after it was empty and Leo promised it would be hers. He slipped the paper band from a fat, fragrant cigar and ceremoniously placed it on Theresa's finger. She studied the band, peering at a miniature picture of the Dutch Masters in their black hats and lace-edged coats, a replica of the Rembrandt painting reproduced on the cigar box lid. She removed the paper ring from her finger and placed it on her thumb, where it fit better.

Leo and Theresa did not discuss what had occurred in Varina's hospital room. They sat in silence, each deep in thought, carefully spooning melting vanilla ice cream from the bell-shaped fountain glasses. Theresa felt a bolt of true love for Leo pierce her chest. She hated Leo, but the hatred lived in her guts, somewhere nameless, dark and smelly. The love she felt for her father pulsed in the center of her heart where it glowed like a big gold nugget. The nugget was her secret, one she never told anyone.

"I kept the good secrets, too," Theresa told an aide, hours later. She stood in line with her fellow ambulatory patients, waiting to receive evening meds. "I loved him in spite of what he did to me."

"I know you must be telling the truff," the aide replied. "I don't know your story, but I praise God that you done what you had to do and that you're here now, by the grace of God!"

Three weeks later, in her pre-exit interview, Theresa showed her notebooks to the review committee.

"So, how are you feeling now, Mrs. Fulton?" Dr. Patel asked.

"I am ready to go home," Theresa replied. "Or, at least, to my daughter's home."

"Ah, good. Are you still experiencing visions or voices?"

"No, Dr. Patel. After I filled these notebooks with all those pictures and memories, they went away. Back where they belong."

"And where do they belong?"

"In my memory," Theresa smiled, confidently, "where everyone's childhood should be."

"Have you experienced any crying episodes?"

"No, none since the first few days after I was admitted to Dix. Honestly, I feel fine. I do."

"Thank you, Theresa. Would you be willing to continue therapy sessions after your release, on an outpatient basis?"

"If you think it's necessary, yes, I would."

"Well, you should know that your daughter is reluctant to have you stay with her. Her minimum requirement is that you continue therapy."

"In other words, Kendra would rather have me stay here," Theresa sighed. "I know how much my condition shocked her. She was counting on my help, especially after her accident."

"You will be free to do whatever you wish," Dr. Patel explained. He wrote furiously in her chart, then snapped it shut. "We don't foresee any problems in your recovery. You are a strong, intelligent woman."

Later that day, Theresa was summoned to the Visitor's Room. "Great," she whispered, as she followed the aide, "Kendra is here to tell me I can't stay at her house. "

She entered the Visitor's Room, then sat at one of several small tables when she did not see Kendra.

"Tireza?"

Startled, she turned and saw Siyit Yigistoy seated at a nearby table. He was amazingly handsome, dressed in tan Dockers, a white gauze shirt and white canvas deck shoes.

"Siyit!" Theresa called, as she hurried to his table. "I can't imagine that I didn't see you! What are you doing here?"

"Am here to see you," Siyit smiled, taking her hand.

Theresa felt every eye in the room upon her and Siyit. She suddenly wished she had taken more care with her hair and make-up. She imagined she must look like his mother, or his frumpy aunt.

"How did you know I was here?"

"Well," he began, smiling, "is interesting story." His voice sounded like chocolate, if chocolate could talk. "You left without telling me good-bye, I am sure you remember. So, all that day, I drive on Interstate 40, look for Tireza's car. Think you were upset with me!"

"I apologize for leaving like I did," Theresa whispered. "I was in real emotional distress, but I didn't realize it. I just woke up and panicked, then took another route to Cary. It had nothing to do with you."

"Good. Am happy to hear from your lips. In Cary, I wait for days for your call. Had feeling you were unhappy."

"Unhappy," Theresa repeated, softly. "That's a nice word to describe what was going on with me. My daughter said I was in 'Bizarro Land', whatever that is."

"Kendra," Siyit said, "yes, we met."

"You found her at Beautifica? I remember telling you where she works."

"No. Stranger than that. I mean, yes, I go to Beautifica, to ask Kendra if you had arrived. At Beautifica, receptionist say Kendra was injured, off work for several days. Would not give her home phone number to me."

"So, how did you manage to find me?"

"Funny thing. Last week, my friend Akin leave me note,"

ask me to go with new neighbor to Wake Medical Center and drive her mother's car to Hampton Court. Say new neighbor had hurt her arm. New neighbor's mother in Dorothea Dixon."

"Dix," Theresa said, laughing.

"Is same, I think," Siyit replied. His jet-black eyes were dancing with good humor. "So, I knock on new neighbor's door. Offer to help. On way to Wake Medical Center, she is tell about how much trouble her mother is cause. How she drove from Texas, got lost along highway. I am thinking it can not be Tireza, but at hospital parking lot, there is your car. Is same, blue Ford Escort, Texas plates! I know that car!"

"So, did you tell Kendra we had met in Tennessee?"

"No. Afraid she think maybe I had harmed you. Might think I am serial murderer. Who could say what she think? She was upset, angry at mother, worried. So, I think I will wait until you are better, then visit. Here I am!"

"This is funny!" Theresa laughed. "How near to Kendra is your friend's house?"

"Next door! Akin only met Kendra when she leave her key, ask him to let repair man in to fix shower door, first day she went back to work. Akin was on vacation that week, so he was at home. Usually not at home, travels to Europe, sometimes Canada, at least two weeks each month. Anyway, Akin thought Kendra very beautiful young woman. Said she was going to kill the contractor."

"Did you tell Kendra anything about knowing me?"

"No, thought it should be your decision. Tell or not tell? I did not know how sick you were. Did not wish to add to your trouble."

"I'm fine, now," Theresa said, softly. "I got well during my stay here. This was a good place for me."

"Good!" Siyit exclaimed. He rubbed his hands together, then stood and pulled Theresa into his arms. "Now, we make plans for good friend, Tireza! When can you leave this Dixon place?"

"Dix," Theresa said. "I will be discharged tomorrow."

"So. My friend Akin and I wish to invite you stay with us, at Akin's new townhouse in Cary."

"Next door to Kendra?"

"Not issue," Siyit said. "Kendra told Akin she has new boyfriend who lives with her. Says no room for you to stay at her house."

"Wow," Theresa whispered, "that's more than she told me."

"Akin's house has four bedrooms, plenty bathrooms. Many village in Turkey have not so many bathrooms as Akin's house. Akin travel, is almost never home. I am work two jobs and enroll in college. You will never see Akin and Siyit. Say yes, Tireza. Stay with us."

"You really mean this, don't you?" Theresa asked. "Why are you being so nice to me?"

"Many years ago, strangers in Sweden help me and Akin. We promise to help other people, to repay kindness debt. You should not be alone now, not so soon after leave hospital. Let us help?"

"Yes," Theresa sighed, "how can I refuse such a generous offer?"

After Siyit's departure, Theresa sat alone at the table, sipping the can of Diet Coke Siyit had insisted on buying. Only then did it dawn on her that Kendra had left her car on the emergency room parking lot at Wake Medical for weeks before moving it to Hampton Court.

"It's a miracle the car wasn't towed," Theresa marveled.

She considered Siyit's offer during the final days of her commitment. It seemed like the ideal answer, considering her situation. She felt physically able to drive back to Texas, but she had promised her therapist and Dr. Patel that she would take care of herself. That she would cease risking her health and safety. That she would carefully plan her activities. In her entire life no one had ever insisted on those things.

"Amazing, isn't it?" Theresa asked herself. "Demetrius, Chris, Teddy and Mary the Mother of Jesus are the first people who ever thought I was worth protecting."

The day of her release, Siyit drove her to his friend's townhouse. He proudly showed her around the sparsely furnished rooms.

"Two extra bedrooms," he beamed, spreading his arms. "You choose which you like. Bathroom connects them, so you will have privacy!"

Theresa chose the room with double windows overlooking Kendra's back yard and patio, where she had watched the sun rise just prior to Kendra's injury.

"Are you sure this room is O.K.? It looks like Akin's home office."

A new computer sat on a desk, trailing its wires onto the hardwood floors. The boxes and packing material were stacked in one corner.

"Is extra computer," Siyit explained. "Akin carries laptop, has computer at work. I have computer in my room. So, is extra."

"Do you think Akin will mind if I hook it up and use it?"

"No. He will not notice. And, will not mind. Please use it, nice woman, if you want."

"I want," Theresa answered.

"Kendra placed all your clothes and suitcases in your car," Siyit explained. "I find your keys lying on top of car one day. I am think she forgot about keys."

"So, there is no reason to ask Kendra for anything today. Is that what you mean?"

"Your choice," Siyit smiled. "Seem like God make it easy for you to have your belongings with not much problem. Now, do you feel like trip to grocery store? We are out of food in kitchen!"

"Let's go," Theresa laughed. She checked her purse for cash and credit cards. "The hospital didn't lose a penny," she observed, "so, I'm buying the groceries. I won't take no for an answer! You don't want me to go into shopper's withdrawal, do you?"

They shopped at Food Lion, then drove down Kildare Farms Road to The Fresh Market for vegetables and meat. She knew she was spending more than Siyit could afford and the gesture felt immensely satisfying. She had survived many penny-pinching days, herself.

Theresa still felt a thrill when she realized she had the

money to splurge, thanks to the recent sale of Devon's ranch land. There was probably more money in the bank at Tisquah, if she was a beneficiary in Gussie's will. She planned to inquire about that in a day or so. At the moment, she simply wanted to enjoy her freedom, to be seen in the company of a very handsome man, and to shop in Cary's pricey, exclusive shops.

Siyit grilled steaks on the Jenn-Aire as Theresa prepared the salad and warmed a loaf of bakery garlic bread. They ate without speaking, as comfortable with each other as life-long friends. After the meal, Siyit loaded the compact disc player with his favorite music and they danced.

"Tireza," Siyit said, as they moved in unison across the hardwood floors, "I do not want you to think I expect sex with you. You are a guest. A friend. You must know this."

"Thank you," Theresa replied. "I honestly hadn't thought about it, but I don't believe I could handle a sex life, right now."

"When you are stronger," Siyit said, softly, "we will talk of it, together. Make deal of it?"

"Deal!"

Life was funny, she thought. She would never have imagined she would be dancing to country western music with a handsome, AWOL Turk on the evening of her release from a mental hospital.

The next day, she used her phone card and contacted the banker, Mr. Woolaver, in Tisquah.

"This is Gussie Abelard's granddaughter, Theresa Fulton. I've just been released from the hospital. I want to know about Gussie's estate. Can we discuss that over the phone?"

"I don't see why not," the old man answered. "When you return to Texas, we will need to have a reading of the will, just to stay perfectly legal. How are you feeling?"

"Fine now," she stated, firmly. "I had an emotional breakdown, of sorts, but I am fully recovered."

"Well, that is good news," her replied. "Your grandmother left you a great deal of money, Theresa. She named only one other beneficiary."

"One?" Theresa asked. She had imagined Gussie would leave each of her grandsons, Theresa's brothers, some part of her estate. "Who?"

"Garvin McElroy, the former sheriff of West County. She left him twenty-five thousand dollars, but specified that amount go towards purchasing band instruments for the Tisquah High School Band in the event that Mr. McElroy died before the will was probated."

"Let me guess," Theresa said. "He's already dead?"

"Last Christmas. He died in the local nursing home."

"Why did she name him in her will?"

"She states that Mr. McElroy 'redeemed' her."

Theresa considered this unexpected bit of news. Gussie had said something about being 'redeemed' in the courthouse. Had she been referring to the sheriff's office? To Garvin McElroy? She felt like kicking herself for not pressing Gussie for an explanation.

"Well, can you tell me how much money Gussie left me?"

"Yes, I can tell you that, at least in the neighborhood, as some of the bequest is invested. Ah, that would be just short of five million."

"Dollars?"

"Yes, five million dollars," Mr. Woolaver replied. Theresa could hear paper rustling, but she doubted the wizened old banker was looking up information. Intuition told her he knew, to the penny, the amount of her inheritance. "Are you in need of an advance at this time? It would be my pleasure to facilitate that for you."

"I'll get back to you in a few days," Theresa said, thoughtfully. "I may need quite a large advance, if my plan works out."

"Plan?"

"Yes. I am considering self-publishing a book, a kind of autobiography. I'll look into it and find out the particulars."

"That sounds intriguing. Please let me know when I may be of service."

Theresa dressed, then went to her car and dialed Kendra's number on the cell phone. A man answered, then called Kendra to the phone.

"Mom?" Theresa heard, in that single word, her

daughter's nervousness, her fear of hurting Theresa, her determination to keep their lives separate. In that one word, their lives changed, forever. "Where are you?"

"I'm in my car at the moment, Kendra," she answered, truthfully. "I was released from the hospital yesterday and got a ride to your place to pick up my car." She paused, giving Kendra an opportunity to make any excuses she wanted for not having visited her for the past several weeks. For not offering her a room, a haven. "I thought you might want to know that I am doing well."

"That is good news, Mom. Look, I know it looks bad that I haven't been to see you lately. But, Mom, you knew before you came out here that I have a hectic schedule. I'm just really busy. Frankly, Mom, I don't have energy enough to live my life and deal with your problems. I'm sorry, Mommy, but that's how it has to be!"

"Kendra," Theresa replied, patiently, "I am sorry to have been such a burden. Before you say anything more, please hear me out. All my life, I wanted to tell Varina exactly what you just said to me. I never had the courage. Varina intruded in my marriages, my homes, my life, without asking. She never learned I was an individual, a human being with a right to live my own life. She dumped all her problems in my lap, all my life. I swear to you that I never intended to do that to you. You don't owe me an apology. I think it is great to defend your life against anyone and anything that might slow you down. I'm proud of you."

"Shit, Mom, you make me feel so rotten. I don't mean to hurt you."

"I know, honey. I know. Don't worry. Look, I'm going to be responsible for handling Gussie's affairs, so don't worry if you don't hear from me for a while."

"Sure, Mom, just don't disappear. Don't scare me again."

"I promise."

Theresa drove to one of Cary's many state-of-the-art computer shops and purchased a flat-bed scanner and software compatible to the computer in her borrowed bedroom. She returned to the townhouse, parked her car in a visitor's area not visible from Kendra's house, then carried her supplies to Akin's apartment.

She was amazed at her energy level. She felt like a teenager, with a wonderful, uncharted life stretched beyond the horizon. She had seldom felt such a sense of freedom.

Theresa assembled the computer, played around with the scanner for an hour, then began transferring her notebooks to disks. She did not know exactly when she had first contemplated publishing her notes and drawings. Events had just fallen into place in a natural manner; a new computer in her room, unlimited funds and all the time in the world.

The scanner made it simple to rearrange her drawings, a necessity since she had not drawn them in strict chronological order. She divided her work into five chapters; from the end of the war until she started to school, grade school, junior high and high school, marriage to Mason, and finally marriage to Devon. As she worked, scanning the drawings and her handwritten notes onto disk, she recalled additional events which she quickly sketched and added to the text.

One such addition, in the chapter devoted to her junior high and high school years, shed light on the strange incident in which Gussie had spit on Michaul's grave.

Theresa sketched herself and Leo checking into a dingy motel in Cuba, New Mexico. Leo turned her amethyst ring on her finger, hiding the stone in her palm, so that only the gold band was visible. As if the cynical night clerk cared in the least whether she was his wife, his daughter, or his dog. Inside the room, Theresa fought Leo as he removed her clothing. With her last strength, she wrapped herself in a coarse wool blanket. Leo, clearly running out of patience, picked up the bedside phone and placed a long distance call to Varina. He lit a cigarette and smoked it as he waited for the call to be completed by the operator. The phone rang, Leo stubbed out the cigarette and spoke into the receiver, smooth as vanilla pudding.

"Hi, honey bunch," he said to Varina. His eyes narrowed, glinting like blue steel. "The damn guy hasn't showed up! Some snafu with the paperwork for that Mercury I'm supposed to pick up and drive back to Belen. Yeah. Yeah, we'll be home by noon, if I have to drive all the way to Farmington and straighten out the paperwork, myself. Yeah, she's right here. Love you, too."

Leo held the phone out for Theresa, secure in the knowledge that she would never refuse to speak to her mother. Theresa clenched her teeth, fought back tears and freed one arm from the blanket's scratchy confines. As she reached for the receiver, Leo's hand circled her wrist in his merciless grip. He smiled. It was a game for Leo, a game he truly loved because he always won.

"Hi, Mom," Theresa said. Her voice trembled and she knew Varina sensed her misery. "I don't want to miss school tomorrow. The principal has already warned me about so many absences." She was crying, could not stop the tears from sliding down her cheeks, onto the blanket. Leo fastened his mouth onto one of her breasts. Theresa's heart stretched over the distance, across mesas and arroyos, above heady, pine-dense mountain ranges. Please, please, please help me, she prayed. "Mom! I want to come home, tonight!"

"Theresa, you should have thought of that before you ran off to Cuba with your daddy. I don't know what you think I can do about it!"

"I didn't want to come, Mom! You know that! You said I had to, because Daddy needed company, so he wouldn't fall asleep driving home!"

"Shut up, Theresa!" Varina snapped. "This call is costing us money!"

Leo replaced the receiver, his eyes never leaving Theresa's face. She lowered her gaze, admitting defeat, and dropped the blanket. Her father unfastened his trousers, sat on the bed and pulled Theresa onto his lap. His penis throbbed against her buttocks, hot, obscene, alive.

"Little guy loves it when you tighten your muscles, honey," Leo crooned into her ear.

Tears rolled down Theresa's face. She nodded, following Leo's instructions. She focused on the dark little room, filled with rawhide furniture, walls splashed with old, vivid, Navajo blankets. The ceiling was supported by peeled cedar logs, vigas, attesting to the age of the building. Theresa loved New Mexican architecture, and allowed her mind to wander, imagining the construction of the low, rambling building that had, finally, evolved into a shabby motel.

"Don't be such a little wildcat, Theresa," Leo cooed. "This is for us both. It's bigger than both of us, it's a universal need, good for what ails you! I can't hurt you! You know that! I'm supposed to do this for your own good, just like my daddy did it for me."

"Your father did this to you? I don't believe it! He died when you were just a little boy!"

"Before he died, he always showed me around. He showed me how things are done. My daddy taught me a lot of things I can teach you, if you will just calm down!"

In Cary, North Carolina, forty years later, Theresa smiled as she typed the conversation from her distant past into the computer. She rested her hands in her lap, thinking of Gussie leaning into the hot wind, spitting onto Michaul's grave.

"That's it!" she cried. "Michaul was a child molester! Gussie knew it! Gussie knew it! I always wondered why she didn't make Leo leave me alone, but it may have been because she didn't blame Leo for the way he was. She blamed Michaul! She must have known, for a fact, that Michaul molested Leo! My God, how many generations of this sick behavior is in my family background? It's almost too much to bear!"

Theresa ran downstairs, snatched a can of Diet Coke from the fridge and paced the kitchen floor as she drank. Something else worried at her mind, something she could not quite piece together. She finished the Coke and returned to her room and the monster computer. As she touched the keyboard, she remembered an incident from her past. Remembered it, in the normal manner.

"I don't need a private movie projector plugged into my head," she whispered, "now that I can deal with what Leo did to me."

Theresa was four-and-a-half years old. Her second baby brother was newborn, just home from Dr. Krohner's clinic. Varina, wearing a pink chenille robe, stood at the tiny cabinet in one of Robert Rice's new rent houses, pouring milk into a vast array of glass baby bottles. The little family had moved to

Tisquah only weeks earlier, after Leo was discharged from the Army Air Corps. Varina was ranting about having been dismissed from the clinic after scarcely three days following the birth, and about leaving a box of tissues in her hospital room.

"Look for yourself, Leo," she cried, "look there, on the bill! 'Tissues, twenty-five cents', that means they charged me for a box of tissues and we didn't bring it home! They cheated us!"

Leo, dressed in a plaid bathrobe, stood between Varina and Theresa, screwing rubber nipples onto the bottles after his wife poured them full of Carnation Evaporated milk and Karo syrup formula. He leaned one hip against the cabinet, turning his lower body in Theresa's direction. His robe parted, revealing his testicles and penis. Theresa's eyes widened in shock. She balled her little hands into fists and punched Leo's privates as hard, as rapidly, as she could. Leo howled in pain, grasped his groin and doubled over. Bottles of baby formula toppled like dominoes across the width of the cabinet top, splashing milk onto the floor.

"Theresa! What on earth?" Varina screamed. She slapped Theresa, sending her tumbling beneath the little drop-leaf dinette table, where she lay, whimpering. "Leo, oh honey! I'm sorry! I'm going to whip Theresa with a belt, if you're hurt! Do you need to go to the doctor?"

"Aaaagggg!" Leo replied.

At that moment, in a scene that always mystified Theresa, Gussie and Aunt Summer entered the house unannounced. They apparently followed the sounds of combat to the kitchen. The two women immediately began screaming at Leo.

"What do you mean, Leo, getting a vasectomy without telling us about it?" Aunt Summer cried.

"Leo," Gussie hissed, "you know we're watching you! If you got this here new-fangled operation just so you can't hurt Theresa the way you hurt Summer, forget about it! We are watching you!"

"Get out of my house," Varina shouted, her hands on her hips. "You trouble-making witches! Get out of my house and stay out! Leo is mine, not yours! Get out!"

Throughout her young life, Theresa pondered the strange scene. She once found the courage to ask Varina what it all meant.

"Gussie and Aunt Summer are jealous because Leo married me," Varina replied, smugly. "They don't respect me, so I don't respect them. If they can act crazy, then so can I! It's none of your business, either, so forget about it!"

Eventually, Theresa did forget the scene, as her life grew more and more complicated. Fifty years later she analyzed the event and it became crystal clear.

"Leo must have molested Summer, maybe even got her pregnant. That's what Gussie meant by 'the same way you hurt Summer.' Leo always told me he couldn't 'hurt' me, but I never realized he meant he was sterile. I was terrified, for years, afraid I was pregnant by my own father. The bastard! 'Hurt' was their euphemism for 'impregnate.' My God! I've got to return to Tisquah and look for Gussie's diaries!"

Theresa saved her work to disk, then turned off the computer. She bathed, changed clothes, then started dinner for three. Akin, who had been absent from Cary since before Theresa's release from the hospital, was due home from France. As she chopped vegetables for stir fry, Theresa suddenly remembered that Gussie's first child, Lorena, had been murdered.

"Gussie always said Mexican rustlers killed Lorena," she whispered. "Is it possible that she was murdered by Michaul? Did Gussie know it?"

Chills ran down Theresa's spine. She had always told people it was a miracle that she had survived her childhood. Perhaps other girls in the Abelard family had not been so fortunate.

"Gussie also told me it was a miracle that Aunt Summer survived, because she was so sick. Maybe, just maybe, she meant Aunt Summer was lucky to have survived life with Leo. Little girls didn't fare well in a house with Abelard men! It's crystal clear now!"

Akin was almost as handsome as Siyit. Theresa compared the two beautiful Turks as they sat around the dining table, eating stir fry with chopsticks. Akin was taller, leaner, more watchful than Siyit. His eyes were a marvelous, dark green, instead of obsidian like Siyit's. Akin's English was more polished than Siyit's, though his conversation was not nearly as warm and revealing.

"Well, Tireza," Akin said, "I hope you are comfortable here. Siyit was very concerned for you."

"It is wonderful here," Theresa responded. "I can't thank you enough! I don't know how to repay your kindness."

"Be kind to someone else," the two men replied, in unison.

Later, preparing for bed, Theresa saw the light come on over Kendra's small patio. She stood behind the white mini blinds in her second floor bedroom, watching, smiling, as Kendra embraced and kissed a dark, muscular young man. Theresa recognized him as the young resident from Wake Medical, Antonio V. Cavaleri, M.D.

"Good for you, Kendra," Theresa whispered. "Good for you!"

"Doctor Patel said I exhibited classic symptoms of post-traumatic stress disorder," Theresa told Siyit, the following afternoon. "He said military personnel have experienced the same syndrome, throughout history."

"I know of this condition," Siyit replied. "I have flashbacks, same thing as disorder! Flashbacks make you feel like you are bad person, because bad things happened to you."

"Yes! Dr. Patel explained that some people get stuck in the memories of things they were forced to endure. Then, as they move on with their lives, everything revolves around those memories, because they are never put into proper perspective."

"I know what it is," Siyit sighed. "Sometimes at night, I dream am back in Turkey. Am tied to wall, scream as my father-in-law hit me on knees with iron pipe. I feel same pain, hear my bones break! Other soldiers watch but do not help, are my friends but do not help."

"God, yes," Theresa whispered, "exactly like that. People watch but do not help."

"For me, soldiers watch," Siyit said, kindly. "Who watch young Tireza, who did not help?"

"Varina," Theresa wept, "my mother watched, but did not help me!"

Varina had simply refused to acknowledge Theresa's stories of Leo's abuse throughout her childhood. In her teen years, Theresa begged Varina to protect her from Leo, but her mother invariably blamed Theresa for Leo's behavior.

"He wants people to think you're his pretty, young wife," Varina often snarled. "You flirt with him and make him forget who you are! Why don't you stop it?"

Theresa believed, for reasons she had never fathomed, that her mother must be protected from knowledge of Leo's actions. It was a false belief system, based partly on Leo's threat that her mother would cease loving her and partly on her devotion to Varina. So, even though Varina was obviously aware, on some level, of Leo's proclivities, Theresa persisted in pretending that her mother played no part in the abuse. She never lost hope that she would, somehow, win her mother's love and protection.

She told Siyit of her sophomore year in high school, when her family lived in Grand Junction, Colorado. They occupied the top floor of a Victorian house converted into several apartments. The house was located in a run-down section of town, one block from the railroad tracks.

"I never liked those teen love songs about rich boys in love with girls from the wrong side of the tracks," she recalled. Siyit raised his brows, unsure of her meaning. "I was always the girl from the wrong side of town. I was the pretty girl nice boys' parents warned them about."

"Is same in Turkey," Siyit replied.

"Which side of the tracks did your family live on?"

"Tracks not important. Family's position is everything. My father teach math at university, my family not rich, not poor. In middle, but good."

"I'll bet your parents wanted you to make a good marriage, with a girl from your own background."

"Did not wish me marry into military family," Siyit admitted, smiling. Theresa sensed his sorrow for having brought disaster to his father's house. "Was not wise to marry a beautiful, spoiled girl whose father could put my father into prison. Not good choice."

Theresa attended Grand Junction High School, by far the newest, most progressive school she had ever known. She made good grades, in spite of the "Migrant Student" label her counselor stamped on her records file. She was absent only when she had a headache.

The migraine headaches had begun the previous year, in Grants, New Mexico, but their severity and frequency increased during the months after their move to Grand Junction. One episode was so severe that Leo called a doctor to make a house visit, stating that he feared Theresa was dying from some mysterious malady.

"She may be experiencing stress," the doctor advised Varina and Leo.

"Well, I'm not surprised!" Varina replied. "I told her not to play field hockey! It should be a boy's sport, in the first place! It's too strenuous for girls! She even insists in playing trombone in the band, and if that's not a boy's instrument, I don't know what is! She's always been a tomboy! I always tried my best to keep her dressed in pretty things, but she wanted to wear jeans and climb trees! It's not my fault! No one can blame me! I'm the one who could tell you about headaches!"

The elderly physician silently wrote a prescription for a sedative, then handed the slip of paper to Leo. He patted Theresa's shoulder, sympathetically, she thought, though his touch sent waves of excruciating pain through her head and eyes. He stared at Leo and Varina for a moment, then picked up his worn, leather bag.

"Get this girl's life in order," he admonished, "or she'll only get worse."

"Sure thing," Leo said, smiling.

"We can't afford to run to the drug store every time your head aches," Varina hissed, as the doctor carefully made his way downstairs. "What if we had to buy medicine every time your brothers walk in their sleep? You didn't see us hauling them to the doctor when they were babies and cried until they held their breath, did you? You're all spoiled, that's what I say! Theresa, you're the worst!"

The prescription was never filled, of course, and the

headaches grew much worse throughout the long winter.

Theresa's twin bed was located in the dining room, and her brothers shared the sofa bed in the living room. Her parents occupied the only bedroom in the apartment. Theresa was terrified of entering that room, even in broad daylight. She felt Leo's presence lurking beneath the bedspread, flattened out like a giant flounder, one huge eye watching his only daughter.

No one in the Abelard household mentioned to the doctor that Varina frequently forced Theresa to go to Leo's bed, no matter how hard Theresa protested. The arguments ended when Varina climbed into Theresa's bed, braced herself against the wall and pushed Theresa onto the linoleum floor.

"Get out of this bed, Theresa, and go in there to see what your daddy wants! If you love your daddy, if you love me, go see what he wants!"

"I just want to help you get over your headaches," Leo whispered, in the dark. "It's my duty and my right. It's why I'm made this way." His rough, mechanic's hands passed over Theresa's body, tried to pry apart her legs. "You need to be loved, Theresa. It will cure those headaches!"

Leo clasped her rigid body, then tried to force his tobacco-stained tongue into her mouth. He eventually settled for forcing her hand to touch his erection.

"See there, Theresa," he whispered, each time. "I'm still wearing my shorts. I'm not going to do anything. I can't hurt you. Calm down, or I'll have to get tough, and then your mother will come in here and see what you're doing!"

Varina was Leo's secret weapon. Though Varina's participation in the dreadful event should have been blindingly apparent to Theresa, she was incapable of causing her mother any pain. She knew Varina was lying awake in her bed, listening, yet pretending ignorance of what transpired in the bedroom with Leo. Theresa would have preferred being kidnapped by strangers.

Sometimes, Theresa fell asleep in Leo's sweaty arms, in spite of her fear and disgust. She always awoke with Leo's mouth on hers, his legs wrapped around her so tightly she could not move. His fingers, rough and hard, as repulsive as his penis, as invasive as his tongue, caressed her private parts. She learned to feign sleep as he moved, silent as a snake, against her body. He eventually ejaculated into a wash cloth, smoked a cigarette, then fell asleep.

When Leo snored, Theresa was free to trade beds with Varina, then lie awake, silently weeping until the sun came up. She dressed for school and sat at the round kitchen table, reading books or writing letters to her friends in New Mexico, until the Baby Ben clock in her parents' room sounded its brassy alarm. The family behaved as if nothing strange had occurred during the long, icy, Rocky Mountain night. As Theresa brushed her teeth before leaving for the walk across town to school, she saw Leo's wash cloth, rinsed and hung to dry on a nail beside the lavatory.

"Don't use that wash rag," Varina warned Theresa's brothers, "it's Leo's personal wash rag, for his skin rash."

"Yes," Theresa told Siyit, forty years later, "I'd say that kindly old doctor was right. I was experiencing some stress."

Theresa knew it was time to leave Cary when she found herself, several weeks later, browsing through a furniture outlet mall, mentally selecting items for Akin's townhouse. She actually contemplated purchasing a white leather seating arrangement and a glass-topped washed oak table. It would look stunning with Akin's Kilim rug, she thought, accented by one enormous brass bowl filled with hand-carved wooden apples. Add several massive, cinnamon-scented candles, dim the lights...

"Theresa, baby, it's time you went back to Texas!"

She returned to the townhouse, packed her things, cleaned her room and bath, then wrote farewell notes to Siyit and Akin. She lingered a while, looking down onto Kendra's patio, hoping in vain for a glimpse of her beautiful daughter. Finally, she unplugged the computer, taped a thank-you note to the scanner, carried her bags to her car and drove out of wonderful little city of Cary, North Carolina.

CHAPTER THIRTEEN

Though she had lived in Lodestone, Texas longer than any other place in her life, Theresa did not feel it was her true home. She had never missed the little ranch town during the many times she left Devon and went to stay with Kendra. Lodestone was Devon's home, not hers. She did not know what home should feel like, other than the sense of great nostalgia she experienced when she thought of the old Rice farm. She had discussed her lack of roots in Dr. Patel's therapy group.

"You're still just living like your fucked-up parents made you live," Chris commented, knowingly. "Like, baby, in Nam, G.I.'s just moved from hole to hole, hootch to hootch, you know, if they were lucky enough to stay alive. It got in their blood, you dig where I'm coming from, and when they got back to the States, no place ever felt right. Like they had concentrated on survival for so friggin' long, they forgot how to enjoy life, to feel like they belonged with the human race. Survival, it can kill you as dead as a bullet, baby!"

As Theresa drove away from Cary, she promised herself she would find a place of her own, where she truly belonged. She had kept Devon's enormous old Victorian house only because Kendra had been happy living here. She hadn't wanted to deprive her daughter of a sense of history, of belonging to a permanent place.

Theresa had done everything she could to dissuade her daughter, who had just turned sixteen, from marrying Ralph, the darling of the community. Ralph, the cutest boy in town, was already an alcoholic and a permanent fixture in high school resource classes. Theresa had begged Kendra to abandon the dysfunctional young man.

"You're jealous!" Kendra cried, whenever Theresa reasoned with her.

"I'm not! I am telling you there is a long history in this family of women throwing away their lives when they rescue screwed-up men. It doesn't work! The men do well and the women fall apart!"

"You are going to lose Kendra," Devon warned, "if you don't stand back and let her do this. Kendra doesn't fit the mold. The only way she learns is through personal, hands-on experience."

So, Theresa consented to the marriage, with great misgivings. Kendra's wedding, held in the front parlor before a blazing log fire, was the talk of the town. An enormous Christmas tree, decorated in Kendra's chosen colors of burgundy and navy, stood in the corner, dominating the scene.

Within six months, Kendra had dropped out of high school, filed for divorce and enrolled in beauty college. Theresa found solace only in the fact that her daughter had not gotten pregnant during the brief, doomed marriage.

"Devon was absolutely right about Kendra," Theresa said, as she remembered those days. "He just didn't understand himself, or know how to deal with me!"

Their marriage had been stormy, sometimes violent, and at the end, tragic. Devon, a life-long alcoholic, also developed congestive heart failure and diabetes. His medical conditions and the medications he took contributed to his deep depression and dangerous mood swings. Theresa left him many times, though she stayed with him in Lodestone after he became seriously ill, caring for him until his death. She knew she should never have married him, but she could not bring herself to abandon him as he waited for death. She had no one to blame but herself, she frequently thought. Even her oldest brother had seen the relationship in a better light than she.

"You know Devon is just like Daddy, don't you? he asked. "Can't you see it? He even looks like Daddy!"

"I don't recall you asking my opinion when you got married," Theresa retorted.

How like Varina she must have sounded, Theresa thought, how defensive, how bitchy. How stupid.

Theresa's bottom-line requirements for a husband had always been that he worked steadily and was not a child molester. Both Mason and Devon met those criteria, but were far from ideal companions.

"I was a fool for love," she told her friends, whenever they discussed their lives and the men who affected them.

"Anyway," Theresa said, as she neared Lodestone, "it's a good thing Kendra married Ralph and got out of that house before Devon went nuts! At least, she didn't have to experience that nightmare!"

Kendra completed beauty school before her eighteenth birthday and immediately moved to Los Angeles. She worked nights at a mortuary, styling hair and applying make-up on corpses in order to have her days free to attend voice and acting classes. A year later, she fell madly in love with an Olympic diving champion, a gorgeous young Hawaiian named Tommy. When he moved to Miami to train with a world-renowned diving coach, Kendra followed.

"I can't believe you just abandoned your singing and acting classes in L.A.!" Theresa said, when Kendra called her from Miami. "I thought you were just about to get a real break."

"Don't sweat it, Mom," Kendra replied. "That wasn't going anywhere. I'm not as talented as you think. I'm interested in sports and personal fitness, now. It's big business!"

Months later, the diver publicly announced his homosexuality and Kendra moved to Boca Raton, where she found work managing a spa. She then met an incredibly talented Cuban artist, Angel Santiago, married him and wound up in a hospital shortly after the honeymoon.

"Mommy?" Kendra said, when Theresa answered a late-night phone call. "Can you fly to Boca and help me? Angel beat me up and I'm in the hospital. He uses drugs, Mommy, and I'm afraid he's going to kill me! His crazy brother went on the honeymoon with us, swear to God, and Angel tried to make me sleep with him! As soon as we got home, they took my car away from me so I couldn't leave town. Then Angel beat me up while his brother watched! They're both fucking crazy! They're in Key West for a few days, so please come and get me before they get back!"

Kendra immediately flew to Boca Raton, rented a car and helped Kendra flee the hospital. They went to Kendra's apartment, packed her things and left town, driving up I-95, uncertain as to their destination. Within three hours, Kendra spotted Angel's car in the rearview mirror.

"Thank God, we're in a rental car," she gasped. "If they get close enough they will recognize us. Pray we can get away from them, Mom. Those freaks will shoot us while we're driving down the highway!"

They escaped with their lives because Kendra had the presence of mind to flag down a Georgia Highway Patrolman and lie about having seen two men in a convertible selling drugs at a convenience store. She gave the cop Angel's Florida license plate number.

"Now, we'll really have to drive like hell," Kendra told Theresa, as the patrol car turned across I-95 and headed south. "I know Angel has drugs in his car because he always does, so they will be arrested and held for at least a few hours. We better fucking well get someplace he won't think to look, and fast!"

"Texas?" Theresa asked.

"Too far, and he might assume we went home."

"Atlanta?"

"Not far enough. Anyway, they may have drug contacts there. You wouldn't believe how many relatives he has in the south!"

They continued driving north, stopping only for gas, until they neared Raleigh, North Carolina.

"Get the map, Mom," Kendra said, suddenly. "Look for a place called Cary, somewhere close to Raleigh."

"I found it," Theresa replied. "Why?"

"When Tommy was training in Miami, before I moved to Boca, I met a sports therapist from Cary. She said it is the place to be."

"Why? I've never heard of the place."

"She said it is just growing like crazy, has lots of job opportunities and people there have all the money in the world. It's near some kind of scientific center or something."

"Hmm, it is near an area called Research Triangle Park. Must be something interesting happening. Will Angel look there for us?" Theresa asked.

"I doubt he's ever heard of Cary. He will probably keep driving up I-95 to Canada, before he realizes he's not going to catch us."

"Is he that stupid?"

"You have no idea!"

They rented an apartment, found work, and Kendra fell in love with Cary.

"This feels like my home, Mom," she announced. "I don't know how to explain it, but I feel like I belong here."

Theresa felt a pang of jealousy. She envied her daughter's certainty about where she belonged on a very slippery planet.

Theresa arrived in Lodestone at dusk, the prettiest time of the day in the autumn months. Great flocks of geese and ducks flew overhead, following their leaders in soaring, v-shaped formations. Their haunting calls filled the air as they settled for the night around Lake Lodestone, two miles south of town. Theresa unloaded her things, bathed, opened a can of soup and contemplated what she would do next.

She had three immediate goals; to search through Gussie's belongings for clues about Leo's early years, to make arrangements to self-publish her memoirs, and to find a home of her own.

The next morning, she drove to Tisquah. Her first stop was at the bank, to see Mr. Woolaver. The old gentleman showed her to a chair opposite his roll-top desk.

"I'm sure you have a lot of documents ready for my signature," she replied. "After that, I want to talk to you about my project."

"Publishing your memoirs?"

"Yes."

She signed a stack of documents pertaining to Gussie's

estate.

"I contacted a self-publishing company," Theresa explained. "They will print my manuscript for a fee. I also contacted a secretarial service in Lubbock, to compile a distribution list and handle the actual mailing of the books. I want to go through Gussie's things before I submit the manuscript, in case she kept material that might shed light on our family history. I don't mean to sound mysterious but my family has lived under a cloud of terrible secrets and I want to get it all out in the open. I thought you might know things I never heard of about my grandmother and my father and my aunt."

"I understand," Mr. Woolaver said, softly. "Tisquah is, and always was, a small town. There were no secrets here, only things we pretended not to know. Pity. Your family's secrets were the reason your grandmother refused to marry me."

"Really?"

"I was much younger than Gustine," the old man explained, "but from the moment I met her she owned my heart. She was the most beautiful woman in town and so vibrant, so full of energy. We went to church together and occasionally to the moving picture shows. We sometimes took Summer with us, for Gustine was reluctant to leave her at home alone. Summer especially enjoyed 'Tarzan' picture shows, as I recall."

"Did you know my father?"

"Everyone knew Leo," he replied. "He was a charming young man, very respectful and considerate. Of course, I understood he had problems at school, but at that time, I had not learned of his depravity."

"Depravity?"

"Yes. I heard later that he was known to have tortured and killed many animals in Tisquah, and there were other things, well..."

"He impregnated his sister?"

"There was that rumor, yes."

"My God, why didn't someone do something?"

"Times were different, then," the old man replied, sadly. "I proposed to Gustine in this very office, one evening after prayer meeting. I taught her to punch in numbers and total them up on a manually operated adding machine I kept beside my desk. She was holding the paper tape when I proposed."

"What did she say?"

"She just shook her head. She held up that tape and said any man who understood how the adding machine worked would soon learn too much about her. She said she and her children would ruin me, and that their burden was hers and hers alone. She was the most courageous woman I ever knew. I love her, still, Theresa. She is the reason I never married."

"My goodness," Theresa sighed. "I had no idea!"

"I want you to have the ruby engagement ring I bought for Gustine," he said, opening a drawer. He placed a velvet covered ring box on the desk top. "Gustine never saw this ring. I kept it all these years in the hope that, somehow, she would reconsider. Please take it. Wear it, if you wish. It will make me happy."

"Thank you," Theresa said. "I will wear it with great pleasure. Thank you for loving Gussie and for not condemning her. She did the best she knew how."

"She had the heart of a tigress," Mr. Woolaver confided.

Theresa spent the next day supervising a crew of local boys who packed everything in Gussie's house and moved the lot to the Goodwill Industries store in Lubbock. The house seemed smaller without the furnishings Theresa had known from childhood.

The old combination record player and radio cabinet, a gift from Summer, was loaded on the truck. Theresa recalled the day Summer and Brendan delivered it to Gussie's little house. Theresa was six years old, spending the month before school started with Gussie.

"You're ungrateful, Mama!" Summer yelled, stamping her foot on the kitchen linoleum. "This is an expensive radio and record player, nicer than anything else in this house! I even brought you some of my favorite records! You make me so mad!"

"Don't yell at me, Summer!" Gussie retorted. She was nervous, Theresa knew, because she twisted the corner of her apron into a taut spiral. "You just want to get this out of your house because it has a scratch on it! I have eyes in my head!

You don't want anything that's not absolutely perfect in your house. That's the only reason you ever bring anything over here for me!"

Aunt Summer and Uncle Brendan drove away in a cloud of dust. Gussie covered the wide, curving gash in the cabinet door with furniture polish, working it into the wood with great care. She then plopped a thick 78 rpm record onto the turntable.

"Theresa," she called, "do you know how to run this thing?"

Theresa plugged the cord into the solitary living room wall outlet, selected '78', turned another switch to 'ON', then gently set the needle into the outside groove of the spinning wax record. Raucous swing music filled the room, 'The Boogie-Woogie Bugle Boy of Company D.'

"Lawsy!" Gussie exclaimed, "Who is that?"

"The Andrews Sisters," Theresa replied.

"Loud, ain't they?"

Theresa kept Gussie's china, silver, crystal, and all the photo albums and personal keepsakes she located as the crew moved from room to room. The upright piano and the stacks of old sheet music had been so dear to Gussie that Theresa could not imagine consigning them to Goodwill. She also decided to keep the treadle Singer sewing machine and, at the last minute, she instructed the boys to unload the dining table, chairs and buffet.

"I can't get rid of the table," she whispered, to herself. "That's the table Gussie lay on when Aunt Summer was born. Gussie said it was in a terrible blizzard and the coyotes ate her pigs. God, what a nightmare!"

In the garage, beneath layers of dust and debris, she found an old trunk. The boys moved it to the back yard, swept off the dust and cobwebs and watched in awe as Theresa opened its curved top.

"Man, I hope there ain't a dead body in that thing," one of the boys said. "Or a vampire!"

"I hope there is a vampire in there," another boy said. "This rotting old town is probably full of them."

"There may actually be ghosts in this trunk," Theresa laughed. "But they're ghosts of old-time Tisquah folks. You guys better get on the road, if you want to beat the Lubbock rush-hour traffic."

Alone, Theresa unpacked the contents of the leather-bound trunk. She carried it all into the house, spreading it over the bedroom floors. She collected the old magazines, seed catalogs and newspapers for later inspection. Her primary interest was in more personal records Gussie might have stored away. Theresa began her search for facts in a tattered scrapbook, its black pages held inside the covers by string.

"Lacy Summer Abelard," Theresa read, smiling at her aunt's schoolgirl handwriting, round and innocent. "Her Keepsake Book." She leafed through the brittle pages filled with school lessons, music scores and a few snapshots, circa 1937. One photo immediately caught Theresa's attention. Leo stood beside one of Gussie's lilac bushes, staring directly into the camera. His teen-aged face was pinched, tortured, miserable, unlike any image of her father she had ever seen.

"God," Theresa cried, staring at the snapshot, "he looks dangerous! How could anyone on earth not suspect that he was dangerous?"

Most of the scrapbook pages were covered with newspaper clippings and Ripley's Believe-It-Or-Not articles.

"Aunt Summer had a morbid curiosity, I'd say," Theresa commented.

She was especially perplexed by one newspaper article, pasted alone on a page, edged with faded red ribbon. She read it twice.

"She must have felt close to the little girl in this story," Theresa whispered. "She must have imagined some kinship with her. Oh, my God, what if Aunt Summer kept this article because she was also pregnant at a very young age? That's what it means! She knew how that little Columbian girl felt because they were both pregnant when they were children!"

The last page of the scrapbook was pasted to the back cover. Theresa ran her fingernail around the edges, dislodging dried bits of paste. The page separated easily from the cover, revealing a folded sheet of lined paper. Chills ran down Theresa's back as she opened the paper and read, in Summer's round penmanship, words that broke her heart.

"To God. Please make my brother stop trying to do it to me. I already had a baby the doctor had to cut out of my belly. It was put in my belly by Leo last summer, when Mama had to work in the cotton fields to pay for my medicine. Leo got into my bed every day and did it and did it over and over, even if I cried. I told Mama and she said it was bad dreams because of the medicine. Dr. Krohner looked at my belly and said a baby was in there.

"Mama nailed the door shut between the bedrooms, but Leo still sneaks through the kitchen at night and puts his hand under the covers. Mama gets up to look for him, but he runs fast, like a spider. He never makes a sound. I can see his eyes shining in the dark like a dog staring at me.

"When I get well enough to go back to school, I will get me a big boyfriend who will beat up Leo and make him be nice to me. If Leo won't act like a Christian, I will tell my big boyfriend to kill him. It is the only way.

Yours truly, Summer Abelard"

"Oh, Aunt Summer," Theresa wept, "I am so sorry!" She read the pitiful note again, thankful she had found it after all the years it had lain, hidden, in Summer's scrapbook. "I'd like to put this note on display," she whispered, "so other people can read it. Aunt Summer suffered too much to be forgotten! Anyone who thinks child molesters don't cause any real damage should read this little girl's note!"

Leo had never changed his ways. He had only changed victims, inflicting his perversion first on his sister, then on his daughter and, years later, his granddaughters. He went after the most vulnerable, available little girls, the ones he had access to.

Theresa briefly examined a bundle of correspondence from the Veterans' Administration, all addressed to Gussie, along with Michaul's insignia patch and obituary notice from the West County News. A small book, a worn McGuffey's Reader, was wrapped in a silk scarf, along with a pair of soft leather women's gloves. A First Baptist Church Sunday Bulletin, dated December 7, 1941, fell from the Reader. Theresa smiled, believing it was a souvenir of Pearl Harbor Day. She noticed writing along the borders, then turned it to read Gussie's message.

"Messkins did not kill Champ. My Daddy kilt him to teach me a lesin. If you love something too much, God will take it away - my Daddy said."

"Oh, Gussie, you always told me not to love Kendra too much because God would take her away. What a hurtful life you had to endure."

She then examined an oval box, decorated with a drawing titled "Be Still, My Beating Heart!" A willowy Southern belle, attended by three slaves, was donning an elaborate wedding dress. Bluebirds held aloft pink ribbons as little rosebuds rained down upon the scene.

"Good grief," Theresa cried. "Things have certainly changed!"

The box held a tattered rag doll, a scrap of brown paper pinned to its faded muslin dress. Theresa read the note.

"Silly Sally, the favrite dolly of my Darling Gurl Lorena. All her dollys burnt by Michaul the day she were burid. Lorena writ on paper dollys how Michaul hurt her, but I did not find them til after she was kilt. Messkins Did Not Kill my darling gurl. Michaul kilt Lorena. Them Abelards was mean, all of them. God help me. I was a Fool for Love."

"I don't know how much more of this sick shit I can take," Theresa whispered. "There's enough here about my father's family to open a museum of horrors! I have a feeling there's more, too!"

The oval box also contained an ornate program for a John Philip Sousa concert held in San Antonio. A faded, crumbling corsage of what appeared to be pansies tied with purple florist's ribbon was pressed inside the brittle paper. Gussie's spidery handwriting filled one margin.

"Sousa The King of Musik. His missus led the singing just like in a church. Me and Mr. Peters to San Antone in the buggy Lawsy was it hot and dry. Mr. Peters got us new things at the dry goods store. Him on accnt of I ruint his old cloths and Me on accnt of us starting over as Mister and Missus Peters. 2 new house dresses 1 church dress and 2 bonnets. Plumb purty. Roomed at fine hotel and ate the downrite best food I evr tasted.

Sartainly hope I kin larn to cook lak that. Cudnt wait to get home and see my darling gurl. Bot piece goods to sew her a new dress."

"Oh, Gussie," Theresa exclaimed. "You never told me you saw John Philip Sousa in person! I would have been so impressed! I remember when you used to take me across town to watch the high school band practice. You bought me that little baton and told me to march beside the drum major. I remember you marched along the sidewalks, too, laughing up a storm! Your garters always slipped down around your ankles."

The last article in the oval box was a little purse, called a reticule in Gussie's youth, Theresa remembered. It was artfully worked in jet beads, closed with a silver clasp. Theresa carefully opened the clasp, felt inside the silk lining and pulled out a scrap of paper rolled around a pencil stub. She read the brief message, her heart pounding as she realized its importance to her and her memoirs.

"It is Lorena's note! The note Gussie told me about the last time I was here. She said Lorena left a note beneath a peanut jar at a gas station, asking for help. She wanted protection from Michaul!"

The trunk had also contained several shoe boxes which, when opened, revealed dozens of rolled-up Rexall Drug calendars. Theresa immediately realized the old paper would crumble if she attempted to flatten out the pages. She decided to take the lot to Lubbock the next day.

"If I have to buy every plastic sleeve in Lubbock," she vowed, "I'll do it, in order to get every page of those calendars on a laser copy machine! It's a good thing I'm rich!"

She loaded the ancient books and messages into her car, drove to Lubbock and rented a hotel suite.

"I've got the money to buy this damned place if I wanted it," she whispered, smiling, as a bellboy escorted her to her room. Her overnight bag sat on one corner of the luggage cart, which was piled high with the dusty old shoe boxes and other items from Gussie's trunk. "I think I'll have the secretarial service pick this stuff up tomorrow, prepare it for copying, then transcribe it onto disk. I feel like shopping for some new clothes to go with this beautiful ruby ring!"

She lived at the hotel for two months, working with the secretarial service to integrate information gleaned from Gussie's calendars and notes into her book. Finally, the manuscript was dispatched by overnight delivery to the press she had selected. A hefty additional fee persuaded the press to give her work priority status. During the weeks the manuscript was at the printer's, the service compiled a list of rape crisis centers and women's shelters throughout the country. Her only objective in publishing her memoirs was to make her experiences available to people who worked with victims of sexual abuse. She prepared a note to accompany each book.

"I am sending you my book of memoirs, 'Memory Book,' in the hope that it may shed some light on the plight of sexually abused children. The fact that these young victims survive their terrible childhood is a miracle, but survival is not enough. They are robbed of every benefit of civilized life and are forced to grow up among monsters. Please consider my own dreadful childhood when you deal with other victims. I began this little book while I was a patient in a mental hospital. Memories of my childhood drove me mad, then healed me as I examined them and faced the truth about what my parents did to me."

The sleek paperbacks arrived at the secretarial agency. Theresa lovingly ran her fingers over the pale blue covers. The cover design was especially pleasing, she thought. The line drawings of a group of nude statues was similar to the embossed Greek family on her baby book, with one exception. A photograph of Theresa as two-year-old was superimposed on the smallest. At the base lay a doll, its eyes brimming with knowledge about which its little painted mouth could not speak.

Theresa decided to keep two dozen copies for herself and requested help in carrying a box of the books to her car. A middle-aged woman was assigned the task. She pulled the box onto a small dolly and followed Theresa to the parking lot. As she transferred the books to the trunk of Theresa's car, she spoke.

"My name is Sylvia Tremaine and I have something I'd like to give you."

"Oh?"

"Yes. I stayed up last night writing it. I've never spoken of this to anyone on earth. My brother molested me and my sisters all our lives. Our parents knew about it and did nothing. My youngest sister was three years old when he raped her and she bled to death in her crib! He was eighteen years old, a star athlete at school and very popular. Our family doctor reported the incident to the police and the judge advised my brother to join the Army before his reputation was ruined. My sisters and I still have never really talked about any of it! We just sit in silence when we're together at funerals or weddings. What can we say?"

"Oh, I know how that is, Sylvia," Theresa sighed. "What can I do to help?"

"Just take this letter I typed last night and keep it," the woman said softly. "I will feel better, knowing there is a written record. Otherwise, our story will go to our graves. Our children know we had bad childhoods, and they've all asked me and my sisters what happened but it's as if our lips are sewn shut! We can't say the words! I wish your book was for sale. I'd buy a copy for each of my sisters and for all our children."

"Let me give you some copies for them," Theresa said. "I hope they help your family." Theresa removed half the books from the box and returned it to the dolly. "Encourage them to talk about your childhood. I promise you it will make things better." She quickly autographed one copy to Sylvia. "Now I feel like a real writer," she said, smiling, "and not just someone with enough money to self-publish her memoirs."

Theresa drove out of Lubbock wondering if her book would, indeed, be helpful to Sylvia Tremaine's sisters and their children. As she left the loop and headed towards Slayton, she shrugged off her concerns for the family she had never met. She reminded herself that she had a list of objectives and enough money to make them all happen. The fact that 'Memory Book' would be in the mail by the end of the week was very satisfying.

"Well, that takes care of the second goal on my list," she said, happily. "I don't have to think about that little book any longer." She slipped the unopened envelope containing Sylvia's letter into her organizer as she made a mental note to read it when she stopped for lunch. She turned south, headed for Abilene and

Lodestone and soon forgot about Sylvia Tremaine and her sad legacy.

Theresa was eager to move on to the third goal on her mental list, finding a place of her own to call home. "I think I'll look in Costa Rica first. I've heard such great things about that little country!"

She drove to Lodestone, unpacked her things, then traveled to Dallas, where she caught a flight out of DFW for Jamaica. She didn't plan to stay in Jamaica long, but it was a destination Devon had promised her over the years, each time they reconciled. For various reasons, he had always failed to keep his promise.

Theresa stayed a week on the western side of the island, pampered beyond belief by the resort plantation's courteous staff. Rested and tanned, she booked passage on a cruise ship bound for Costa Rica. At times, she simply could not believe her new life was really happening to her, to Leona Theresa Abelard Mitchell Fulton.

"I love this," she said, again and again, "I love having enough money to travel. It's all I ever wanted to do!" Her fantasies had all been based on movement, she realized, never on putting down roots. "Survival, it can kill you dead as bullets, baby," she said, reciting Chris' words from group therapy. "It's a wonder I didn't wind up living in a box under some bridge."

She began searching for a house the day of her arrival in Costa Rica. The real estate broker showed her a series of expensive properties in various enclaves throughout the little country.

"You must take your time, Senora," he instructed, knowingly. "A house is not a home unless it strikes a chord in your heart. I am confident there is at least one perfect place for you in Costa Rica. We will find it, I promise!"

A week later they inspected a rambling, tan stucco house situated on a tiny peninsula jutting into the Pacific. Decorated and furnished in neutral colors, pale tan and gray against white interior walls, the house was obviously designed to invoke a great sense of calmness. Each room opened to the gentle breezes, each wide door framed blue sky melting into aqua waters.

Bougainvillea and poinsettia draped the privacy fences, blinding Theresa's senses with their brilliant pink, purple and red blossoms. The air was laden with the mysterious scent of night-blooming jasmine.

"I don't know if this is my permanent home," she told the real estate broker. "I do know it looks and feels like paradise. At this moment I can't imagine ever wanting to be any place else!"

"Many Americans live in this area," the broker replied. "You will find every modern convenience, as well as world-class shopping near here."

"Enough said," she laughed. "Heaven and a shopping mall!"

Theresa called Kendra from her new house, planning to invite her and her doctor friend down for a luxurious vacation. She located Kendra at home.

"Where in the hell have you been?" Kendra shouted. "Are you trying to drive me crazy?"

"Kendra," Theresa replied, "didn't we have this same conversation a few months ago? What's the problem now?"

"It's that old fart banker, Woolaver, again," Kendra said. "I don't see why you can't take care of your own business! I don't expect you to look after mine! Just call him, will you, and tell him to leave me the hell alone! You promised you wouldn't drop out of sight again! For all I knew you were in another nut house! Where are you?"

"I'm in Costa Rica, Kendra, in my new villa."

"Oh," Kendra breathed. "Costa Rica. Cool. Let me have your number, and for God's sake, don't go anywhere before I call you back! I have to tell you who my boyfriend is. In fact, I'm planning to marry him."

"Is it Antonio V. Cavaleri, M.D.?"

"Christ, how do you do that?"

"Mother's intuition," Theresa replied. "Let's talk tomorrow, O.K.? I'd like to fly you and the doctor to Costa Rica for a few days. It's lovely here."

"O.K.," Kendra agreed, suspiciously, "but don't pull your disappearing act again, ever. I mean it! Don't make me lose my patience!"

"God forbid!"

Hands trembling, Theresa called Mr. Woolaver. In her gut, she feared he would only have bad news, perhaps concerning her inheritance. What if the money wasn't hers, after all? She felt sick.

"Theresa," Woolaver said, "how nice to hear your voice."

"What's wrong?"

"Oh, I don't think anything is wrong, dear. I have received several telephone calls from various New York publishing houses. Seems your little book is all the rage in the Big Apple. Someone at one of the shelters was very impressed with your work and showed it around. Now, apparently, the big publishing houses are eager to find you and obtain publishing rights. Someone named Ms. Tremaine at the secretarial service gave the houses my number when they traced the books to their point of origin. I thought you might want to see what it is all about. There's quite a list of calls."

"Sylvia Tremaine!" Theresa cried. "My goodness, I'd forgotten about her! Well, I guess I'd better look into this right away. Would you be kind enough to fax the information to me?"

"Certainly," Mr. Woolaver replied. "I greatly enjoy using the fax machine. This is a wonderful era, don't you think?"

"Yes, I do," she replied. "Definitely."

Theresa waited in her office, a room filled with state-of-the-art equipment, until the old gentleman's fax came through. The office was one reason she had purchased the villa, though she had not expected to use it for quite some time.

"I need an agent," she said, examining the list of editors, "or someone who knows about the publishing business."

She placed a call to a prestigious agency in New York City, explaining her situation to three different receptionists and two secretaries before she was finally transferred to the office of someone named Zinnia Gertz.

"Hello, doll?" Zinnia Gertz shouted. "Theresa Fulton, the Theresa Fulton who wrote and illustrated that marvelous little book? What's it called? I Remember Something or Other...?"

"'Memory Book,'" Theresa replied.

"Yeah, doll, that's it. Look, do you have any idea what's

happening to your book right now?"

"I believe several publishers are interested in obtaining rights to the book."

"Yeah. Right. You were smart to call us, doll. You can make a lot of money if this thing is handled properly."

"Meaning?"

"Don't talk to any of the publishing houses. Let me talk to them. That is, if you want us to represent you. Where are you?"

"Costa Rica," Theresa said. "I just bought a house here."

"Right," Zinnia said. "Look, stay put and don't talk to anyone until I get there."

"You're coming to Costa Rica? When?"

"Now, sugar! I'm practically out the door! Stay put! I'll call you from the plane with my arrival time. You will sign a contract if I bring one down?"

"Yes. Yes, I'll sign."

Theresa spent the night on one of the oversized sofas in the living room, watching white-capped waves come to life as a full moon inched across the star-studded sky. The surf was muted by thick glass doors but Theresa sensed each wave break against the sand.

"I always thought I remembered the ocean, even before I saw it for the first time."

As a child she had secretly kept a paper bag packed with a box of Cracker Jacks, a change of panties for herself and a blanket for Suda, part of her little girl plans to run away to the Pacific Ocean. An aunt showing off her new Chevrolet appeared in Tisqua early one August day and persuaded Varina to allow her to take five-year-old Theresa to Corpus Christi for a week's visit. Theresa, dressed in her yellow taffeta Easter dress and sporting a Roy Rogers Fan Club pin, sat perfectly still on the car seat, convinced she was living a dream.

They arrived in Corpus Christi at sunset and drove directly to the bluff overlooking the Gulf of Mexico. The sun, a perfect red ball, hovered on the horizon, casting ripples of fire across the green waves. Theresa breathed deeply the exotic smell of the sea, sand, rotting vegetation and beach-front oyster houses as gulls pierced the air with frantic cries. Her heart lurched in recognition and she quickly climbed out the open window, then plunged down the bluff and across the sandy beach. She splashed into the surf, stopping only when a wave broke across her chest. Her hysterical aunt parked the car and sprinted across the sand, begging onlookers for help. A man plucked Theresa from the water and carried her to safety. Water poured from her sandals, wetting the sand as her aunt knelt and examined her for injuries.

"Theresa!" she screamed. "Did you lose your mind?"

"No," Theresa answered, "I was going home!"

"You're going to the nut house, young lady," her aunt tearfully replied. "And your mama is going to thrash you for ruining your Easter dress and shoes."

Both predictions eventually proved accurate.

"When I was very young I thought I left the sea to grow in my mother's body," she whispered, all those years later, sitting in her beautiful new house. "My life seemed so precious, so special. I thought my own beginning must have been just as dark and mysterious as this night. I imagined having lived in a pink shell castle beneath the water, like a princess. I thought I was a gift to the world, to my parents and to all my relatives."

She recalled the day she first met Leo and how, from that moment on, she had struggled to maintain her own identity, her sense of self apart from the lunacy that permeated every aspect of her world. As an adult, she had always known that her weaknesses and emotional scars were the results of a childhood lived in total dysfunction. Still, she had always blamed herself for not achieving more.

"I hated feeling so weak and helpless," she whispered. "I obsessed about my failures because I thought everyone else cared about what I did. I had to write my little book to understand that no one had ever cared enough to protect me. No one. I managed to stay alive, that's all! My survival is my gift to myself."

At dawn, she signed the contract of representation delivered the previous day by Zinnia Gertz. The brash little woman, a total stranger, had cared enough about Theresa's work to fly to Costa Rica from New York City. The Big Apple, Mr.

Woolaver had called it, a huge, vital city where professionals had read her innermost secrets and deemed them worthy of a big-time book contract. An awful lot of people would soon read of her struggle to survive life with Varina and Leo. Leo had always won, Theresa thought. Always. But now her father was dead and she was embarking on uncharted, fabulous seas.

Theresa slid open the glass doors leading onto the verandah. She walked outside, savoring the salty, humid air and stood for a moment, smiling at the glorious colors of her new world. She stretched her arms wide, laughing.

"Hey, Leo," she shouted. "Look at me, you bastard! I win this time! I win!"

EPILOGUE
2001

From The New Orleans Times-Picayune
August 2, 2001
by Sheila Roussell-Ngamba

Today marks the opening of a unique museum within walking distance of the French Quarter, though no one is yet willing to predict whether or not it will earn a spot on the "places to visit while in New Orleans" maps. Called "Neutral Ground" and located on Tchoupitoulas Street, the museum fills a century-old coffee warehouse.

"My grandmother, Gustine Abelard, would have been one hundred and eight years old today," Neutral Ground's founder Theresa Fulton explains. "For purely sentimental reasons, I chose her birthday as our opening date."

Ms. Fulton's grandmother and other relatives owned many of the objects displayed on the museum's lower level. A collection of faded photographs, an old upright piano, a treadle sewing machine and various clothing, scrapbooks, toys and newspaper clippings tell the story of what appears to be a typical West Texas family. What distinguishes the family history is Ms. Fulton's brutally honest revelations of life as an Abelard child.

"I was sexually abused by my father until I was sixteen years old," Ms. Fulton claims. "Two years ago I spent time in a mental hospital as I recalled my earliest childhood experiences. Later, in the course of researching my father's family, I uncovered evidence of generations of incest and sexual abuse, even murder of children. I published my story and was immediately besieged by other people who had experienced similar trauma. Eventually, it seemed necessary to provide a place to gather and preserve my readers' stories. Most of the feedback I've received indicates that regardless of the abuse my readers endured, their homes and families appeared fairly normal. So, I thought it appropriate to use my own family's artifacts as background for our generational story of abuse. When I first visited New Orleans, I was intrigued with the term 'neutral ground.'"

Ms. Fulton named her museum after the grassy areas in the middle of New Orleans' boulevards, the neutral grounds between the old French and American neighborhoods where citizens could seek safety during duels. She initially envisioned an interactive site similar to the Murrah Building Memorial in Oklahoma City.

"I was stunned when I visited the Murrah Building temporary memorial," she says. "I spent hours reading the handwritten notes and touching the stuffed toys and flowers that visitors had placed in the chain link fences. The whole experience felt so personal. There was a sense of shared agony, of the horror and outrage that anyone could harm so many innocent people who were just going about their daily routines. Before Memory Book was released, a secretary who worked on the project gave me a typed history of her family. Later, readers inundated me with letters and other items they wanted to share. Their common statement was, 'I've never told anyone about what happened to me.' When it became obvious that my readers would continue sending me a tremendous amount of material and that I would put it on public display, I wanted that same feeling for Neutral Ground. I wanted to convey the terror of innocent, helpless children as they are attacked by sexual deviants and predators. I wanted to explain that those children never forget the experiences and seldom overcome the effects of abuse. Believe me, there are other millions of victims who have never told anyone about what happened to them but who feel that their stories should be told."

The second level of the warehouse is filled with the

memorabilia of approximately one hundred and fifty thousand victims of childhood sexual abuse. Written material, drawings, photographs and newspaper clippings are displayed in Plexiglas frames, arranged as nearly as possible according to dates the abuses occurred. Ms. Fulton explains that any material received from minors is referred to local officials if there is a sufficient address or identity. The identity of minors is concealed from the public when the items go on display.

"I want to stress that Neutral Ground is not, in and of itself, a law enforcement entity, though we gladly help whenever we can in order to protect children. Our primary focus is to provide a national venue for victims to simply tell their stories. Nothing else quite like Neutral Ground exists, so we are learning as we go along. Some people have compared Neutral Ground with the Holocaust memorial in Washington, D.C., but there are vast differences. The most obvious is that the majority of children are abused in their homes by family members or friends. And, of course, there is no political doctrine promoting their abuse, other than apathy. The public response has been overwhelming, so we can only believe there is a great need for what we're doing here."

Ms. Fulton denies any expertise in child psychology or the legal field.

"I'm expert only in how not to deal with molestation," she says. "I protected my parents and even allowed my daughter to spend time with them. She and my nieces were molested by my father, and that, unfortunately, is a common progression in this type of family dysfunction. My father should have gone to prison for what he did to me, to my nieces and to his sister. My mother also would be prosecuted in today's legal climate, for allowing him to continue his perversions. My daughter's father and I were criminally negligent when we left her in their care. It was only after I had a complete emotional breakdown that I was able to see clearly how dangerous it was to keep such terrible secrets, to maintain the appearance that our family was, in any way, normal. Once the problem is identified and looked at in the light of day it is easier to see the danger. I hope Neutral Ground provides that light."

She firmly believes that there is sufficient legislation in every state to punish child molesters and that the current trend to make their presence publicly known after release from prison is beneficial. She feels that with intensive public education and awareness, more families and institutions will refuse to shelter pedophiles.

"Anyone who says children aren't harmed by sexual abuse is uninformed," Ms. Fulton says. "Anyone who believes it is a one-time event is also uninformed and playing with fire. Pedophiles look for vulnerability and opportunity. Always. And they repeat the offense, usually as often as humanly possible. Some molesters report thousands of episodes during their lives. Where do they find their victims? Where but among their families, their neighbors, their students and parishioners? When a child has the courage to report abuse, that child should be protected from further incidents. Always. Always. No matter what."

Ms. Fulton decided to establish Neutral Ground in New Orleans because so many tourists visit the city each year. She claims that there was no initial concern expressed by the City concerning the subject-matter of her project, though as the museum neared completion, several groups picketed the area.

"Some people honestly felt it was inappropriate," she says, "but we expected a certain degree of opposition. It is something new and frightening to many people. I believe there is no substitute for public awareness, so the pickets were not all bad. You know what they say, 'there's no such thing as bad publicity'. I knew from my experience on the road as I promoted my book that many, many people wanted to share their childhood stories. I was on the book tour in New Orleans when I learned of Ann Rice's doll museum. It dawned on me then that I was also a writer, that I had the means to open a museum of my own and that this beautiful old city is the perfect setting."

When asked if she was an Ann Rice fan prior to learning of her Uptown doll museum, Ms. Fulton says she began reading the Vampire Lestat books many years ago.

"I made the connection between vampires and pedophiles early on," she says. "I found it interesting that a vast reading audience was horrified by the very thought of fictional creatures preying on victims in the dark. Later, as I pondered just how I wanted to present my readers' stories, I recalled the Lestat atmosphere. It is easy to imagine the terror of a child who is afraid to fall asleep each night because someone regularly crawls into his or her bed. It should be simple for adults to imagine the fear a child feels when a trusted relative, teacher, pastor or family friend repeatedly assaults them! Unless they receive protection and intensive help, they will be changed for life, as surely as if a vampire had bitten them."

When asked what she hopes the long-range legacy of Neutral Ground will be, Ms. Fulton becomes very serious, indeed.

"Those children whom we allow to lie awake in the dark will someday grow to adulthood. They may be crippled in horrible ways because we ignored their suffering. We can no longer claim we don't know what is happening! A silent holocaust is destroying the soul of our nation. Why is this so difficult to grasp? Child sexual abuse makes young children insane and very little attention has ever been devoted to its effects or prevention. I hope every adult who tours Neutral Ground will leave here asking two things. What can be done? And when?"

The Storyteller must inspire humans
To walk the Great Spirit's Path,
For when a human heart forgets to love,
It shrivels to the size of a walnut.
                                    - Cherokee Legend

Jackie is a native Texan, born during World War II while her father was stationed in the Pacific. During the tumultuous years following the war's end, she often lived with relatives. The stories told by her grandparents as well as her own traumatic childhood continued to haunt her as she matured. She took notes on family history from the time she was allowed to possess pencils and paper. At age nine she announced her intention to become a writer. Her school years were spent moving across several western states, caught up in a nomadic existence with her parents and siblings. She found solace in reading and music, imagining her future as a novelist and/or a storytelling trombone player - it was difficult for girls in that era to visualize a future other than marriage and babies.

Married to three men - the first divorced her, she divorced the second, and the third died - Jackie's life followed a pattern familiar to adult victims of childhood abuse. Though she believed she was choosing very different men, she was inevitably forced to focus her energy on the debris they left as they exited her life. She had two children, a son and daughter. Her dream of becoming a writer was always just beneath the surface, and when she stopped working as a secretary in order to take care of her dying husband, she began "Walnut Hearts". Following her husband's death, Jackie attended nursing school and has worked in psychiatric settings. She currently resides in Texas.

Order These Great Books Directly From Limitless, Dare 2 Dream Publishing

Cat on the Couch by Cathy L. Parker	16.00	Hilarious
Kara: Lady Rogue by j. taylor Anderson	15.00	Adventure
The Amazon Nation by C. A. Osborne	15.00	Reference
A Woman's Ring by Rea Frey	16.00	NEW
Sweet Melody by Liana M. Scott	16.00	NEW
Deadly Rumors by Jeanne Foguth- OUT OF PRINT	15.00	VERY Limited
Walnut Hearts by Jackie Glover	17.00	NEW
Soldiers Now by Dean Krystek	16.00	November 2004
Home to Ohio by Deborah E. Warr	15.00	Mystery
The Mysterious Cave	12.00	Children's Adventure
Where Love is Not by Deborah E. Warr	16.00	NEW Ellen Richardson Mystery
		Total

South Carolina residents add 5% sales tax.
Domestic shipping is $3.50 per book

Visit our website at: http://limitlessd2d.net

Please mail orders with credit card info, check or money order to:

Limitless, Dare 2 Dream Publishing
100 Pin Oak Ct.
Lexington, SC 29073-7911

Please make checks or money orders payable to **Limitless**.

I

Printed in the United States
25900LVS00003B/244-249